AMERICAN FOLKLORE

American

THE CHICAGO HISTORY OF AMERICAN CIVILIZATION

Daniel J. Boorstin, EDITOR

Folklore

Richard M. Dorson

With revised Bibliographical Notes, 1977

THE UNIVERSITY OF CHICAGO PRESS

CHICAGO AND LONDON

The University of Chicago Press, Chicago 60637
The University of Chicago Press, Ltd., London

© 1959, 1977 by The University of Chicago
All rights reserved. Published in 1959
Printed in the United States of America

81 80 79 78 77   15 14 13 12 11

ISBN: 0–226–15859–4
Library of Congress Catalog Card Number: 77–77491

For
GLORIA

Table of Contents

Preface

Although we are all actually sources and carriers of folklore, few of us know what we mean by it. In everyday speech we use "folklore" to include everything—printed or spoken—that is folksy or romantic or inauthentic about our past. But until we cease to think of "folklore" as this miscellany of charming misinformation we cannot learn what it has to teach us about American civilization.

In this book, Mr. Dorson is careful to define what he means by "folklore." By showing us what we can learn by examining American Folklore in his specific sense, Mr. Dorson helps us separate out what he calls "fakelore"—which, instead of originating as anonymous tradition, is concocted by particular individuals, usually for profit. In this way, Mr. Dorson helps us understand how books can bury the very facts which they purport to expound. To grasp the elusive experience of living people and their spoken words, we have to free ourselves from clichés that are really not folklore at all.

The desire to tell a story is, of course, universal. But the folklore of a people is as distinctive as anything else about

Preface

them. The new American places—the colonial fireside, the backwoods bearhunt, the city slum, or the college campus—make a difference. American literacy and the American standard of living change the channels of folklore. It becomes more difficult than ever to disentangle printed from oral sources when the "folktale" comes to us in books and magazines, over radio or television, instead of in conversation. All this makes the task of the American folklorist even more complex and subtle than that of his fellow specialists elsewhere.

We have seen so many saccharine movies and television shows for "children of all ages" offered up as "folklore" that we are tempted to think of it as a commodity that offends nobody, that is non-controversial, that does not describe in uncomplimentary terms any race, religion, or immigrant group, and that certainly avoids reference to bodily functions or to sex. Mr. Dorson shows us how inaccurate is this prettified picture. One of the reasons why folklore was communicated orally rather than in print was, as Mr. Dorson explains, because much of it was coarse and obscene—in a word, "unprintable." In other ways, too, folklore bore the mark of the spoken rather than the printed word. How can we recapture its spirit?

The author of this book has the great advantage of having traveled widely with notebook and tape-recorder. He is a skilled and patient listener, as well as a careful scholar and a brilliant raconteur. He has the sound of the spoken word in his ear. There is no substitute for this firsthandness, or for the native wit and human warmth which have enabled the author to hear universal sentiments in national and regional accents.

The "Chicago History of American Civilization" aims to bring to the general reader, in compact and readable form, the insights of scholars who write from different points of

Preface

view. The series contains two kinds of books: a *chronological* group, which will provide a coherent narrative of American history from its beginning to the present day, and a *topical* group—including this volume by Mr. Dorson—which will deal with the history of varied and significant aspects of American life.

DANIEL J. BOORSTIN

A Foreword on Folklore

Folklore is a word with a short but turbulent history. An Englishman named William John Thoms coined it in 1846, to replace the cumbersome "popular antiquities" then in vogue to designate the loving study of old customs, usages, and superstitions. Five years later the first book appeared with "Folklore" in its title, *The Dialect and Folk-Lore of Northamptonshire*, by Thomas Sternberg. Interest in the new subject gathered momentum, especially after Darwin's theory of biological evolution pumped fresh blood into the young sciences of anthropology and folklore. Following Darwin's lead, folklorists sought to reconstruct the prehistory of mankind from the traditions of savages and the ancient practices surviving among peasants. A talented group of scholarly enthusiasts in London formed the Folk-Lore Society in 1878, and began publishing a journal, *Folk-Lore*, which endures to the present day.

Meanwhile the word and the subject had spread to the Continent and rapidly acquired a following. The Romance tongues adopted the term "Folklore," while the Teutonic countries preferred the German *Volkskunde*, covering the traditional arts and crafts of the folk. In different lands the subject has tended to follow one or the other of the emphases implicit in these labels. *Volkskunde* embraces the total rural folk life, including the physical objects produced by household artisans; "folklore" usually suggests the oral traditions channeled across the centuries through human mouths. In its flexible uses folklore may refer to types of barns, bread molds, or quilts; to orally inherited tales, songs, sayings, and beliefs; or to village festivals, household customs, and peasant rituals. The common element in all these matters is tradition. Since the arc of tradition in a given culture may vary considerably from country to country, it is only right that the study of folklore should follow the contours of a particular civilization. The scientific folklorist seeks out, observes, collects, and describes the inherited traditions of the community, whatsoever forms they take.

In the United States, folklore has customarily meant the spoken and sung traditions. After an initial thrust of interest propelled from England, which led to the founding of an American Folklore Society in 1888, the subject languished, going by default to the anthropologists, who concentrated on North American Indian tales. In the first two decades of the present century interest picked up, with the publication of cowboy songs in 1910 by John A. Lomax and of old English ballads from the southern Appalachians by Cecil Sharp in 1917. The collectors of folksongs were joined by collectors of tales in the 1930's and 40's, when the nation rather suddenly awoke to find itself the proud possessor of its very own body of so-called American folklore.

In Europe, Asia, and North and South America, the growth

A Foreword on Folklore

of interest in folklore reveals an intimate dependence upon the rise of a nationalistic spirit. Tiny countries like Finland and Ireland assumed the leadership in folklore studies, receiving support from their governments, as part of their endeavor to demonstrate their cultural independence. Evil colossi like Nazi Germany and Soviet Russia have found in folklore an effective propaganda instrument for proclaiming the uniqueness of the master race, and asserting the kinship of a conglomerate people. So seriously do the Russians take their folklore that the standard book on the subject, edited by Bogatyrev in 1954, was reissued in a new edition upon the change of regime in 1956, and over two hundred references to Stalin were expunged. Shortly after Nasser became established in Egypt and began his campaign for pan-Arabism, a Folklore Center arose in Cairo.

Romantic nationalism has colored American folklore in still a different way. Neither the intensive scholarship of a Finland nor the aggressive progaganda of a Russia has developed, but rather a naïve proclamation of America's boundless folklore treasures, comparable in richness to her unequaled agricultural and mineral resources. America, the land of plenty, must indubitably own plenty of folklore. Now, in the era of their world eminence, Americans should proudly unfurl their folk heritage. Hence the popularity of largely manufactured "folk heroes" like Paul Bunyan, exuding 100 per cent Americanism, of "folk singers" titillating urban audiences in Town Hall and the Broadway cabaret; of mammoth treasuries cramming together anecdotal slabs of local color, jocularity, sentiment, and nostalgia in the name of folklore; of guided folk dance and folk art revivals; of what in short one critic has called the "cult of the folksy." Ironically the lore of the folk was strained

3

and trumpeted through the mass media as a patriotic act. Why should American youths read continually about Greek and Roman and Norse gods and myths? Surely the most important nation in the world could offer its children some homegrown heroics and mythology. So the writers went to work to meet the demand.

For this contrived, romantic picture of folklore I coined, in 1950, the term "fakelore." Fakelore falsifies the raw data of folklore by invention, selection, fabrication, and similar refining processes, but for capitalistic gain rather than for totalitarian conquest. The end result is a conception of the folk as quaint, eccentric, whimsical, droll, primeval. Beware of the adjectives "charming" and "delightful" when applied to folktales and folksongs. The fact is that much folklore is coarse and obscene, and in its true form is often meaningless and dull to the casual reader, though absorbing to the serious student of culture. Beware, too, of the defensive argument now used by "folklore" writers to justify their tampering with sources: "We have the same right as the original storytellers to tell a folktale in our own way." There is no more fundamental fallacy in the presentation of folk materials than this notion. The carrier of oral folk traditions continually alters the tale, song, or saying he has heard; such change is at the very heart of oral, unrehearsed narration. But the calculating money-writer, using the very different medium of print in a self-conscious effort to reach readers who already associate "folklore" with froth and fun, is the voice not of the folk but of the mass culture. Of course the creative artist employs folk themes imaginatively, but he makes no claim to present pristine folklore.

If the popularizers have simply reinforced the prejudices of

A Foreword on Folklore

the public about folk stereotypes, what have the professional folklorists been doing? Regional collectors and literary scholars have made available splendid materials from various corners and sectors of the American scene. However, the professionals come to American folklore from their own special interests, in medieval literature, German, ethnomusicology, Spanish, sociology, and they plow a restricted field. The current approaches are those of the comparative folklorists, who are primarily Europe-centered; cultural anthropologists, who are chiefly concerned with non-literate peoples; special pleaders, following in the steps of Sir James Frazer and his *Golden Bough,* and now Freud and Jung, who would interpret all folklore in the light of one universal theme; regional collectors, who drift into parochialism; literary scholars untrained in folklore; folksong and folk music specialists; and popularizers and entertainers. No overarching synthesis has integrated the study of folklore with the history of American civilization. It is my conviction that the only meaningful approach to the folk traditions of the United States must be made against the background of American history, with its unique circumstances and environment. What other history—or folklore—grapples in the same measure with the factors of colonization, immigration, Negro slavery, the westward movement, or mass culture?

If folklore scholars are not yet united by a general theory for American folklore, they fully agree on the methods necessary for accurate collecting and documenting of folk materials. Texts must be secured literally from informants; full background information should be provided on these human sources of folklore; all traditions, whether collected currently in the field, or excavated from the printed sources of an earlier day, need to be verified through the great indexes and reference works which form the scientific tools of the folklorist. Only with these proofs can we be reasonably sure of the oral, traditional character of our assumed folklore.

The present book thus rests on a special theory for American folklore and a general method for all folklore. Its outline follows the broad sweep of American history, and its materials come from authentic collections and studies. If this book leads new readers to these works, it will have served its purpose.

I

Colonial Folklore

A new nation, born suddenly in a seventeenth-century wilderness, possessed neither cultural nor folk traditions to call its own. Yet in a relatively short span an American civilization has arisen on the naked earth, endowed with distinctive institutions, literature, behavior, and folklore. The shaping of this folklore commenced with the first landings of explorers, and drew from two heritages, the uprooted European and the native Indian, blended in the crucible of a strange, fierce land.

The European settlers who crossed the Atlantic in the seventeenth century brought with them a host of supernatural beliefs which colored their views of the universe. Learned men and common folk alike gave credence to demons and hags, ghouls and specters of the midnight darkness and regulated their lives with signs, charms, and exorcisms innumerable. In the eighteenth century the tides of rationalism would sweep away many "vulgar errors," as Sir Thomas Browne had called the grosser superstitions. But for the first hundred years

of colonization, supernatural explanations in terms of God and
the Devil ruled the thinking of governor and cleric as well
as farmer and servant. English colonists viewed the fantastic
world they encountered, and interpreted their novel experiences through the concepts of witchcraft, demonology, and
divine providences. Hence the settlement of America generated powerful folk traditions which would form an enduring,
if little understood, legacy of American civilization. What we
may call American folklore resulted from the grafting of Old
World beliefs onto the New World environment, and the
generation of new folk fancies within old forms.

The Age of Exploration encouraged wild stories and vivid
fantasies, for truth itself was wonderful. Twin images rose
about America that would persist across the continental frontier, the conceits of an Earthly Paradise and a Howling
Wilderness, and the wake of these images threw up a spume
of fabulous tales.

We can see these marvelous stories being exchanged, in the
gossipy report of one seventeenth-century traveler to New
England, John Josselyn. Approaching the American coast in
1638, his ship sighted two sail bound for Newfoundland and
hove to for news. "They told us of a general earthquake in
New England, of the birth of a monster at Boston, in the
Massachusetts Bay a mortality." After landing and joining a
group of "Neighboring gentlemen" who came to welcome him
into the new country, Josselyn heard more of these wondrous
occurrences in fuller detail. One told of a young lion killed
at Piscataway by an Indian, and another of a sea serpent
coiled up like a cable on a rock at Cape Ann, which an Englishman in a passing boat would have shot, had not two Indians
dissuaded him, saying if he were not killed outright they

would all be in danger of their lives. Thereupon a Mr. Mittin capped them both with an account of a merman who tried to clamber into his canoe while he was out fowling in Maine's Casco Bay; he chopped off the creature's hand with a hatchet, and the merman sunk beneath the water, staining it with purple blood. Now under the heat of the story-swapping, Mr. Foxwell came forth and related how he had passed a night at sea in a small shallop, hugging the shore but afraid to land; suddenly at midnight a loud voice called him, "Foxwell, Foxwell, come ashore," and upon the beach he beheld a great fire ringed by dancing men and women. After an hour they vanished, and next morning Foxwell put ashore and found their footprints and brands' ends on the sand. But no living Englishman or Indian could he find on shore or in the woods.

Throughout the seventeenth century many such knots of hardy settlers, bold in the face of physical danger but wise enough to run from specters, must have gathered to exchange marvels and wonders. The American setting supplied three special themes for their narrations. The land itself, with its strange denizens and luxuriant, unfamiliar growths, furnished the stuff of sensational reports. The savages who inhabited the land reveled in barbarous customs and diabolical sorceries astounding to Europeans. And the hazards of life in a wilderness providentially governed by God as His special preserve inspired awesome "relations."

From the coastal wilderness issued a steady stream of travelers' and settlers' tales of natural history. Exotic creatures and a giant terrain dazzled European eyes, untrained in empirical observation and inflamed with the excitement of their momentous enterprise. Colonists readily credited accounts of New

World fertility and fecundity, lushness and abundance, and transmitted them to their transatlantic kinfolk who waited cautiously before investing in or emigrating to these newborn settlements. Ecstatically Francis Higginson wrote from Massachusetts Bay in 1630 that "of one corn there springeth four or five hundred," colored red, blue, and yellow, and even little children could more than earn their keep by planting the seed. He spoke of twenty-five-pound lobsters, "great and fat and luscious," and a partridge so heavy it could scarcely fly. A sup of New England's air was equal to a draft of old England's ale, averred Higginson in an oft-quoted phrase. The king's evil (scrofula), which only royal touch could cure in England, had dried up on his afflicted son under the wholesome air, and the physic that had tormented Higginson with melancholic humors had vanished, leaving him an iron constitution. For the first time in many years he had thrown away his cap and double waistcoats, and went about "thin-clad as any." Alas, poor Higginson died the following August.

Perhaps the most lyrical individual tribute to New World vegetation was John Josselyn's hymn to tobacco, the weed brought to the court of King James the First by Sir Walter Raleigh, which "hath made more slaves than Mahomet." In 1675 Josselyn recited its virtues. "It helps digestion, the gout, the toothache, prevents infection by scents; it heats the cold, and cools them that sweat, feedeth the hungry, spent spirits restoreth, purgeth the stomach, killeth nits and lice; the juice of the green leaf healeth green wounds, although poisoned; the syrup for many diseases, the smoke for the phthisic, cough of the lungs, distillations of rheum, and all diseases of a cold and moist cause; good for all bodies cold and moist taken upon an empty stomach; taken upon a full stomach it precipitates digestion."

To show his objectivity, Josselyn also pointed out the dangers of excess. "Immoderately taken it drieth the body, inflameth the blood, hurteth the brain, weakens the eyes and the sinews."

The historian of the Carolinas, John Lawson, told of a tulip tree so large that a lusty man moved his bed and household furniture inside. Virginia's historian, Robert Beverley, described the "Jamestown Weed," a diabolical plant looking like the thorny apple of Peru, which some soldiers at the time of Bacon's Rebellion (1675) ate in a boiled salad, and consequently for the next eleven days played the fool. "One would blow up a feather in the air; another would dart straws at it with much fury; and another stark naked was sitting up in a corner like a monkey grinning and making mows at them; a fourth would fondly kiss and paw his companions and sneer in their faces." Had they not been prevented, these witless men would have wallowed in their own excrement. When the madness suddenly passed, they remembered nothing of what had occurred.

Old wives' tales still current about the habits of native beasts originated in colonial times, particularly of bears and snakes. An early traveler to New England, William Wood, spoke of bears hibernating through the cold, lean winters and staying alive by "sleeping and sucking their paws, which keepeth them as fat as they are in summer." Since they sang while they sucked, Indians easily found their lairs and killed them. Another popular bear myth, that the mother licks her lumpy, formless cubs into proper shape, had anciently been noted by Pliny. The Swedish traveler Peter Kalm heard from the Quaker botanist John Bartram that a bear killed a cow by biting into her hide and blowing air into the wound until she burst. However, the eminent Virginia planter and diarist, William Byrd II, asserted that bears devoured their prey from the rump forwards, collop by collop, "till they come to the Vitals, the poor Animal crying all the while, for several Minutes together."

Snakes literally fascinated travelers, for the reptiles were reported to hypnotize their prey by gazing upon their victims. Colonial writers set down numerous instances of snakes charming birds, animals, and even men. A farmer in New Jersey, tearing down a haystack with a pitchfork, was transfixed for two hours by the beady eye of a rattlesnake, and saved only by the appearance of his wife, distracting to the reptile. Observers repeated cases of two-headed snakes (amphisboena), brittle snakes that reunited their broken parts, snakes that drank milk out of the same bowl with children (a familiar European legend), snakes with glittering carbuncles on their foreheads. In their love bouts serpents engaged in sinuous and supple embraces almost human in intensity. Indeed Peter Kalm heard of a young lady in Albany who sat down in the woods, attended by her Negro servant, when

a Black Snake being disturbed in its amours, ran under her petticoats, and twisted round her waist, so that she fell backwards in a swoon. . . . The negro came up to her, and . . . lifted up her cloaths, and really found the snake wound about her body as close as possible; the negro was not able to tear it away, and therefore cut it, and the girl came to herself again; but she conceived so great an aversion to the negro, that she could not bear the sight of him afterwards, and died of a consumption.

Colonial Folklore

The horn snake achieved even greater celebrity than the rattlesnake, thanks to the horny knob like a cock's spur on its tail, from which it gained its name and infamy. "I have heard it credibly reported," wrote John Lawson in 1709, "by those who said they were eye-witnesses, that a small locust tree, about the thickness of a man's arm, being struck by one of these snakes in the morning, then verdant and flourishing, at four in the afternoon was dead, and the leaves red and withered." Cotton Mather reported to the Royal Society in London how a rattlesnake bit a broadax, discoloring the steel, which chipped at the next stroke. The horn snake merged into the hoop snake, which rolled tail-over-head to chase its enemies and strike them with its lethal horn.

Medieval bestiaries, the illustrated booklets that perpetuated zoölogical myths about fabled animals, contributed to the folklore of American natural history. A popular Dutch author who never visited America but wrote a lavish treatise on the New World in 1671, Arnoldus Montanus, plucked a fable from the bestiaries when he declared that eagles in New Netherlands, in old age, "fly to the highest regions towards the sun, tumble down into the coldest stream, pluck out their feathers, clammy with sweat, and thus breathe their last." So lascivious were eagles, said Montanus, that they consorted with each other more than thirty times a day, and failing their own kind, resorted to the she-hawks and she-wolves. Another bestiary tradition, originally told on elephants, emerged in the eighteenth-century journal of James Kenny, who reported that large horses in the far-away country beyond the Mississippi slept standing up against trees. A new American bestiary could well have been compiled. Josselyn first told of porcupines "shooting a whole shower of quills when aroused at their enemies." The North Carolina doctor John Brickell alleged that whales copulated standing upright with their heads out of the water—a hypothesis argued from every angle by colonial naturalists. A punitive beaver king, according to Byrd and Beverley, watched over his industrious colony while they built dams, using their tails for trowels. A French traveler to America, Bossu, perhaps mindful of Münchausen, wrote of tree-bearing alligators, into whose bullet-pocked hides the seeds of river-bank trees dropped and sprouted.

Fertility, fecundity, lushness, abundance—these were the hallmarks of the New World. All nature contributed to the human powers of reproduction and regeneration. Childless mothers and their husbands drank the waters of the Mississippi and brought forth young; unproductive men in North Carolina ate the teeth of the alligator's right jaw, "to provoke Venery"; and other sterile colonists devoured the beaver's tail, the hare's eggs, the cod's head, with gratifying results. William Byrd in 1728 verified the Indian belief in the potency of bear's meat, for among his party of surveyors who partook heavily of bear's flesh, "all the Marryed men of our Company were joyful Fathers within forty weeks after they got Home, and most of the Single men had children sworn to them within the same time, our chaplain always excepted."

The travelers' tale of natural wonders survived deep into the eighteenth century and turns up, somewhat rationalized, in the writings of famous men. John Adams found a healing spring at Stafford Springs, Connecticut, which in a few days cured a sickly man who had languished for thirty years under doctors' care. The mysterious fossil remains at Big Bone Lick in Kentucky attracted, among other commentators, Thomas

Colonial Folklore

Jefferson, who knew the Delaware Indian tradition: The Great Man above sent his lightning bolts at these mammoths, destroying the lesser animals, and the print of his seat and feet can still be seen on the mountain where he rested. But as the new empirical sciences probed into the phenomena of nature, the extravagances of the wonder tale soared into outright hoax. Benjamin Franklin twisted the travelers' tale into the lying tale when he pictured for English readers how sheep in America trailed carts to carry their heavy wool, and whales flung themselves over Niagara Falls in pursuit of the cod.

Not all accounts of the colonial scene presented a glowing picture. Some delighted in portraying the terrors of the untamed land. To protect their colony against the slanders of "scum" and "pirates" who had deserted Virginia and scandalized Englishmen with the story of a starving colonist forced to eat his dead wife, the Council for Virginia in 1610 issued this denial: "There was one of the company who mortally hated his wife and therefore secretly killed her, then cut her in pieces and hid her in divers parts of his house. When the woman was missing, the man was suspected, his house searched, and parts of her mangled body were discovered. To excuse himself he said that his wife died, that he hid her to satisfy his hunger, and that he fed daily upon her." Ample provisions of meal, beans, and peas were found in his house, and the man was burned for his villainy. A spokesman for the Council for New England in 1628 explained away another case of a starving colonist with a strange story he heard from the man's companion. A Londoner named Chapman sailing for America spent seven to eight pounds weekly on wine, tobacco, and whores while his ship lay at anchor in Plymouth. On the voyage he exchanged a fifty-shilling suit for a pipeful of tobacco, and at last became servant to his own servant, who offered him one biscuit cake a day if he worked, and half a cake if he preferred to idle. Chapman chose to be idle and starved to death. "Where was the fault now, in the man or in the country?"

Indians in their turn pictured the horrendous dangers of the inland country, hoping to deter the white man from further explorations. A chief of the Illinois, Nikanape, sought to dissuade Father Hennepin from traveling down the Mississippi, saying that the river was full of dread monsters and serpents and that if his craft survived them, it would surely be drawn into a rapid current at the mouth leading "into a horrid whirlpool that swallows up everything that comes near it, and even the river itself, which appears no more, losing itself in that hideous and bottomless gulf."

From rumors, reports, slanders, and counter-slanders such as these, grew the extravagant narratives about geography, climate, flora, and fauna which have characterized American folklore to the present day.

Colonists in America faced not only the hazards of nature but also the sorceries of the red natives who roamed the woods. In the light of Christian doctrine, Europeans were intellectually prepared to equate savages with devils, and hence to credit the conjurations and divinations of Indian shamans as fully as did their own tribesmen. Cotton Mather, New England's foremost divine, explicitly linked the shamans or "powaws" with infernal spirits, from whom they derived powers of fortune-telling, enchantment, and miraculous healing. The wizardry of Pissacannawa reached the ears of one early New England chronicler, William Wood, who related that "he can make the water burn, the rocks move, the trees dance, metamorphize himself into a flaming man." Should some object that this is hallucination, Pissacannawa can do more, "for in winter, when there is no green leaves to be got, he will burn an old one to ashes, and putting those into the water, produce a new green leaf, which you shall not only see but substantially handle and carry away; and make of a dead snake's skin a living snake, both to be seen, felt, and heard." An eyewitness, "an honest gentleman," told Wood how through God's permission, with the Devil's help, another powaw had sucked forth a sliver from the foot of a lame man, and spat it into a tray of water.

English settlers must often have repeated tales of these marvels, for Beverley introduces one as "The latest story of conjuration." It concerned the well-known Virginian planter Colonel William Byrd, whose lands at the head of the James River were suffering from a severe drought. An Indian approached one of the Colonel's overseers, professing great friendship for his master, and offered to bring a rainfall to save the tobacco crop, in return for two bottles of rum. The sky being cloudless, the overseer agreed. "Upon this the Indian went immediately a-powawing, as they call it; and in about half an hour there came up a black cloud into the sky that showered down rain enough upon this gentleman's corn and tobacco, but none at all upon any of the neighbors', except a few drops of the skirt of the shower." The overseer jumped on a horse and rode nearly forty miles to tell Colonel Byrd the marvel.

After noting several Indian cures conjured upon white men, in his breezy history of North Carolina, Lawson recalled a particularly dramatic example from Maryland. A poor planter there had grown increasingly emaciated from a lingering distemper, and also impoverished, having given all his Negro slaves in payment to the English doctors, who purged him to no avail. Finally an Indian friend named Jack offered to treat this disease, for a blanket and powder and shot. Jack prepared a decoction of herbs and roots which he gave the planter to drink in bed. Toward evening he returned with a live rattlesnake in his hand, which he insisted the sick man take to bed with him, saying the fangs had been removed. The distressed planter at first preferred to die of distemper, but finally consented to have Jack gird the snake about his middle. The rattler drew itself tight as a belt around the planter's waist. Eventually its twitches grew weaker, and by morning it died, and the man's distemper had disappeared, gone into the reptile.

Seeing such performances by the powaws, American colonists gave heed to Indian stories of their gods and demons, from whom the powaws drew their occult strength. "Cheepie," their most ghoulish demon, so terrified the New England Indians they would not stir out at night, a reaction quite comprehensible to Devil-fearing English settlers. "One Black Robin, an Indian, sitting down in the cornfield belonging to the house where I resided," Josselyn wrote, "ran out of his wigwam frighted with the apparition of two infernal spirits in the shape of Mohawks. Another time two Indians and an Indess came running into our house crying out they should all die—Cheepie was gone over the field gliding in the air with a long rope hanging from one of his legs. We asked them what he was like. They said, all one Englishman, clothed with hat and coat, shoes and stockings." (Indians too equated the Devil with their enemy!) Josselyn saw for himself one of their apparitions, a flame appearing upon a wigwam, when some Indians called him out at dead of night. The flame mounted into the air over the settlement church, on the north side, signifying a death shortly in that quarter.

Along with powaw magic and demon sorcery, the colonists marveled at the fanciful myths of the red man. The Indian god had left his giant footprints in a rock by the falls of the James River, in Virginia, about five feet apart. On seeing them Beverley was reminded "what the fathers of the Romish Church tell us, that our Lord left the print of his feet on the stone whereon he stood while he talked with St. Peter; which stone was afterward preserved as a very sacred relic."

A Dutch agent for the Labadist sect, Jasper Danckaerts, asked a Long Island Indian eighty years old where his people came from. The red man drew on the floor with a hot coal a little circle, with four paws, a head, and a tail. "This is a tortoise lying in the water," he said, and moved his hand around the figure. "This was all water, and so at first was the world of the earth, when the tortoise gradually raised its round back up high, and the water ran off of it, and thus the earth became dry." Then he took a little straw and placed it in the middle of the figure. "There grew a tree in the middle of the earth, and the root of this tree sent forth a sprout beside it and there grew upon it a man, who was the first male. This man was then alone, and would have remained alone, but the tree bent over until its top touched the earth, and there shot therein another root, from which came forth another sprout, and there grew upon it the woman; and from these two are all men produced."

John Gyles, a settler in Maine captured by Indians, lived with them a number of years and learned their language and legends of an enchanted mountain called Teddon. An Indian beauty who spurned any human consort disappeared from her family while they lived at the head of Penobscot River, by the Teddon. After much search and distress, they finally discovered her sporting and swimming with a handsome youth, whose hair, like hers, flowed down below his waist. The two vanished at their approach, but the parents considered their son-in-law a kind spirit of the Teddon, and called upon him for moose, bear, or other game at the waterside, and the animals would immediately come swimming toward them. Gyles heard another wonder from an Indian who lived by the river at the foot of the Teddon. Seeing its summit through the smoke-hole in his wigwam he was tempted to travel there, and spent a whole day laboriously attempting to ascend the hill, but the peak seemed as remote as ever, and he finally concluded the spirits were present and so turned back. Three other young Indians became "disordered and delirious" after several days touring the Teddon, and upon their minds clearing, found themselves already one day's journey toward home, conveyed, no doubt, by the genii of the place.

A comic as well as a supernatural folklore developed about the red man in the minds of the settlers. In their personal relations with the lordly white man, Indians often played the part of the fool, ignorant of such furnishings of civilization as pistols and powder, books and rum. As one chronicler after another recorded Indian antics and accidents, a folk stereotype took shape, antedating the Yankee, of a red-skinned booby, complete even to pidgin English dialect. Cotton Mather ridiculed one tawny brave who mounted the horse of a Maine colonist for sport, had himself strapped on for security, and was promptly ridden out of sight by the mettlesome steed, nothing ever being found of him but a leg. In Virginia one of Powhatan's savages dried gunpowder on a piece of armor plate, as he had seen the English do, but dried it too long, and blew himself and one or two of his fellows to eternity. The numskull Indian was easily duped. A lone settler, Thomas Bickford, held off a marauding band by appearing at his windows in a variety of liveries, thus causing them to think a strong garrison occupied the place. Another group, plotting to kill the English in Plymouth for their provisions, gave up their design when they saw Thomas Willett, master of the trading house, solemnly reading the Bible; for from the gravity of his countenance they realized he had detected their scheme from the book. New England settlers spoofed a friendly Indian who asked what they kept in the hole in the ground (where they stored their powder), by telling him "The plague." Later he asked them to let the plague out to destroy a hostile tribe. A chronicle of 1675 relates how Captain Mosely with sixty men faced three hundred Indians in battle; the captain plucked off his periwig and tucked it into his breeches, preparatory to fighting, whereupon the red men turned tail and fled, crying out "Umh, umh, me no stay more fight Engismon, Engismon got two head, if me cut off un head he got noder a put on beder as dis." This theme persisted across the frontier, and we hear of a Yankee on the western plains, confronted by hostile Indians, pulling out his false teeth and unstrapping his cork leg, then making a move as if to unscrew his head, the while informing the braves he could similarly dismember them; they fled in terror.

This anecdotal portrait of the doltish Indian early began to show another side. Again like the Yankee, the folk Indian concealed a low cunning beneath his rude appearance. He engaged in a battle of wits that proved more successful than his forest warfare. In one oft-repeated colonial anecdote, the white man triumphs, but over a shrewd, not a stupid, redskin. Hendrick, chief of the Mohawks, in a council meeting told the British superintendent of Indian affairs in America, Sir William Johnson, that the previous night he had dreamed Sir William had given him a fine laced coat. Knowing the Indian commitment to dreams, Johnson immediately pulled off his rich garment and gave it to the delighted chief, who departed crying out "Who-ah" in great good humor. At the next council meeting, Sir William informed the Mohawk that he too had dreamed, namely that the chieftain had given him a fertile five-thousand-acre tract along the Mohawk River. Hendrick accordingly deeded over the land, but remarked ruefully, "Now, Sir William, I will never dream with you again; you dream too hard for me."

The outlines of the sly, underdog, dialect-speaking Indian appear in fugitive colonial sources. In a poem written in 1676 on King Philip's War, "New-England's Crisis," the poet, Benjamin Tompson, reproduces a speech of King Philip to his counselors and followers, inciting them against the English. Some Indian phrasings occur, particularly in one passage where King Philip points out the double standard of the white man's justice.

> We drink, we so big whipt; but english they
> Go sneep, no more, or else a little pay.
> Me meddle Squaw, me hang'd; our fathers kept
> What Squaws they would. . . .

In 1946 I heard a very similar anecdote in northern Michigan, where Ojibwa Indian reservations are located, in which an Irishman quoted the words of a plaintive Indian sentenced to six months in jail for chasing a white woman. "White man come out, have all squaw he want. That all right, all right, all right. Indian try same thing and get hell kicked out of him. Now what's the matter, judge?"

An early newspaper story, from the Boston *Evening Post* for August 2, 1736, shows a poker-faced Indian regurgitating the white man's culture. Lord Lovelace, newly arrived from England, interrogates a Christian Indian on the principles of true religion and divine revelation. He asks, "Well, tell me then, how came this World, and how came Man at first?" In reply the Indian gives this synopsis of Genesis:

Well—now me tell you what me tink: When first Time God make dis World, he make one Man and one Woman, den he make one clebber Orchard, den he tell em dat Man and dat Woman,— "See, me gib you dis Orchard, best way you lib here and eat Apples, only dat one Tree grow dere dat side, be sure you no eat, cause so big Poison, if you eat dat sure you poisoned, you run mad and turn Rogue presently, therefore sure you no eat."

He say "No." So when go it away God, dat Man his squaw she look dat Tree, see, 'tis clebber Apples, all red one side, and smell sweet, she good mind taste, she taste. Oh clebber sweet. Den she speak dat Man her Sannup [husband, master], "Here you—you nebber taste all one such sweet Apples, best way you taste too." See den he taste too. Den presently both on 'em turn Rogue, quite Rogue, and ebber since all his Children Rogue too. Now ebbery body Rogue, now I Rogue, and you Rogue, too, and ebbery body Rogue.

Here the comic Indian secures revenge on the white man who sneers at Indian myths as childish, by reducing the Christian myth to the same skeletal absurdity. A more direct form of the rebuff has the Indian tell the missionary, "You come across the water to tell us you killed your god, and then you blame us for it."

In the era of settlement, Indian supernaturalism entered deeply into American thinking. Puritans regarded Indian sorcery and mythology as certain proof of the Devil's presence, linked with the witchcraft in their own midst. The Pequot War of 1636 and King Philip's War of 1675 were not simply struggles against a savage foe but part of their perpetual battle against the malignant, occult forces of Satan.

Englishmen brought to America their own inheritance of supernatural convictions. One form of English supernaturalism, newly evolved since the Reformation, found its most appropriate environment in the New England colonies, for it reinforced the special interpretation Puritans gave their history. This was the belief in remarkable providences.

The Puritans who emigrated to Massachusetts Bay in 1630 regarded themselves as chief actors in a world drama being staged under God's direct supervision in the American wilderness. In line with Calvin's rigorous determinism, the Puritans believed that God controlled every event in the universe, even to the falling of a sparrow; that he had doomed all mankind to damnation for Adam's sin, but requited an arbitrarily chosen few upon Christ's Atonement; and that these "elect" constituted his own saints who would persevere in grace and resist all Satan's blandishments. Puritan saints in old England gathered together and removed to their chartered colony in New England, to live in isolation from the world's sinners and erect a Bible Commonwealth of sanctified citizens obeying his revealed Word as laid down in Scripture. Thus would a community of "visible saints" come into being, the only one in the world. Under the inspiration of this grand motive, the Puritans planted their colony and sought to achieve a holy society.

The progress of their venture became their all-consuming interest. God communicated to his saints through providences which he insinuated into the daily flow of routine events. To extract the meaning of these divine messages, the Puritans assiduously collected and deciphered the remarkable disasters and deliverances, omens and prodigies, and accidents and mishaps transpiring in their midst. A plague or an Indian foray might signal God's displeasure and admonish the saints to scrutinize their behavior still more closely, to see wherein they were falling short of his commands. Marvelous escapes from shipwreck, Indian captivity, or starvation reassured the elect that the Lord was guarding their fortunes under his watchful eye.

The material for the providences came from the heady lives of the settlers bent on conquering a new and untamed world. But the threads of wonder and shock that tied together the providences into little fabliaux were drawn from the storehouse of Old World folklore motifs. The providences are replete with ghosts and apparitions, heavenly signs and pernicious omens, which had permeated British folklore for centuries. Since providences by their very nature involved extraordinary happenings, they were much talked about, repeated and enlarged upon, and rendered still more awesome, in the manner of all oral legends. The absorbing interest of Puritan ministers and congregations in providential manifestations of the Divine Will further stimulated the normal human interest in sensational events, and caused them to be bruited all the more. New England saints did more than talk about providences. They also noted them down in diaries and posted reports to the two leading Massachusetts divines, Increase Mather and his son Cotton. In 1684 Increase wrote *An Essay for the Recording of Illustrious Providences*, and when Cotton published his providential history of the Puritan commonwealth in 1702, *Magnalia Christi Americana*, he devoted one of its six sections to expanding his father's collection. Certain of these providences became tenacious New England legends enduring to the present day.

A typical miscellany of providences appears in the diary of John Hull, mintmaster of Massachusetts, who titled it "Some Observable Passages of Providence toward the Country." Two women go raving mad and refuse to eat; another walks naked to church; a man dreams of fighting with devils. The heavens are continually perturbed with great storms of hail as big as duck eggs, flaming comets and stars, the blare of guns and drums. A boy shoots his father in the bowels, an Indian slays a pregnant housewife, a tailor is found dead on Lord's day morning after a night in a wine cellar—"a tippling fellow, profanely malignant against the ways of people and God." Burning homes, smallpox epidemics, lightning bolts, and Pequot raids carry off the settlers with swift and sudden blows. "The Lord teaches us what such sad providences speak unto us all," Hull penned in 1657.

These assorted providences follow definite patterns. God smote the profane, seditious, and heretic with just and dreadful punishments. The saints took solid comfort from the swift vengeance meted out to their manifold enemies in such "judgments." John Winthrop, first governor of Massachusetts, described in his journal a monster born to a follower of the antinomian heretic Mrs. Hutchinson, having a face but no head, two mouths, horns over the eyes, pricks and scales all over the breast and back, and three claws on each foot. Increase Mather, noting "The hand of God was very remarkable in that which came to pass in the Narragansett country in New England, not many weeks since" (1683), set down a string of providential judgments. A lying atheist, accused of doing mischief to his neighbor's cattle, said "He wished to God he might never stir out of that place, if he had done that which he was charged with." Instantly he sunk down dead into the arms of his son-in-law. A man on the isle of Providence, similarly under accusation, blasphemed that "the Devil might put out his eyes if he had done as was suspected concerning him." That very night a rheum fell into his eyes, and within a few days he became stark blind. A notorious drunkard on Long Island fell into a fire, and on awakening cried "Fire! Fire!" as if he were in hell, and so continued yelling, in spite of water being thrown upon him, until he died in torment a day or two later. The missionary John Eliot told of two ungodly servants who drowned on an oyster bank, "A dreadful example of God's displeasure against obstinate servants." Winthrop reported a dastardly seaman who swore he would take one pipe of tobacco, "if the Devil should carry him away quick," and lit his pipe while sitting on a barrel of powder; he was blown to the sky and later found with his hands and feet torn off. Increase Mather recorded various afflictions laid upon the "singing and dancing Quakers" who were particular anathema to Puritans. Even a New Haven church member of twenty years standing, presumably a holy saint but actually, in the words of Cotton Mather, a "diabolical creature" and "hellhound," met his judgment when he was hanged in 1662 along with a cow, two heifers, three sheep, and two sows, with whom he had committed "infandous buggeries." Yet heaven had sent him remarkable warnings to repent of his impieties, for many years previous his daughter had dreamed she saw her father being executed among a great multitude.

God's judgments blasted not only sinners who broke the

holy law, but also critics and enemies of the state. Governor Winthrop hammered home the lesson of such seditious conduct. Had not the "Mary Rose" mysteriously blown up in Charlestown harbor, causing death to the master and a number of the company, profane scoffers all, who refused to attend church and complained about Boston's low prices for their commodities? "This judgment of God upon these scorners of his ordinances and the ways of his servants gives occasion to mention other examples of like kind," commented the governor, "by which it will appear how the Lord hath owned this work, and preserved and prospered his people here beyond ordinary ways of providence." So he cited Mason and Georges, promoters of a rival colony in Maine, whose costly ship was broken at launching; Austin, a dissatisfied colonist who quitted New England but was captured with his family by the Turks and sold into slavery; the group of malcontents lashed by a tempest on their return to England and spared only because one, Phillips of Wrentham, had praised New England. Increase Mather noted the miserable fates of two Indians, Simon and Squando, who had shed much innocent blood of the settlers. Simon was accidentally shot in the arm and lived two years in such pain that other Indians called him "worse than dead." Squando thought the Englishman's God had promised he would never die more if he took his own life, so he hanged himself, and "This was the end of the man that disturbed the peace of New England."

As he annihilated their enemies, so did the Lord providentially preserve his elect. "Remarkable was the preservation and restoration which the gracious providence of God vouchsafed to Abigail Eliot, the daughter of elder Eliot, of Boston in New England," wrote Increase Mather. When a child of five, the iron hinge of a cart under which she was playing pierced her skull and brain, and on its being drawn forth bits of bloody brains oozed out. A bunch the size of a small egg appeared above the wound, which the surgeon pressed back into the opening and covered with a silver plate. "The brains of the child did swell and swage according to the tides. When it was spring tide her brain would heave up the tender skin, and fill the place sometimes; when it was neap tide, they would be sunk and fallen within the skull." Abigail lived to be the healthy mother of two children.

Massachusetts Puritans did not monopolize all providential reports of judgments and deliverances, which other Protestant colonies and Roman Catholic missions also recorded as marks of God's special concern with their plantations. A great plague of weevils struck the "godless and profane" planters of Maryland and Virginia. According to Jasper Danckaerts, a Dutch agent and Labadist missionary in America, those planters listened neither to God nor his commandments, squandered their money on wine and brandy, and quarreled with their Dutch neighbors in New Netherlands. During the English war with the Dutch, the Lord caused weevils to eat up all the grain and vegetables of the field and create a famine in Maryland and Virginia. Many died, and one woman was reduced to eating her own child. On the scaffold she cried out, in his hearing, that the governor of Maryland alone should bear the guilt of her crime, for he had led an expedition against the Dutch and burned their crops, and God had therefore smitten the English with this visitation of weevils.

Still the Lord smiled providentially on Virginian Anglicans. The Council for Virginia called public attention to his marvelous deliverances in the Starving Time of 1609–10. First Sir

American Folklore

Thomas Gates and Sir George Somers were preserved through a fearful tempest, by sighting the enchanted isles of the Bermudas, whose devils turned into herds of swine, while fat and fair fowls perched on the shoulders of the men when they whistled. "An accident, I take it, that cannot be paralleled by any history, except when God sent abundance of quail to feed his Israel in the barren wilderness." Then as a second providential design, the company thus marvelously delivered built two pinnaces and sailed for the Virginia colony just in time, in the spring of 1610, to rescue the despairing and near starving Jamestown colonists. "This was not Ariadne's thread, but the direct line of God's providence."

From Maryland, the Roman Catholic colony, came miracles to equal the providences. Father White was called to the death-bed of a Christian Indian pierced near the heart by a wooden spear. The Jesuit father received his confession, recited the gospel for the sick, and applied sacred relics of the most holy cross on each side of the wound, two fingers broad. The following day he beheld this same Indian paddling a canoe. Seeing the father, he threw open his cloak and revealed the scar of the wound, now fully healed. Father Edward Knott wrote his superiors of a high-born planter in Maryland reduced to poverty by his own licentiousness, and then recalled to the right faith by a Jesuit father. He took all the sacraments at the point of death, and after his burial a brilliant light was seen at night around his tomb, "even by Protestants."

In the folklore of all peoples appear such acts of the gods in punishing the ungodly and rewarding the faithful. The Calvinistic theory of providences gave universal folklore motifs direct and special application to American history, which commenced indeed under providential direction. Besides the miracles of the deities, other folk beliefs, in dreams, signs, apparitions, enchantments, were brought within the concept of providences.

The idea that a corpse bleeds when touched by its murderer is anciently known throughout the Western world. Cotton Mather recounted the unmasking of Mary Martin, in 1646, who yielded three times to the temptations of a married man, withal pleading each time to God that "she would leave herself unto his justice, to be made a public example," were she ever overtaken again. She conceived, and murdered the infant, "hiding it in a chest from the eyes of all but the jealous God." When she was made to touch the dead babe before the jury, the blood came fresh upon it, and she confessed all. And what was remarkable at her execution, as she had twice essayed to kill the child, so the unskilful executioner twice turned her off the ladder before she died.

Cotton Mather described another case occurring in 1674, with ominous implications for all New England. A Christian Indian, John Sausaman, informed the governor of Plymouth colony that King Philip was plotting to lead several Indian nations against the English. Shortly after, Sausaman was "barbarously murdered" by certain Indians, who cut a hole in the ice and disposed of his body there, to make it seem he had drowned. But a jury discovered that his neck was broken in the Indian way of murdering. "One Tobias, a counselor of King Philip's whom they suspected as the author of this murder, approaching to the dead body, it would still *fall a-bleeding afresh*, as if it had newly been slain." Other evidence then confirmed this test, and Tobias was hanged. Sausaman's rumor proved true, and King Philip's War broke out the following year.

American Folklore

In one of the English and Scottish traditional ballads, "Young Hunting," the corpse of Young Hunting (or Earl Richard) flows with blood when touched by his jealous murderess.

> White, white waur his wounds washen,
>   As white as ony lawn;
> But sune's the traitor stude afore,
>   Then oot the red blude sprang.

The *Niebelungenlied* and Shakespeare's *Richard III* contain the same folk belief, and so do registries of legal trials. A case in the Scottish courts in 1687 shows a close parallel with that of John Sausaman. Philip Standfield, profligate son of Sir James Standfield, stood by when the body of his father, who presumably drowned himself in a pond, was disinterred. Philip placed his hand on the corpse's head, when the mouth and nostrils instantly gushed with blood, *"according to God's usual mode of discovering murder."* With little other evidence Philip was found guilty of being accessory to the murder. Another Scottish instance concerned two youths who quarreled while fishing in the river Yarrow; one killed the other and buried him deep in the sands. Fifty years later a smith uncovered a curious bone, which he showed to a group in the smithy, among them an old white-headed man, who no sooner touched it than the bone streamed with purple blood. He confessed the crime, but died before he could be executed.

As late as 1875 the belief in a murderer being revealed by his victim's blood is reported from North Carolina newspapers, when two white men accused of killing a Negro in a barroom brawl were compelled to touch the corpse. A current oral tradition from Ashe County, North Carolina, states that when the murderer touched his victim, laid out in a stiff white shirt and a black suit, blood spurted forth on the white shirt, and he yelled out, "Good Gawd A'mighty, I done hit," then fell down in a fit.

The test-by-blood that disclosed the murderer of the Christian Indian was linked with other prodigies by which God signaled to his elect the forthcoming of King Philip's War. After discussing Sausaman, Cotton Mather in his next breath spoke of "divers persons in Malden who heard in the air . . . a great gun go off," with the singing of bullets over their heads and the sound of drums, while the same day in Plymouth colony "invisible troops of horses were heard riding to and fro." Down in Virginia, where in the same year of 1675 Bacon's Rebellion was impending, three prodigies were "looked upon as ominous presages." A large comet resembling a horse tail streamed westward; swarms of flies about an inch long rose out of spigot holes in the earth and ate new-sprouted leaves from tree tops; and flights of pigeons whose weight when roosting broke the limbs of large trees, passed overhead without visible end—a sight that "put the old planters under the more portentous apprehensions, because the like was seen (as they said) in the year 1640 when the Indians committed the last massacre."

Apparitions loomed large and fearfully in the English folklore brought by the colonists to America and grafted onto the New World by the theory of providences. At five in the morning of May 2, 1687, Joseph Beacon in Boston saw his brother, then living in London, appear before him in a Bengal gown he usually wore, with a napkin tied about a bloody wound on his head, looking "pale, ghastly, deadly." Said the apparition, "Brother! I have been most barbarously and inhumanely murdered by a debauched fellow, to whom I never did any wrong in my life." So saying he vanished. In great astonishment Joseph related the matter to his family. The following June he learned by post that his brother had the preceding April run afoul of a drunken fellow who smote Beacon on the skull with a fire-fork, from which grievous wound he died at five in the morning of May 2. Joseph Beacon, "a most ingenious, accomplished, and well-disposed young gentleman," gave his minister, Cotton Mather, a signed testimonial to the vision.

New England's most famous apparition was witnessed by a whole throng of saints, and remained the subject of wonder for at least half a century. Governor Winthrop referred in his journal to the spectral ship sighted over New Haven harbor in 1647, and Cotton Mather in the *Magnalia* gave a more extended account in 1702, including a testimonial letter from the minister at New Haven. In January of 1647 a richly laden ship had sailed from New Haven, never to be seen again. The godly people of the town earnestly prayed the Lord to "Let them hear what he had done with their dear friends, and prepare them with a suitable submission to his Holy Will." In June a great thunderstorm arose out of the northwest, and when it cleared, a ship like the lost vessel appeared in the air at the harbor's mouth, and sailed against the wind for half an hour. "Many were drawn to behold this great work of God; yea, the very children cried out, 'There's a brave ship!'" At length her topsails seemed blown off, her hulk overset, and she vanished into a smoky cloud. The Reverend Mr. Davenport declared that God had granted to his grieving saints this "extraordinary account of his sovereign disposal of those for whom so many fervent prayers were made continually." "Reader," concluded Mather, "there being yet living so many credible gentlemen that were eyewitnesses of this wonderful thing, I venture to publish it for a thing as undoubted as 'tis wonderful."

Still other spectral ships sailed before the seaboard settlers. Lawson reported in 1709 having heard in Carolina, from "men of the best credit in the country," that Sir Walter Raleigh's ship, which had brought the very first colonists to the lost plantation of Roanoke, often appeared among them "in a gallant posture."

Providences issued from God and witchcrafts from the Devil, and they marked the tide of battle between the forces of Christ and the minions of Satan. Witches sneaked aboard the ships headed for America, and murmurings of their evil work rumbled throughout the seventeenth century, as they attempted to subvert the cities of the Lord. As the end of the first century of colonization neared, the disturbances created by the Devil gave point to an oft-told jest, set down by a substantial Puritan citizen, Lawrence Hammond, in his diary for 1688, as a true incident.

In New England, one J. Bradbent, an exciseman and a hectoring debauchee resident in Boston (where too many of the same stamp have lately multiplied), meeting an honest, ingenious countryman upon the road, inquired of him, "What news, countryman?" Who replied, "I know none."

The other then replied, "I'll tell you, son. The Devil is dead."

"How?" said the countryman. "I believe not that."

"Yes," said the other, "he is dead for certain."

"Well, then," said the countryman, "if he be dead, he hath left many fatherless children in Boston."

In truth the Devil and his witches appeared to be making heavy inroads into the congregations of saints. The gossipy Josselyn noted, "There are none that beg in the country, but there be witches too many, bottle-bellied witches amongst the

Quakers, and others that produce many strange apparitions, if you will believe report. Of a shallop at sea manned with women. Of a ship and a great red horse standing by the mainmast. . . . Of a witch that appeared aboard of a ship twenty leagues to sea to a mariner, who took up the carpenter's broadax and cleft her head with it, the witch dying of the wound at home." And Danckaerts in 1680 wrote of Boston, "I have never been in a place where more was said about witchcraft and witches."

Sometimes Satan and his demons caused objects in a house to fly about. An example of such a poltergeist occurred at Portsmouth, New Hampshire, in 1682, and was duly communicated to Increase Mather. Showers of stones rained inside the house of George Walton; the spit was carried up the chimney; a nimble black cat was seen; a dismal hollow whistling was heard, and sometimes the noise of a horse snorting and trotting; the anchor leaped overboard Walton's boat; cocks of hay were hung upon trees; a hand appeared at the hall window. Increase wrote up the deviltry as "Lithobolia, or the Stone-Throwing Demon."

The mischief of poltergeists paled before the torments and deaths wrought by the witches. Aghast, Cotton Mather recorded the fate in 1684 of Philip Smith, a deacon of Hadley, member of the General Court, justice, selectman, militia lieutenant, a man exemplary for "devotion, sanctity, gravity," who was "murdered with an hideous witchcraft." Knowing that a wretched woman in town had threatened him, the deacon cried out, "There shall be a wonder in Hadley! I shall not be dead, when 'tis thought I am!" Strange mischiefs occurred at his bedside; galley pots of medicine were unaccountably emptied; a flame was seen upon the bed, which shook unaccountably. After his death the jury found his body punctured with holes, his privates burned, his back bruised, but his countenance lively as if he still lived. A clattering of stools and chairs was heard around the corpse.

When sufficient of such cases had been faithfully recorded, Cotton Mather stated his conviction of New England's jeopardy. "That the Devil is come down unto us with great wrath, we find, we feel, we now deplore." Appearing like a small, black man among the proud, ignorant, and envious, he had decoyed sinners into signing his book, whereupon these witches "have met in hellish rendezvous" to perform "diabolical sacraments, imitating the baptism and the supper of our Lord." In view of the Puritan design to found a Bible commonwealth, this multiplication of witchcrafts pointed in one ominous direction. Clearly Satan and his agents were plotting *"to destroy the kingdom of our Lord Jesus Christ in these parts of the world."* Other Protestants in New York and Virginia, and the Roman Catholics in Maryland, spoke of witchery, but the neurotic intensity of the New England witch scare, climaxed in the Salem trials of 1692, grew from the providential aura the Puritans gave their colonial enterprise. In Massachusetts Bay the dark powers of the Devil were assaulting the citadel of God's saints.

Many folklore tales entered court records in the accusation and trial of Susanna Martin at Salem, June 29, 1692. When John Allen of Salisbury had refused to let his oxen carry her staves, she had threatened the beasts, and they had all run into the sea. Bernard Peache testified that he heard a scrabbling at the window while he lay abed, when Susanna Martin entered, took hold of his feet and drew his body in a heap, then lay on him for near two hours. The likeness of a cat had flown at

Robert Downer and seized him by the throat, till he remembered that Susanna Martin had threatened him the day before, so he cried out, "Avoid, thou she-devil! In the name of God the Father, the Son, and the Holy Ghost, avoid!" Whereupon it flew out the window. And among other wonders, Sarah Atkinson swore that Susanna Martin came to her house on foot from a long distance in dismal weather, and yet not even the soles of her shoes were wet. Atkinson professed amazement that Martin was not wet to her knees, whereon Martin replied, *"She scorned to be drabbled!"* In court this testimony threw her into singular confusion.

The witch hysteria reached its crescendo in a panicky purge of respected citizens along with old crones, and receded abruptly before the eighteenth-century winds of rationalism. But the witch tales had seeded themselves deeply into the colonial soil, and ever since have continued to sprout in weedy patches of the backcountry. Scarcely a New England town history but contains its legend of the local goodwife who ill-wishes her neighbors, and plagues them in the form of a cat, or other beast or bird. In the present day the old witch stories are still told with deep conviction by Southern Negroes, Ozark hillfolk, and down-East fishermen.

A minute examination of colonial writings might uncover many more samples of folklore. Bloody ballads, old wives' cures, pithy proverbs, children's pastimes, sailor superstitions —all these entered the lives of the settlers. But in the travelers' tales and Indian conjurations, the divine providences and satanic witchcrafts, we see the multiplicity of universal folklore motifs pervading colonial life and thought and powerfully influencing the course of early American history.

II

The Rise of Native Folk Humor

1780–1825

After a century and a half in the New World, Americans began to center their folk invention upon themselves. The novelties of quill-throwing porcupines and paw-sucking bears lost their freshness as civilization became established along the seaboard, and the travelers' tales of natural wonders migrated into the fabulous West. By the time of the Revolution the Indian tribes had largely been ejected from the midst of the colonists, and relegated to the alien frontier. The force and zeal of supernatural Calvinism spent itself, fading in the sober climate of the Enlightenment. A mounting skepticism now tamed the wild accounts of prodigies and marvels that had filled the air since the early settlements. The Boston *Evening Post* on August 4, 1766, in a dispatch from New Haven, began in a customary vein: "A report prevails that some unaccountable noises were lately heard near Hartford; and 'tis said, via

Derby, that a few men being lately at work in a wood, they were terrified with an extraordinary Voice, commanding them to read the seventh chapter of Ezekiel." Then in a sudden switch the column professed rank disbelief in the marvel: "After the cause of any wonderful thing is discovered, astonishment, perplexity and fear commonly cease." This verse follows:

> Nature well-known, no Prodigies remain:
> Comets are regular, Eclipses plain.

For proof the article proffered an incident of a skeptical housewife disturbed in bed by a violent series of rappings. She searched the kitchen, and "beheld the Cat jump on one handle of a long cross-cut saw, while the other lay upon a Pine-Board Dresser, and the main body on another thing. The weight of the Cat lifted the handle which lay on the Dresser, and made it quiver so as to give three raps. . . ." Thus a simple natural explanation blew away another poltergeist.

So the providences and wonders passed from general attention. The penchant for yarning and tall talk continued with ever mounting vigor but now drew its materials from a new source, the odd grain of American character. Regional types, whom English travelers and American aristocrats viewed with amused disdain, evolved—or degenerated—in the New England hills and Carolina swamps. William Byrd already in 1728 had spied out the shiftless creatures of "Lubberland" on the backwoods border of Virginia and North Carolina.

These new American breeds exhibited the traits of colonials, falling somewhere between wild and civilized men on the ladder of cultural refinement. Isolated in mountain pockets or forest clearings, lacking education and contact with centers of culture such as even the lower classes enjoyed in the English towns, they provided natural butts for the wit of the educated. In a sense the down-Easter and Kentuckian supplant the Indian after the Revolution as examples of the grotesque human beings found in the American wilderness.

Yet the Yankee bumpkin, southern clay-eater, and western roarer contained the stuff of homespun American heroes. They turned the ridicule of high-toned English and eastern travelers to glory in brags about themselves during their Revolutionary triumph. The arduous struggle from 1775 to 1783 crystallized the sense of American identity, supplying heroes, symbols, and traditions to cement the new nation. "Yankee Doodle" emanated from the Revolution, originally intended to caricature the hayseed rebel, but then adopted by the patriots as a badge of independence. English officers and Tory traitors were effete gentlemen in finery, American patriots were ragged daredevils. A Revolutionary narrative of 1781 catches these images, and voices the rising spirit of rough-hewn American braggadocio.

We were the bravest of the brave; we were a formidable set of blue hen's chickens of the game blood, of indomitable courage, and strangers to fear. We were well provided with sticks; we made the egg shells—British and Tory skulls—fly, like onion peelings in a windy day; the blue cocks flapped their wings and crowed—"we are all for Liberty these times"; and all was over; our equals were scarce, and our superiors hard to find.

Throughout the chronicle the references ring to the "blue hen's chickens" from Delaware, precursors of the half-horse, half-alligator breed of the western woods and waters. A Tory refuses to believe that a few hundred scraggly colonials have defeated the picked troops of Colonel Ferguson in South Carolina. The patriots reply simply, "But we were all of us blue hen's chickens." The account breaks into a dialogue between two British officers, suggestive of later stage plays presenting Yankee and Kentucky heroes.

FIRST OFFICER: Some of them were South Carolina and Georgia Refugees, some from Virginia, some from the head of the Yadkin, some from the head of Catawba, some from over the Mountains, and some from everywhere else. They met at Gilbert Town, about 2000 desperadoes on horseback, calling themselves blue hen's chickens—started in pursuit of Ferguson, leaving as many footmen to follow. They overtook Col. Ferguson at a place called King's Mountain; there they killed Col. Ferguson after surrounding his army, defeated them and took them prisoners.
OFFICER OF GUARD: Can this be true?
FIRST OFFICER: As true as the gospel, and we may look out for breakers.
OFFICER OF GUARD: God bless us!
Whereupon David Knox jumped on a pile of firewood in the street, slapped his hands and thighs, and crowed like a cock, exclaiming "Day is at hand!"

The surprising and decisive American victory at King's Mountain gave substance to Yankee brag and shape to the newly forming image of "the gamecock of the wilderness." On the trans-Appalachian frontier that attracted hardy souls after the Revolution, these gamecocks startled decorous strangers, like the English traveler Thomas Ashe, who in 1806 descended into the Southwest "for the Purpose of Exploring the Rivers Allegheny, Monongahela, Ohio, and Mississippi, and Ascertaining the Produce and Condition of their Banks and Vicinity." While passing through a Kentucky hamlet, Ashe witnessed a favorite backwoods recreation, in the form of a vicious rough-and-tumble fight between a Kentuckian and a Virginian, which he recorded to the last grisly detail of gouged eye, chewed ear, and stomped bowel. That evening Ashe went to a backwoods ball, which ended in a general melee, whereupon the horrified Englishman retreated to his tavern, to hear his landlord expand luridly on the events of the day. Ashe remarked that "mine host . . . went so far as to tell me a variety of anecdotes, which from a respect for human nature, I suppress."

Accompanying the backwoods fight as a ritual prelude, so travelers observed, came an exchange of highly colored brags salted with bold metaphors. In 1808 Christian Schulz, Jr., overheard two drunken boatmen matching boasts in a pattern later to become commonplace in frontier humor.

> One said, "I am a man; I am a horse; I am a team. I can whip any man *in all Kentucky*, by G——d." The other replied, "I am an alligator, half man half horse; can whip any man *on the Mississippi*, by G——d." The first one again, "I am a man; have the best horse, best dog, best gun, and the handsomest wife in all Kentucky, by G——d." The other, "I am a Mississippi snapping turtle; have bear's claws, alligator's teeth, and the devil's tail; can whip *any man*, by G——d." This was too much for the first, and at it they went like two bulls. [Quoted in Walter Blair, *Native American Humor (1800–1900)* (New York, 1937), p. 30.]

A Knickerbocker man of letters traveling through the South noticed and faithfully described in 1817 a similar encounter between a "batteauxman" and a wagoner, with the preamble to fisticuffs still further elaborated. The wagoner chaws tobacco and cocks his eye; the boatman swigs from his whiskey bottle and leers. "The wagoner flapped his hands against his hips, and crowed like a cock; the batteauxman curved his neck, and neighed like a horse." Then came the boasts, about sweethearts, horses, and rifles, and finally the fracas.

Elsewhere in these *Letters from the South*, James K. Paulding sets down tall stories about rattlesnakes, hunters, and thick fog. Such tall tales had already appeared on the American scene, finding congenial company among Western brags. A jestbook published in 1808 provides excellent evidence of this fact. It bore the revealing title, *The American Magazine of Wit; A Collection of Anecdotes, Stories, and Narratives, Humorous, Marvellous, Witty, Queer, Remarkable, and Interesting. Partly Selected, and Partly Original.* One piece realistically describes "The Diverting Club," a group of bons vivants who gathered in New York to regale themselves with fierce yarns of hunting, fishing, and outdoor pursuits. Three complete texts are given from two of the storytellers present, localized in New York and Virginia, and they provide the earliest examples of now well-known American windies. The Split Dog, cut in twain by a sapling and patched hastily with two legs up and two down, is told independently and in conjunction with the Paul Bunyan cycle, where the reversible canine is called Elmer. The Wooly Horse, whose own skin, mistakenly replaced with sheepskins, turns into a fleecy hide, recurs in 1890 in Vermont on the lips of a local Münchausen, who also related the Split Dog. The third tale was volunteered by an elderly gentleman bent on topping these twin outrages. He recalled a fishing party in 1788, where a lady lost a gold earbob; a year later at the same spot she caught a large fish and opening it found inside—nothing but guts. This gives a negative twist to the tall tale of the fish found with lost objects that have grown astonishingly in its belly.

A year later Robert B. Thomas included in *The Farmer's Almanack* for 1809 a "Wonderful Story related by George Howell, a mighty Hunter, and known in that part of the country where he lived by the name of the Vermont Nimrod."

The Rise of Native Folk Humor

With one lucky shot Howell procured a deer, a sturgeon, a rabbit, three partridges, and a woodcock, and laid bare a honey tree. This is the first recording of America's favorite tall tale, the Wonderful Hunt, also well liked in Europe.

Yankee tricks rivalled backwoods boasts and hunting fictions in oral popularity. Travelers down East and out West reported hearing tales of slick and knavish Yankees peddling wares. Such yarns developed from a long tradition of European and English rogue tales, but acquired their own special sauce. The (Northampton) *Hampshire Gazette*, for July 8, 1789, printed this little story of "The Dreamer," lacking in any New World flavor.

A farmer, overhearing a conversation of two of his neighbours, in which they expressed much faith in dreams, took occasion to tell them, with great secrecy and strict injunctions not to mention it, that he had dreamed there was a large sum of money buried in a dung hill in his field, and promised them a share in the booty if they would help him search for it. It was agreed to carry the dung out upon the land for the better certainty of examination, and they brought their carts and set to work; but not finding the expected prize, one of them expressed a persuasion that it must be under the ground where the dung hill lay, and was proceeding to dig for it, when the farmer told them his dream went no farther than the removal of the dung hill, which he was much obliged to them for doing, as he could not himself have effected it before the snow came on.

The agricultural setting of this trickster tale suits American colonial life, but the language is literary and the narration contains no Americanism of speech or place name or character type. Anecdotes in this vein appeared regularly in English jestbooks of the eighteenth century.

Eleven years later "An Original Anecdote" appeared in Nathan Daboll's *The New-England Almanac* for 1800, setting forth a Yankee trick in conversational style and with local references.

Not long since a gentleman from Connecticut, (whom I shall designate by the letter B.)—being on his way to the westward, was stopped in York state, on Sunday, by a miserly Dutchman, who was invested with civil authority. Mr. B. in vain plead the necessity of pursuing his journey unmolested. At length, taking a five dollar bill from his pocket book:—"Sir," said he, "this is at your service, on condition you will give me a *pass*."

After a few minutes' pause, this mercenary character replied, "*Yes, I give you von pass for five Tollars;* you may write de pass, and I make my mark X." Mr. B. accordingly sat down, and drew an order on a merchant in town, for 50 dollars in cash, and 50 dollars worth of English goods; with the Dutch signature; and takes his leave, with, "Your humble servant."

Calls on the merchant, who cheerfully loaned 50 dollars with the idea of 50 per cent gain on the goods. Soon after, the merchant calls on our noble Dutchman for the balance of the order; at which he started and exclaimed: "*By Got I oze you noting,* ize got moneys, and *always* pay."

The merchant produced the order; and on seeing his mark (the Dutchman) exclaimed, "*Dis is dat dam Yankee pass!*" But found himself reluctantly obliged to cancel the demand; swearing, "*dat if he could see dat damn rascal, he would give him von horse lickin.*"

Here the ingenious Connecticut traveler is identified as a Yankee, and perpetrates a "sell" in the manner later associated with all Yankees. His victim is an early American comic type, the pompous, obtuse Dutchman surviving from New Netherlands in the early republic. Like later comic stereotypes, including the low-class Yankee, the Dutchman speaks in a thick-tongued dialect. In this "original anecdote" the gentleman from Connecticut does not yet display the buffoonish traits of the later Yankee caricature.

The Yankee character emerged not only as a crafty fellow

in yarns but also as a comic figure in plays. A bumpkin named Jonathan made his appearance in 1787 in Royall Tyler's *The Contrast,* as the "waiter"—he objects to being called a servant —to Colonel Manly. Unused to the ways of the big city, he talks companionably with a harlot, whom he takes to be the deacon's daughter. Courting Jenny on first acquaintance, he sputters "Burning rivers! cooling flames! red-hot roses! pig-nuts! hasty-pudding and ambrosia!" yet to his wonder fails to captivate her. When his colonel is attacked he rushes to his side declaring, "I feel chock-full of fight," and, "I'd shew him Yankee boys play, pretty quick." These themes of the "ver-dant" confounded by the city, and the Yankee as ludicrous swain, echoed through countless anecdotes and farces in the following decades. Jonathan the patriot-hero, whistling "Yan-kee Doodle" and proclaiming himself a "true blue son of lib-erty," belongs chiefly to the theater.

Yankees in minor roles continually held the stage following *The Contrast,* and by 1809 three more named Jonathan had appeared. A drama of 1815, *The Yankey in England* by David Humphreys, transported the lubber overseas, where he was introduced as an "Original! A character little known here. A full-blooded Yankey." A full-blown Yankee cried his wares in a three-act farce titled *The Pedlar,* written for the St. Louis Thespians in 1821 by the paymaster of the United States Army, Alphonso Wetmore. All the regional comic types meet in this western play produced and set across the mountains: Nutmeg, the wily down-East peddler with his cart full of notions; Op-possum, the backwoods roarer, boasting of his hunting dogs and coonskins and hungry for an eye-gouging fight—a pre-liminary Davy Crockett; Boatman, in red shirt and tow trou-sers, the river counterpart of Oppossum and stage reflection of Mike Fink, the name indeed that Oppossum calls him in the last line of the play. Even Old Continental, the Revolutionary veteran reminiscing about Bunker Hill, and Harry Emigrant, a roving tar who won't give up the ship, present dimmer native comic figures.

Nutmeg, Oppossum, and Boatman speak in perfect character. In the opening lines Nutmeg calls himself "the greatest genius in the universe," ready to cheat Old Prairie the settler out of half he is worth. To Old Prairie he introduces himself as "A travelling merchant, sir—all the way over the mountains, from the town of New Haven, with a cart load of very useful, very desirable and very pretty notions: such as, tin cups and nutmegs, candlesticks and onion seed, wooden clocks, flax seed and lanterns, Japanned coffee pots, and tea *sarcers,* together with a variety of cordage and other dry goods." Then he perpetrates a "Yankee trick," selling three lanterns to different members of the same family. Nutmeg in the end performs an honorable act, suggestive of noble Yankees to come. The peddler of wooden clocks, the "half sea-horse half sea-serpent" coon hunter, and the drunken "steamboat," who rastle each other and match boasts, are three aspects of the same linsey-woolsey folk hero, already fully visible by 1821.

In the first thirty years of the Republic, the rising swell of an indigenous folk humor comes into view. Three main tributaries fed this humor, often mingling their currents: the boastful speech and eccentricities of frontiersmen, the drolleries of Yankees, and the stock fictions of roguery and mendacity. In stage coaches and taverns, during husking and raising bees, at militia musters, around hunters' campfires, in New England village squares and on Southern verandas, tongues wagged and stories flew. Alert reporters and receptive media would now bring this backcountry oral humor prominently before the public.

1825–55

Following the War of 1812, the nation embarked on a century of internal expansion in which the sense of Manifest Destiny and the spirit of national exuberance rode high. The rise to the presidency of Andrew Jackson in 1828 symbolized the emergence of the common man into the center of American life. In the West new states entered the Union permitting free suffrage. In the East public schools begun under the Republic graduated a literate middle class. The crossings into the trans-Appalachian frontier and the growth of river and turnpike travel enlarged the area of physical democracy, while the Jacksonian philosophy broadened the base of political democracy. A new audience had come into existence responsive to the "delineation of American character and scenery," in Audubon's phrase, and for the three decades from the triumph of Jackson to the crisis of Civil War, the popular media supplied this audience with regional humor and local color. Nor was the comic lore dispensed with the patronizing air of Colonel Byrd viewing the squatters of Lubberland; folk heroes rose from the backwoods and city slums.

During the decade of the 1830's, the channels feeding the oral humor of the countryside into the subliterary levels of print expanded and multiplied. In 1825, for the first time in the New York theater, a Yankee pre-empted the central role of a drama, as Jonathan Ploughboy in Samuel Woodworth's *The Forest Rose*, and thereafter a succession of Yankee heroes bestrode the boards. In 1831 the ringtailed roarer made his first stage appearance as Nimrod Wildfire in Paulding's success, *The Lion of the West.* Also in 1831 were published the first numbers of a weekly sporting paper, the *Spirit of the Times,* whose New York editor, William T. Porter, would make it for the next thirty years the leading medium for a new kind of writing, the humorous backcountry sketch. In 1835 appeared the first book collection of such newspaper sketches, *Georgia Scenes,* by A. B. Longstreet, the precursor of many similar volumes issued chiefly in cheap paperback editions. Parodying the farmers' almanacs, an illustrated Crockett almanac series commenced in 1835 and soon carried the fame of Davy Crockett across the land. At no other period in American history did a flourishing oral humor enjoy such intimate and fruitful connections with the popular culture of journalism, literature, and the stage.

Newspapers.—Especially did the daily newspaper change its character during the 1820's. The eighteenth-century newspaper was a four-page production on good rag stock, printed in eastern seaboard cities, addressed to the educated upper class, and given over largely to foreign news. With the advent of Jacksonian democracy, a personal, chatty newspaper emerged, run by an individualistic editor in close touch with the local community he served, and conscious of his function as a dispenser of entertainment as well as news. Wire services did not exist to standardize news, and no radio, television, or movies purveyed laughs and thrills. The ante-bellum newspapers are crammed full of waggish humor, ranging from conundrums to elaborate vignettes. Editors hoped for local contributions while ceaselessly pilfering choice morsels from their exchanges. A felicitous yarn traveled the rounds of the press, sometimes repeating the circuit at a later day. The "original" anecdote

The Rise of Native Folk Humor

and "capital" story commanded a premium. Hundreds of files of the ante-bellum papers contain stores of humorous narratives, but only a handful are as yet mined: the St. Louis *Reveille*, the New Orleans *Picayune*, the Burlington, Vermont, *Free Press*, the Norwalk, Ohio, *Observer*, the Columbus, Georgia, *Enquirer*.

A sampling of the folk matter in the Tarboro, North Carolina, *Free Press*, founded and edited from 1824 to 1850 by George Howard, who enjoyed a lengthy career in North Carolina politics and the law, may illustrate the reading fare of the period. The columns of the Tarboro paper carried sundry freaks of nature, from monstrous births to gargantuan people, animals, and vegetables; imbroglios involving husbands, wives, and lovers; tall accounts of snakes and domestic animals; public stunts; western exaggerations; innumerable stories of cute and inventive Yankees; dreams of death and charms for lovers; references to clairvoyance and weird celestial phenomena; pseudo-science and folk medicine galore; cure-all patent nostrums. The bleeding corpse test appears, in a Missouri case where the suspect was adjudged guilty. A witch-doctor from Rockingham persuades a family to keep a dead body at home, in the expectation that it will come to life. Judgments on drunkards, after the colonial tradition, are still found, but now with a comic touch of pseudo-science; some verses, entitled "Spontaneous Combustion: A Warning to Dram Drinkers," conclude

> But when he stooped to light his pipe,
> Which had by chance expired,
> His alcoholic body was
> Spontaneously fired.

American Folklore

Folktales keep cropping up, under the guise of news items or choice stories. A Negro dialect sermon offers a variation on the theme of how the colored man came to be. Satan emulated God, who had just made a fine white man of clay, but Satan used moss for hair and was so disgusted with his handiwork he kicked his man in the shins and struck him on the nose. Michigan is the locale for the popular American tall tale or "windy" of big mosquitoes flying off with a kettle under which a frightened man has hidden; he had clinched their stingers with his hammer from the inside. The mythical land of Cockaigne, a fairy-tale glutton's paradise, is grafted onto the Great West, where pigs' tails planted in the rich bottom lands produce a crop of young porkers, pieces of steel sprout into jackknives, and even the deer obligingly carry a bucket of salt on their rumps and turn them to the squatter's fire until their hind parts are juicily cooked.

As the Tarboro *Free Press* files suggest, many comic folktales are scattered through the newspapers of the day, sometimes deceptively disguised as local legends. A story titled "How Sandusky Was Saved from Famine" appeared in the Norwalk, Ohio, *Experiment* for January 27, 1857, credited to the Buffalo *Republic*. The piece described a famine in the early days of Sandusky. A drought had so lowered the water level in the port that vessels could not enter, and no land routes into Sandusky then existed. Wild hogs from the neighboring woods tantalizingly trotted down to the bay for water. All soon became blind from the vast fields of fine sand that lined the bay, save for one dim-sighted leader. A blind hog took the leader's tail in his mouth, another followed suit behind the second, and so on until the whole drove was accounted for. One day while the line of hogs was making its way to the bay, a bold Sanduskian fired at the leader's tail and amputated it close to the body. Rushing forward, the man grasped the remnant still hanging from the second hog's mouth, and began gently pulling. The drove of hogs started forward like a train of cars, and the sharpshooter led them back to the famished natives.

In spite of all the local detail, this is a far-traveled fiction, having crossed over from Europe, and is popular in America as a hunter's whopper. I collected variants in northern Michigan and on the Maine coast. As Aaron Kinney of Iron River, Michigan, told me the yarn, he saw a cow moose leading her blind mate by the tail, shot the cow with his last bullet, and led the bull back to town by the cow's tail. There he tied the beast to a hitching post while he ambled into the store, bought some more bullets, and in a leisurely manner shot the bull moose.

Some newspaper stories no longer found in current oral tradition clearly belong to a buried layer of humorous folk-tales preserved only in these ante-bellum files. A vanished cycle of tall tales deals with fearful examples of fever and ague in the backwoods. The New Orleans Sunday *Delta* carried a yarn on April 20, 1856, "Some Shaking," about the severity of chills and fever in Anne Arundel County, Maryland. A "queer genius" named Tom reported that men building a house down on Severn River took a chill and shook all the bricks down, and then shook the bricks into a dust that obscured the sun for two hours; farmers in apple-picking season leaned a slave against a tree to shake down the apples, but cautiously placed a man on each side to remove him after the fruit had fallen, lest he shake the tree down; a little boy seized with a chill at the dinner table shook off all his buttons and then his pants.

American Folklore

While traveling by stage from Wheeling to Zanesville, Ohio, James Silk Buckingham overheard a conversation concerning the effects of ague along the Illinois River. One told of a sufferer who had shaken all the teeth out of his head; a second knew of a victim who shook off his clothes and even unraveled them thread by thread; a third had a friend who developed fits of such intensity he shook his house down and perished in the ruins. This scene, written in 1842, captures an actual story-matching contest on the subject of the ague.

Examples could be multiplied. In "Sister Nance and the Ager," printed in the New York *Spirit of the Times* in 1840, from the St. Louis *Pennant*, a squatter tells an educated traveler that the folks were planning on having the shakes that afternoon, all save Sister Nance, who was so contrary the ague wouldn't take her, and if it did, she wouldn't shake. This suggests the European folktale of the obstinate wife who drowned in a river; her husband searched for the body upstream, knowing she was too contrary to go with the current. A story "Chills and Fever" in the same paper in 1852 relates how a Tennessee squatter switched the shakes right out of his boy, who had previously shaken himself out of his breeches and into the fire. From these journalistic windies we can reconstruct a once popular but now forgotten theme of back-country tall tales.

Weeklies.—A special type of humorous sporting weekly arose during the ante-bellum period that attracted the most and the best original sketches of the day. Resembling an over-sized newspaper in appearance, the weekly really bore closer kinship to a magazine in its contents. The two most celebrated, the New York *Spirit of the Times* and the Boston *Yankee Blade*—there were others lesser known and shorter lived—

appealed primarily to sporting gentry and men-about-town. William T. Porter, who founded the *Spirit* in 1831, covered horse racing, the New York theater, hunting and fishing, and related topics of masculine entertainment and pastimes. Increasingly his pages became filled with backwoods scenes and sketches written by sportsmen describing a hunting or camping trip. In time the emphasis shifted to the characters and customs of frontier communities, and the formula altered from straightforward observation to humorous and imaginative depiction. The *Spirit's* only close rival, the *Yankee Blade*, emerged from a local literary and family newspaper first published in Waterville, Maine, in 1841, and at its height in Boston from 1847 to 1856. Its publisher, William Mathews, a Harvard graduate and practicing lawyer, later moved to Chicago and enjoyed a productive career as journalist, professor of rhetoric and literature, and author of many popular works on literary and self-help themes.

The *Spirit* and the *Blade*, as they were familiarly called in the popular press, relied extensively on the contributions of talented correspondents from the field. Although they reprinted "good ones" from their exchanges and from each other, they set in motion far more original humorous pieces than any other papers. Porter and Mathews carefully cultivated the lawyers, doctors, editors, and other educated easterners resident in the backcountry who daily observed squatters and peddlers. Many of the *Spirit's* cleverest correspondents lived in the Old Southwest, and the *Blade* concentrated on New England, but both journals were national in circulation and coverage. The *Spirit* developed, and the *Blade* successfully emulated, a distinctive style of writing appropriate for the humorous journalistic sketch of regional characters. A breezy, conversational, colloquial air brought the reader into the circle of witty fellows swapping yarns about the verdants of Yankeeland and the clay-eaters of the swamps. Frequently the correspondent introduced the scene from his own eyewitness position, and then let his slatternly characters talk in their natural dialect. A *Blade* or *Spirit* sketch contained much dialogue, marked by frequent italics to convey verbal emphases, and liberally strewn with local idioms and turns of phrase. Also the two papers went in for a good deal of archness, expressed through frequent quotation marks around pet phrases, the printed equivalent of sly winks and knowing nudges to the inner circle of gay "spirits" and sharp "blades."

Contributors drew heavily upon oral yarns for the material of their sketches, which were indeed intended to read like yarns-in-print. A folklorist can identify a good many twice-told tales among the thousands of stories in the *Spirit* and the *Blade*, although he must tread warily, for an observed incident, a created piece, or a traveled folktale is written in the same form and style. Folktales in these literary family weeklies usually contain more detail of setting and verisimilitude of actual speech than those found in the daily papers. The whole milieu of the storytelling scene is presented, and the tale appears in its proper frame.

Sometimes the evidence for direct reporting of oral humor is very clear. The *Spirit of the Times* for April 24, 1847, reprints a piece from the *Yankee Blade* titled "Tough Stories, or, Some Reminiscences of Uncle Charles." The sketch is devoted to a master fabulist from a small town near Augusta, Maine, who "as a regular out-and-out-story-teller . . . 'flogged down' all competition—distancing Major Longbow 'all hollow,' beating Sam Hyde into 'shoe-strings,' and leaving

The Rise of Native Folk Humor

Münchausen '*no whar.*' " Two lengthy and two short texts are given, including such well-known windies as the severed snake that reunites, fat hens that burst open on their roosts, and the hero's underwater journey along the riverbed. Again in the *Blade* for October 25, 1851, the correspondent catches the convivial glow of "Yarn-Spinning" around the hotel fireside by sea captains wind-bound at Wood's Hole in Martha's Vineyard. One Captain Benson topped all the rest, relating among other exploits how he ran his hand down a dog's throat, seized the inside of his tail, and turned him inside out; and how from the street he heard a mouse trot on St. Paul's steeple.

Many American folktales of tricksters and scapegraces appear in the *Spirit* and the *Blade* as actual incidents. "How Big Lige Got the Liquor" was printed in the *Spirit* for July 27, 1850, as an original contribution from Robin Roughead of Greenville, Mississippi. Big Lige Shattuck, a character in other *Spirit* sketches, is a crew member poling a broadhorn down the Mississippi with other boatmen. His captain finds the whiskey keg empty, and instructs Lige to fill it half full of river water and to seek the other half in whiskey from the next wooding-up station on shore. (When full, the keg holds six gallons of liquor plus two teaspoonfuls of Mississippi water.) At the next stop Lige lands and orders three gallons of whiskey, but the dealer makes Lige pour them back on learning that the boatman lacks ready cash. However the three gallons remaining in the keg contain a strong enough dilution of whiskey and water to cheer the captain and crew on the remainder of their voyage.

This elaborately detailed sketch is a roving American trickster tale attached to local scalawags all over the country. A shorter variation had already appeared in the *Spirit* in 1845, from the St. Louis *Reveille*, about a "bruiser" named Bill. In 1860 the New York *Atlas* ascribed the deceit to General Tay of Laconia, and in 1902 a regional magazine of western Massachusetts, the *Berkshire Hills*, told it on Captain Elisha Smart. The blind Vermont author, Rowland Robinson, who constructed his book *Uncle Lisha's Shop* (1887) around actual storytelling sessions in a shoemaker's shop in Vergennes, Vermont, put the tale in the mouth of one of his Green Mountain raconteurs, Sam Lovel. A twentieth-century writer and collector of New Hampshire traditions, Cornelius Weygandt, caught the trick twice, in *The White Hills* (1934) and *New Hampshire Neighbors* (1937), first as performed by Uncle Sam of Sandwich, and then by a twin named Theophilus. Finally a collection of folklore from New York State, the *Body, Boots and Britches* of Harold W. Thompson (1940), similarly relates how raftsman-hero "Boney" Quillan obtained rum without credit.

So the sell has drifted along the rivers and into the hills and added to the luster of some minor rogue. It takes two forms, one where the rascal fills his jug half full of water ahead of time, and the other where he exchanges a bottle of water hidden on his person for one of spirits whose return the proprietor demands. The liquor varies, from rum to brandy to whiskey to gin, but always the thirsty one is penniless and lacking in credit. This relished American folk yarn is one of a goodly number appreciated and "done brown" by the waggish correspondents of the *Spirit* and the *Blade*.

Paperbacks.—Many of the best newspaper sketches were gathered from the files and reprinted in cheap paperback and cloth editions. Two Philadelphia publishers, Carey and Hart, and T. B. Peterson and Brothers, issued a "Library of Humorous American Works" in the 1840's and 50's which included several volumes of choice *Spirit* pieces, two edited by Porter himself. The "humor of the Old Southwest," rediscovered since 1930 by literary scholars, refers to the editions of reprinted journalistic sketches beginning with Longstreet's *Georgia Scenes* in 1835 and culminating in Harris's *Sut Lovingood's Yarns* in 1867.

Folklore elements are strewn throughout this literature, but one volume particularly reveals a dependence on oral tradition. *Fisher's River (North Carolina) Scenes and Characters*, written in 1859 by Harden E. Taliaferro (which did not first appear in newspapers but emulates the *Georgia Scenes*), presents a model format for a folktale collector's field report. The setting is mountainous Surry County high in the Blue Hills, the structure is a series of earthy character portraits followed by quoted narratives from each storyteller, and the tales often belong to well-known types. Those of Uncle Davy Lane, a gunsmith with "a great fund of long-winded stories and incidents," mingle classic Münchausen themes of the steeple-tethered horse and the deer-bearing-a-peach-tree with hallowed colonial reports of hoopsnakes and rattlesnakes. The language in which Taliaferro, a Baptist minister raised in Surry County, recounted the tales of his mountain folk, faithfully captured their gamey locutions and traditional sayings. Typical utterances are: "Didn't care a dried-apple cuss whether I lived ur died"; "I felt like I could a whipped a string o'wildcats long as Tar River"; "And at it we went like a whirlygust uv woodpeckers." The loyalty of the mountain folk toward their own speech is vehemently illustrated in the sketch of "Uncle Frost Snow," who caught his lone slave using quality words.

"Pantaloons! pantaloons!!" says I; "who larnt you to call 'um pantaloons?" says I. "Gittin' above yer master? Talkin' like the Franklins and all the big quality folks, you lamper-jawed, cat-hamed puke," says I. "You nuver hearn yer master call 'um any thing but britches, nur you shan't," says I. "I'll larn you to puke up big quality words, you varmunt," says I; and I larruped him well, I tell you.

The fact that the individual and family names in Surry County have been corroborated from other sources further authenticates the value of Taliaferro's book as a folklore document.

A classic composition of southwestern humor gave its title to a paperback volume of collected *Spirit* sketches. "The Big Bear of Arkansas" by T. B. Thorpe bears all the outward evidence of a retold hunter's yarn. Actually it testifies to the powerful influence of the oral backwoods tale on fiction. The scene is a Mississippi River steamboat, the central figure a loquacious Arkansas backwoodsman, the story a long narration by hunter Jim Doggett to the gaping steamboat audience. Jim commences with brief tall tales extolling the fecundity of Arkansas soil and leads into an epical hunt for a "creation b'ar." The pursuit of Jim Doggett after the mammoth bear takes on transcendental overtones that lift this backwoods hunt into the symbolic realm of man's combat with awesome creatures of the night: St. George's fight with the dragon, Beowulf's grapple with Grendel, Ahab's quest for Moby Dick.

Almanacs.—Along with the daily newspaper, the sporting weekly, and the paperback reprint, the lowly almanac too captured floating folk humor. Almanacs had long served as a repository for fugitive items of folklore. In the eighteenth century Nathaniel Ames and his son had issued a yeasty *Astronomical Diary and Almanac*, and Benjamin Franklin larded *Poor Richard's Almanac* with wise saws. Robert B. Thomas began publishing *The Old Farmer's Almanac* in 1793. Weather sayings, facetiae, Yankee anecdotes, and pithy proverbs provided reading matter for the farmer and his family between the pages of astronomical calculations. In 1831 New York and Boston printers began issuing comic almanacs filled with artificial jokes and rhymes about Englishmen, Irishmen, Negroes, and Yankees, which make insipid reading today. One notable series evolved within this format, however, of signal interest to folklorists—the spate of comic almanacs bearing the name and dealing with the backwoods adventures and exploits of Davy Crockett. These were first published in Nashville in 1835, the year before Crockett's death, through 1841, but New York printers of regular joke almanacs followed the lead in 1836 and continued the cycle until 1856. The Crockett almanacs contained increasingly fantastic accounts by and about Davy, concerning his encounters with pukes and peddlers, b'ars and pant'ers in the canebrakes, and pirates and cannibals in distant corners of the globe. Their language abounded in extravagant word coinages—slantendicklar, teetotaciously, boliterated—giving a mock literary flavor to Crockett's oratory. Woodcuts of Crockett in action accompanied the tales.

These almanac fictions extended the legend of Davy Crockett that had grown apace since the Tennessee backwoodsman entered Congress in 1829. Crockett himself was a humorist and storyteller, but he speedily became the subject of many floating anecdotes in the daily press and in his alleged autobiographies. The best known had him playing a Yankee trick by giving the barkeep the same coonskin for each fresh round of drinks. A substratum of oral jests no doubt lay under the mass of journalistic yarns, politically inspired by both Whigs and Democrats, that made the name of Crockett a household word in the 1830's and 40's. The almanac stories follow the universal patterns of heroic legend and occasionally show a clear affinity with oral tradition.

The Crockett almanac for 1840 contains the tale of "Col. Crockett, the Bear, and the Swallows." Davy begins by disputing the superstition that swallows fly away in the fall and come back in the spring when white oak leaves are the size of a mouse's ear. He knows they winter in the hollow of a rotten old sycamore. Hunting early one spring on the banks of the Tennessee, he heard a noise like thunder and saw a swarm of swallows fly out of a sycamore. Climbing up to investigate, he tumbled into the hollow and landed on a pile of swallows' dung. Davy groped around in the darkness and felt the fur of a hibernating bear. He seized the bear's tail with his teeth, prodded his rump with his butcher knife, and so ascended the steep hole by bear power. Although realistically set on the Tennessee frontier, this yarn closely follows a European folktale, "How the Man Came Out of the Tree Stump," pulled by the bear's tail.

Another characteristic almanac scrape finds Davy in Washington being entertained by a senator. Crockett, smoking a cigar, keeps spitting on the carpet, while a Negro servant places a cuspidor where he has spit. Finally Davy roars at him in wrath that if he places the painted box in his way once again, he'll spit right in it. This tale is hung on the Far West guide and trapper, Jim Baker; Vance Randolph has collected it currently in the Ozarks, told on a "country fellow"; and it precedes Davy, for the *Western Citizen* of Paris, Kentucky, in 1831 placed the incident six years earlier, when uncouth Governor James Ray of Kentucky entertained Lafayette.

A few tales appear in the Crockett almanacs about Mike Fink, the legendary keelboatman of the Ohio and Mississippi waters during the 1820's, whose prowess as bully-boy and sharpshooter spread up and down the river towns. The Fink legends drifted into print through various channels, sometimes giftbook annuals or newspaper stories of pioneer reminiscences. In the almanacs he rivals Crockett as a doughty demigod, and indeed bests Davy in one memorable shooting match.

The Theater.—In the ebullient years from 1825 to 1855, the popular stage rivaled the popular press as a medium for transmitting native folk humor to urban audiences. Through the vehicle of the traveling troupe, the theater radiated out from Broadway to every city in the land. Up and down the country the canny down-Easter, the ranting Kentuckian, and the dandified Bowery tough cavorted in farce and melodrama. The "real, live Yankee" capered on the stage in red wig, bell-shaped hat, and striped coat and trousers. Nimrod Wildfire, the stage representation of Davy Crockett, uttered his brags in coonskin cap and fringed buckskin breeches, carrying his long rifle and powder horn. Mose the Bowery "b'hoy," darling of the New York fire laddies, strutted the boards in stovepipe hat, bright red shirt, pearl-buttoned pea jacket, and rolled-up trousers tucked in his boots, puffing away at his rakishly tilted "long nine."

Life, art, and folklore all meshed in these comic stage heroes. Journeyman playwrights, accustomed to fashioning knockabout pieces for quick production by the troupes, collaborated with type actors portraying stock characters who in turn reflected actual regional figures recognizable to the audience. Playwright, comedian, audience, and folk tradition shared in the creative process.

This cross-fertilization is plainly seen in the celebrated comic melodrama, *The Lion of the West,* which in 1831 projected the image of Davy Crockett onto the boards, under the name of Nimrod Wildfire. The well-known Yankee actor, James H. Hackett, had offered a prize for a play in which he could act the western roarer, and its winner, James K. Paulding, drew upon his earlier first-hand acquaintance with the half-horse, half-alligator breed down South. Two play-doctors reworked the script, under Hackett's direction, so that at least four scripts were used during the twenty-year life of the play. A close contact with oral folktale and the Crockett legend can be seen. One set-to in the drama, where Wildfire exchanges boasts and threats with a Mississippi "snag," nearly duplicates an 1837 Crockett almanac tale, which also appeared in the newspapers. Elsewhere Nimrod astonishes the visiting Englishwoman, Mrs. Wollope, with the statement that the soil of Old Kentucky is so rich one can travel under it, and he tells about the time he spied a hat in the muddy swamp, covering a mired traveler who disclaimed any need of aid, since he was astride a sound horse. Nimrod has here told a familiar American tall tale.

A similar evolution produced Mose the Bowery "b'hoy," hero of the sensationally popular *A Glance at New York,* which opened in New York in 1848 and took the country by storm. The actor Chanfrau conceived the notion of representing on the stage the loafer-dandy, volunteer-fireman type known throughout his Bowery haunts as the "b'hoy." Very likely he chose Moses Humphries, who ran with the Lady Washington engine number forty, as his model. Benjamin A. Baker hammered out a plot for Chanfrau, based on a London melodrama depicting the lurid and seamy side of the metropolis. Mose swaggered through the Bowery vanquishing sharpers and swindlers much as Davy Crockett conquered pukes and

The Rise of Native Folk Humor

squatters in the backwoods. Upon its initial success the *Glance* proliferated into a series of piecemeal Mose skits that carried the swashbuckling "b'hoy" out of the Bowery to California, France, and Arabia. So had the Crockett of the almanacs left the canebrakes for Brazil, the South Seas, and Japan. Bowery bums continued to tell fantastic tales about Mose into the present century, long after the plays had perished.

In 1829 Sam Patch jumped over Niagara Falls, but shortly he leaped to his death over the Genesee Falls at Rochester. In the following years a swarm of comic verses, hoaxes, sayings, and tall tales clustered around the cotton-spinner from Pawtucket, Rhode Island. The legend of the stunt-jumper who announced, "There's no mistake in Sam Patch," and, "Some things can be done as well as others," reached its apogee on the stage. In 1836 the renowned Yankee actor Dan Marble played the part of the daredevil in *Sam Patch, or the Daring Yankee,* and followed this with a sequel, *Sam Patch in France.* Like the historic Sam, the stage Patch leaped mightily over Niagara Falls in each performance.

No single hero, but a mock-heroic type, evolved in the long spate of Yankee plays. From his beginnings as a loutish servant in *The Contrast* in 1787 to his blackguard role in *The Pedlar* in 1821, the stage Yankee appeared as bumpkin or knave. But from 1825 on, when Jonathan Ploughboy emerged as hero in *The Forest Rose,* and "Yankee" Hill became indentified with the part, the Yankee assumed increasingly heroic stature. His odyssey carried him ever farther from his New England base, to France, England, Cuba, Poland, Algiers, Spain, and China. He sails with Captain Kidd, fights for Polish freedom against the Russians, and rescues Senorita Miralda from the clutches of Count Almonte in a Cuban mansion. Jonathans boast like ringtailed roarers: "I'll whip the hull boodle of you at once. Make me mad, and I'll lick a thunderstorm," crows Deuteronomy Dutiful in C. A. Logan's *Vermont Wool Dealer* (1840). In Morris Barnett's *The Yankee Peddler*, Hiram Dodge utters a Crockett almanac brag: "I'll swallow one of your niggers hull, if you'll grease his head and pin his ears back."

Yankee actors formed a living bridge between stage comedy and oral humor. Favorite comedians like George H. Hill and Dan Marble played the Yankee offstage as well as on. Between the scenes of a Yankee play they stepped forward before the curtain and recited a Yankee story in down-East dialect. *Hill's Yankee Stories and Reciter's Own Book of Popular Recitations* was issued in pocket size format by Turner and Fisher, publishers of the Crockett and other comic almanacs. "Ichabod's New Year, a Yankee Story, written and recited by Mr. Hill," described an adventure of the greenhorn in the big city, a constant theme of printed Yankee yarns. Two other selections, "Simon Slow's Visit to Boston," and "Ben's First Visit to the Theatre," dealt with a popular subdivision of this theme, the "verdant's" astonishment on beholding his first theatrical performance. In his biography, Hill tells of playing a farce in an upstate New York town without eliciting a single laugh from the audience. A rawboned native approached him as he was sitting disconsolately in his hotel room. The actor inquired if he had been entertained. "I swow, I guess I was. I tell you what it is, now; my mouth won't be straight for the next month, straining to keep from larfing. If it hadn't a been fer the women, I should a snorted right out in the meetin'."

The popular press carried the latest "good ones" credited to Hill and Marble, a recognition of their status as professional

The Rise of Native Folk Humor

storytellers. Under the caption, "Climate of California," the New Orleans *Weekly Delta* for January 15, 1849, recounted a crisp dialogue between Dan Marble and a newly returned Californian describing the wonders of that "blessed land." There the hunter climbed a mountain top with a double-barreled gun, and killed summer game in one valley and winter game in the other—although unfortunately his dog's tail froze off while his head was pointing on the summer side. At least three papers, the *Spirit* among them, in 1849 ran Yankee Hill's tale of "The Yankee Fox Skin," in which a down-East trader extols the virtues of his fox fur, alternately picturing reynard as greasy with fat, and again as "tremenjus lean," in hopes of making a sale. The contemporary biographies of Marble and Hill are rife with their droll stories, told on all occasions. In effect they became individual examples of the genus Yankee they were portraying on the stage in imitation of down-East countrymen.

Pictorial Humor.—A word should be said about graphic humor as an extension to the popular press and the popular stage in depicting comic folk types and folk heroes. If the humble literature of journalism and paperbacks struck a realistic new note in American letters, so did the lower levels of illustration—woodcuts, engravings, etchings, lithographs—bring an earthy, homely strain into the American graphic arts. The new lithographic process invented in 1791 began flooding American book stalls in the 1830's, at the same time that humorous cartoons of Jacksonian politics titillated the public.

The fame of Felix O. C. Darley, who illustrated the "Library of Humorous American Works," often eclipsed that of the authors. Darley's black-and-white line drawings transfixed

67

the southern squatter as a cadaverous, fever-and-ague-ridden, slovenly rapscallion. He drew fleshy, frizzy-haired, petrified Negro servants, bug-eyed innkeepers in nightdress, long-jawed sanctimonious preachers, unshaven sheriffs, rotund, bonneted dames—the whole slatternly backwoods gallery.

The copious woodcuts in the Crockett almanacs visualized the legendary adventures of Davy. In the early Nashville almanacs, from 1835 to 1838, the image of Crockett takes the form of a noble primitive. In 1839 the image abruptly changes, to a sly and self-assured woodsman. The links between almanac, play, and woodcut are strikingly seen in the identical stance and dress of James H. Hackett in the part of Nimrod Wildfire (in a portrait now in the Crawford Theater Collection of the Yale University Library), and the likeness of Crockett in an 1837 almanac story, "A Corn Cracker's Account of His Encounter with an Eelskin." Clad in regal coonskin cap—the coon's face dangling over his right ear and its tail hanging alongside the left—fringed buckskin jacket and breeches, a broad loop of fur circling neck and bosom, Betsy, his long rifle, clasped across the chest, feet planted firmly apart, the whole attitude one of tension and resolution—so the legendary Crockett confronted almanac readers and theater goers.

Mose too flowered in pictorial humor, modeled after the stage role created by Chanfrau, which in turn copied the Bowery "b'hoys" of Chatham Square. Flaming posters, lithographs, drawings, and playbills limned Mose in his shiny stovepipe hat and long soaplocks leaning insolently against a fireplug; or atop a ladder poised precariously against a burning building, about to rescue Linda the Cigar Girl from the flames; or driving with his gal Lize through the park in a sulky, sportily togged and a trifle looped. A twenty-page booklet of hand-colored lithographs by Thomas Gunn, *Mose among the Britishers: The B'hoy in London,* was issued in Philadelphia in 1850, showing Mose cockily viewing the sights of London.

1855–65

The regional humor that flourished in newspaper sketches, dramatic farces, and stone engravings in the 1830's and 40's slackened off in the late 1850's as the rumble of sectional strife grew louder. In 1856 the Crockett almanacs came to an end, Porter left the *Spirit of the Times,* which lingered on until 1861, and Mathews sold the *Yankee Blade.* A new breed of professional humorists came into vogue, Artemus Ward and Petroleum V. Nasby and Orpheus C. Kerr, who looked to Washington and the political arena for their material. But the backwoods oral yarn found one final supreme mode of expression during the Civil War holocaust, in the person of its central actor, Abraham Lincoln.

Lincoln's fame as a storyteller attracted wide attention during his later political career, and numerous friends, reporters, and visitors recorded the circumstances and texts of his salty fables. The celebrated correspondent of the London *Times,* William Howard Russell, meeting the President at the White House early in 1861, remarked on his adept employment of the humorous anecdote to lighten an awkward situation, where the professional diplomat would rely on a silken compliment or sly evasion. When his Attorney-General remonstrated before the assembled guests against the appointment of an incompetent judge, Lincoln turned him aside with a little story. The judge had recently offered Lincoln a lift in his carriage. The driver handled the horses poorly and the carriage swayed and lurched. Finally the judge yelled out, "Why, you infernal scoundrel, you are drunk!" With aplomb the coachman replied, "By gorra! that's the first rightful decision you have given for the last twelve-month." As the party laughed, Lincoln moved off to another circle, having tacitly agreed with his cabinet minister's judgment, while insinuating his point about the obligations of patronage.

Abe Lincoln grew up in the pioneer farm country of western Kentucky, southern Indiana, and central Illinois in the decades of westward migration following the War of 1812. The *Spirit* correspondents had culled their narratives chiefly from the older southern frontier, the land of dense canebrakes, bears and coons, cotton plantations, and Negro slaves. Lincoln's country was the prairie and depended on corn and cattle. His yarns smacked of the barnyard and cornfield and were laid against the plowed earth and general store rather than the forest clearing and hunter's cabin.

Storytellers of the folk belong by definition to the unknown and anonymous depths of society, and only the chance foray of a collector throws a shaft of light on some talented folk artist. By a seemingly impossible chance, a star backwoods humorist became a famous statesman. We can readily tell that Lincoln belonged to the select group of master narrators who relate folktales. He possessed a vast repertoire of yarns at his tongue's tip, and relished reciting them at any hour; once in the White House he rose in the middle of the night and roused a friend to uncork a good one that came to his mind. He knew and responded to the folk ritual of matching tales and the folk manner of narrating; he acted out his stories with apposite gesture and inflection, and observers commented how his countenance glowed and became almost handsome under the illumination of tale-telling.

Few farm tales are reported in American folklore collections, but certain of Lincoln's yarns can promptly be spotted as oft-told. Tall tales of speedy runners are evoked by his windy of the boy who sparks the farmer's daughter, is chased by her irate father with a shotgun, and outruns a rabbit. In a horse-trading story Lincoln told, a balky horse, praised by its seller as a bird-hunter, squats stubbornly in the middle of a stream. "Ride him! Ride him! He's as good for fish as he is for birds," cries out the trader to his dupe. This jest is current today as a shaggy-dog story. The first trace of a local anecdote I heard in northern Michigan came in Lincoln's sally about an unpopular candidate in Illinois who told his wife on election morning she would sleep with the township supervisor that night. Accordingly she dressed up to visit her husband's rival, who indeed proved victor at the polls. "I say to them again: 'Go it, husband!—Go it, bear!' " joked Lincoln in his Alton debate of 1858 with Douglas. The Republican nominee, jesting at the mutual recriminations between Douglas and President Buchanan over the slavery question in Kansas, applied the folktale known from Kentucky to Vermont about the squatter's wife who cheers impartially for her shiftless husband and the bear embracing him.

Like other expert yarn-spinners, Lincoln strewed his recitations with the homely metaphor and backwoods phrase, into which indeed he continually lapsed in his ordinary speech. "My young friend, have I *hunkered* you out of your chair?" he inquired of a telegraph operator. "Every man must skin his own skunk," his father had told Abe, who remembered the proverb. "Some of my generals are so slow that molasses in the coldest days of winter is a race horse compared to them," he sighed, falling into a traditional form of tall-tale comparison. The historical importance of Lincoln the storyteller lies in the uncanny pertinence with which he tied a homely anecdote to a vexing problem, and drove home his point with a laugh. Seemingly for each thorny dilemma he knew an appropriate story, which served him as a political fable. The structure of a Lincoln yarn falls into three parts: the political problem posed to Lincoln; his recollection of an old tale involving a comparable situation; and the application of its evident moral to the question at hand. Lincoln thus gave an unexpected new function to backwoods anecdotes, which now served to lighten the tension of overwhelming moments, while pointing to wise solutions. The pompous platitude or pious homily would never have hit the mark so well.

Numerous illustrations of Lincoln's technique could be given, but three may suffice. From his inept cabinet Lincoln finally dismissed his Secretary of War, Cameron, and was promptly asked why he hadn't fired the whole lot. Lincoln was reminded of a western farmer who trapped nine skunks and then let eight go because the one he killed made such a stench. After the collapse of the Confederacy a citizen asked Lincoln, then on tour, what he intended to do with Jeff Davis. The President thought of the small boy who had caught a coon and hoped it would escape so he wouldn't have to kill it. A harassed senator from Kentucky begged Lincoln to advise him how to deal with the two-faced constituents of his border state. Thereupon Lincoln launched into a graphic account of a cockfight in Kentucky presided over by a loud-talking squire. The squire hedged his bets on the high-combed and low-combed cocks, until the high-combed cock had gained the victory, whereupon he pronounced himself as having favored that gamebird all along. So, concluded Lincoln, the Kentuckians want to be on both sides of this struggle until the winner is assured. "I think we have got the high-combed cock in this fight," he said seriously. "We must see to it that our rooster wins and then in the end we will be all right."

The humorous anecdote of the pioneer farm became on the lips of Lincoln an invaluable political asset. During his years of national prominence, from 1858 until 1865, Lincoln related hundreds of yarns in political speeches, to White House circles, to his cabinet, to patronage-seekers, to his generals. By the sixth decade of the nineteenth century the backwoods jest had penetrated deeply into the American consciousness, propelled by newspapers, almanacs, and plays, and Lincoln's stories met with immediate comprehension. In turn, Lincoln jokebooks appeared in the wake of his election, providing yet another channel between folk humor and subliterature. After the Civil War the patterns of popular culture drastically changed, and the homespun yarn never again became nationally intelligible. A century later literary scholars and folklorists would unearth specimens as antiquarian curiosities.

III

Regional Folk Cultures

During the drama of settlement and the saga of western expansion between 1607 and 1850, sharply defined regional zones planted themselves on the American landscape. A variety of causes explain the formation and tenacity of these minority cultures, sometimes speaking different languages, practicing strange religions, following peculiar customs, in defiance of the main stream of American civilization. Some became established during the Colonial period, and remain as relics of the German settlements in Pennsylvania, the French foothold in Louisiana, and the Spanish empire in the Southwest. The Mormons in Utah arose from a unique American messiahship, and found their ultimate home after a tortured western trek in the second quarter of the nineteenth century. The wake of the westward push to the Pacific and the urban pull from industrial cities left pockets of hillfolk stranded in the Pine Mountain of eastern Kentucky, the southern Appalachians in Virginia and North Carolina, and the Ozarks in northern

Regional Folk Cultures

Arkansas. Forgotten settlements persist in the cutover pine barrens of eastern New Jersey and sequestered fishing inlets along the Atlantic and Gulf coasts. Historical and geographical circumstances have set apart the Upper Peninsula of Michigan and "Egypt" in southern Illinois. In all these areas folklorists have reaped rich harvests.

Such nooks and byways resist the relentless forces of change and mobility in contemporary American life. In place of mass culture, they represent folk cultures, whose roots and traditions contrast oddly with the standardized glitter of American urban industrial society. In the folk region, people are wedded to the land, and the land holds memories. The people themselves possess identity and ancestry, through continuous occupation of the same soil. Local events can flower into legend and ballad and proverb, and village ways can harden into custom. Extended and inbred families form smaller units within the area that strengthen the sense of community.

These folk regions become important reservoirs of traditional lore. Much of their folklore will be common to other parts of the country and to other countries, but they stand out in the density and abundance of their oral traditions. The floating tale or song, drama or festival, belief or saying, eddy toward the folk culture, and cluster thickly in that congenial harbor. Each regional complex contains its own genius, inclining perhaps toward material folk crafts, or festival drama, or bardic songs, depending upon the historical and ethnic and geographical elements that have shaped its character. In this chapter, four of the richest regional folk cultures in the United States will be quickly scanned for their pre-eminent traits, and the author will describe a fifth folk region from his own field experience.

American Folklore

Late in the seventeenth century German farmer-folk began emigrating to the environs of Philadelphia. While the Spaniards, French, and Dutch permitted only their own nationals to colonize their overseas possessions, England threw wide her doors, allowing the holders of colonial charters to determine the qualifications of their settlers. William Penn, the friend of King George II, intended his colony of Pennyslvania for the Quaker sect whose religious convictions he had himself espoused. To fill up its fertile reaches, Penn needed additional settlers and dispatched his agents to the Palatine valley of southwestern Germany, where German Protestant peasants with sentiments akin to Quakerism were being sorely harassed. The military ravages of the Thirty Years' War, heavy feudal taxes of petty nobles aping the French court at Versailles, restrictive measures of the Roman Catholic clergy, all helped uproot the passive peasants. The first contingent arrived to found Germantown (now absorbed by Philadelphia) in 1683, and a great mass exodus of Rhinelanders sailed from London and Bristol in 1709. From Philadelphia they fanned north into the lush counties lying between the Susquehanna and Delaware rivers, Lancaster, Berks, Lehigh, Bucks, and Montgomery, to share Pennsylvania with English Quakers and Scotch-Irish Presbyterians. Where the Holland Dutch who first settled New Netherlands were destined for cultural submersion by the English, the Pennsylvania Germans stoutly held their own and eventually expanded into outlying colonies in mideastern states.

These Palatine emigrants comprised a peasant stock from manorial villages in petty German baronies. Their ranks in-

76

cluded no aspiring yeomanry or middle-class merchants or impoverished gentry. Bound to the soil in their homeland, indifferent by their religious tenets to educational development, dependent on traditional crafts for their self-sustaining feudal economy, the Palatines brought to America a medieval folk culture, which acquired American hues. In Pennsylvania they resumed the practice of agriculture, but now as independent landowners and free citizens. The individual farm replaced the medieval village with its common fields; the European serf became an American farmer. Yet if the compact, close-knit manorial village disappeared, the strong bonds of religion, language, and occupation held the Rhenish settlers together.

The people now known as the Pennsylvania Dutch originally included a gamut of Protestant groups, ranging in theology from orthodox Calvinism and Lutheranism to extreme Anabaptism, and displaying a whole spectrum of cultural behavior. Farthest from the American norms are the Old Order or House Amish, rejecting the world and its machines, schools, organizations, wearing their broad-brimmed hats and bonnets, hook-and-eye jackets, beards, driving to town in their buggies and carriages. The Church Amish have departed from the precepts of Jacob Amman enough to permit assembling in church buildings, whose interiors must not be photographed. The liberal wing has drawn close to the Mennonites from whom they originally withdrew. The Mennonites and their splinter groups still retain the outlook of "plain people" in dress and piety, but some will drive automobiles and support colleges. In a middle ground between the plain people and orthodox Protestants fall the Moravians, whose eighteenth-century communities at Nazareth and Bethlehem were distinguished by their communal society, ritual love feasts, musical concerts, and daily singing, and marriage by lot rather than by choice. But the impact of the nineteenth century brought the Moravians ever closer to their Lutheran and Reformed countrymen.

The one cultural element that binds all these groups together is the dialect, spoken by nearly a million persons, and the Pennsylvania German dialect becomes involved with folklore. This speech developed from the mixing of Palatine and Swiss dialects in America, and the intrusion of English terms. The dialect took various comic directions, such as the Germanized spelling of American loan-words—*balledicks* for "politics," *leifinschurings* for "life insurance." The use of German word order in American English gives rise to repeated tidbits. "Go look the window out and see who is coming the yard in," the mother tells the child. Or she salts her imperatives with German verbs: "Are you fressin (eating) yet?" and "Spritz the grass, Yohnny." The dialect spread to Scotch-Irish and Welsh, Negroes, and gypsies living alongside the Germans. In his book *The Pennsylvania Dutch*, Klees tells of the Italian immigrant digging a ditch who thought he was learning English from his fellow laborer. " 'Dunnerwetter,' he says; 'dunnerwetter,' I say. 'Ha, I thought, now I learn English; I real American. But no, I no learn English, I learn Pennsylvania Dutch!' "

A conspicuous feature of the dialect is its resort to proverbs and aphorisms, to confirm a judgment, point a moral, or impart advice. The proverb is "the very bone and sinew of the dialect," writes Fogel, the assiduous collector of Pennsylvania German lore. Along with the usual stock of European sayings appear less familiar saws obviously congenial to an agricultural people. Cattle and other domestic animals loom prominently in the homely injunctions; the dog indeed is an object of reference in thirty-three different proverbs. "No matter how lousy the dog, it has its hangers-on," conveys the idea that even the despised man has supporters. The loudmouth is advised, "If you cackle, lay," suggestive of the modern "Put up or shut up." The idea that mistakes are made by the best of men issues in barnyard metaphor as "Even a clever hen will lay outside the nest."

The values of the Pennyslvania German farmer can be read in proverbs. "A big wife and a big barn will never do a man any harm," and "As the man so his cattle" succinctly state his goals: the fertile farm, ample livestock, large family. An exhortation to work is given in "Every man must carry his own hide to the tanner," and a criticism of sloth appears in "It's a poor sheep that can't carry its own wool." Some proverbs suggest the homely wisdom of Franklin: "Empty ears of wheat stand upright, full ones droop" and "A loaded wagon creaks, an empty one rattles." Proverbial comparisons too abound with farming similes: "As welcome as a pig in a turnip patch," and "As stupid as horse-bean straw." Numerous euphemisms for bearing a bastard invoke the horse: "She lost a heel"; "She cast a shoe"; "A mule kicked it out of the wall"; "Why should she brag, she lost a horseshoe"; or for a man, "He is also pasturing a few."

One distinctive trait of Pennsylvania German proverbs, the frequent allusion to obscure persons, suggests the recent local origin of traditional expressions. The farmer says: "Like Drumbore's bakeoven, well planned but a failure"; "Holds out like Butz' bread, all eaten two weeks before the cheese"; "Old Hammel said he always was a back number—when he was young the old folks knew it all, and now the young know it all"; "Like Dietz's funeral—went to nothing"; "Like Joe Schneck, who dragged his wife by the hair for love";

" 'Thanks, I am not hungry, I have "schnitz" in my pocket,' said old man Moser when invited to take pot luck"; "When Gackenbach's pigs have enough to drink they do not need any feed"; "Do you know how Girard became so rich?—He minded his own business." Again the reflection of farm life is seen, but the intriguing point here is that eccentric local characters give rise to local tales and anecdotes, now lost save for their condensation in proverbs.

Riddles too convey the aroma of the barnyard. "Flesh at both ends, iron and wood in the middle?" (A farmer plowing.) "How did buckwheat come across the ocean?" (Three-cornered.) "What grows on its own tail?" (Turnip.) "What stands on its foot and has its heart in its head?" (Cabbage head.) "Why does the farmer go to the mill?" (Because the mill will not come to the farmer.) "What uses the largest handkerchief in the world?" (A hen, for it wipes its nose anywhere on the earth.)

From their homeland the Palatine settlers brought a bountiful supply in their native tongue of old tales and legends, which after two centuries across the sea show American stripings. The malevolent trickster of Germanic tradition, Tyl Eulenspiegel, takes on a friendlier, pixie-like character in Pennsylvania as "Eilischpijjel" and similar names, even "Eirisch Bickel," suggesting Irish association. Frequently the Pennsylvania Germans speak familiarly of Eilischpijjel, as a friend of their father and grandfather. In versions of well-known European tales, the mischief-maker bests the Devil in wagers and partnerships, while other stories show him as a literal fool carrying out his master's instructions to the letter. As hired man to a farmer, Eilischpijjel continually exasperates his master with his follies. Told to hitch up the sorrel horses in front and the blacks in back, he ties the sorrel span to the front of the wagon and the black pair behind; ordered to grease the wagon, he greases the body instead of the spindles.

Sometimes the stories hinge on bilingual meanings. A farmer who had sent his sons to college was asked about their progress by a neighbor. "Du Buwe? Well dar eent is en Schpart, awwer ar schpart nix, un dar anner is en Dud awwer ar dud nix." (One is a sport, but he saves nothing, and the other is a dude, but he does nothing.) The jest turns on the resemblance of the English words sport and dude to the dialect verb forms *schpart*, "to save," and *dud*, "to perform." Again, the place name Hosensack, of Indian origin, has acquired the folk etymology that a teamster, lost in the valley one night, exclaimed in dialect, "It is as dark as in a pants' pocket" (*hosensack*).

A surprising number of frontier tall tales and southern Negro stories crop up in dialect variants. The popular American windy of Elmer the Reversible Dog, which we encountered at the Diverting Club, gets attached to Eilischpijjel. From Lehigh County comes another American perennial, of the snake which strikes a hoe handle that swells to great size, but the Pennsylvania Germans have given it their own twist. A poor farmer contemplating suicide while hoeing his scraggly corn sees his snake-bit handle swell to the size of a rail, a post, a log, and finally a thick tree trunk; he rolls the log to the saw mill and secures enough shingles to cover all his buildings. Again, the best-known of all American tall tales, the Wonderful Hunt, appears in Montgomery County in more fantastic form than ever. Not merely does old Beltz, the champion hunter, shoot into a tree trunk to split a limb and clamp the toes of seven pigeons, in a standard feat, but he adds the novelty of exciting the pigeons to pull up the tree and fly off;

American Folklore

Beltz jumps on the butt, and by waving his hat from side to side guides the pigeons to his home across the Schuylkill River. True, the butt occasionally dipped into the water. Reaching home old Beltz found his trousers full of suckers, adding to his pigeons and winter's wood.

Certain tales common among American Negroes are equally familiar to the Pennsylvania Dutch (although whether this correspondence results from the presence of Negroes in Lancaster County, or from common tale origins in Europe, cannot easily be determined). A popular Negro jest not found in English white tradition explains the origin of the expression "Mhm." The Devil was carrying souls in his hands and mouth, when asked a question by a passerby. Instead of replying "Yes," and losing the soul in his mouth, the devil mumbled "Mhm." Among the Pennsylvania Dutch he is reported to have grunted "U-hu," and ever since they have followed suit. The ignorant countryman who buys a pumpkin thinking it a mule's egg, tries to hatch it, takes a scurrying rabbit for the new-born colt, and calls to it, "Hee-haw little colt, here is your mammy," becomes Eilischpijjel, who cries "Hie-ha Hutchelli, do is dei Mudderli."

The dialect readily handles the tale of the stupid wife who gave her husband's savings to a beggar she believed to be Mr. "Time of Need." In the Pennsylvania German form the dialect expression for famine, *Die gross Not*, fits well the pun on "Time of Need." Disgusted at his spouse, the husband sets off to find someone more stupid; he meets a woman living in a valley who asks him where he comes from. "Down from above," he replies, which in the dialect, *Vun owwe runner*, can mean "Down from a hill," or "Down from Heaven." Taking it in the latter sense, the woman asks about her dead son Michael, and gives the stranger food, clothes and money for Michael. Satisfied, he returns to his wife. The double meaning of the dialect phrase provides a sharper twist to the tale than the customary European form, in which the woman confuses Paris and Paradise.

Folktales reflect the importance of the church to the Pennsylvania German farmers in cycles of anecdotes about ministers. Whereas in Europe the arrogant clergyman is the butt of the jest which turns on his discomfiture, in Pennsylvania no latent hostilities flare out in tales, and the pastor appears as a heroic if somewhat eccentric servant of the Lord. The most celebrated minister was Moses Dissinger, born in Lebanon County in 1825, who preached in the Pennsylvania German counties from 1856 to 1879, before heading west for Kansas. An unlettered carpenter called to the ministry, he spellbound his congregations with the force of his sermons and the originality of his expressions. "Only with the weapons the Lord has given me can I whip the devil," he explained, "even if he does come upon me on stilts as high as a three story house." He preached in the dialect, while Lutheran and Reformed ministers spoke in High German, and so made his points in the language of the people. Castigating drunkards, he fumed: "They have noses like red peppers, ears like doughnuts, bellies like barrels, and they make faces like foxes eating wasps; but in spite of it all they go on drinking; they jump for the rum bottle like bullfrogs for red rags." One time Mose visited the filthy home of a church member whom other ministers had scrupulously avoided. For grace he said, "God bless this dirty woman; God bless this dirty food; and God bless poor Mose who must eat it. Amen."

Mose possessed an element of the ringtailed roarer. To a set of rowdies interrupting his preaching he bellowed: "Listen now, you fellows, back there; you are all dogs, every part of you except the skin, you must keep quiet or I will come down and throw you out of doors, that you break your necks. I can lick a half dozen such Gadarenes and stuck-up chaps as you are before breakfast. Do you hear? Dissinger is my name." Once challenged to fight by a hostile blacksmith, he hung his clerical coat on the fence, saying "There hangs Dissinger the preacher, and here stands Dissinger the man. Now come on and fight." Then he thrashed the smith.

Widely told retorts float into the Moses Dissinger cycle. Walking down the street in Allentown, Moses met a group of loafers, who jeered, "Mose, how is the devil today?" Quickly he replied, "It always gives me great joy to meet one who like you is concerned about his father's welfare." This anecdote (as we saw in chapter I) was bruited in seventeenth-century Boston. Another time a friend asked him, "What are you doing today?" "Today," said Mose, "I am going to do something that the devil never did." "What is that?" "Leave Allentown." This jest is also told in proverbial form.

A profusion of folk beliefs circulate among the Pennsylvania Germans, many of which like the proverbs and tales reflect their agricultural economy and peasant earthiness. If a cow gives scanty milk, the farmer should arise early and before speaking to anyone milk the cow and then pour the milk into the privy or the fire. If the milk is bloody, he must milk the cow through the atlas bone of a pig. Esoteric beliefs contain suggestions for increasing the fertility of gardens, fields, and orchards. If a pregnant woman helps plant a fruit tree by holding it with both hands, the tree will bear doubly well. Urinate into the hole where parsley is planted to make it grow. Flax will grow tall if you show it your buttocks. When sowing radish seed say, "As long as my arm and as big as my buttocks." Potatoes planted on St. Patrick's Day will grow large and bountifully (clearly the Pennsylvania Germans carried over no prejudice into their beliefs!). Sit on thyme after planting to make it grow. It is time to plant corn when women throw off the blankets in bed at night.

A wide variety of charms and prescriptions for convulsions reflect the concern over this dread killer of children on the pioneer farm. Eleven Pennsylvania German counties report that convulsions can be stopped by laying on the child's chest a piece of rope with which someone has hanged himself. In all fourteen counties the cure is known of placing under the head of the child a horseshoe with eight nails found in the road. Ten counties yield the remedy of tying yarn never wet and spun by a child under seven around the sick infant's neck, to be worn till it falls off. All have the remedy of placing under the child's head a part of the parents' bridal trousseau.

To counteract evil spells something more potent than household formulas were needed, and here the shaman figure appears, possessing occult arts of "powwowing." This term curiously crept into Pennsylvania but not New England usage from the Indian "powaw," to denote enchantment and witchcraft, or "hexerei" in the German. In the folklore about the Amish held by their Scotch-Irish neighbors, three special notions prevailed: that the Amish painted hex signs on their barns to frighten off witches; that they painted their gates blue to indicate the presence of a marriageable daughter; and that they resorted to powwow doctors. In his biographical story, *Rosanna of the Amish*, Joseph Yoder has an Amishwoman strongly dismiss the first two ideas when questioned by an

Irishman from Philadelphia, but readily admit to faith in pow-wowing. Proverbially the wise man or "braucher" was described as "one who could do more than eat bread." The "braucher" effected cures and warded off evil spirits by his charms and conjurations, and on occasion perpetrated "hexe" or black magic. Two favorite types of "braucher" stories show the one-who-can-do-more-than-eat-bread in different lights. In one formula, he detects a witch by advising the tormented person to drive a nail or peg gently into the floor, door sill, or a tree in the yard; the aggrieved one angrily smites the peg, and the witch dies. In the other, rationalizing pattern, the "braucher" is called on to drive off evil spirits afflicting the cattle of a shiftless farmer. The "braucher" advises the farmer to plug up and clean out his drafty stables, and fill the hay racks. The prescriptions work marvelously and the cattle fatten.

In folksong and folk music the little-known stores of the Pennsylvania Germans have only recently been gathered and examined. At applebutter frolics, quilting bees, husking and play parties, during the festive New Year's season, old and young sang imported, indigenous, and hybrid folksongs. Some came straight from Germany with the early settlers, pleasant humorous pieces like the spinning song "Schpinn, schpinn" where the mother promises her daughter, complaining of a sore finger at the spinning wheel, various presents, but only the promise of a husband allayed the pain. Other songs originating in the late colonial period conveyed the sentiments of emigrants about to journey to America. Some ballads contained both Old Country quatrains and verses composed in America, as the Schelmlieder or roguish song "Drei Wochen vor Ochsdren" ("Three Weeks before Easter"), where members of the convivial group in turn contribute lighthearted stanzas about dancing maidens and summer roses. Occasionally songs from Germany include American loan-words when transplanted to Pennsylvania, as "D'r zwitzerich Danzer" ("The Flashy Dancer"), about a proud young fellow displaying his handsome clothes, who points to the "jacketle" and "beltelle" (little jacket and little belt) in his wardrobe.

Purely local ballads also sprouted in Pennsylvania. A rollicking caricature of the personalities in the Merztown village band ("Di Matztown Cornet Band") spread to other localities, and incorporated such Americanisms as "Yankee Doodle," "Dixie Land," and "Kutztown Fair" in its ribbing dialect. Indistinguishable, save for its dialect, from English broadside ballads of criminal laments, is the dirge of "Susanna Cox," a servant maid seduced by a neighbor. Susanna killed her bastard child and was executed at Reading. The lengthy broadside was printed in 1810, translated into English in 1845, and survives today in folk tradition.

If the oral folklore of the Pennsylvania Germans is abundant, their material folk art is lavish and indeed outstrips the craftsmanship of any other region. Their self-sustaining agrarian economy and cultural insulation nourished handicrafts and decorative arts that made gay their cooking and eating utensils, their clothing, their houses and barns, their furniture, their writing. These folk arts flowered from the decade before the Revolution to the Civil War, following the period of rude pioneer living, and preceding the deluge of mass production. In recent years a revival of interest in Pennsylvania Dutch folk crafts has led to the collection and reproduction of nineteenth-century craft products.

The forms of Pennsylvania Dutch folk art were shaped by

memories of decorative devices used in the Rhineland, influenced by British craft traditions such as fine cabinet-making, and infiltrated by American symbols like the eagle. Bringing few worldly goods with them, the woodcarvers and tinsmiths, potters and weavers, worked from mental images and thus simplified the Old Country designs, sometimes painting motifs which in Europe had been carved. Ornamentation was never practiced for its own sake, but rather to enhance the everyday objects of living, and yet the multiplicity of crafts permitted ample opportunity for naïve artistic endeavor. John J. Stoudt has enumerated the objects bearing folk decoration: "chests, birth-certificates, hymn-books, *haus-segen*, barns, butter-molds, waffle-irons, tea pots, clocks, tombstones, date-stones, cooking-dishes, pie-plates, towels, samplers, baking-molds, irons for Conestoga schooners, coverlets, quilts, weaving-stools, tumblers, tin-ware, stove-plates, tiles, hinges, tavern-signs, chairs, cradles."

Whether on wood or tin, rag paper or clay, woolen or linen, stone or iron, the traditional motifs recurred. Always there appeared bell-shaped tulips, fancy hearts, stiff but often brightly colored birds and flowers, solemn mermaids and unicorns. Geometric designs based on the compass were especially popular on barns. The human figure when it appeared, as a soldier or an angel, looked like a misshapen doll. Some American themes entered the repertoire. A gaudy Carolina parrot, now extinct, was introduced in the woodcut birth records printed by Heinrich Otto in the late eighteenth century, while after the Revolution eagles flourished. In the words of Frances Lichten, "Eagles spread their wings on pottery, screamed on birth certificates, were painted on dower chests and shaped in tin as cookie cutters. Women even appliqued large eagles on quilts."

Regional Folk Cultures

Exuberant art forms and creative folk artists flourished from 1750 to 1850 on the farms and in the market towns. The glassware initiated by Henry William Stiegel between 1756 and 1772 evoked nationwide desire for its skilfully blown and colorfully ornamented mugs and tumblers and jiggers and decanters. *Sgraffito* pottery provided a technique for scratching peacocks and eagles, tulips and pomegranates and the ever present tree of life through a white clay coat laid over red clay plates and dishes. "Fraktur" writing produced beautifully illustrated baptismal certificates and bookplates, often drawn by schoolmasters expert in the calligraphy based on medieval manuscript lettering. (*Fraktur* was the name of a German type face derived from calligraphy.) New American objects received the traditional decoration, like the curved, rimless earthenware pie-dish designed for fruit pies, and the pie-cupboard or "safe," fashioned to hold the rash of home-made pies, a wooden piece with ventilated tin panels.

Few individual folksingers or folktale tellers are ever individually honored, but certain of the Pennsylvania folk artists have left their mark for posterity. Christian Selzer (1749–1831) painted panels on the massive wooden chests so important in farmhouse storage, with a distinctive pattern of red, blue, and gold tulips with dark brown leaves set in solid urns. Lewis Miller (1796–1882) left numerous drawings of farm life among the Pennsylvania Germans. Even into the present century the creative urge has lingered, as with Noah Weis (1842–1907), who filled the walls of his country inn with wooden carvings of biblical and hunting scenes.

Eventually the maudlin taste of the mid-nineteenth century, when *Godey's Lady's Book* set the fashions, and the stultifying effect of factory production, withered the native folk crafts.

The passing of the peasant art can be seen, for instance, in the transition of tombstone designs, from the fecund tree of life embracing a variety of trees and animals, a symbol imported from Europe, to the weeping willow chiseled on the tomb of Joseph Bahl in 1846, a motto typifying the teardrop sentiment of ladies' annuals.

THE OZARKS

Victory in the revolution against England brought Americans a new slice of territory west of the Appalachian chain, sealed off by the British Proclamation Line of 1763. In 1803 another vast chunk of the continent expanded the western domain, in the Louisiana Purchase from France. With these extensions to the republic came a solitary range of hills to interrupt the flat prairielands stretching from the Appalachians to the Rockies, the Ozark plateau of northwestern Arkansas, southern Missouri, and a piece of eastern Oklahoma. Today a million people live in this wooded land of eroded limestone ridges and sunken "hollers," three-fifths of them on scrubby submarginal soil. The Ozark hillfolk are twice a mountain people, for their forebears moved to northern Arkansas from the southern Appalachians of Kentucky, Tennessee, and North Carolina in the 1830's and 40's, after planters and farmers had gobbled up the rich bottoms of the Mississippi Delta and the waving Missouri prairies to the south and north. For a century thereafter these people of British stock lived an isolated and inbred life, cut off from the highways of commerce and the quickening currents of immigration.

The classical elements of the folk community seemed present here: isolation, illiteracy, marginal living, close contact with nature.

The Ozarks have indeed revealed a vast reservoir of oral folk traditions. America's foremost collector, Vance Randolph, has ladled them into his voluminous collections of Ozark folk-songs, legends, tall tales, folk speech, beliefs, riddles, obscene jokes, ballads, rhymes, fiddle tunes, and dance calls. Yet folk-lore flourishes in the modern metropolis as well as in the backwoods, and isolation pays a price. The movements of history have little affected the hillfolk, and their lore is lean in historical legend. Even the Civil War, while producing some local balladry, was unknown in certain parts of the Ozarks. Where in New England the Yankee bumpkin gave way before new comic stereotypes arising out of the immigration flood after the Civil War, the Ozark hillman remained the bottom man on the totem pole, sinking deeper into his hillbilly role as the tides of American material prosperity raced past him.

The Arkansawyer himself became a legend, growing from realities. An idle squatter drinking corn liquor in a log cabin buried in the holler, surrounded by a stringy-haired wife, a passel of barefooted young uns, and a couple of razor-backed hogs—such was the picture drawn in the most famous piece of Ozark folklore, "The Arkansaw Traveler." By 1850 this humorous dialogue and fiddle tune was already in circulation, and it has retained oral appeal right up to the present. A well-dressed traveler rides up to the squatter's home, asks directions, and gets shifty replies from the fiddling hillman, until he volunteers to finish the tune for the ragged old fellow. Delighted, the fiddler gives the traveler whiskey and every hospitality. This scene burgeoned into print, drawing, and farce, but its basic form is the oral recitation, both in song and dialogue. Humorous colloquies between travelers and inquisitive Yankees preceded the Arkansas version, which incorporated floating bits of anecdotal repartee. Its most celebrated snatch, the reply of the squatter when asked why he does not repair his leaking roof (when it's raining he can't and when it isn't he doesn't need to), has endured in Maine from 1832 until today.

An actual traveler to Arkansas, Marion Hughes, crystallized the outside attitudes toward Ozarkers in a pamphlet of 1904, *Three Years in Arkansas.* A roving farmer and storekeeper, Hughes spent his three years in tiny Ozark settlements, and described the ignorance and primitive living of Arkansawyers in a caricature larded with folktales, which many readers accepted in full, and which indeed contained a spine of truth. Hughes pictured an Ozark family with whom he stopped. The old woman's hair was covered with goose feathers, and her dress was made of flour sacks. The children went barefoot. The old man wore a coonskin cap, striped shirt, and high-water pants patched with a tobacco sign. The old woman kept a frog in the churn to kick the cream into butter, and then picked hairs from the butter, as easier than straining the milk. Two shirts spread over a stump in the center of the cabin made a supper table; the old man sat on a box, the old woman on the churn, and the two children stood. During the meal a sound came from under the table cloth, and the old man lifted a cat and her kittens out of the stump. Before going to bed on the floor, the old woman "turned" the chickens; that is, she turned their heads into and their tails out of the meal barrel, so they wouldn't nasty the meal during the night. Such a scene, with an accompanying illustration, helped fix the image of hillbilly life.

Regional Folk Cultures

In ballads, tall tales, ribald jokes, and local legends, the hill people expanded on the backwardness of Arkansas reported by travelers, much as second generation Jews tell Jewish dialect stories. A mournful song recounting the sad experiences of a hobo in the Ozarks in the 1870's or 80's has lived on in the country he defamed. Usually called "The State of Arkansaw," the ballad details the miserable food, the poor pay, and the unhealthful climate of the region, and leaves this unflattering portrait of a typical inhabitant:

I worked six weeks for the son of a gun, Jesse Herring was his name.
He was six foot seven in his stocking feet and taller than any crane;
His hair hung down in strings over his long and lantern jaw,—
He was a photograph of all the gents who lived in Arkansaw.

In the end the hobo frantically fled Arkansas. Instead of countering these calumnies, the Ozarkers inflated them, appropriating current tall tales to astound "foreigners" with the steepness of their hills and poverty of their soil, the leanness of their razorback hogs, the severity of their storms, and the fierceness of their forest beasts. In the last thirty years Vance Randolph has collected many such tales. A hillman claimed he could shave with the bony ridge of his starved razorback; another sighed that his coon dogs were so poor they had to lean against a stump to bark; one told of a summer so dry the trees followed the dogs around, and a snowstorm so deep he had to dig forty feet looking for his privy. A straight-faced yarn that embroiders the Ozark legend, "Big Knives in Arkansas," has a Yankee wander into a hill settlement where a frolic was being held in a log cabin with a puncheon floor. The boys wore long hair, kept their hats on while they danced, hooped and hollered every so often, and at the end of the dance escorted their gals to a bench and pulled their long Bowie knives out of their belts. The frightened Yankee bolted into a corner, but when he finally peeked out, he saw the gallant hill lads picking splinters out of their partners' feet.

Unprintable tall tales and jests gibe at the primitive morality of hillbilly families and church cults in the hollers. They run strongly to adultery and incest, to the virility of country boys and the credulity of country girls. For a mild example, a husky lad helps a rich city lady change her tire. She offers him pay, but he says that in the hills people swap. Looking him over, she leads him behind a bush and undresses, saying, "You can have anything I've got." He fingers her dress and remarks, "It ain't wool," eyes her panties scornfully, saying "They ain't worth anything," and concludes, "Just give me twenty-five cents and we'll call it even." In all the sexual jokes, not an instance of homosexual perversion occurs, a theme popular in urban jests, nor is any hint of petting or dalliance suggested. In line with Kinsey's findings, the lower-class Ozarkers go straight for the target. However they are perfectly willing to include heifers, ewes, sows, and lady jackrabbits as targets.

These shady stories reflect not only the mores of the backwoods but something of their deeper belief system as well. Nakedness and copulation symbolized fertility, and Randolph reports evidence of hillfolk insuring the abundant growth of their crops with intercourse on the planting ground.

Much Ozark humor turns on the ignorance by hillfolk of modern refinements. A young hillman took his bride to a hotel, asked the clerk if they had any private rooms, was given one, and came flying downstairs. "There's a toilet up there," he said; "Why people will be coming and going all night." An old fellow was amazed to hear that city people had bathrooms in their homes, and said to Randolph, "You mean they dung right in the house?" The conception of an animal-like creature interested only in women and whiskey recurs through tale after tale. In one story called "The Necessities of Life," a party of deer hunters traipsing through wild country comes across a lonely rundown shack where a solitary old codger lives. "He didn't even know how the election turned out, or the war, or even the World Series." The old fellow had no garden or livestock, and didn't farm, hunt, or cut wood, so one of the hunters asked him, wasn't it difficult to obtain the necessities of life. "It sure is, stranger," the old chap quickly replied, "and half the time, when you do get it, the damn stuff ain't fit to drink!"

The exaggeration of this Ozark self-portrait becomes evident from the Victorian verbal taboos of the hill people, whose sense of propriety far exceeds that of city dwellers. Off-color stories are never told in mixed company, and even references to the sex of animals brings a blush to a fair cheek. This attitude leads to such delicate euphemisms as rumpsafetida for asafetida, limb for leg, dinners (!) for breasts, hoe-handle for penis, rooster for the cock of a shotgun. Great embarrassment was caused an Ozark congregation when a circuit preacher asked, "How many Peters are there here?" speaking of Peter denying Christ. An old woman vigorously objected to the phrase "Passion of Christ," asserting that the Lord was without sin.

The creative genius of Ozark folk expression lies in the short anecdotal legend. For all their abundance, folksongs in the Ozarks fail to reveal much of a regional imprint; the old English ballads found in New England and the southern Appalachians are closer than the Ozark versions to the fine British texts gathered by the Harvard scholar Francis James Child. The rich Ozark idiom of folk speech that flavors the tales little affects the balladry, and surprisingly few native ballads originate in the Ozarks. But the repertoire of tales is fresh and distinctively regional, even though one constant form refashions all the varieties of narrative. Märchen, legends, jokes, supernatural experiences, stories of local characters, neighborhood events, all emerge as actual incidents that transpired somewhere in the next holler or on the other side of the mountain. "One time there was. . . ." the Ozark storytellers begin, and launch into a brief true narration, localized like an anecdote, believed like a legend, but structured, with opening and closing formulas and action in the middle, like a formal folktale. The world of the hillman comes into focus in these narratives, which served him in lieu of newspapers and radio. Gossip of the hills, sensational matters, pranks and antics and tomfoolery, circulate as local stories. The European wonder tale that wanders in from the southern Appalachians is cut down to size and given an Ozark setting; the abbreviated jest from the city is expanded and tied onto an appropriate personality; the Negro story from the Mississippi Delta takes on a hill country hue. Because the tales are so splashed with local color, only the comparative folklorist discovers that the great majority are widely traveled.

A few examples must suffice from a hundred possible illustrations. In the story "The Two White Springs," a criminal is sentenced to death unless he can construct an unanswerable riddle. He proposes the following riddle in the court room:

> I got my dinner at two white springs
> A-running through a yellow gold ring.

The champion riddlers confess defeat, and the accused explains how he drank the mother's milk of a soldier's wife through her gold wedding ring. The criminal was released, though the soldier was not pleased. This riddle has been traced back to classical times by Archer Taylor. In his *Natural History*, Pliny tells how Pero saved her father Cimon from starvation by suckling him in prison, a scene painted in Pompeii and by Rubens and both Breughels (and we think too of the final tableau in Steinbeck's *The Grapes of Wrath*). In the Middle Ages the episode turned into a riddle, spread all over Europe, and was carried by the Spanish to Latin America. Versions in England and North America take the form of the "neck riddle," in which a doomed person can avoid the gallows only by constructing an unanswerable riddle. Taylor gives a North Carolina version with this riddle:

> Good morning, Mr. King! [*Three times.*]
> I took a drink from your morning spring.
> In your garden it was done;
> Through a gold ring it did run.
> Now if you can solve this riddle,
> You may hang me before tomorrow's sun.

The play on a personal name, typical of neck riddles, appears here, the king's wife being called Morning-Spring. In the Ozark text, the figure of the king and the pun on the queen's name have disappeared, in the interest of realism. Since the Ozarkers gave much attention to riddles, to sharpen the wits of their children, and provide an adult game of mental skill, the tale takes on an added plausibility.

Migratory American legends as well as international fictions turn up in Ozark dress. An unpretentious yarn tells of a circuit-riding preacher who thrashes a contentious blacksmith, Colonel Dockett, and converts him. In similar fashion the celebrated frontier preacher, Peter Cartwright, is supposed to have smacked down rowdy Mike Fink at a Methodist camp meeting in Missouri in 1833, and forced the bully to repeat the Lord's Prayer after him. We have seen how the Pennsylvania Dutch preacher-hero, Moses Dissinger, licked a blacksmith, a performance perhaps picked up from the Scotch-Irish on the frontier. Connected with different names, the same incident is reported in east Tennessee, possibly brought down by the Pennsylvania Germans, and then taken west from the southern Appalachians to the Ozarks.

Sometimes a tale, though bearing all the apparent characteristics of legend, withholds its secret. The grisly yarn of "The Bloody Miller," who killed his wife and smoked her meat into sausage, and thus began a flourishing human sausage business, fits readily into the wild Ozark setting, where outlaws and murderers were accustomed to hole up. In Randolph's account, heard in Joplin, Missouri, in 1937, as current since 1900, the sausage-vendor's name is Bland. A separate tradition from southern Missouri gives the cannibal's name as Dunderbeck, describing him as a mean old man living alone in a ramshackle cabin, who constructed a large sausage mill, invited visitors, chiefly small children, to peer within, then tossed them into the hopper and started grinding. Men investigated, tied Dunderbeck to a tree, circled around him and sang out:

> Old Mister Dunderbeck, what makes you be so mean?
> You're going to be ground to sausage meat in
> Dunderbeck's machine.

Whereupon the cannibal was ground in his own mill, and the sausage fed to the hogs. But children continued to chant the jingle.

Also in Joplin, Randolph collected a song, "Donderback's

Machine," in 1922, with a less sordid climax, since Donderback grinds up only cats and dogs, and is accidentally ground up himself by his wife when he has crawled inside to fix the machine. Across the Arkansas line, in Fayetteville, Randolph recorded the song in 1941 as "Johnny Berbeck." As Sigmund Spaeth notes, in *Read 'em and Weep*, this song, often with Germanic dialect phrases, has enjoyed considerable popularity to a tune borrowed from an Irish vagabond song, "The Son of a Gambolier," which appears in college songbooks. The parody of "Johnny Verbeck" is widely sung today at camps and on college beer busts. In Michigan's Upper Peninsula I heard of a sausage-maker named Reutgert who pushed his wife into the machine, her ring later being found in a sausage. Hence lumberjacks at the meal table were accustomed to say, "Please pass Mrs. Reutgert."

A Negro informant of mine, Mrs. Mary Richardson, told me for true a horrible business of a colored man in Clarksdale, Mississippi, who slaughtered his wife and sold beefsteaks from her carcass to his neighbors. When they all began vomiting, he was tracked down, chained in a dungeon, hanged, and buried in a shallow grave which the dogs dug up. The structure of this narration runs parallel to "The Bloody Miller," save that the Ozark woman tasted delicious as sausage, whereas the sharecropper's wife cooked into beef patties made people throw up. In both cases the husband-murderer buried the bony parts of the skeleton. Natives in Haiti speak of an Austrian visitor who paid two shoeshine boys four dollars per head to kill peasants, whom he sold as sausage. The Ozark story clearly has affinities with the popular folksong and the Negro legend, but the exact relationship is uncertain.

The prevalence of the legendary yarn in the Ozarks reflects

the wide area of supernatural belief still current in the hills. Since belief in witchcraft strongly persists, a European witch-tale will be told as a true experience rather than as a bedtime story. So the drying up of cows by a stranger woman who calls their owners' names while milking a towel into a bucket, or the transformation of a husband and sons into alligators, or the spoiling of a strawberry bed by a rejected peddler-woman, or the initiation of a hillwoman at a witch's sabbath, are all related as real happenings. The old English ballad of "Sir Hugh and the Jew's Daughter" (Child 155) becomes an actual murder of the little boy chasing his ball over the wall, by a witch and her daughter who ghoulishly suck his blood.

The tenacious and secretive witch-lore pervading the Ozarks involves spells and poppets, the initiation of witches through orgiastic rites, and the preparation of counter-spells by witch-masters. In his "Unprintable Collections," Randolph reveals lascivious traditions about the nineteenth-century Arkansas poet, editor, and public figure, Albert Pike, covenanting with the Devil. The virile Pike sat on a throne in the woods, while naked women danced about in wild orgies. The naked women were all witches, a Confederate veteran told Randolph, and some of them were the wives of Pike's best friends.

Witchcraft and other supernatural beliefs in the Ozarks follow the English inheritance. In the hills the "power doctors" staunch blood, heal burns, and locate water by esoteric formulas. Ghosts walk, and haunted houses terrify. Innumerable superstitions of daily life abound. But the evil eye of the Mediterranean, the fairies of Ireland, the trolls of Scandinavia, have no place. This is an Anglo-Saxon folklore, molded and colored by the American backwoods environment.

Regional Folk Cultures

Resting directly athwart the westward advance of the young republic lay the northern properties of Mexico. If Manifest Destiny were to be consummated, Mexico must sell, cede, or yield her weakly held outlying provinces that blocked the American advance to the Pacific. The matter came to a head in 1846. Expansionist President James K. Polk engineered a skirmish on the Rio Grande border, and by 1848 the territory from New Mexico to California was flying the United States flag.

The new territory of New Mexico, destined to become the forty-seventh state of the Union in 1912, boasted a history going back to the early sixteenth century. In 1528 the Spanish conquistadores entered the land, greedily drank in treasure stories of the fabled "Seven Cities of Cibola" from Indians, and took formal occupation by 1539. Coronado never found the riches he sought, and the settlement of New Mexico slackened off until 1598, when Don Juan de Oñate founded the capital at San Juan, and missionary and agricultural work began in earnest. For more than two centuries Spain ruled the vast, bare tract of mesa and canyon and arid plain sprinkled with Indian pueblos and Franciscan missions. For twenty-five years more, from 1821 to 1846, Mexico governed the area, following her independence from Spain.

Now with a century of United States possession behind her, New Mexico remains in large part a Spanish-Mexican *paisano* culture. Particularly in the isolated plateau country north of Santa Fe have language and traditions retained their ancient forms. The center of the state, cushioned in the Rio Grande river basin, has passed most noticeably under "Anglo" influence. Here the Americans crossed in their westward march, and developed trading centers. South in the Mesilla valley the proximity with Mexico has kept fresh and fluid the Spanish tongue and the Mexican civilization. With all these regional variations, the conditions of folk culture cover most of the state: a rich Old World legacy of sung and spoken traditions; a marginal society living close to an austere yet compelling land; a strong sense of ethnic exclusiveness. Today Spanish New Mexicans comprise nearly half the population of the state. They live in segregated areas in the cities—like "Old Town" in Las Vegas—and in tiny villages, like Hot Springs on a high mesa in the northeast, which Helen Zunser has so sensitively described. Only twenty families, amounting to sixty people, live in Hot Springs, and there is but one American among them, manager of the ice company which provides the sole regular employment. They are condemned to hunger and poverty on their dusty plateaus and to seclusion in the mountains, with only two wheezy Fords to carry them from the village. Their loves and hates, pleasures and hopes, beliefs and fears, are governed by tradition.

Folklore wraps around the lives of the community at every point. Women steal husbands with love magic, or strike down the wives with witch poison. Counter enchantments and herbs cure the sick. Religious miracles are performed by the hermit of Hermit's Peak. Mystery cloaks the secret flagellant order of "The Penitentes," who flail themselves with *yucca* whips and parade naked during Holy Week. For excitement and the prospect of wealth, parties hunt for treasure, carrying a little picture of St. Ignatius to ward off witches. The Devil lurks about the 'dobe houses, perhaps as a fireball seen near the home of a bewitched woman. "My body afraid but my soul not afraid. I take my cross in my hand and hold it and go outside. It don't come near me." For recreation there are community dances in large rooms of the 'dobe homes, with fiddle and guitar accompaniment; games of agility, sometimes with horses; volumes of storytelling; feasts with traditional recipes, on the rare occasions of plenty. Some influence from cheap phonograph records and readers has entered the song and tale repertoires, but the major part is purely oral. Proverbs and riddles abound, closely keyed to the immediate life. "Two places when you know your friend, in bed [sick] and in jail," summarizes the complacent attitude toward jail sentences, an experience shared by most of the menfolk. "What is it, an old woman with her belly on her face?" Answer: a guitar. "What has a tall grandfather and a short father, a black mother and a white child?" Answer: the piñon nut; grandfather is the bush, stem the father, shell the mother, and the nut is the child.

The people of Hot Springs draw a sharp line between themselves and Old Mexico, whose inhabitants they regard as knife-fighting brawlers and bandits. Though they call their language Mexican, they speak of themselves as Spanish-Americans. In the Southwest, Mexicans rank well below Anglos, and the natives of Hot Springs suffer discrimination in town. Their relations with *Americanos* have failed to bridge the chasm of cultures. In turn they hold aloof from the nearby heathen Indians. These *paisanos* are a people apart.

The vigor and vitality of folk tradition in Spanish New Mexico, with its special Hispanic-Mexican-Catholic hue, has found a unique expression for the United States in religious folk theater. In particular the play of *Los Pastores* (*The Shepherds*) has penetrated "the entire American Southwest from

California to the lower Texas-Mexican border and from the border to Spanish-speaking pockets scattered over the mid-Rocky Mountain area," in the words of John Englekirk. New Mexico provides the center of its appearances, and those of other Nativity dramas and even of secular plays produced by the folk. Although a treasured manuscript lies behind the performance, *Los Pastores* is in very essence a folk creation.

On Christmas the players in Las Vegas or Santa Fe, Socorro or San Rafael, or tiny hamlets in the valleys, gather for the enactment. Gardeners, sheepherders, auto mechanics, laborers, they come in traditional costume of starched pantaloons, colored ribbons, and grotesque masks, carrying the crooks of shepherds. Their stage is a drafty town hall, the open plaza, somebody's backyard. Decorations and properties are strictly impromptu: a cross made from corncobs; a booth for the Holy Family draped with flags; picture cards, apples, striped candy, baubles for the crib of the Child. The audience is roped off on both sides of the hall, and the players roam down the middle.

To the shepherds come the Hermit and Lucifer, seeking information about the Messiah. In a humorous colloquy between Lucifer and young Cucharon, the shepherd boy mistakes "Messiah" for the man "Matias," and gives ludicrous cross-answers, something like the Arkansas-traveler dialogue. He is saved from Lucifer's burning wrath only by accidentally invoking the name of God. In later scenes an angel protects the shepherds from Lucifer, and they all journey to the manger to adore the Babe. Hymns intersperse the speeches.

Los Pastores blends ritual, devotion, theatrics, music and song and dance, pageantry, seasonal festival, and social gaiety. The Christmas story is pushed to the background, and the antics of the shepherds and the Devil come to the fore, permitting some secular jollity and clowning. To the traditional Hispanic feast-day ceremonials—baptisms and weddings and church holidays—*Los Pastores* adds a thespian note, and the opportunity for spectacle, in costuming, decorations, home-made properties. The Archangel Michael descends from heaven by a rope and pulley, sometimes jerkily; devils prance in red-jawed masks hammered out by the local tinsmith; a tinsel Star of Bethlehem slides on a cord across the plaza guiding the Magi.

Why does this manuscript-based drama qualify as a form of folklore? Unlike the pretentious "folk plays" of university drama departments, which are sophisticated attempts to write and produce plays with quaint folk backgrounds, *Los Pastores* springs genuinely from the folk community. A traveling troupe from Mexico performs the spectacle in some New Mexican village, and instills the desire for an annual production. With effort a manuscript is procured, perhaps written down from the memory of an actor, or copied from another manuscript in a neighboring village, or stitched together with several threads of recollection and the loose ends tied up by the *maestro*. Each village stages its own version, and from one year to another the script changes, according to the local talent, the physical facilities, the successes of improvisation, the garbling of lines learned from one single, battered script. Episodes from one play move to another; thus *The Shepherds* has lifted the clattering swordplay of Lucifer from *The Moors and the Christians*. As Frances Gillmor observes, there is fluidity at many points; the plays move from books to manuscripts to oral tradition; from village to village; from one generation to the next. Topical and national sentiments alter the texts; the war of the Moors and Christians may change to strife between French and Mexicans, who call on Our Lady of Guadalupe when the invaders try to convert them! In still a further sense these Nativity dramas are folk, for the whole Hispanic community participates in their preparation and staging and in observing their performance.

In its music and dance interludes, *Los Pastores* reveals other folk processes. Texts of speeches for Michael and Lucifer and the shepherds are written down in the manuscripts, but the music of their solo and choral songs and marches lives by ear and memory. The musical numbers share in the story; the shepherds march to Bethlehem to irregular musical rhythms, and there sing their adoration to the Christ child; when one shepherd has no gift to offer, he performs a dance. In the different performances, texts and tunes separate and recombine. Old Spanish forms tenaciously persist. A singing chorus accompanies Lucifer mourning his fall from grace, in the *decima-glosada* style typical in sixteenth-century Spain; the chorus sings the four lines of *glosa* and the tenth *decima* line after Lucifer has uttered the first nine. Yet the authority on southwestern Hispanic music, John D. Robb, finds in *Los Pastores* musical imitations neither of Spain or Mexico, but an indigenous New Mexican quality.

The miracle plays arise from the Middle Ages, and a performance of *The Moors and the Christians* in New Mexico dates from 1598, when Don Juan de Oñate dedicated the first church in the new land. Not until 1889, however, did the New Mexican religious folk-theater attract the attention of outside observers, when Honora de Busk beheld *Los Pastores* at San Rafael in New Mexico. Two years later Captain John G. Bourke witnessed *Los Pastores* at Rio Grande City in Texas. Their texts with Bourke's lantern slides were published by M. R. Cole as a memoir of the American Folklore Society in

Regional Folk Cultures

1907. In the 1920's Mary Austin wrote popular articles about these Nativity dramas, and in the 1930's scholars began studying them in earnest, engaging in arduous detective work to uncover and date manuscripts. Over one hundred such manuscripts have been located in New Mexico. The evidence indicates that a Mexican shoemaker from Durango or Guadalajara brought the original manuscript with him to Las Vegas in 1871, and copies, chiefly from this script, proliferated throughout the state.

A vast horde of folk narratives lingers on the lips of Spanish-speaking sheepherders and farmworkers and farmwives in New Mexico. A recent two-volume collection, *Cuentos españoles de Colorado y de Nuevo Méjico* by Juan B. Rael, who first heard *cuentos* and riddles from his aunt in New Mexico, contains over five hundred tales of all kinds. Most of them stem from Europe and the Middle East, and retain the Old World plots about enchanted princes, talking animals, and the underdog hero who conquers ogres with the aid of supernatural helpers. There are Boccaccio-like bedroom farces, miraculous deeds credited to the Virgin Mary or St. Peter, and cycles about powerful and picaresque heroes, particularly Pedro de Ordimalas, a diabolical and sadistic rogue.

In the midst of the old narratives new American notes intrude. Bilingual jests mirror the collision of cultures and tongues. A Mexican lad knowing no English tries to make purchases in an American department store. "What you want?" asks the clerk. "Sí, guante" (Yes, a glove), replies Juan. "What you say?" "Sí, pa José" (Yes, father Joe), answers Juan, and so on, until the exasperated clerk cries out, "Oh, you go to hell." "Sí, de ésos me mandó él" (Yes, he sent me some of those things). Similarly, a Mexican thinking he knows English says "Yes," when an American asks him if he wants to fight, and "No," to the question "Did you have enough?" The popular Negro jest based on misunderstood cries of barnyard fowls is adapted to the local setting. A Mexican returns to his native country complaining that even the animals speak English in the United States; the rooster crows "Get out of here," the pig grunts "Go on," and the duck says "Quick, quick."

Cowboys and corrals, priests and Indians, fiestas and *brujas* (witches), spice the tales with local color. A New Mexicanized account of the reversible dog paints in the western locale:

My uncle have a puppy, very fast runner. One day he see a jackrabbit and chase it. Rabbit run too fast, come to a wire fence and jump through. My uncle say that he very fast runner. Puppy came to the fence, jump, cut hisself on the wire, cut right in half. Half fall this side, half other side. My uncle José come up and feel bad when he see the puppy. Pick up two pieces and weld them together. Puppy fine, only got two legs up, two down. Then he run after jackrabbit, when tired turn around on other two legs. He catch him too.

An Arabian tale told on the trickster Abu Nawas is localized in the sheep country. A rich man offers his daughter to any suitor who can endure the night outdoors and naked. A hardy sheepherder passes the test, pretending to warm himself by a campfire on a distant mountain. Therefore the wealthy man disqualifies him. Peeved, his daughter cooks dinner holding the meat several feet from the stove, and serves it to her father, who then consents to the marriage.

The venerable spate of Jew and Catholic conflicts takes on a new Far West wrinkle. A priest trying to convert a Jew shows him many beautiful flowers, symbolizing Christian faiths, while the cactus stands for Judaism. "Well," said the Jew, "I can use those lovely flowers for toilet paper, but you try using cactus." A time-honored insult recurs when a skunk flees from the smell of a sheepherder. The popular American windies of the stretching buckskin harness, and the Indian-fighter who tells how he was killed by redskins, make their appearance. The New Mexican outsmarts the Californian in another brace of anecdotes. Ranchers behave ridiculously in church, and an Indian takes a hundred sheep from a priest after hearing the sermon that his gift will be returned a hundredfold. In these tales we see the impact of the American environment on an age-old repertoire.

The field of Hispanic folksong and folk poetry in New Mexico in turn offers an abundant and varied harvest. Narratives of the old aristocracy and the common people appear in *romance* and *corrido*, religious sentiment in the *alabado*, poetic imagery in the *canción*, Indian elements in the *indita*. Musical streams from Spain and Mexico, from the Indian and the frontier and the Roman Catholic faith have mingled in New Mexico.

The *corrido*, best-known type of Hispanic folksong, came to popularity in Mexico late in the nineteenth century. There it supplanted the imported ballad form of the *romance*, replacing its heroic and romantic mood with immediacy and earthiness, in a flexible mold of *coplas* (four-line octosyllabic verses) strung together for as long as the narrative demanded. Much like the English broadside balladry of the seventeenth century, the *corrido* performed the services of journalism, in reporting the latest catastrophe and adultery to the illiterate masses. Where the English broadside was first printed and later found its way occasionally into oral tradition, the *corrido* was first sung by street corner composers, at fiestas or in cafes, and then made the rounds of colored sheet, radio song, and even movie plot. In New Mexico less need existed for transmitting general news and historical events through *corridos*, in the absence of a national Mexican community, and given the ubiquity of American newspapers, so the *corrido* assumed a more personal function, commemorating an episode of family or neighborhood interest. Such is the *corrido* on the death of Antonio Mestas.

In 1946 John D. Robb heard a blind singer near Abiquiu, New Mexico, sing twenty-four *coplas* of the song, which described the death of Mestas near Santa Cruz in 1889. "The melody was one of peculiar beauty and interest," Robb noted. "Each phrase followed a descending line starting on its highest note and ending on its lowest. It had an almost immeasurable quality, defying attempts to beat time." This was the medieval Dorian mode. Following the trail of the place names in the *corrido*, Robb traced the incident to a still existing ranch, talked with old men who had known Mestas and recalled his death, secured three more versions, and identified the composer as Gino Gonzales, an uneducated but prolific composer knowing both Spanish and English. The text had remained fairly constant, though it ranged from nine to twenty-four stanzas, but each made use of different melodic phrase patterns. The story, closely following the actual event, relates how young, handsome Antonio rode off from the "Rancho de los Ingleses" at dawn to round up a head of cattle. A premonition intrudes; he had dreamed of death beside a running stream, and his friend the cook had seen a similar vision. Three days later Mestas' body was found, swollen and rotten and torn by crows, where he had been thrown from his horse. A crow revealed its location. The remainder of the *corrido* describes the laments of his father and wife on hearing the news, and the funeral held on the mountainside, because the swollen body would not fit in a coffin. From this moving but undramatic accident, the *poetas* fashioned his *corrido,* to honor a fine representative of a respected family.

Other kinds of folksongs thrive in New Mexico, from *canciones* praising Billy the Kid, and *alabados* sung by flagellant cults of the Penitentes, to *relaciones* about worthless jalopies. An Albuquerque composer made up a political song for the lumberman's union criticizing a proposed constitutional amendment against the closed shop. Stephen Collins Foster's "Oh Susannah" has become a thoroughly New Mexicanized "Susanita," with a languorous six-eight meter. Before the turn of the century Charles F. Lummis set down words and music of indigenous songs composed and sung by the New Mexican sheepherders in the mountain snows around the campfires. He found mournful love songs, sprightly drinking songs, local compositions addressed to the coyote and the railroad.

> Up from the town on the line
> Come running the *Americanos,*
> Earning us everyone money—
> Money for all us *paisanos.*

Lummis has described the peculiar art of the New Mexican folksinger:

Clear-voiced or husky, the Mexican is always a master of time. His technique may fail at other points, but the *tempo* is faultless. It is so in his singing and in his playing. To certain simple instruments he seems to have been born. He can always play the *musica,* or harmonica, and he learns the concertina with great ease, and also the guitar. He has, too, a rude musical apology of his own, invented in and confined to the sheep camp—the *bijuela.* This is a giant jews-harp made of a bow with a key and one string. When he can afford it, this string is a guitar-gut and the bow made of hard wood and three feet long. But in case of need a *bijuela* can be constructed of a fairly stiff weed-stalk and a linen thread. One end of the bow is held between the teeth, with the string outward, and it is "fanned" in the precise manner of a jews-harp. The resultant air is more audible and not without sweetness.

Folksinging enjoys a valued position in the lives of the New Mexican Spanish-speaking people. In the nineteenth century, troubadours sang with the wagon trains along the Santa Fe trail, and on occasion matched repertoires in all-night contests. At dance parties, in taverns, sheepherding in the hills, the troubadours plucked their guitars to accompany traditional and original songs. Some became individually renowned, like Apolinario Almanzares, reared by the Comanches, a hard-riding bronco-buster, who roamed the hills around Las Vegas as cowpuncher and horse jockey, composing and singing *versos* wherever he went, until his death at ninety-eight. Besides these bards who contributed songs of their own to the stream of folk tradition, talented singers in each village, the local *cantadores*, absorbed and dispensed all the regional songs. In recent times a new type of singing performer has emerged who appears in colorful caballero costume to sing for a fee at banquets and dinners and over the radio.

UTAH MORMONS

Along with the expected booty from Mexico in the Treaty of Guadalupe Hidalgo in 1848 came an unexpected bonus. Utah, far north of the Mexican borderlands, held in its boundaries no Spanish-speaking *paisanos* but a hardy, well-organized colony of disgruntled Americans who had sought a haven outside the territorial boundaries of the United States. Now the fortunes of peace brought them back under the flag they had desperately relinquished.

Alone among American regional groups, the Mormons have developed much of their folklore from stirring events in American history. Mountain ranges penned in the hillfolk of the southern Appalachians and the Ozarks from the industrial culture, and language walls immured German Pennsylvania, French Louisiana, and Spanish New Mexico, but the Mormons sprang into being on American soil before the astonished gaze of the American public, fought bloodily with their neighbors and the federal government, and trekked dramatically westward across the continent in their search for Zion.

An original theology and a new-founded church gave the Mormons unity and strength, and marked them as a people apart. Like the Puritans, the Latter-Day Saints enjoyed special providential protection for their unique destiny. Unlike the earlier saints, the Mormons themselves became the objects of a widespread folklore about their alleged peculiarities of creed and organization.

The striking occurrences that determined the existence of the Church of Latter-Day Saints all gave rise to folk legends and folksongs. Joseph Smith, the founder of the church, received visions and visitations from the Lord and his angels in Palmyra, New York, between 1820 and 1823, which led him to discover the gold plates of the Book of Mormon, and translate them with the aid of the magic spectacles Urim and Thummin. This sacred work gave the followers of Joseph Smith a special revelation extending the Old and New Testaments. Prophet Smith led his people through persecutions in Ohio and Missouri to a new headquarters at Nauvoo, Illinois, until he met his death in 1844 at the hands of an anti-Mormon mob. Brigham Young assumed the leadership, and conducted an advance guard to Salt Lake City in Utah in 1847, then outside the territory of the United States. Here the Saints took possession of the Great Basin of northwestern Utah, spreading out in orderly, well-planned settlements in the one fertile farming area west of the Wasatch Mountains that cleave the state. Today some two-thirds of Utah's close-packed population, about eight hundred thousand people, are Mormon, still largely farmers in a country of red deserts and salt flats and snowy mountains.

A legendary history of Mormonism developed simultaneously with the factual history. The collective survival of the Saints in itself amounted to a miracle. As they hewed their way across the continent, the religious traditions gathered into a dense volume of testimony: prophecies and visions, deliverances and judgments, the healing of the faithful and the conversion of cynics. Joseph Smith and Brigham Young became the center of glowing cycles, though all the elders possessed spiritual gifts which formed the basis for legends. The inviolability of the Book of Mormon furnished a theme for repeated stories. Persecution by the Gentiles, who vilified, threatened, and murdered the Saints all along their route to Zion, from New York to Utah, set the stage for acts of providence. Nature offered its hazards after the pioneers reached the Promised Land. The best-known Mormon providence occurred in the summer of 1848, when a plague of crickets descended on the first grain planted in the Great Salt Lake valley by the Saints. All efforts to dispel them proved fruitless, until miraculously wave on wave of gulls from the lake hove into view and devoured the insects. Because the obligations of the church required young Mormon men to spend a year or two abroad in a foreign country, ignorant of the language and untrained in proselytizing, accounts of their spectacular successes in converting cynical Gentiles passed into general Mormon tradition.

Mormon theology invited folklore of the supernatural with its strong commitment to intuitive knowledge and extrasensory experience. The church dogmas supported the reality of spirits and miracles, the rewards for prayer and zeal, the genuineness of inspiration, and the uniqueness of the Saints in the eyes of the Lord. In the course of their pioneer history, Mormon families encountered innumerable situations when these articles of faith could be tested and confirmed.

One supreme legend arose soon after the establishment of the Church of Latter-Day Saints in Utah, which came to symbolize the whole Mormon experience. In time of distress, physical or spiritual, one, two, or three elderly strangers appeared at a Mormon home, or by the roadside, or even in the desert, proffering aid to a Saint. Only when they were gone, leaving perhaps a full larder behind, did the faithful realize that the three Nephites had given them succor. The ubiquitous three, who usually materialized singly, devoted their powers to humble individual cases, making no attempt to interfere with divinely foreordained persecutions and martyrdoms.

The year 1855 marks the emergence of the Nephite tradition. In a sermon before a conference of Saints, Apostle Orson Pratt declared "how pleasing—how glorious it would be, could we see those three old Nephites whose prayers have ascended up, for something like 1800 years, in behalf of the children of men in the last days, and have them return to their old native land. . . . Do you suppose that these three Nephites have any knowledge of what is going on in this land? They know all about it; they are filled with the spirit of prophecy. Why do they not come into our midst?"

These three Nephites familiarly referred to by the apostle appear in the Book of Mormon, whose plates Joseph Smith received from the angel Moroni. The race of Nephites sprang from the followers of Nephi, son of Lehi, a good man who sailed from Jerusalem for South America six centuries before the birth of Christ. After his resurrection, Christ visited the Nephites in the New World and preached to twelve chosen disciples. Nine asked to live seventy-two years, and enter heaven. To the others, however, Jesus granted everlasting life, transfigured them, and brought them to heaven. For three hundred years they ministered to the Jews and Gentiles on earth, and suffered extreme tortures, when they were withdrawn because of the wickedness of man. Meanwhile the fair and virtuous Nephites in South America had been pushed north into North America and there had been conquered by the dark and evil Lamanites, followers of Laman, the other son of Lehi, who are today known as the Indians. Moroni, the angel who delivered the Book of Mormon to Joseph Smith in 1827, had sealed the sacred record in A.D. 421, then in his human person, as the last Nephite historian.

Angels and spirits had visited Mormons in the years from 1827 to 1855, according to testimony of the church fathers. But after the sermon of Apostle Pratt dramatically invoking the three Nephites, the common folk in Utah began to perceive the transfigured ones. Instances multiplied, reaching a peak between 1875 and 1900 and gradually dwindling, until after 1925 only scattered experiences are reported, although the Nephites still appear. In the pioneer period of Mormon settlement, the Nephites brought food to the hungry and healed the sick, but as the communities prospered, their mission changed, and they turned to bringing spiritual messages. With the church now so successfully established there is less work for the Nephites. As one elderly woman explained, "Things are so easy for us now that we don't have the need for those Nephites that we once had when we were pioneering and homesteading." However, appearances of the Nephites are now extended back in time, and Columbus is supposed to have encountered the Three.

The trio of Nephite legends most widely told and printed display a wide variety in circumstance. A professor at the University of Utah, Maud May Babcock, while riding through the Silver Lake country in Utah with a schoolteacher friend in 1900, found herself crawling with her horse on a jagged mountain peak covered with slippery shale. In her hopeless plight she prayed, and found herself with her horse on a path below the peak facing a courteous stranger, in Van Dyke beard and blue overalls, with clean white hands. He directed her back to camp and vanished. Miss Babcock's friend joined the Mormon church.

While helping erect a temple at Logan, Utah, in 1884, Brother Ballard sought for the genealogical information prerequisite to his performing services for his English ancestors. The day before the temple dedication, two elderly strangers thrust a newspaper into the hands of Ballard's daughters, telling them to take it posthaste to their father. He found it to be an English newspaper printed three days before, giving all the data he needed.

In the early days of Payson, Utah, a Mormon farmwife, living alone while her husband served his missionary term in Germany, saw an elderly stranger materialize at her remote doorstep. He requested something to eat. She wrapped bread in a cloth of peculiar pattern, and he disappeared. Several years later her husband related how, on that same day, when he was hungry and penniless in Germany, a stranger had thrust upon him a parcel of bread in a cloth of the same pattern, urging him to call at the post office, where indeed he found money waiting for him.

In all these accounts one special folk touch intrudes, the sudden disappearance of the strangers, a motif not sanctioned by the church but characteristic of other folktale cycles. The legend of the Three Nephites shows some affinity with that of the Wandering Jew, and of myths about gods visiting mortals in disguise and requiting their hospitality, best known in the Greek tale of Philemon and Baucis. During the 1940's it became entangled with the contemporary legend of the Ghostly Hitchhiker. Mormons driving in their car picked up a stranger who uttered mystic predictions that they would shortly transport a corpse and that the war would end in the following August. Both prophecies come true.

The traditions of the three Nephites belong exclusively to Mormonism. The bulk are placed in Utah, although the Nephites appear wherever Saints reside. All ethnic groups who belong to the church (they are chiefly Anglo-Scandinavian) share in the legend, but non-Mormons have no idea who or what the Nephites are.

Curiously the three elderly strangers inspired no folksongs, but every other aspect of Mormon history and tradition seems to have given rise to ballads, lyrics, and hymns. There are songs of the westward trek, songs in praise of Brigham Young, a song about the miracle of the gulls and crickets, song of Mormon participation in the Mexican War, comic songs about husbands with multiple wives, like Zack the Mormon engineer who had a wife in every station.

The ballad-making process in Mormon history is dramatically illustrated in the folksong retelling of "The Mountain Meadows Massacre," a blot on the Mormon record equal to any perfidy inflicted by Gentiles on the Saints. In 1857, ten years after their settlement in the Great Salt Lake basin, the Mormons learned of a United States army approaching to suppress their "rebellion." In their anger the church leaders planned to wipe out a Gentile emigrant train that had recently passed through Salt Lake City, as many California-bound parties needs must do. Mormon scouts contacted the Fancher party in southwestern Utah, promised them safe conduct against the Indians, and then butchered all save eighteen children. Not until after the Civil War was one scapegoat, John. D. Lee, tried and executed. Grisly legends grew around the site of Mountain Meadows. Screams of women and the ghostly creak of wagon wheels were heard; the Devil was seen thereabouts smoking his pipe; vegetation did not grow on the meadow. A ballad arose of the "bloody massacre," perhaps composed by the federal soldiers wintering in Wyoming. In its early form it portrayed the events fairly accurately. Later variants shift the blame from Brigham Young to Lee and indicate an acceptance and revision of the ballad by Mormon singers. The charges against Lee in the song may well have stirred up popular feeling against him.

> On a crisp October morning
> At the Mountain Meadows green
> By the light of bright campfires
> Lee's Mormon bullets screamed.

> .   .   .   .

American Folklore

At a word from Lee the pistols blazed,
The women and children came.
They shot them down in Indian style.
O Utah, where's your shame!

In spite of its theological context, Mormon folklore abounds in humor. The theme of polygamy has given rise to countless jests, about the failure of a father to recognize his own child, of the courtship of plural wives by an ardent husband, on the intricate relationships resulting from multiple matrimony, concerning the escape of "cohabs" from federal deputies. Polygamy yarns have traveled far and wide, and this one somehow came to my ears. Brigham Young slept in a mammoth bed with five wives on each side. At the head of the bed he placed a gong, which he struck when he was ready to turn over. All his wives simultaneously shifted, and in this way avoided difficulties. Alas, one grew deaf, failed to hear the gong, and was permanently lamed when she neglected to turn with the tide. Many songs have gathered around Brigham Young and his menage.

Old Brigham Young was a stout man once
    But now he is thin and old,
And I love to state, there's no hair on his pate
    Which once wore a covering of gold.
For his youngest wives won't have white wool
    And his old ones won't take red,
So in tearing it out they have taken turn about,
    'Till they've pulled all the wool from his head.

A lusty spate of yarns has recently formed about a preacher uncontrollably addicted to cuss-words and plain talk, J. Golden Kimball. Only his obvious sincerity saved him from ecclesiastical punishment. Castigating some cocky youths, he yelled: "Go to hell! That's where you're going to anyhow if you don't quit your damn foolishness! I hear you're all going around with a six-shooter on your hip! Better watch out. The damn thing'll go off and blow your brains out!" One time Senator Reed Smoot informed Brother Kimball that he had just received permission to marry Sister Sheets. "You're a pretty old man, you know," mused Kimball. "And Sister Sheets, she's a pretty young woman. And she'll expect more from you than just the laying on of hands." These jests, revolving around church figures in a pious society, display the bite and earthiness of secular folk humor.

MAINE COAST YANKEES

The earliest English explorers in North America probed along the indented and island-sprinkled Maine coast, eyeing likely sites for fishing and trading posts. With the planting of the Massachusetts Bay colony in 1630, a fringe of such posts came into uneasy existence. Not until after the Revolution did Massachusetts encourage the settlement of her Maine lands, hitherto regarded chiefly as a buffer strip against the French and Indians. Then fishermen and sailors from Cape Cod, Plymouth, and New Hampshire ports moved up the coastline between Kittery and the Androscoggin River. A century later the older Maine settlements in turn spawned maritime villages farther "down East." Through most of the nineteenth century the shipbuilding and commerce of harbor towns from Portland to Calais contributed mightily to the supremacy of the American merchant marine. Their bays teemed with oceangoing clippers and coastal schooners.

But with the era of steel and steam the Maine shipyards languished. The course of American history lay west, after

Canada had successfully blunted two northern thrusts by the United States in the Revolution and the War of 1812. Northern New England, lying above the main routes of east-west traffic, slowly stagnated, and the Maine coast towns, deprived both of inland and oceangoing trade, sank into backwater communities of small fishermen. Today they form an inbred coast-and-island culture, untouched by immigration or industry, unnoticed by the big world outside.

In one of these communities, the little town of Jonesport, fieldworkers for the Linguistic Atlas of America encountered in 1932 a remarkable ninety-one-year-old narrator, Joshua Alley. Did his meaty repertoire of tale and song reflect a pervasive folk tradition? To find out I drove to Jonesport and its offshoot, Beals Island, in July, 1956.

Much-traveled Route 1 follows the scenic Maine coast faithfully, but it bypasses the Jonesport elbow—at the desire of the natives, I was told—to pursue a direct course from Columbia Falls to Machias. North of Bar Harbor, Route 1 loses its air of tourism and traffic lessens; the countryside becomes wilder, the towns sparser, the road narrower, and the summer colonies thinner. Turning off from Columbia Falls to Jonesport, one sees scrub woods and verdant growth for twelve miles, when suddenly a dense, cold fog heralds the presence of the coastal sea. The little town of eleven hundred souls fronts a wide bay, dotted with islands of all sizes and shapes, which extends to a depth of ten miles until the unbroken Atlantic stretches before the eye. Directly across from the mainland, and reached in fifteen minutes by a makeshift ferry that holds four cars, lies Beals Island, whose five hundred residents separately incorporated in 1925. In this coast-and-island community live pure-bred Yankee fishermen, whose survival depends upon the lobsters, clams, and herring of the waters, and related trades of the sea, boat-building, twine-knitting, and sardine-canning. Outsiders have never penetrated, since the natives themselves can barely maintain subsistence; one GI brought back an Italian bride, who constitutes the single transplanted blossom in the township. True, my landlady indignantly denied being a native, saying she was born in Columbia Falls, and the fact soon became apparent that a stranger in Jonesport came not from across the sea, or out of the state, or even out of the county, but from an adjoining township. A person from out of state is a "foreigner," from out of the country an "outlandishman."

No one in Jonesport and Beals is wealthy, but a definite economic hierarchy exists. Old men and boys go clamming with the tides and sell clams for cash to waiting trucks. At home they shuck clams with the housewives, knit "heads" for lobster traps, and mend twine. Women work in the three sardine factories packing the fish, and when the factory whistle blows to announce a sardine ship is in, they drop everything and run to the job. An able-bodied fisherman owns his own lobster boat and traps, and enjoys the status of an independent operator. If he prospers, he may invest in a sardine weir or a sardine boat, and at the pinnacle of piscatorial capitalism he owns the sardine factory. Maine's major summer industry, the tourist trade, has pumped some blood into Jonesport, but the icy waters, fog blankets, and modest facilities have so far deterred all but hardy vacationers. When the sun shines through, the coves and bays and inlets of the curving coast radiate beauty.

Two extended families permeate Jonesport and Beals Island, the Alleys and the Beals, who have intermarried over the generations in a complicated web of intrarelationships, so that double cousins are common. The clan of Joshua Alley originally lived on Head Harbor Island in the bay, and there were born all his sons and nephews and their sons with whom I talked. In the early years of the present century the families began moving to Jonesport, chiefly to avoid the hard winters, and today Head Harbor is a ghost island. A number of Joshua Alley's line took up residence in a narrow lane, a stone's throw from our cabin, popularly known as Alley's Lane, where they continue to live their island ways. In the mysterious fashion of folklore, these island fisherfolk (who shared a common culture and family tradition, belonged to the Reorganized Church of the Latter Day Saints, and married one another) still show sharp individual variations of folk fancy. James Alley, nephew of Joshua, alone spewed forth Irishman tales and local anecdotes in an incessant spray; his older brother Frank sang one local sea ballad and told one wonderful yarn traceable to the *Odyssey*, but otherwise confined himself to personal narratives; Frank's son Maurice specialized in supernatural experiences and superstitions of the coastal waters; Stuart Alley, a nephew to James and Frank, alone among the clan composed ballads of local events and characters.

In three weeks I recorded over four hundred tales and songs from these Yankee lobstermen. Some specimens of their traditions follow.

Barney Beal, Folk Hero.—Every man, woman, and child in Jonesport and on Beals with whom I spoke knew legends about Tall Barney (so called in distinction from Short Barney, a distant kinsman). In fact, ten minutes after arriving in Jonesport I heard remarks about Barney from robust Thurman Alley and his son Findey, who served as fishing guides for

McCollum's Camps. "Barney Beal could lug a barrel of flour under each arm. He was a giant—a real giant. No one could lay him on his back. He heard a horse whicker in town and he said, 'You do that again and I'll kill you. The horse whickered again and he went back and hit it with his fist and killed it. Barney Beal could rest his hands on the floor sitting down in a common chair. He was about six foot four, but not an ounce of fat on him, all rawboned." These are the commonplaces of the coastal and island people when Barney's name is mentioned. Not one failed to mention that he could drum on the floor with his fingers from a sitting position. And each recited some marvelous feat of strength that he performed.

Barney Beal is a hero endowed with strength who endures by word-of-mouth tradition in the close-knit community of coastal fishermen. True, the fame of Barney has reached print, in feature articles in Bangor and Portland newspapers, and my own *Jonathan Draws the Long Bow* reprints a newspaper broadside ballad about the giant. But the local tales cascade from a pure oral source, traceable back to eyewitness accounts of Barney's awesome deeds. I recorded one of Barney's two living sons, Napoleon Beal, and two grandsons, and other old men who had seen Barney before he died fifty-seven years ago. Barney himself was the son of a giant, Manwaring Beal, a remoter and dimmer patriarchal hero of the same herculean dimensions, who pioneered on Beals Island. Most of the island families bore the name of Beal and had at least some misty relationship with Barney. Both the father and mother of Riley Beal, the boat-builder and hymn-singer, were named Beal— and his mother was a daughter of Barney. Only Riley, of all my informants, accounted for the broken nose of Barney which I saw in a large elliptical photograph owned by son Napoleon. Drifting within the three-mile limit of Canada, Riley said, Barney found himself accosted by Englishmen, one of whom smote him across the nose with an oar. Barney grabbed the oar and split it in two across his knee, seized the Englishman's shoulder and wrenched it from the socket, then picked up his gun and bent it with his bare hands. Some, like eighty-two-year-old Ami Beal, report that he said, "You can use this to shoot around corners with."

Riley Beal dug into his papers and brought forth a gem: an ancient tintype of Barney and his son Napoleon. The boy stood on a chair, and reached the waist of his father, who stood beside him on the floor. A long face, a long body, in no whit bizarre or malformed but massive, solid, and leonine— that was Barney, gazing at the camera with Indian inscrutability. He exuded power in his dangling arms and oaken torso, adorned by hip boots, rough fishing garments, and the "pea bouncer" (derby hat) he always wore.

Some tales about Barney Beal are based on direct observation by their tellers, but their dissemination to newer generations over the past half-century has sown the seeds of legend. Variants of individual stories appear, and universal folklore motifs intrude. These emphatic comments by Curt Morse of Kennebec, who as a lad knew the giant, convey their flavor.

Barney Beal was a freak. His hands hung down to the floor setting in a common chair. He'd drum his fingers on the floor. He was around seven foot, weighed three hundred and ninety, four hundred pounds but it was bone and muscle.

Barney was in Boston and he had a drink and a horse bit at him. He let go a barnyard swing and the horse just hauled up his feet and died.

He'd go down to Rockland—that's as far as you can go in a little two-master, about forty-five feet long. He was taking kiln

Regional Folk Cultures

wood to the lime kilns, and was going to bring some flour home for winter. The fellow told him, "I'm sorry, the delivery horse is gone." He said, "That's all right, I'll take it right along with me." He took a barrel under each arm and scuffed right off.

They was all standing around on the wharf chewing the rag at Rockland. There was an anchor there weighed twelve, fifteen hundred pounds. Fellow said, "I'll give five dollars to anybody who'll lift it." "Well," Barney said, "I'll lift it but it'll spoil my shoes." It would squat his feet out—he had to wear special shoes. The fellow said, "I'll give you five dollars and buy you a new pair of shoes too." So Barney lifted the anchor. Then the fellow squealed out [wouldn't pay]. So Barney carried it over to the edge of the wharf and dropped it right through the fellow's sailboat.

He sat in the bottom of a dory and rowed that way because he was too long-geared to sit on the seat.

He'd reach out and take a common man by the breast and break his head right back over.

We went into an old blacksmith's shop in Kennebec to get out of the shower. It lightninged, and he was superstitious, he thought the steel of the plough would draw the lightning. So he picked the plough up by the handle and swung it around his head and threw it fifty feet—I wouldn't say fifty yards. It must have weighed five, six hundred pounds. I couldn't up end the beam on it.

He filled an eighteen-foot dory with clams and mud, and he wanted to push off so he could go home out of the rain, up to the Great Bar. He put his shoulder down under the bow of the boat. She was stuck and wouldn't move. He pushed her so hard she broke right in two.

He had shoulders that broad [gesture] and he tapered down to about thirty-eight, forty inches. When he doubled up his arm it would fill right up like a two-quart kettle.

He wore short boots and he'd stand up straight and hook his fingers right in the ears of 'em.

He was the best feller ever was till you crossed him and then he'd spank your ass till you cried.

How did Barney die? No informant knew, until grandson Riley told me he strained his heart lifting a sixteen-foot dory by the beckets over the sea wall day after day at his camp on

Plum Island. Some tendency exists to apotheosize Barney as father-protector of Beals Island, and Riley stated that in the hard winters Barney looked after the needy and luckless. Barney Beal possesses all the folklore attributes customarily, and erroneously, credited to Paul Bunyan. As the owner of the little grocery, Charles Kilton, put it, "He was really the giant of these parts for all time."

Calling the Spirits.—An unusual form of folk belief pervaded the minds of the older Head Harbor and Beals Island natives. All the elderly people with whom I spoke knew the ritualistic procedure of "calling up the spirits," sometimes referred to as "table-tipping," and clearly a folk cousin to the spiritualistic seance. The preceding generation had possessed this art, and the seventy- and eighty-year-old men and women of today vividly remembered seeing their fathers and mothers and uncles call the spirits and make the table move. But they themselves lacked the power and no longer continued the practice. Calling the spirits served a crucial function in the older island culture, for in lieu of policemen and courts, the infallible answers of the spirits located thieves and paramours.

As Frank Alley described the practice of his mother and father: "They'd take and set up the table, and get a hymn book and sing a hymn, and put their hands on the table, and say, 'If there's any spirits in this room please move the table.' And that table would move, up and down. And it was twice for 'yes' and once for 'no.' "

The spirits unerringly apprehended thieves. Frank's father and mother called up the spirits when they were living in Warren Kelley's house to see who had stolen a brand new fishing line, and they named everyone on the island until they came to Warren Kelley. Then the table said "yes," and Warren

Regional Folk Cultures

Kelley owned right up to it. Another time Frank discovered that his own brother-in-law had stolen lobsters from his traps, so Frank wouldn't beat him lobstering, and he wouldn't speak to Frank for a year after the spirits gave him away.

Cuckolds too could be ruthlessly exposed by the omniscient spirits. A patriarch of Beals Island, eighty-two-year-old Ami B. Beal, offered this example:

It used to be common to call up the spirits. 'Cause I know one time there was three men down to east'ard, and they called up the spirits to see who had an honest wife. They said "yes" to the first man, and "yes" to the second man. And the third one, who was supposed to have the best wife, they told "no." He wouldn't believe them, and if he hadn't apologized the table would have killed him. Two weeks later his wife left him and married another man.

Coastal Legends.—The coastal fishermen share some beliefs held by deep-sea sailors, and possess others linked with the shipyards and fishing coves. An oceanic tradition astonishingly diffused along the Washington County coast deals with the buying of wind in a calm sea by throwing a coin overboard. Twelve persons in Jonesport, Beals Island, Columbia Falls, and Machias told me of wicked individuals in the neighborhood who had bought wind and repented when a gale promptly sprang up. Half of these texts center on Paris Kaler, a notorious blasphemer, and others on George Beal, Captain Belmore, Nick Bryant, Malcolm Lowell, and Cam Crowley, impious men all. The most striking version was told me by Lee Smith of Indian River, a mason and whiskey-drinking bachelor, whose very own uncle had sailed on the memorable voyage with Paris Kaler.

Paris Kaler's first wife was my aunt. Her husband, uncle Edwin Smith, sailed with him. He was a tough nut. Paris had a threetopmast schooner called "The Sawyer Brothers," almost brand new. He was sailing coastwise and hit a calm off Cape Hatteras. Paris was an awful man to swear. "Goddam this calm, throw me down half a dollar's worth of wind," he said, and scaled half a dollar into the sea. A gale came up that most knocked the sails overboard. Then Paris got down on his knees and cried baby after he asked for it. Uncle Ed told Paris to get up. He said, "You can do more on your feet than on your knees. You asked for this wind, now you're going to get a dose of it." And he threw another half dollar overboard.

It's a wonder Uncle Ed didn't knock him overboard. He never sailed with Paris again. Uncle Ed died in the Gulf of Mexico in 1912 or 1913. I remember him telling about that to my father.

From the lips of humorist "Uncle Curt" Morse came a strangely somber story explaining how Yoho Cove obtained its name. Though Curt did not know it, this experience supposedly occurring two miles from his home is known in French Canada, the Pine Mountain of Kentucky, Italy, Portugal, and Persia.

Cove about two mile below where I live called Yoho Cove and the old fellas years ago allus said there was some kind of wild man lived there, and all they could understand he holler, "Yoho, yoho" all the time, especially at night. So he kinda slacked off and there was some of the natives down around the shore, don't 'cha know, and took kinda of a dugout canoe I call it, dug out of tree, went across there raspberryin'. Well they got about ready to come home and they heard this Yoho hollerin'—they call him a Yoho. So before they reached the boat this fella, this man, ran out and grabbed this girl and took her back in the woods with him and left the rest screechin'. So they went home, and a little while afterwards why it kinda died out, don't you know? They missed the girl a lot.

Well they thought she was dead and about two years afterwards, or about a year and a half afterwards, they had kinda forgot about it and they was over there raspberryin' or blueberryin' again and they heard this screechin' and they looked up and this girl there, their relation, was runnin' and screechin' for help. So she had a baby with her chasin' along—a year old—some little year old baby somethin' like that. And they got her in the canoe anyway, started off from the shore. And the Yoho come down on the shore and caught the baby, or took the baby, tore it apart, tore it to pieces, throwed one part at the canoe as it was leavin', and took the other part back in the woods. So it's been called Yoho Cove ever since. That's all of it that I know about. It's always been called Yoho Cove.

Local Characters.—Two hundred comic stories were poured into my tape-recorder by James Alley and Curt Morse. They embraced international folktales, tall tales, humorous personal experiences, anecdotes and sayings of local characters, and jokes about Irishmen. Curt Morse, who in real life continually acts the part of a character, tells a number of yarns on himself. He is the victim of mishaps, frights, and general misfortune. There was the time he visited a booby hatch.

Oh yes, I went up to that darn place up there called the insane asylum. I was in Bangor and I thought I'd call up and see an old fella, a neighbor of ours that they'd sent up there. I don't know much about it anyhow, but there was a couple of guards had some fellas out along there with pruning shears and sickles and different things that they had in their hands, cutting the grass around the bushes. So this big fella, black whiskers, he had a sickle. And he looked at me and I thought he looked pretty wild, and he started after me on the run and I started running. And I was scairt. So I caught my toe and fell down and I could almost feel that sickle around me neck. And he says, "Tag." And the guards come and get him and I never did get to that darn place.

Conceivably this laughable incident could have happened to Curt. I had a peculiar experience myself once when I entered that same asylum to meet a mentally sick folklore collector. However, the same episode with a different locale was recorded in 1944 by an Indiana University student who heard it from his grandfather in Morganfield, Kentucky, two years before.

Sometimes the anecdotes attached to odd local characters in the neighborhood have traveled widely. Art Church of Indian River enjoyed considerable reputation as a wag and liar. When asked one time to tell a lie, he pleaded haste, for he must see his critically injured father. Later it turned out that he had lied. Though Jim Alley told this on Art Church, the same jest is connected with Gib Morgan and other liars around the country.

Jim recounted a little cycle of incidents about another character, Frank Addison, who during the World or Revolutionary War (Jim equates them) was found by his sergeant fishing in the stream with the ramrod of an old muzzle-loader. The sergeant recommended him for discharge as mentally unfit; given his civilian papers, Frank explained, "That's what I was fishing for." One of the popular folktales to come out of World War II concerns the pretended psychopath who walks around all day looking for invisible pieces of paper. Receiving his discharge paper, he says, "That's what I was looking for."

Jim also told how John Fleet finally, on the solicitation of neighbors, spoke to his brother Timothy, with whom he had conducted a long-standing feud. John had broken silence by asking Timothy to kiss his nether parts. A like scene involving two stubborn Hazard brothers appears in *The Jonny-Cake Papers* of "Shepherd Tom" Hazard, and Lincoln told a similar yarn.

One of Curt Morse's comic portraits caricatures a hermit in Kennebec known as Willie the Racker, from the resemblance of his walk to a horse's gait. Curt constantly wavers between reality and fantasy in his sketch.

DORSON: Now who was this hermit Willie Racker you were telling me about?

CURT: Oh that's an old fellow lived about a mile down in back, down in Duck Cove where I lived. He was a character. He was a hermit, a dirty old fellow, and wore his hair long, kinda looked like pencils hanging down where it was twisted. In fact he'd get up some days—it was a disease or something because he'd sleep two or three days at a time—and the little mice would nest in his hair, lugging pieces of paper and stuff. That's no lie, that's a fact. It's been proven.

So I asked some people in town one day, I was telling them that Willie had a couple or three mice that used to come eating out of the same plate with him. And they kind of contradicted it. So one day I got Colby Johnson—a fellow and his wife over in our other district—to take a camera and went down and sure enough they caught the pictures of the mice and they put them in the Bangor paper.

DORSON: How did he get his name?

CURT: Oh he kind of weaved back and forth when he walked and they called him Willie Racker. His name was Willie Foss.

DORSON: You said he could play the fiddle.

CURT: Oh boy he was a wonderful violin player. Oh I'm telling you that he'd play "The Mocking Bird" so real that you'd have to take a stick to keep driving off the birds from the strings, you know what I mean.

DORSON: How did he die?

CURT: Well I guess as far as we know he froze to death, right down by his camp. He was found with the door open and snow covered him and he was froze stiff. That was last winter.

A unified body of regional folklore, with clearly marked themes and patterns, thrives among the Maine coastal Yankees. Some traditions grow from the sea, and are generally shared by coastal sailors and fishermen. The seventeenth century contributes its supernatural vein, in the lingering awe of witches and the esoteric ritual of spirit calling. Legends of buried treasure inflame the down-Easters and set them digging with the same ardor as southern Negroes and poor whites, and grubstakers out west. Anecdotes and rhymes about local characters provide much home-made entertainment, and mingle with imported European jest-tales. A true superman folk hero flourishes in the oral traditions radiating out from Beals Island, in the personage of Barney Beal, the giant lobsterman. The occult experience and the comic oddity stand out in this blend of old English, rural American, and general maritime folklore.

Some of these folklore forms appear also in the other regions, but in varying contexts. Among the Mormons, the latter-day revelation molds the lore, so that supernatural apparitions deal with angels and spirits and the Three Nephites, and humorous anecdotes gather around an outspoken elder. With the Pennsylvania Germans, preachers become comic heroes, and the invisible world manifests itself in a thousand household and barnyard remedies and formulas. The agricultural and artisan focus of Pennsylvania Dutch culture finds expression in folk decoration of the utensils and furnishings of daily usage. In the Spanish Southwest, religious folk drama offers in one form the spectacle, fellowship, song and dance, and ritual devotion equally cherished in the *paisano* culture. The Ozark hillfolk, like the Maine coast Yankees, hark back to Anglo-Saxon forebears, but they are landlocked, not seagirt, and look to rolling country and wooded hollers rather than choppy seas and placid bays. Hence the legends of the one area are tied to scrubby soil and razor-backed hogs, and those of the other are dashed with salt spray and high winds. Each regional lore displays its own hues and preferences, according to its local history and terrain and people.

IV

Immigrant Folklore

Following the Civil War a flood of immigration swept into the United States, rapidly replacing the giant human losses of that holocaust. The Irish cop, the Italian fruit merchant, the Chinese laundryman, the Hungarian steelworker, the Jewish clothing salesman, the Armenian rug merchant, become stock figures of the American metropolis. New nationalities, little known in the American population, continued to pour into the northern states from the 1870's to the First World War. Scandinavians and East Europeans swarmed into the cities where the demands of industry had created huge labor markets, and drifted into the countryside from Massachusetts to Oregon, to harvest crops on the farms, shovel ore in the mines, cut timber in the forests. With them they brought every species of European folklore, even to the Slovenian, the Basque, the Luxembourger.

What happens to the inherited traditions of European and Asiatic folk after they settle in the United States and learn a new language and new ways? How much of the old lore is retained and transmitted to their children? What parts are sloughed off, what intrusions appear, what accommodation is made between Old Country beliefs and the American physical scene? These are the large questions that confront the assessor of immigrant folk traditions.

The impact of the immigrant differs considerably in rural regions and urban centers, for in the country he enters into regional folk culture. By contrast with the Louisiana French, Pennsylvania Germans, and New Mexican Spanish, who settled on virgin land in the sixteenth and seventeenth centuries, these later arrivals enjoyed less than a single century to leave their imprint on an already established population. Still, in a regional area such as the Upper Peninsula of Michigan, the immigrant has already stamped the folk culture with indelible contributions. Into the Peninsula, colonized by the French early in the seventeenth century, came miners from Cornwall, nicknamed "Cousin Jacks," hard upon copper and iron booms of the 1840's. French Canadians from Quebec moved down to the white pine lumber camps of the Peninsula, sustaining the original French tradition. After the Civil War the Finns and the Swedes streamed into the country resembling their own, along with smaller groups from most of Europe: Italians, Germans, Irish, Belgians, Danes, Slovenians, Croats, Luxembourgers, Syrians. In the small, fraternal, easygoing, hard-drinking Upper Peninsula towns they mingled and intermarried. Meanwhile the Ojibwa Indians, whose legends Schoolcraft had collected and bequeathed to Longfellow for *The Song of Hiawatha*, stolidly held their reservation grants.

By 1940 the Peninsula presented a rich population complex of the aborigine, the pioneer, and the immigrant, channeled into the American occupations of farming, mining, lumbering, and sailing and fishing on the Great Lakes. A spate of separate folk traditions, both ethnic and occupational, coexisted, while arching over all a new regional folklore had emerged, in the dialect humor common to the whole Peninsula.

In a single day the collector can hear traditional tales that are scattered across Europe. Elderly French-Canadian residents of St. Ignace speak in awe of *loup-garou* sorcerers taking the shape of owls and bears to torture their enemies. "Finlanders" talk of *noita* wizards cut down from the gallows after several days, who rub their necks and walk casually away. Cousin Jacks tell "plods" of the first four-wheel buggy seen in Cornwall, astounding the Cornishmen, who ran alongside the front wheels cheering, "Go along little feller, you're 'head, keep 'head." Swedes declare they have seen the *tomteguber*, a household elf who curried their horses. In spite of their close contacts, the members of the different nationality groups make no exchange of their European folk traditions, which remain in completely separate compartments. Norman Johnson, born in the Swedish settlement of Skandia in the Peninsula, told me not to bother writing down legends of Gustav Vasa, the Swedish king, which he had heard from his immigrant father, since these were so commonplace. I turned to his wife Aili Kolehmainen, Peninsula-born of Finnish parents, herself a student of Finnish folklore, and asked if she had heard the Gustav Vasa tales. "Never." But both savored the dialect jests spawned in their region, which no person unfamiliar to the Peninsula can properly appreciate.

Comic malapropisms uttered by clumsy-tongued immigrants learning English generated these dialect jokes, "lingoes," rhymes, and songs. Each dominant group—the Finns, Swedes, French Canadians, and even the Cornishmen, who brought

over their own English county dialect—bred its special variation, based on errors of grammar and accent, but all the
dialects made fun of the hapless immigrant. A brace of comic
foils emerged for each nationality, echoing Pat and Mike, who
had penetrated deeply into American popular culture following the Irish invasion of the mid-nineteenth century. The
Finnish Eino and Weino, the Cornish Jan and Bill, the Swedish
Ole and Yon, engaged in comparable antics and mouthed
equally absurd dialogues. Often the mishaps and escapades
grew from actual experiences and expressions connected with
notorious local characters, to whom other floating jests quickly
gravitated.

As the dialect story grew in popularity in the Upper Peninsula, adept "dialecticians" sprang up in each town who were
called on to give "lingoes" before lodges, socials, stag parties,
and church suppers. Their own nationality and occupation
were irrelevant to their art; they might or might not belong to
the group whose speech they mimicked; usually they had
mastered several dialects; but every raconteur had grown up
in the Peninsula, learning his English in the American school
system and his comic dialect from the immigrant speech he
heard all about him. Noted dialecticians throughout the Peninsula include an undertaker, an auto mechanic, a tavern-keeper,
a ticket agent, a county treasurer, a company superintendent,
a mason, the owner of a bottling works. Perhaps the best
known of all is Walter Gries, of German ancestry, an executive
with an iron mining company in Ishpeming, whose political
prominence is not hindered by the dialect stories with which
he sauces high school commencement addresses and after-
dinner speeches to fraternal orders. Everyone in the Peninsula
—man, woman, and child—relishes the dialect joke and can

tell at least a few; the comic immigrant stereotypes have welded the region into an in-group. A girl of Swedish background recited this jingle:

> Oh my darling, never you mind,
> I gotta yob in de Athens mine,
> Big chunk fall on de Coozie Yackie's head,
> Finnie mannie laugh when de Coozie Yackie dead.

Here in epitome is the regional, occupational, and immigrant folk culture of the Upper Peninsula. The dialect rhyme from the Swedish coed bring together the Finn and the Cousin Jack in the Negaunee iron mine with grisly humor. Every Peninsularite would respond instantly to this silly-seeming verse.

Dialect narratives, while consistent in their humorous elements, range widely in length. They may run to several thousand words, as the reciter describes the bobbles of the immigrant on his first visit to the big city, the baseball game, or the carnival. Again they may take the form of brief pointed jests, such as the following:

Finnish.—Finnish fellow running for coroner was told by the candidate for sheriff, who was also a Finn, that he should have a campaign slogan. So after working on it for several days he met the candidate for sheriff on the street and said, "Well Toivo, I got it. My campaign slogan is, 'A new suit of clothes for every gorpse, wid two bair of bants.' "

Finnish-Chinese.—The Finns and Irish always used to feud in early days. Finns called the Irish "Irish booger," as a term of contempt. A Finn went into a Chinese laundry and asked for his laundry. The Chinaman said, "No leady yet." "Vassa matter, I bring dis laundry one veek ago, and no ready yet." "No can help, he come next week." "I vant laundry now, not next veek, you Irish booger."

French.—In the early days of Escanaba there was much French-Irish rivalry. A French mayor had been elected, Munizippe Perron.

American Folklore

The whole town was celebrating Saint Batiste day. He was asked to make a speech. He got up on top of the bandstand and said, "Ladies and gentle*men*. You can talk about your Saint Pat*rick*, but Saint Batchees is de boy."

Swedish-French.—The Scandinavians are very proud of their native heritage. A Swede does not like to be called a Norwegian and so on. A Swedish farmer at Ensign staggers home from a Grange meeting—his wife had left him because of his drinking— and he falls asleep in a neighbor's pigpen. In the morning cool breezes wake him up, he blinks and finds his arm wrapped around a pig. "Ar du Svensk?" he asks. The pig rustles a little bit, grunts, "Norsk, Norsk."

The Frenchman, in a similar position, says, "Good morning, mistaire, what time is eet?" Pig says, "Neuf, neuf." "Jesus Chris'! That late alreadee." The little pig alongside says, "Oui, oui." Frenchman says, "Tank you, mistaire."

Swedish.—A Swede goes back to the Old Country and is asked how he liked America. "Py Yesus, it take me twenty year to learn to say yelly and den dey call it yam."

Yon met Ole on the street, and the following conversation took place:

Yon: "Mey gudeness Ole min [but] jur luking fine. Vat iss ju doing now?"

Ole: "Ay have gude yob wit da Soo Line."

Yon: "Vat kind yob ju gat?"

Ole: "Ets gude yob. All day ay load steel rails; gude pay, fifty cents a day. Avery night ay buy beer wit' et. Eassy come, eassy go."

Irish.—An Irishman had a brother in the Old Country and wrote him to come to America. "You can pick up money in the strait." The brother comes over. Walking along the street, he picks up a piece of tin, it looked like money to him. So he went into a saloon, and says to the bartender, "Give me a beer." So he drank the beer, and put the tin up on the bar. The bartender says, "That's tin." He says, "Excuse me, I thought it was five. Give me another one."

Cornish.—This is a true one, it happened up at 5th St. "I going up 5th St., I looked up by 'arper and Thomas's and I see father coming down the street, and father seed I too. Damme when we got up to each other, 'twasn't neither one of us."

Italian.—Some Italians were working on a construction job where

Immigrant Folklore

they were using dynamite, blasting. After the blast was set off, one of the Italians come running down the road hollering, "Tony, Angelo, Joe. Come queek. Bringa da shovel, bringa da two pick. Pete she stuck in de mud." "How deep she stuck in de mud?" "Up to his knee." "Well, tell heem to walk out." He said, "No, no can he walk out. He de wronga way up."

While dialect humor abounds in the Upper Peninsula, similar jest patterns appear all over the United States, wherever thick clusters of colonial and immigrant ethnic groups rub shoulders with Yankee Americans. The Yiddish dialect story in particular flourishes in eastern cities and by now has attained a nationwide distribution, carried by the sons and daughters of Yiddish-speaking immigrants to all corners of the land, and to the Gentiles. A southern belle mimicking Abie and Ikie produces a strange medley of accents!

A sophisticated acculturation is evident in one well-liked cycle of Yiddish stories, in which Jewish youths gently ridicule the oversensitivity to anti-Semitism of their orthodox parents. One favorite example has the Jewish salesman, who has forgotten his toilet kit, borrow soap, towel, and shaving accessories from a courteous stranger in the Pullman car washroom. After shaving he asks once more, "Maybe you mind I'm borrowing your toot'brush, I'm slick up my tootsies a little?" The stranger, who gets off at the next station, denies this request in irritation and walks out. Wagging his finger at the departing back, the Jew yells out, "Enti-Semite!"

With all the incalculable riches of immigrant folklore available in the United States, one would expect to encounter an exciting series of studies on the transfer of Old Country traditions to the New World. Ironically, only one extensive treatment exists, and this was undertaken by a sociologist as a

141

handbook for social workers, visiting nurses, schoolteachers, and physicians dealing with the practical problems posed by Italian immigrants. Nevertheless, in *South Italian Folkways in Europe and America* (1938), Phyllis H. Williams executed a model study of immigrant folk culture. She provides the indispensable baseline information about the Sicilians and the villagers from the boot of Italy's peninsula. We remember how sharply Carlos Levi cleft Italy's civilization in twain, in *Christ Stopped at Eboli*, a work itself permeated with lore of the South Italian peasant. South Italy in turn splinters into numerous regional subcultures, whose horizons are bounded by *campanilismo*—the sound limits of the village bell. Derogatory folk rhymes and sayings display antagonisms and differences among villages. In America these townsfolk settle in clusters, perpetuating their local variations in custom. Having sketched this baseline, Miss Williams discusses a dozen aspects of the social and cultural life of South Italians, such as diet, housing, education, religion and superstition, and marriage and the family, giving first the European practices and then the American retentions or adjustments.

Folk belief enters into nearly every phase of the daily round, conspicuously in matters of health and the *rites de passage*. Wary of hospitals, suspicious of doctors, aghast at psychiatrists, the South Italian peasant relied heavily in the new environment on his traditional remedies and nostrums. An immigrant woman, under pressure to visit a psychiatrist, at length consented, and after the interview triumphantly revealed to her friends a quantity of amulets she had amassed from her family and neighbors, and stowed in her handbag. They had indeed protected her. "The doctor he no hurt me." Forced by his American doctor to observe continence with his invalid wife, a South Italian greatly feared he would succumb to tuberculosis, according to the prevalent folk notion. The husband now found a use for the hospital, and repaired to it regularly with a specimen of his sputum to see if he were contracting the disease. Italian women in labor, utterly loath in the Old Country to bear their children in hospitals, made a surprising turnabout in the United States. For admission into the maternity wards made impossible the practice of ritual intercourse always performed at home at the onset of labor. Only the strongest revulsion against their own ritual enabled the immigrant mothers to overcome their dread of the strange admissions procedure, unfamiliar diet, and family separation involved in hospitalization.

A case on record of a five-year-old girl afflicted with infantile paralysis illustrates the conflict between modern medicine and ancient tradition in the minds of the Italian immigrants. Although a physician was treating the girl, the parents took her to a *maga*, who had sold her soul to the Devil for the power to cure other people's children, after her own two had died. The *maga* diagnosed the malady as a spell inflicted by *iannare* (Neapolitan for witches) who had flown in the window and attacked the child as she lay asleep between her parents. They were immune, explained the mother, "because one of my ancestors once caught one of them and would not let her go until she promised not to harm my family for seven generations. I am the seventh. When we woke in the morning, my husband and I, we were black with bruises where the *iannare* had pinched us." The *maga* rubbed the girl with salve, muttered words, and predicted that a crisis would come, giving the child a fit. This happened the following night, while a horrible noise sounded outside the window. The child recovered, and in spite of the doctor's ridicule, the parents gave all the credit to the *maga.*

Feast days of the saints continue in the New World as in the Old to serve both a religious and a social function. The fact that the immigrants came over in clumps made possible the transference of their celebrations for local saints. Two such saints' days annually observed in New York City are described by Miss Williams. The Feast of the Madonna del Carmine, held on July 16, pays tribute to the healing powers of the Madonna, who receives offerings of wax limbs at morning masses, in return for a scapular. People buy red and pink legs, arms, eyes, hearts, and long candles bearing pictures, at stalls near the church. After mass they buy traditional foods at these stalls, such as tomato pies, peppers, sausages, *torrone* (almond candy), and fried cakes and long loaves. Also they can purchase "The Only True Letter of Jesus Christ," a copy of a letter of prayer found in the Holy Sepulcher of the Lord, which brings miraculous power to the possessor. The Feast of San Gandolfo honors the patron saint of the little Sicilian town of Polizzi Generosa. Band concerts, a parade, a display of lights from Mott Street to the Bowery, fireworks, and drawing of prizes are climaxed with the Flight of Angels. Two young girls, the angels, are drawn by rope and pulley across the street from one fire escape to another, and suspended over the statue of the saint as it passes by. Such feast days draw many celebrants, even from out of state.

Though a valuable pioneering study, the handbook by Miss Williams only suggests the possibilities for investigating immigrant folklore. The bulk of its materials is restricted to South Italians in New Haven. A full comparative study would consider both North and South Italians, in contrasting parts of the United States, from Providence to San Francisco, and in small-town and rural districts, and would trace the process of acculturation from the immigrants through their children and grandchildren. Miss Williams provides but a handful of folklore texts, and these are written as case history records for the social worker and hospital attendant.

The transplanted folklore of one immigrant group was given attention as early as 1892. In a brief, meaty article, "The Portuguese Element in New England," in the *Journal of American Folklore*, Henry R. Lang presented an excellent bird's-eye view of this nationality group. Close to two thousand Portuguese from the Azores were then landing in Boston and New Bedford annually, drawn to seven Portuguese colonies scattered through eastern Massachusetts. Probably Portuguese sailors had first drifted into New Bedford during the heyday of the whaling fisheries. Today as one drives through the city, Portuguese names and faces are everywhere evident.

New Bedford in 1892 maintained the Azorian traditions and sense of community, dating back to the fifteenth century, when the Azores were occupied by the Portuguese. In the Portuguese quarter of Fayal sprang up a Roman Catholic church, the "Monte Pio" hall where national feast days and entertainments were staged, and the Club Social Lusitano which celebrated in the "Monte Pio" on each December 1 with banquet and ball the liberation of Portugal from Spain in 1640. The illiterate Azorian cotton-mill workers, street cleaners, barbers, and seamstresses preserved songs, tales, and games from their island homes amid the alien culture. Lang provides examples of these surviving forms: the historical song, or *aravias*, reflecting old Arabic influences; the *aravenga*, a children's rhyme with Moorish overtones; the love song or *cantiga d'amor*, in which, as in the Japanese haiku, a general sentiment is balanced by a personal application; satirical epigrams, accompanied by the viola or rabeca and sung to the popular dance, the *chama-Rita;* popular tales, known as *contos da carouchinha;* proverbs, sometimes incorporating a tale, such as, "It is faith that saves us, not the wood of the ship," referring to a maiden who recovered when her lover gave her a sliver of wood supposedly from the Cross, but actually from his vessel; jocular replies, a favorite form in Azorian speech— "What time is it?" "Time to eat bread." Lang remarked on the disappearance of certain types of tradition, such as the battle-pageant of the Moors and Christians, which continues in the Spanish Southwest. The ancient historical ballad was vanishing, while the popular love lyric increased in vitality. Language change reflected the mingling of cultures, as American words in frequent usage entered the Portuguese (*bordar*, "to board", for *hospedar; offas*, "office" for *escritorio*), or Portuguese forms carried over to English, as "I had cabbages for dinner," not cabbage, since *couves* is plural.

In 1916 and 1917 the enterprising collector Elsie Clews Parsons turned her attention to Portuguese-speaking Negroes from the Cape Verde Islands, who had come to Massachusetts, Rhode Island, and Connecticut seaports in the mid-nineteenth century. Visiting these communities in Newport, Nantucket, Cape Cod, and New Bedford, she discovered colonies within colonies, based on the individual islands of origin, Fogo or Boa Vista or San Nicolao. A Fogo Islander betrayed shyness when calling on a family from another island. Parsons collected one hundred and thirty-three tales, exhibiting a blend of

Immigrant Folklore

European and African features, with wonder tales of kings and giants jostling animal stories about Wolf and his Nephew. Some American influences can be detected in these exotic adventures. Three tales were told in English, by a fourteen-year-old boy born on Cape Cod and a twenty-two-year-old girl who had come to the Cape at the age of three, and whose mother prompted her in Portuguese. American place names occasionally creep in, as when robbers announce they are going to Providence, Newport, and San Francisco to steal. One narrative from a Fogo Islander, told in the native dialect, shows more Americanization than any other. Basically it is the tale of "The Youth Who Wanted To Learn What Fear Is." Pedr' Quadrad undergoes a series of eerie experiences in his quest for fear, in the course of which goats give him cheeses costing twenty cents apiece; he meets enchanted princesses, "even prettier than Americans," to whom he gives apples so sweet "you could smell them from here to California"; he views a tower that stretches to heaven, at whose foot he sees a pile of nails the size of "that oil-tank there" (this was told in New Bedford); he sleeps in a bed with sixteen feather mattresses costing three thousand dollars; and finally Pedr' outwrestles a giant, who rewards him with a diamond "as big as from here to Boston, and as long as from here to California."

If one Old World narrative had assumed this much local coloration in 1917, what is the state of the Cape Verde tradition in America today, if indeed it still survives?

The few students of immigrant folklore tend to agree that imported folk customs and ideas rapidly wither under the merciless glare of American life. One intriguing study furnishes strong evidence for this oft-repeated generalization. As community analyst at the segregation center in Tule Lake, California, from 1943 to 1946, Marvin K. Opler closely observed the behavior of 19,000 Japanese torn from their homes along the Pacific Coast and herded together for the duration of the war. He reported a strong revival of Japanese folk beliefs and practices at the center, extending even to the Nisei, under the pressure of wartime tensions and the close confinement of Issei with American-born Japanese. In the barracks of the center, inmates saw ghost-fire, or *hinotama,* known from their childhoods in Japan, and shortly thereafter residents of the center died. The older Japanese immigrants commenced retelling the familiar village legends of foxes and badgers deceiving human beings, and a badger was actually captured in Tule Lake. At this same time a woman was accused of fox-possession—*kitsune-tsuki*—and neighbors heard her talking noisily with the animal. Throughout the center there circulated with increasing force stories of pre-Meiji swordsmen with supernatural powers, the *ninjitsu* magicians who could snatch arrows from the air and catch flies with chopsticks, and they led to talk about a swordsman in Los Angeles who could cleave twelve telephone books with one stroke. Conversations turned to good-luck amulets, death omens, pregnancy taboos (avoid dark pets, or the baby will be dark complexioned; eat seaweed, so the baby will have thick hair). The practice of non-medical therapy known as *chiryo,* making use of such treatments as the application of dried and ignited *mogusa* (a kind of moss) to ailing parts of the body, revived during the life of the center.

As soon as the war ended and the center disbanded, these traditions evaporated, according to Opler. Resuming their normal lives, the Japanese families soon forgot or rationalized away the folk ideas they had accepted while residing at Tule Lake. I find this statement most unlikely. It neatly fits Opler's hypothesis that the unusual psychic tensions at the segregation center stimulated a short-lived revival of the Old Country supernaturalism. But Opler merely gives unsupported statements that the old beliefs sank into limbo after Tule Lake. Daily family life among Japanese-Americans at home should be observed with the thoroughness with which activities at the center were scrutinized. The very fact that so rich a stock of traditional lore could be documented at Tule Lake demonstrates its persistence and adaptability to the American environment. There are tensions in peacetime as well as in wartime living. Nationality enclaves certainly feel the need for security and reassurance from the traditions of the in-group during the ordinary round of American life, and they build institutions to conserve their Old World culture: foreign-language publications, ethnic societies, nationality churches. Festivals and exhibits publicly display traditional foods, costumes, songs, and dances. If immigrants do not live under the forced association of a Tule Lake Center, they reside voluntarily in their own part of town. The forces for acculturation are balanced by forces for cultural conservation. In particular the commentators on immigrant folklore have neglected to notice that the Atlantic and Pacific are two-way avenues.

The Atlantic Ocean was not only a wall that immigrant traditions must surmount; at times it was a highway for the crossing back and forth of song, legend, and belief. Finns living in Michigan's Upper Peninsula often visited a seer in Marquette County, Emmanuel Salminen, to obtain information about their relatives in Finland. The mystic would place his hands over his eyes, call up his second thoughts, and send them dancing over the sea. Only with those whose spirit was "away," because they were drinking or otherwise carrying on in ways they wished to keep secret from their families, did Salminen have trouble in making contact. Salminen once made Herman Maki a map of Herman's home in Finland which the seer had never seen—perfect down to the last rowan tree. The house, barns, trees, the distance from the main road, were all indicated in exact detail, even to the color of the neighbor's house, yellow. But here Herman objected, saying the color was red. Suddenly he remembered the house had been painted yellow the year before he left for America.

Immigrants did not always remain in the United States, and a full consideration of the impact of America on Old Country lore should also consider the backwash. The America theme entered traditions in the homeland with returning immigrants, and through correspondence and news flowing across the Atlantic. In Norway the ballad "Oleana" soared to popularity following the collapse of a settlement planned in Potter County, Pennsylvania, in 1852, by the celebrated Norwegian violinist, Ole Bull. Although composed by the editor of a humorous journal, the song drew upon tall tales linked with the myth of American fertility, and with the European fantasy of *Schlauraffenland*, and it passed into folk circulation all over Norway. A few verses in English translation will convey the spirit:

> In Oleana, that's where I'd like to be,
> And not drag the chains of slavery in Norway.
>
> In Oleana they give you land for nothing,
> And the grain just pops out of the ground.
> Golly, that's easy.

Immigrant Folklore

And Münchener beer, as sweet as Ytteborg's,
Runs in the creeks for the poor man's delectation.

And the salmon, they leap like mad in the rivers,
And hop into the kettles, and cry out for a cover.

And little roasted piggies rush about the streets,
Politely inquiring if you wish for ham.

Each verse ended with the refrain, "Ole—Ole—Ole—Oh! Oleana."

"Oleana" belongs to a type of immigrant folksong known as "The America Ballad," popular also among the Swedes and Danes, and sung on both sides of the water. The constant theme is the lushness of America, as the following translated verses from an early Swedish version bear witness:

Brethren, we have far to go over the salt waters
And there is America on the other shore.
Can it be possible?

Alas, yes, it is so peaceful!
Too bad that America, too bad that America
Lies so far away from here.

The trees which stand on the ground
Are as sweet as sugar.
The country is filled with girls,
Beautiful dolls.

If you wish to have one of them
Immediately you have four or five.
On the ground and in the meadows
Grows English money.

Chickens and ducks shower down,
Roast geese and even others

American Folklore

Fly in on the table
With knife and fork between their legs.

Ireland more than any other European country possesses a deep sense of community with the "Yanks." Scarcely an Irish family but has kinsfolk in the States, and the dream of American riches which drained off Ireland's thousands ever since the mid-nineteenth century still lingers on in the Emerald Isle. On a brief collecting trip to Ireland in 1951 I encountered a striking instance of the America theme encased in a traditional Irish tale, the journey of a mortal to distant lands accompanied by the fairies. Seán Palmer of County Kerry, the westernmost county in Ireland, facing across the sea to America, related in Gaelic in 1933 an extended, dramatic account of his overnight visit to America in a small sailboat manned by the fairies. He called on relatives and friends and his old flame in New York and Boston, and returned to Rineen Ban in the morning with a fistful of dollars, a fine box of tobacco, and a grand new suit of clothes as documentary proof of his expedition. In due time letters came from the people in America to their friends in Rineen Ban, saying how they had seen and talked with Seán Palmer in America.

Of special interest to the folklorist is the question whether the traditions of the immigrant leap the language wall. If they remain locked in the mother tongue, the chances are they will die with the immigrant generation. On one field trip I had the opportunity to collect Old World Märchen told for the first time in English by an excellent Polish folk narrator. In Crystal Falls, a mining town in Michigan's Upper Peninsula, Joe Woods (born Wojtowicz) recited a spate of European wonder tales, novelle, heroic legends, jests, moral tales, and riddles, some running to several thousand words. He had come to America from the town of Csanok in Austrian Poland in 1904, at the age of twenty-one, joining the great Polish tide to Milwaukee and the Midwest at the turn of the century. After working in a blast furnace in Milwaukee, he started roaming the north country, picking up jobs on the harvests, in the lumberwoods, down in the iron mines. Stubborn, independent, razor sharp, Joe Woods seemed too bitter and unsociable to regale a group with stories, but he had the master's touch, and delivered his lengthy texts unerringly. He served as a purveyor of tales from the Old World to the New, and he told exactly where he had learned and how he had distributed his narrations.

There was a beggar with a wooden leg goes from house to house, singing Cossack songs. At night he come to our house, and he tell stories to everybody. I wasn't supposed to listen, but I opened the door a crack. And I always remember. He have a lyre, like a violin, with a wooden box you wind up. He had a voice too. His name was Andrew Bakus. Somebody give him eggs, some potatoes, some money—not much. For a couple of years he didn't come; somebody kill him in the woods. They find twelve hundred thousand kronen sewed up in his coat under the lining.

Also Woods heard men tell stories at the fairs, where he stayed all night tending the horses. "I hear it once and I remember it. I was hungry for stories."

Then in America he poured out what he had drunk in as a youth in Poland. "When I was night shift at Balkan mine at Alpha, I used to tell stories to the trammer boss—easy job. When I got tired working in the mines, I went in the lumber camps and told stories there. Wouldn't finish one night, so next night the boys would put cigarettes, tobacco in my mouth, ask me to finish. I told them in Polish and Slavish.

American Folklore

In the Sawyer-Goodman camp here, in Flannegan's camp at Sagola."

On hearing Joe's stories one could readily understand the interest of his audience. Although he spoke English with the thick tongue of the immigrant, fumbling his *th*'s, misplacing accents, twisting his *v*'s and *w*'s, his speech pulsed with lively idioms and the fresh vernacular of everyday talk. None of the artificial language of the fairy-tale books diluted his texts.

Riddles gave him more trouble, and he complained about the difficulty of transferring images from Polish into English. Still he managed eight. One is based on the same idea as the Cornish *plod* we mentioned earlier. "Two brothers run away, the other two try to catch them but never can. Answer: Four wheels of a car or wagon." Seven of the eight riddles he put into English appear in the standard Polish riddle collection.

In the United States, the older Americans lump together each new immigrant strain under general labels—Bohunks, Eyetalians, Polocks, Finlanders—as if a nationality group emigrated en masse from a single Old World town. A clever and sophisticated essay on "Folklore of the Greeks in America," by Dorothy Demetracopoulou Lee, demonstrates the wide variety in folk-cultural backgrounds of one immigrant people. Collecting from Greek families in and around Boston in 1934 and 1935, she distinguished among them three areas of origin, in which, moving westward from the Black Sea to the Peloponnesus, the Turkish language and cultural influence gradually dwindled to zero.

Each area displayed a distinctive quality in its folklore. The bilingual Pontics, living along the Black Sea, saw life in cold, rational terms. They related their ghost tales with a skeptic air, and explained away appearances of *magisses* (female magicians) as hallucinations caused by fireflies dancing on stone. Like the Turks, the Pontics enjoyed comic stories about the supreme jester Malastradi (elsewhere Nasreddin) Hodja, whose witty sayings—the point of the jest—were told in Turkish. Tales of the priest and priestwife contained a cruel Asiatic humor. Coffee-house minstrels related realistic adventures in Greek prose interspersed with Turkish songs. The Pontic storyteller always stressed the moral element in his narrative.

On the island of Lesbos and the adjacent Asia Minor coast, a lively alert people spoke no Turkish, but did converse with Greek-speaking Turks. They related European fairy tales and told of amusing encounters with demons.

The third group, from mountainous Arcadia in the Peloponnesus, were stolid and unimaginative, lean in fairy tales but rich in local traditions. A man from Selemna recalled how a rope followed a boy when he passed the house of an evil old woman, right up to his home, where the boy fell ill and died. The Arcadians spoke much about unnatural creatures like the *vrykólakas* and the *neraidos*. Taboos filled their fear-haunted lives.

How meaningful is this transplanted folklore in America? Lee found the men reluctant and the women eager to talk about Old Country notions. The men now concentrated on their immediate American affairs, but the women enjoyed recapturing their quondam importance as relayers of village tales and gossip on long winter evenings. In the complex mechanized culture to which they had moved—Lee concludes—the legend and fairy tale had lost their function.

This essay offers striking suggestions for appraising the Old World bases of immigrant folklore, but it errs in its gloomy forecast for the ancient legacies. Lee fails to consider the forces for conservatism operating in new-fangled America. A solid and cohesive Greek-American community takes root within the metropolis, buttressed by its Greek Orthodox Church, parochial schools teaching modern Greek, Greek social and religious clubs, Greek language newspapers distributed from New York. Ties with the homeland remain strong and constant, a fact easily overlooked by the outsider. Members of the family revisit their homeland and birth town, correspond with their kinsmen in Greece and assist them to immigrate, make vows to their patron saints in the Old Country. In such an atmosphere, certain folk traditions endure and prosper. This was my discovery when I visited the Corombos family in northern Michigan one fall day in 1955.

John Corombos had emigrated to America in 1903 and his brother George followed in 1907, from Bambakou, Greece. George brought their mother back from Bambakou in 1918, and a wife, aunt to John's wife, all born in Bambakou. In 1933 a son was born to John, by then living in Iron Mountain, Michigan, and this son, Ted, turned up in my American Folklore class at Michigan State University in the spring of 1955. He handed in a family collection of such unusual interest that I arranged to drive the five hundred miles to Iron Mountain in order to meet his father and uncle and their wives. Ted's grandmother Demetra was no longer alive, but the influence of her spirit could still be observed in the frequent allusions to her wisdom. Three generations of Coromboses had lived under the same roof in Michigan. The old grandmother represented the fountainhead of ancient lore. When Ted was stricken by the evil eye, she knew the proper formula for detecting the culprit. Her sons spanned the two cultures, speaking fair and rapid-fire English, adapting themselves to American business ways, but withal respecting the old heritage. Their wives, residing in the home and not meeting the public like their husbands, spoke only broken English, and appeared timid and withdrawn. Young Ted, bushy-haired and solemn, handled Greek and English with equal facility, and listened with respect to the family tales. But Ted had now graduated from an American college and had taken a course in comparative folklore; he had never seen Greece or Bambakou, and he could look at the traditions with some degree of detachment.

The Corombos family followed the pattern in the United States common to many Greeks who became restaurant owners in midwestern towns and cities. Why do so many Greeks own restaurants? John Corombos spelled out the answer with the broad insight of a folk historian. In "Old Country" the men stayed out of the kitchen, which was their wives' domain. Coming to America with only a few dollars in their pockets, they remained in their port of debarkation, Boston, scrambling for odd jobs, or going off to the Lowell mills. John Corombos earned a dollar and sixty-seven cents a week in Lowell in 1903, while a seven-year-old girl interpreted for him, explaining how to take the last out of the shoe. With their wages, the Greeks bought apples and bananas and sold them outside factories. John remembers one compatriot whose only English words were, "Sixteen for a quarter." Eventually the vendors opened their own little fruit and candy stores. Above all, they wanted to be in business for themselves. Fanning out to the Midwest, they found small demand for candy stores, but a need for restaurants, which required little capital and no special skill. John opened a restaurant in Racine, Wisconsin, in 1911 with seven hundred dollars he borrowed from a shoemaker friend. He moved to Iron Mountain in 1923, when he read that Ford was opening a factory there.

Old Country traditions have remained fresh and vivid in the minds of these Greek immigrants, who rely on their heritage for sustenance and stability in alien surroundings. In America the Coromboses retain a compelling sense of their Greek identity, and display active loyalties to their homeland, their village of birth, and their family clan. They are proud of being Greeks, Bambaketes, and Coromboses. "The Greeks have done better on the average than any other people who came to this country," said John sincerely. "They have more lawyers, doctors, judges, mayors in the cities, senators from the states; they are in business for themselves, and have sent their children to school." John regularly read the two Greek-language newspapers published in New York and possessed a ready supply of intimate anecdotes about prominent Greek-Americans. He related the career of Spyros Skouras, the multimillionaire Hollywood magnate, who came to America later than John, and told how he himself had a chance to become a wealthy movie exhibitor. Jim Bardis asked him to join forces in opening a movie house in a livery stable, back in 1917. "I didn't know what a movie was so I said 'no.'" When Bardis died he left fifteen theaters in New Hampshire and Vermont, the two newest ones costing half a million dollars apiece.

American Greeks maintain active ties with their homeland. Both John and George have revisited Bambakou, and recently they brought over a family of kinsmen, who stayed with them a year in Iron Mountain but now reside in Long Island. They still own their home in Bambakou, renting it through a relative, and they showed me a photograph of the hillside dwelling. Nor are their links with "Old Country" unusual. A restaurant owner in Lansing, Michigan, George Spanos, vowed to give his church on the island of Lesbos a silver hand if he survived a serious abdominal operation. He weathered it, and accordingly returned in 1928 to donate the hand, even knowing the authorities would fine him for the military service he had avoided by leaving Greece nineteen years before.

Emotionally involved with "Old Country," the Greeks continue to hate the Turks who ruled them for four hundred years. Angrily George Corombos told how a Greek liberation army entered Smyrna after the First World War, to the enthusiastic cheers of the three hundred thousand Greeks among the population of three hundred and fifty thousand. But the English, French, and Americans assisted the Turks with battleships and planes, in order to prevent Greece from regaining Constantinople and becoming once again a great nation. When the outnumbered Greek soldiers swam for refuge to the Allied battleships, the Allied sailors cut off the hands of the Greek fugitives as they tried to climb aboard. The Turks tied the Archbishop of Smyrna to four horses and let them pull him to pieces. All this the Comboses learned from a dishwasher who could speak English and talked his way on board an Allied ship.

If the Comboses are proud of being Greeks, they are thrilled to come from Bambakou. The world at large may never have heard of their modest village, but in their fond imagination it eclipses Athens and dwarfs Sparta. John mentioned a wealthy Athenian who customarily vacationed in Switzerland, and happened one time to pass through Bambakou. "This beats Switzerland a thousand times," he declared, and thereafter regularly summered in Bambakou. His children, who had no appetites in Athens, gorged themselves on bread and water in Bambakou. (Seeing my surprise at this meager fare, John explained that a piece of bread, an onion, and a handful of olives make a meal in Greece.) Drinking the water at a spring in Bambakou, a traveler developed such a thirst that he ate seven loaves of bread one right after the other, big round flat German loaves, each weighing two and a half pounds. Thereafter the spot bore the name "Seven Bread Loaf Spring." Tuberculosis patients who came to the sanitarium in town drank life-giving water at the spring. The curative water, the climate, and the scenery combined to make Bambakou a paradise. "If Bambakou were a little more in the center, it would be the mecca of Greece," John stated.

Every Greek village took pride and comfort in its patron saint, and quite naturally St. Haralampos of Bambakou led all the rest. In 1944 the German army invading Greece entered Bambakou on a bright, clear day. A German had been killed in the district, and in reprisal the lives of fifty Greeks were forfeit. The people crowded into the church of St. Haralampos, two hundred feet from the home of the Comboses. All of a sudden a fog descended on the town, and the German guns sprayed the town at random, hitting everything but the church. As soon as the Germans pulled out, the fog lifted. "Her brother," said George Corombos, pointing to his wife, "was right there, and he come from Greece and tell us all that story."

St. Haralampos possessed the special power of delivering his people from pestilences. In 1880 a smallpox epidemic ravaged the town, and deaths ran to ten or fifteen daily. A woman walked outside of town, trying to get away from the plague. She met a monk, who said, "You go back to town, and the epidemic will have all gone away." She returned to find his words true and then recognized the monk by the picture of St. Haralampos hanging in the church. "So they worship him all the more after that because they claim he save the town from the total destruction of the smallpox." Again, during the First World War, the whole country was suffering from flu. The Bambaketes prayed, "Saint Haralampos, you saved us from the epidemic of smallpox, save us again from the epidemic of flu." All the other towns continued to suffer, but not a single person in Bambakou died of flu.

"Don't all the other towns have their saints too?" I asked.

"Yes indeed," replied John. "But maybe the people in Bambakou had more faith."

Janaikis, Ted's great-grandfather, performed a notable exploit against the Turks in 1828. The Turkish emperor dispatched from Egypt a pasha against the people of Bambakou. Janaikis sent the women and children into hiding, and then stationed the men on both sides of a ravine leading through the cliffs. When the pasha's troops entered the ravine, the Bambaketes nearest the entrance called out to their leader on the opposite side, "Janaikis, oh Janaikis, hide, the red fezzes are coming." A Turk heard Janaikis answer and climbed up to his hiding place, a cave with a stone in the opening. Pretending to be Greek, he asked Janaikis to open up. The Greek leader shot him dead, and his body rolled down the mountainside. The Turks, below, thinking he was slipping, yelled to him to grab hold of the bushes. Now the Bambaketes rolled rocks down from the top of the cliff, lacking guns, and crushed the mass of horsemen in the ravine below. The Turkish army suffered its first defeat, and the battle for Greek freedom was launched. In 1841 the first king of Greece awarded Janaikis a medal for his heroism, and his grandsons pointed out to me on the wall a commemorative inscription to Janaikis signed by the king.

Another Bambaketis distinguished himself in the war for freedom. The Greek general Kolokotronis desired a second in command to take his place if he were killed, and called for volunteers unafraid of suffering or death. To test their fearlessness, he proposed to shave their heads without soap or water, using a straight razor. Only one man stood up, and submitted successfully to the test. Thenceforth he was known as Kakokefalos, or "Tough Head." A family in Bath, Maine, where immigrants from Bambakou have settled, bears that name today.

Certain unnatural beings omnipresent in Greece lingered sharply in the memories of the Coromboses. They described the *vrykólakas*, half a dead man and half a devil, who returned from the grave to terrify the living. Once a bad man died, and Christ and Saint Peter rejected him, so he returned to his wife, and sought to sleep with her. She refused him, and he whipped her black and blue, so that she died a few days later. Her mistake was to speak to the *vrykólakas*. Had she remained silent, the *vrykólakas* would have had to depart. Evil men, excommunicated by the church, assume this spectral form after death. "In other words," explained John Corombos, "they were bad enough when living, and still when they were dead the ground couldn't even hold 'em. Even the ground wanted to kick 'em outa there."

Another spirit-being to beware of is the *neraidos*, a beautiful woman, nicely dressed, who lives in mountain caves and comes out in the nighttime to dance. If a passerby sees a *neraidos,* he should fall face down on the ground and lie still. For if he speaks to her, he loses his voice, and can only regain it by returning to the same spot. A man named Skousis from Bambakou lost his voice to the *neraidos.* Some years later he happened to pass the same place, and a strong wind blew his hat off. "Gee," he cried, "I lost my hat." And his voice came back. The Skousis family now lives in Detroit.

I asked if the *vrykólakas* or *neraidos* appeared in this country. The family group laughed a little, shaking their heads, and said they were never seen on this side of the water. "See, the Christ or the Apostles didn't come to this country," mused George Corombos. "They're scared to pass the ocean, it's too far," Mrs. John Corombos added, giggling.

Nevertheless some Old Country beliefs have indeed spanned the Atlantic. The most prevalent notion in all Greek folk knowledge, the curse of the evil eye, has come to roost in the homes of the immigrants. In fact, Ted Corombos himself when a boy of three had suffered from the malignant effects of the *mati,* the evil eye. Down at his father's restaurant someone had remarked, "Oh my, what a nice boy, what a beautiful boy he is." When Ted came out he could hardly breathe, and nearly fell dead. His grandmother, then living, immediately recognized the symptoms, and resorted to Old Country divination. She secured a live charcoal, placed a whole clove upon it, made the sign of the cross, and said in Greek, "In the name of the Father, the Son, and the Holy Spirit." Thereupon she uttered the names of all possible suspects. When she came to Jim Voris, cook at the restaurant, the coal exploded with a blast.

Two procedures were now possible. The family could have gone to Voris and explained what he had done. Voris would then go to Ted, spit, and say, "Ptu, I didn't mean to do that." This action would cure the child. To avoid embarrassing their cook, the family chose the other expedient. They sneaked away a glass from which Jim Voris had drunk some water, brought it home, made Ted drink from the same glass, and then washed his face from the chin upward three times with the remaining water. This cured him. Not till fifteen years later did John Corombos inform his employee how he had nearly killed his boss's son. Jim was shocked. The bearer of the evil eye may be quite unconscious of his power to injure. Hence people must not admire children too much and should always spit toward the devil before commenting about a baby, saying "Ptu, and I hope you don't get my evil eye."

Besides their myriad accounts of saints' legends and miracles and black magic, the Corombos brothers spouted forth lighter tales of entertainment, from the old wonder stories to modern jests. A prize specimen from George showed an American veneer coating the venerable European tale of the valiant hero overcoming the stupid ogres. George introduced the story as an account of how baseball was invented in Greece two thousand years ago. Giants eight and ten feet tall then lived in Greece, and from them the New York Giants took their name. A weak, lazy fellow joined the giants and outwitted them in trials of strength. When night fell he placed his overcoat over a pile of stones, to simulate a man sleeping, and hid in the hills. The giants attempted to kill the little fellow by pounding his bed with an ax. But in the morning the youth, whom they had presumably chopped in a thousand pieces, reappeared, complaining that the bedbugs had been scratching him all night long. Impressed and overawed, the giants named him captain, and thenceforth carried out his orders. The Americans picked up baseball from this adventure, and the New York Giants began swinging bats two thousand years after the Greek giants had swung axes.

Insofar as one family can represent a national folk heritage, the Coromboses indeed qualify. In spite of their isolation in Iron Mountain, where no other Greek families live, Bambakou and the saints and icons in Greece remain a powerful reality in their lives, to which they return on occasion.

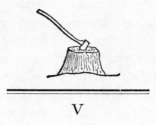

V

The Negro

While the Indian met the white man on fairly equal terms in the seventeenth century, and gradually slipped down the social and cultural scale to the position of a frontier savage and a government ward, the Negro has steadily moved upward from slavery. Torn from his West African culture and denied education, the slave commenced life in America bereft of his own institutions and traditions, and barred from those of his master. Yet while the cultural inheritance of the Indian tribes steadily dwindled, the cultural possessions of Negro bondsmen steadily grew. The mythology and art of Navaho and Zuñi, Cherokee and Ojibwa, have drifted outside the mainstream of American civilization, to become the object of anthropological study and the subject of tourist curiosity. In Colonial times the white man and the Indian had exchanged economic practices and supernatural conceptions. But unlike the Spanish and French colonizers, Englishmen refused to wed the dusky natives and failed to coerce them into Christianity. Ejected from the settled area

The Negro

of the Republic and thrust beyond the frontier—as the Cherokees were uprooted from Georgia by President Jackson and consigned to Oklahoma—the Indian tribes sank into a condition of dependency upon their conquerors.

But the Negro from the beginning lived inside the white man's society. Willy-nilly he acquired the tongue of his master, some of his blood, and segments of his culture. The white planter graced the beds of his slaves and herded them into his churches. The mulatto children and the shouting congregations that resulted, though denied full and equal recognition by their progenitors, still tacitly betrayed some degree of intimacy between the races.

The lesson for folklore is clearly written. When Longfellow wrote *The Song of Hiawatha* in 1855, basing his narrative poem upon the reasonably accurate Ojibwa tales collected by Schoolcraft, he transformed them extensively to suit the reading taste of the American public. His poetical image of the Noble Savage bore little relation to the original forms of the tribal narratives, whose alien style and esoteric ideas carried no meaning for white Americans. The Indian has absorbed medieval wonder tales of magic and transformation from Frenchmen and Spaniards, often clothing them with the details of his tribal culture. But the tales of the Indian are never retold by whites.

The case of the Negro is just the reverse. When the first collection of *Slave Songs of the United States* was published in 1867, and the first book of Uncle Remus stories appeared in 1880, they were alike greeted with enormous interest. Joel Chandler Harris became an international figure, the correspondent of Rudyard Kipling and Mark Twain. But the appeal of these songs and tales lay in their unexpected familiarity to the white audience, not in the allure of an exotic primeval lore. With a shock the white man recognized the Christian spirituals and animal fictions as vaguely his own. Manabozho the Ojibwa shape-shifter meant nothing to him, but gospel songs praising the Lord, and beast tales dramatizing the triumph of a weak creature over powerful ones came from his very own traditions. How had the slaves obtained them?

The yeasty oral traditions of the American Negro took form in the plantation culture of the Old South. Northern freedmen who settled in free states before emancipation possess none of this folklore. The Negro song and narrative lore of the West Indies, Brazil, and Surinam, heavy in African elements, shows little correspondence with that of southern colored folk. Southern slave lore developed along its own lines under the particular conditions of the cotton plantation economy. Cotton cultivation from Georgia to Texas, with the growing of rice on the Carolina and Georgia coast, sugar cane in Louisiana, and tobacco in Virginia and Kentucky, molded the southern slaves into homogeneity. After the importation of African slaves ceased in 1808, the Negro community in the United States grew entirely from its own procreation.

Negro folklore remained largely invisible during the existence of slavery, simply for lack of interest and understanding on the part of white observers. In his richly detailed books on the Cotton Kingdom during the decade preceding the Civil War, the traveler Frederick Law Olmsted paid little heed to Negro folk traditions. The word "folklore" had after all only been coined in England in 1846. Still Olmsted incidentally described the milieu shaping the folk expression of slaves. Often he cites the importance of revivalistic religion and the exhorting preacher in the lives of the blacks, saying "On many plantations, religious exercises are almost the only habitual recreation not purely sensual." He speaks of the poetic utterances of slave preachers, and the scriptural language of their congregations. He remarks on the shouting and jumping in the praise-houses, and the excited singing and dancing in the slave cabins after Sunday service. Slaves openly avow personal possession by the Spirit and the Devil. At one religious service he attended in the rice country of eastern Georgia, crackers and slaves occupied the same meeting house, and the Negroes watched white people crying and groaning in response to the wild salvos of the preacher. Though he fails to mention storytelling, Olmsted clipped a passage from the *Southern Cultivator* of June, 1855, referring to "the simple tales, and the witch and ghost stories, so common among negroes." He observed the slaves constantly among beasts: plowing with mules, tending hogs and hens, trapping raccoons, rabbits, turkeys, deer, but the agrarian economist understandably failed to see in livestock the characters of folktales.

Occasionally ante-bellum writers set down snatches of slave songs and other lore in novels, diaries, travel books, and autobiographies by ex-slaves. These specimens include corn-shucking songs and rowing chants, gospel hymns, songs praising and satirizing Old Marster, "patting" dance songs accompanied by rhythmic handclaps, nonsense refrains, and jingles. Visiting a South Carolina plantation in 1843, William Cullen Bryant heard several Negro melodies, among them a corn-husking song "set to a singularly wild and plaintive air." The words fell into the fluid pattern later to become widely known, single lines of action capped by a shouted refrain:

> De nigger-trader got me.
> Oh, hollow!

American Folklore

In the end the singer announces his intention to escape.

Fanny Kemble, the celebrated actress, in her *Journal of a Residence on a Georgian Plantation in 1838–1839* (published in 1863), described in some detail the singing of slaves as they rowed a planter from one coastal island to another.

I believe I have mentioned to you before the peculiar characteristics of this veritable negro minstrelsy—how they all sing in unison, having never, it appears, attempted or heard anything like part-singing. Their voices seem oftener tenor than any other quality, and the tune and time they keep something quite wonderful; such truth of intonation and accent would make almost any music agreeable. That which I have heard these people sing is often plaintive and pretty, but almost always has some resemblance to tunes with which they must have become acquainted through the instrumentality of white men; their overseers or masters whistling Scotch or Irish airs, of which they have produced by ear these *rifacciamenti*.

The Philadelphia actress went on to express her puzzlement at the meaningless words to such songs.

There is no mistaking the meaning in the "Jubilee-Beaters" song which Frederick Douglass included in his autobiography, *My Bondage and My Freedom,* in 1855.

> We raise de wheat
> Dey gib us de corn;
> We bake de bread
> Dey gib us de cruss;
> We sif de meal
> Dey gib us de huss;
> We peel de meat
> Dey gib us de skin,
> And dat's de way
> Dey takes us in.
> We skim de pot
> Dey gib us the liquor
> And say dat's good enough for nigger.

The Negro

Walk over! Walk over!
Tom butter and de fat;
Poor nigger you can't get over dat;
Walk over!

From ante-bellum plantations we can see emerging characteristic patterns of American Negro folklore. Tales and rhymes about animals, cleverly mimicking the sounds and cries of birds and beasts; the music and dance of spirituals, gang-labor songs, shouts, breakdowns, jigs; a cycle of stories about Old Marster, the despotic plantation owner, and John, the roguish slave, who engaged in a continual battle of wits; a mountain of beliefs, charms, omens, cures, signs from the poor whites; folk history of the ordeal of slavery, with its whippings, killings, escapes, and pursuits; a folk speech flavored with barnyard and biblical imagery. These dimly perceived forms of Negro tradition gathered momentum in the rural, cotton-growing South of "befo' de Wa'."

Before the war a folk Negro did indeed parade in public view, but in distorted and ludicrous guise. In the 1830's and 40's theater audiences constantly beheld the blackface minstrel show and the comic Sambo of stage plays. Jokebooks and newspapers carried numerous dialogues between Sambo and Rastus, along with jocularities about the down-East peddler, the French exquisite, and the Irish drunkard. The dull-witted Ethiopian thus joined the gallery of comic native types circulating in the popular humor preceding the Civil War. "Daddy" Rice introduced the Jim Crow dance, modeled on a limping slave's shuffle, to the New York theater in 1832, initiating a series of vogues for pseudo-Negro and Negro-derived song, dance, and humor that has persisted to the present day. Eleven years later, the first blackface minstrel band performed the *Virginia Minstrels* for New York and Boston audiences, ushering in a half-century of high popularity for minstrelsy. Unquestionably Negro folk sources contributed to this entertainment. Rice supposedly modeled his Jim Crow number upon the dance-hop of a lame old colored hostler in Louisville. Dan Emmett and his three fellows in the Virginia Minstrel Band employed the instruments familiarly handled by slaves in their cabins: the fiddle, banjo, tambourine, and bones. Snatches of Negro rhymes and copies of Negro breakdowns spiced the choral songs, dance routines, humorous lectures, and dialect colloquies of the evening-long minstrel show. But the blackface performers who capered and sputtered before paleface audiences rarely studied their originals, and could hardly live among them, as did Yankee Hill when he returned to Massachusetts to observe real live down-Easters. Jim Crow and Sambo, eating watermelons and grinning vacuously, grew into broad and ridiculous caricatures of the darky, a travesty on, rather than a simulacrum of, his folklore.

The War between the States brought deep inside the South northern men who in 1867 produced the first collection of Negro folksongs. With the publication of *Slave Songs of the United States,* by William F. Allen, Charles P. Ware, and Lucy M. Garrison, Negro plantation spirituals came into full glory. The interest in collecting, analyzing, and performing Negro folk music, among both the white and colored population, has never since abated.

The *Slave Songs* came about as a joint enterprise of Union agents stationed on the Carolina coast during the war. Ware and Allen pooled the sheaves of spirituals they garnered on the sea island of St. Helena, South Carolina. In addition they drew

The Negro

from the trove of Thomas Wentworth Higginson, the New
England author who printed Negro spirituals in the *Atlantic
Monthly* for June, 1867, as he had heard them sung by the
colored troops in the first South Carolina Volunteers, whom
he commanded as colonel. Already in 1862 one of the authors,
Mrs. Garrison (then Lucy McKim, of Philadelphia) had discussed the musical qualities of Negro folksong in an article
in *Dwight's Journal of Music* on "Songs of the Port Royal
Contrabands." Making contact with the colored population
of the Port Royal Islands through the Freedmen's Commission,
Ware and Allen saw the serious, sober side of the Negro and
heard chiefly religious songs.

In terms of cultural history, the *Slave Songs* erected a
bridge from the obscure subculture of Negro folk music to
the broad light of American civilization. This was to prove
a two-way bridge, for the interest of the white public infected
Negro singers and scholars. Though a pioneer volume, the
Slave Songs set high standards. Unlike a good many later
collections, it included musical scores with its one hundred and
thirty-six texts. The bulk came from the Carolina coastal
islands whose conservative Negro culture, with African overtones, subsequently attracted much attention from students of
the "Gullah" Negro. Still the authors included songs from
other southern seaboard and inland states, and discussed regional
characteristics of Negro folk music throughout the Cotton
Kingdom, a point virtually ignored by their successors. They
described the unique "shout" of the Port Royal Islanders,
represented in their book by several choice texts. A kind of
shuffling, rhythmic ring dance performed in the cabins and
praise-houses after the regular service, the shout blended dance
movements with repeated snatches of chorus or stanzas from

spirituals, often accompanied by knee-patting claps from by-standers, the whole exercise gathering momentum and steam as the night hours wore on.

The date of the *Slave Songs*, 1867, made the volume a marker between the ante-bellum and post-bellum eras. The collection established a canon for Negro spirituals of the Old South; already the vibrant energies of Negro improvisation could be seen in new songs reflecting the war.

In 1880 a second immense portal into the hidden domain of Negro folklore swung open. In this year Joel Chandler Harris gave to the white world his animal tales of the old plantation, in *Uncle Remus: His Songs and His Sayings*. A lifelong jour-nalist, who had grown up in central Georgia, Harris began writing his Uncle Remus stories in the *Atlanta Constitution* after reading an article in the December, 1877, number of *Lippincott's Magazine*, "Folk-lore of Southern Negroes," by William Owens, which he found inaccurate. He drew upon his own recollection of Negro stories he had heard in his thirteen years of life before the outbreak of war, but he also secured new examples from ex-slaves at the time he was writ-ing his books. Still the source of his narratives, like their set-ting, clearly lies in slavery times.

With the publication of the *Slave Songs* and the Uncle Remus stories, Negro folklore assumed a conspicuous place in American culture. On three different fronts it commanded attention: in the fields of creative literature and music, which found inspiration in Negro folk sources; in the world of popular entertainment and performance; and in scholarly col-lections and studies, which raged over the question of African versus white origins. These three areas of interest constantly overlapped and contributed to each other, making the average

The Negro

American uncommonly aware of Negro song, dance, tale, and belief. The last area chiefly concerns us here.

As early as 1872 Fisk University decided to capitalize on the newborn interest in Negro spirituals, and formed a choir of musically trained "Jubilee Singers," who toured the country giving concerts and raising funds for their institution. Other Negro universities, Hampton and Tuskegee Institutes, followed suit. Under such stimulus these universities also became centers for Negro study of Negro folklore. At Fisk, Frederick J. Work, director of the Jubilee Singers from 1892 to 1916, began issuing collections of Negro songs early in the present century, assisted by his scholarly son, John Wesley Work. At Hampton Institute a folklore group held regular meetings and published their findings during the 1880's and 90's, in a department in the *Southern Workman*, in whose files valuable early texts of Negro folktales may still be uncovered.

The decade of the 1880's saw a lively interest in Negro animal stories. Following the appearance of his first Uncle Remus book, Harris found himself willy-nilly in the midst of an excited discussion about the folklore nature of the Brer Rabbit stories. Harris himself possessed no prior knowledge of folklore; he had simply stumbled on an appealing vein of oral narratives and written them up with a master's touch. The benign, autocratic figure of Uncle Remus spinning the animal fables to the little white boy in the shadow of the big house, and dodging his troublesome questions with a pontifical authority, captivated readers as much as the tales themselves. These too bore the stamp of the creative author, who transformed a simple text into an artistically complete little fiction. Still, readers readily spotted the folktale cores, and Harris was "bleedged" to read up and write about folklore matters. In his second volume, *Nights with Uncle Remus*, published in 1883, he devoted a lengthy introduction to pointing out analogues between the Brer Rabbit cycle and Kaffir, Hottentot, Amazon Indian, and Creek animal tales. That same year he wrote to the English folklore scholar, G. L. Gomme, "They are all genuine folk-lore tales," and elsewhere he makes the quite erroneous statement about origins, still largely credited, "One thing is certain—the negroes did not get them from the whites: probably they are of remote African origin."

Casting about for additional material, Harris enlisted the aid of friends from the Georgia coast to obtain samples of the Gullah dialect and tales. One of his later storytellers, African-born Daddy Jake, relates these as a contrast to Uncle Remus. Stimulated by his collecting for Harris, the lawyer Charles C. Jones gathered together Gullah tales in their oral forms for his *Negro Myths from the Georgia Coast*, issued in 1888. Another volume of field texts from the same area followed in 1892, *Afro-American Folk-Lore*, by Mrs. A. M. H. Christensen, who resided in Beaufort on Port Royal Island, South Carolina, after the war. Influenced by Harris, these and subsequent collections emphasized animal tales. Actually Harris presented only a portion of the Negro folktale repertoire, which ranges over many themes besides talking animals. Of the fascinating tale cycle about Old Marster, he lamely presented but one sample. On the other hand, he has received too little credit for other aspects of plantation folklore he placed in the mouth of Uncle Remus, rhymes and songs and wise sayings, which make Uncle Remus a well-rounded carrier of Negro lore.

The bibliography of works dealing with Negro folklore mounted rapidly. The *Journal of American Folklore*, founded in 1888, published over a hundred articles and notes dealing with Negro song, tale, and superstition in its first twenty-five volumes. Newman I. White counted fifty-nine books on Negro folksong alone issued between 1914 and 1927, nineteen by Negro authors. The decade of the 1920's witnessed the publication of a baker's dozen of major works on Negro folklore, with the university presses of North Carolina and Harvard taking the lead. From Chapel Hill came two thoroughgoing analyses of southern Negro values and social attitudes as reflected in folksong, by two sociologists of the University of North Carolina faculty, Howard W. Odum and Guy B. Johnson: *The Negro and His Songs* (1925) and *Negro Workaday Songs* (1926). The same press also published in 1926 the monumental *Folk Beliefs of the Southern Negro* by another sociologist, Mississippi-born Newbell N. Puckett, who gathered his data through extensive use of questionnaires and by personal interviews. Two independent studies by Johnson came from Chapel Hill in 1929 and 1930, *John Henry: Tracking Down a Negro Legend*, his inquiry into the genesis of the ballad that produced a folk hero, and *Folk Culture on St. Helena Island, South Carolina*, an intensive field study.

This last work was only one of several volumes during the decade to consider the folklore of the Gullah Negroes. On the same island the African N. G. J. Ballanta collected *Saint Helena Island Spirituals* in 1925. Elsie Clews Parsons, the millionaire feminist, sociologist, and angel of the American Folklore Society, who did much of her fieldwork cruising in her yacht to Caribbean islands, in 1923 published her important collection of Negro tales and riddles, *Folk-Lore of the Sea Islands, South Carolina*. Faithful to the dialect, though influenced by humorous treatments of the darky, Ambrose E.

Gonzales issued *The Black Border, Gullah Stories of the Carolina Coast*, in 1923 and *With Aesop Along the Black Border*, in 1924.

Meanwhile the Harvard University Press was taking note of folksong down East and in the Deep South, in a sudden outpouring of field collections. Among these, the press in 1925 brought out Dorothy Scarborough's *On the Trail of Negro Folk-Songs*, splotched by the adolescent enthusiasm of the literary clubwoman, but capturing useful texts. In 1928 Harvard issued the comprehensive and scholarly collection by Newman I. White of Duke University, *American Negro Folk-Songs*, notable for an introductory chapter on the history of popular and academic interest in Negro folk music.

During the decade, the New York trade publishers also cultivated Negro folklore, and their most successful titles were executed by Negro authors. In *Negro Folk Rhymes* (1922), Thomas W. Talley of Fisk University assembled an unusual body of secular jingles, chants, teasing rhymes, and party songs, sometimes sung, sometimes recited. An instant best-seller upon publication in 1925, *The Book of American Negro Spirituals* by James Weldon Johnson eloquently affirmed the artistic elaboration of African rhymes by colored southern singers. Johnson promptly followed this the next year with *The Second Book of Negro Spirituals*, and in 1927 he turned to a new form, the Negro folk sermon, in *God's Trombones*. Meanwhile the blues came into its own, with *Blues: An Anthology*, by its creator, W. C. Handy, with notes by Abbe Niles (1926).

The important works that appeared in the 1930's, 40's, and 50's centered upon one controversial theme, the question of white versus Negro origins of the spiritual. Southern white scholars maintained white cultural supremacy against the new

The Negro

generation of college-educated Negroes, who found support in the Africanist anthropologists of Northwestern University led by Melville J. Herskovits. Fresh ammunition for the master-race position was provided by George Pullen Jackson of Vanderbilt University, through carefully annotated collections of "White" spirituals taken from nineteenth-century Baptist and Methodist country singing books. From these early revival hymns and other religious folksongs, the colored man borrowed both texts and tunes, Jackson argued in *White Spirituals in the Southern Uplands* (1933) and later books. This position was foreshadowed by Newman I. White and Guy B. Johnson. The southerners sought to destroy the theory of African origins espoused in technical terms in 1914 by the musicologist Henry E. Krehbiel, in his *Afro-American Folksongs: A Study in Racial and National Music*. Krehbiel had himself refuted Wallaschek, an earlier white supremacist. In 1940 John W. Work of the music department of Fisk University, who had been issuing Negro song collections since 1901, struck back at Newman White and Jackson in a new edition of *American Negro Songs*. Work advanced the theory that American Negroes "reassembled" the gospel song texts they had borrowed from white gospel-singers, so revising them according to their own social outlook and musical taste that these Negro spirituals long outlived their white originals.

By far the most sweeping turn of the argument appeared in 1953 under the imprint of the American Historical Association. *Negro Slave Songs in the United States*, by the Negro theological scholar, Miles Mark Fisher, relied on the 1867 volume of *Slave Songs* for its basic text, but bolstered its position with ample documentation from ante-bellum writings and post-bellum collections. Fisher contended that African slaves carried to the United States their cultural trait of using songs for historical records and for satirical purposes. The editors of the 1867 *Slave Songs* recognized them as historical documents. Slavery spirituals served as a clarion call to southern slaves throughout the cotton plantations. They summoned the bondsmen for African-type secret meetings, encouraged them to flee via the underground railroad, cautioned them to subservience after Nat Turner's abortive rebellion in 1831. All the time they employed the white man's phrases for their own meanings. "Freedom" which to the Christian signified freedom from sin, to the slave meant physical freedom; the white man's "Canaan" was for him the North. Although the idea of double meanings in spirituals was understood as far back as Thomas Wentworth Higginson, Fisher refurbished and garnished the theory, stretching it indeed to tenuous limits.

Interest in the Negro folktale never matched the consuming absorption in folksong, but recent collections have uncovered new vistas of Negro storytelling art. The talented Negro novelist, Zora Neale Hurston, unfolded a splendid exhibit of Florida Negro tales in *Mules and Men* (1935). A Negro folklorist, J. Mason Brewer, also stylizing tales, with an excessive dialect suggestive of Uncle Remus, presented two hauls from the Brazos Bottoms of east Texas, in *The Word on the Brazos* (1953) and *Dog Ghosts and Other Texas Negro Folk Tales* (1958), unfortunately lacking comparative notes. My own collections of modern tales told by Negroes who went north, and whose horizons have vastly widened since slavery times, appeared as *Negro Folktales in Michigan* (1956) and *Negro Tales from Pine Bluff, Arkansas, and Calvin, Michigan* (1958). These field trips to northern and southern Negro communities proved conclusively, to me at any rate, that American Negro

The Negro

folklore belongs to the plantation culture of the Old South. Free Negroes living north of the Ohio River possessed no traditions, and indeed rejected their southern heritage, reminiscent of "Uncle Tomism." Negroes from the deep South pouring into northern cities encountered chilly winds that froze their old, leisurely, gregarious habits and dissipated the ante-bellum lore common to southern colored folk.

Although cradled in the Old South, the lore of the Negro has not stood still. The South did not change so drastically after the Civil War, and the plantation stories need make only the slight adjustment from Old Marster to Old Boss. But the new mobility of the freedman, who could now romp in the city on Saturday night and take a sporting excursion up North, perhaps settling there permanently, did affect and expand his lore. Further, the folk Negro, rather than his white imitator, could now penetrate the entertainment world of radio, recordings, theatricals, movies, cabarets, television, and fiction writing. A web of interrelationships between the folk and the mass culture began to crisscross.

In post-bellum Negro folklore, the note of protest sounded ever more overtly. From the new city life opened to him in the twentieth century, the Negro of the South developed the blues, to express his cry of anguish. The blues were officially launched in 1909 by W. C. Handy in Memphis, Tennessee, although as with other inventions the signs of the approaching bomb-burst can now be read back to an earlier day. Handy himself has written that his blues were "already used by Negro roustabouts, honky-tonk piano players, wanderers and others of their underprivileged but undaunted class from Missouri to the Gulf." A set, three-line stanza, with the second line echoing the first, the blues seemed to regiment the Negro creative genius, but in fact they opened the floodgates to all manner of throbbing emotions, and to the fresh, natural imagery of Negro folk metaphor. Where the spiritual had flowed from the camp ground, the blues streamed from haunts of sin. In dives and brothels, gin palaces and honky-tonks, Negro performers sang the blues, and from their piano, trombone, and trumpet accompaniments, jazz burgeoned in New Orleans sporting houses.

The blues furnished merely one outlet for the torment and frustration of the Negro, whose accents, long muffled under slavery, became increasingly strident under freedom. Songs of protest voiced his plaints against Jim Crow, sometimes in two- or four-line jingles, or gang-chants, or even lullabies, echoing one basic thought:

> Ought's a' ought and a figure's a figur',
> All for the white folks and none for the nigger.

Even the newer balladry arising from topical incidents carried its overtones of social protest. The celebrated ballads of "John Henry," "The Boll Weevil," and "The Titanic" all conveyed a similar message: John Henry successfully pitted his massive strength with only a hammer and his bare hands against the white man's steam drill; the despised boll weevil, like the Negro, lived off cotton and was always looking for a home; Shine, the one colored man on the "Titanic," swam to safety with superman strokes while white millionaires cried to him for help.

Unrecognized until very recently, a whole body of jests, some bitter, some mocking, some merely wry, have vented the hurt of colored Americans at their un-American treatment.

The Negro

These tales of protest frequently revolve about a generic character, called "Colored Man," who is discomfited and humiliated by White Man, but whose very arrogance he can sometimes turn to account. Arrested for crossing against a red light, the Mississippi Negro tells the judge, "I saw all the white folks going on the green light, so I thought the red light was for us colored folks."

Not merely the content, but the personality of Negro folklore shows change in freedom times. The blurred and anonymous folk darky has suddenly sharpened into an individual. Consider the saga of Lead Belly, who performed before the Modern Language Association and in Town Hall. Huddie Ledbetter, who became known as Lead Belly, was born in 1885 on a tenant farm in west Louisiana. He was big and strong, and he could play a twelve-stringed guitar and sing sinful songs all night. He lived a life of violence and sex, which he has described in his own words: carousing and suky dancing with yellow gals in the gin mills of Shreveport, Dallas, and New Orleans; chasing women, and dumping them from his car if they wouldn't " 'commodate" him a little; brawling with knives, serving two jail sentences, and earning reprieves both times after composing pardon songs to the governors of Texas and Louisiana. On the chain gang he hoed harder and faster than any other convict, immediately won his place as lead man, and worked his fellow prisoners till they dropped. Like the frontier roarer of old, Lead Belly could out-sing, out-drink, out-work, out-love any of his fellows. John Lomax, recording folksongs in southern Negro penitentiaries, found Lead Belly in the Angola, Louisiana, prison, and after his release Lead Belly served the Texas folklorist as his chauffeur and folksinging decoy on prison visits. Eventually Huddie went north with his mentor, to become in 1935 an overnight sensation on the lecture platforms and concert stages. Today the record albums made by Lead Belly, and the book of his songs assembled by John and Alan Lomax, preserve his extensive repertoire and husky, intoxicating voice. Lead Belly sang straight blues and talking blues, work songs and work hollers, fiddle sings and reels, and lustful songs too broad for any recording. The most hypnotic melody he left on wax is a paean to a "yaller gal." In his songs and his career Lead Belly represents the new Negro folklore of the twentieth century. Only a long history of interest in Negro songs, both academic and popular, can account for his spectacular admission to the pages of *Time* and the portals of Harvard.

The effects of the southern Negro's diaspora upon his traditions are yet to be tallied. Already from Harlem a new, sophisticated note can be heard, jangling oddly with the older southern tones in *The Book of Negro Folklore,* assembled in 1958 by the northern Negro authors Langston Hughes and Arna Bontemps. Simple, the literary and theatrical creation of Hughes, is pure Harlem and a century removed from Uncle Remus; he is no storyteller, but a social folk critic; not the Georgia plantation, but the Harlem bar, is the scene of his oracles.

With all the wealth of Negro lore to consider, we can here discuss only the disputed question of origins, and the central trait of fluidity, two teasing aspects of Negro folk utterance.

The heated controversy over origins of the spiritual never extended to other forms of folk material, such as tales and superstitions. All sides assumed without fuss that these traditions came straight from Africa. Spirituals sung by the

The Negro

Negroes had won admiration for their beauty of melody and poignancy of sentiment, and hence the question arose, could savages create art? But animal tales and ghostly superstitions belonged naturally to a childlike, primitive race, and so through the fallacy of what Melville Herskovits has called the "myth of the Negro past," these evidences of the African savage state were readily allowed to American Negroes.

The fact is that their beliefs and folktales are in large part directly traceable to Europe and England. The luminous ghosts who alarm colored folk at dusk dark, and the shape-shifting witches who straddle them in bed, are English not African creations. Indeed a twentieth-century recording of southern Negroes exchanging witch-encounters strongly echoes the Salem witchcraft records of seventeenth-century New England. Many of the Brer Rabbit tales, such as the account of how the bear lost his tail fishing through the ice, are standard European types. Even though such stories traveled to Africa, they must have reached America from Europe, for little correspondence exists between African and American Negro tale harvests. Slaves would scarcely have singled out imported European fictions to carry with them to the New World, leaving their own cultural stock behind. The sharp break between African and American tradition occurs at the West Indies, where Anansi the spider dominates hundreds of cante-fables, the tales that inclose songs. But no Anansi stories are found in the United States.

The argument for African origins is fully as racist as that for white origins, for it assumes that an original American Negro tradition can only emanate from black-skinned Africans. Some spokesmen, such as Sterling Brown in his fine essay "Spirituals" in *The Book of Negro Folklore,* have emphasized the mold of Negro church songs, rather than their sources, as the creative contribution of the American Negro, and here indeed lies the rightful answer. Taking their raw material from a variety of sources, European, British, African, Caribbean, and white American, the colored folk have selected, squeezed, and shaped this dough into their very own folk property. This process can be viewed in the recently uncovered story-cycle of Old Marster and his roguish slave John.

This group of tales is set on the old plantation. John performs customary slave labor, plowing the new ground, milking the cows, killing hogs, planting corn, cutting wood, toting water. At the same time he enjoys a favored position with Old Marster, for whom he does personal chores, like saddling his horse; Marster visits his quarters and calls him to the big house for special errands. John does not chop cotton like a common field hand but mediates between Old Marster and the rest of the hands. As one story begins, "Old Marster had this main fellow on his farm he put his confidence in, John." In the anecdotes, John and his master constantly spar for advantage, John seeking idleness and good pickings, and Old Marse attempting to frustrate his schemes. A tally of the reported tales shows roughly a draw in the contest of wits.

Several narratives in the cycle hinge on a wager made by Old Marster with a neighboring planter who doubts John's talents. In the best-known John story, Old Marse bets on the fortunetelling powers of his prize slave. Actually all John has done is to eavesdrop by the big house and learn of Old Marster's plans ahead of time. Now he is on the spot, because all the planters and a crowd from round about have gathered to see the test. The planters have concealed a raccoon under a pot, and John must guess what's hidden. "You done caught de ole coon at last," he acknowledges sadly. Marster grins broadly and rakes in the money, his faith in John vindicated.

In the Household Tales of the Brothers Grimm, a "False Diviner" who has deluded many persons with his pretended knowledge of medicine extricates himself from a challenge to his powers by a lucky pun on his name. "Poor Krebs" (German for crab) he mourns, and has guessed the hidden object, a crab. This incident from the full tale has traveled widely; it is found in India and Africa, as well as all over Europe, and is popular in the West Indies, with the pun usually turning on the name Cricket. American Negroes pivot the episode on the generic label for the colored man, "coon," which makes a better pun than a surname. Slaves had no surname in any event, and after freedom took their family name from their former owner.

In another wager tale, John is pitted against the strong slave of the adjoining plantation in a contest of strength. Customarily on the large plantations the most powerful slave acted as foreman. John, who is tough but little, rides his master's horse to town and there sees his giant opponent tearing up trees four feet through the butt, and tossing a thousand-pound maul half a mile in the air to limber up. John reaches for the maul, looks heavenward, and cries, "Saint Peter, move over, and tell Sister Mary to move out the way, and move baby Jesus." The big fellow runs away.

The idea of a small hero bluffing a giant or ogre by his pretended strength is one of the commonest traits in European folktales. (See for instance the story of "How Baseball Was Invented in Greece," in chapter iv.) This particular motif, in which the trickster prepares to hurl a missile skyward, occurs in both American white and Negro tradition.

187

The fight between the two strong slaves takes still a different turn. When John rides down to the fight ground, where a big crowd has already gathered, he sees Jim chained to an iron stake, wearing an iron ring in his nose, pawing the dirt, and running excitedly back and forward, while his master attempts to restrain him until fight time. As John views this fearsome sight, his Old Miss comes over and asks him sharply, "What kept you? Why you so late?" John slaps her face. Jim pulls up the stake and runs away. While pleased at winning the bet, John's master still doesn't like the idea of his slave striking his wife. John explains, "Well, Marster, Jim knowed if I slapped a white woman I'd a killed him, so he run."

For this version, so cleverly capturing the values of the Old South, I find no parallel anywhere.

Yet appearances can prove highly deceiving. Another tale begins with a perfectly factual historical statement. "They [the planters and overseers] used to carry the slaves out in the woods and leave them there, if they killed them—just like dead animals. There wasn't any burying then. It used to be a secret, between one plantation and another, when they beat up their hands and carried them off." The tale continues with John finding a skeleton at the edge of the woods, which says, "Tongue is the cause of my being here." John rushes back to Old Marster, and tells him the skeleton has talked. Marster is skeptical, but he goes along with John, and a crowd gathers to hear the bones talk. But now they remain silent. Old Marster beats John to death, and leaves his corpse beside the skeleton. When all have left, the bones talk again. "Tongue brought us here, and tongue brought you here."

Despite the specific association with the plantation scene, this tale comes straight from West Africa. Among the Nupe, a skull talks to a warrior, who then relays the startling information to his chieftain; but the skull keeps silence before the chief, and the warrior suffers death.

Our point could be buttressed with many more illustrations. A longish narrative contains serial episodes in which Nigger Sam steals objects seemingly impossible to filch. Each time Old Marster promises Sam his freedom if he accomplishes the theft. This is the complex European tale of "The Master Thief," combined with other independent stories like the coon under the pot, the whole cleverly structured around the goal of freedom in place of the usual monetary reward. In "The Mojo," John purchases a medium-priced mojo (a charm-bag, perhaps of African origin) which enables him to change into a rabbit, a quail, and a snake. Then he lies late abed, shirking his chores, and when Old Marster comes storming to the slave quarters, John assumes these animal forms. But Old Marster owns an expensive mojo, and pursues John as a greyhound, a chicken hawk, and a stick, catching and whipping him. This fantasy dramatizes the superior knowledge and resources of the planter over his slave. Yet in previous contexts the same transformation combat has appeared in Egyptian, Greek, and Finnish mythology, in the *Arabian Nights,* in the Welsh *Mabinogion,* and in the Child ballad of "The Twa Magicians." In one characteristic incident John steals a pig from Old Marster, conceals it in a crib, and covers it with a blanket. Old Marster, stopping by John's cabin, wants to see the baby. John warns him that the baby has the measles and will be killed if he is uncovered. Old Marster persists. As he reaches for the cover, John moans, "If that baby is turned to a pig now, don't blame me." Virtually the same scene occurs in an English shepherd's play of the fourteenth century, where a shepherd tries to disguise a stolen sheep as a baby. The Old Marster cycle draws from multiple sources, but the finished product bears the special imprint of the southern Negro.

This selective talent of the Negro storyteller leads us to our second point, the extreme fluidity of all Negro folk expression. Accustomed to look for rigid categories of folk tradition, no doubt from his literary training, the folklorist divides his collected lore into separate pigeonholes, oblivious of the fact that his informants make no such distinctions and that these arbitrarily fixed forms continually overflow their compartments. The strength and variety of Negro folklore derives from the vast common reservoir of folk phrases, notions, verses, incidents from which the individual folk artist can select for his own composing.

For one thing, the individual Negro frequently possesses a well-rounded store of traditions rubbing against each other. Not he, but the collector, specializes in tales or songs, or even in particular kinds of tales or songs. In white folklore the evidence points to a clear division between folksinger and folk narrator, but my own field experience with the Negro indicates the opposite. The outstanding storyteller I encountered, J. D. Suggs, also proved a fluent singer, with and without a guitar in his hands. He knew "church" songs from the services conducted in Mississippi by his preacher father, and later he himself sang in a choir in Saxon, Missouri. Secular songs he picked up while traveling for two years with a Negro minstrel show. He could shift from gospel hymns like "What Are They Doing Up in Heaven Today?" and "You've Got To Reap Just What You Sow," to the ubiquitous parody revolving around the refrain, "When the Good Lord Sets You Free."

The Negro

If you wanta go to Heaven, tell you what you better do.
Grease your feet with hog-eye lard,
You can slip right over in the promised land.
Going to Heaven now, shall be free,
Having a good time, you shall be free,
When the good Lord sets you free.

He sang the "Memphis Blues," which he claimed to have heard from a girl named Rosie on Beale Street in Memphis, and the ballad of "Casey Jones," whom he knew personally and whose fireman became his engineer when Suggs worked as a railroad brakeman. From the First World War came "Onct I Had a Sweetheart," a song hit about the soldier boy who died in the "Germany" war, and a one-stanza lyric Suggs titled "When Uncle Sam Calls Your Man":

When Uncle Sam call out your man
Don't cry and cry because he can't, simply can't refuse.
Don't hold him back, it will make him sad,
Please no, don't hold him back.

His minstrel experience bequeathed to him comic pieces like "The Preacher and the Grizzly Bear," "Wasn't That a Travelin' Man!" and "Red River Side," all of which he learned in New Orleans, in the tent shows where colored "ministers" practiced their song and dance routines before going on the road. Sometimes he remembered vividly the occasion of his first hearing a song. In New Orleans twenty-five or thirty years previously, he had heard Al Barney sing "What Are They Doing Up in Heaven Today?" Suggs recalled:

Now I can't sing it like he could. But he could sing that so's he could never get to the end of it. He would just go wild, and he just commenced screamin' and hollerin' and they'd have to set him down. And he had such expression: when he sang, he look like he's lookin' right at heaven, you know. And he got red hair, and his face was just as white as yours, but his hair was red and the bead in his eyes looked like the chicken in the egg.

Besides his mixed bag of songs, Suggs gave me during my visits to him in 1952 and 1953 one hundred and seventy assorted narratives representing all the characteristic forms of Negro storytelling. They included fictions of the Rabbit and the Buzzard, and of Old Marster and John, laid in slavery times; true hant, hoodoo, and ghost experiences; cruel folk histories dealing with the white man's treatment of his colored brother; biblical and apocryphal lessons; European noodle stories about silly old maids and quarrelsome couples; jokes in profusion, concerning Colored Man, preachers, Irishmen; American tall tales; Jim Crow protest tales. In addition to stories and songs, Suggs knew riddles, charms, signs, toasties, cures, rhymes, minstrel dialogues.

The mobile life and variegated folklore of James Douglas Suggs reflect the troubadour career of the twentieth-century southern Negro. He matches Left Wing Gordon, the wandering laborer who traversed the country accumulating a storehouse of blues, chants, and personal ballads, around which Howard Odum constructed three books of poetic sociology. Born in Kosciusko in northern Mississippi in 1887, Suggs traveled through thirty-nine states and saw Europe as a private in the First World War. A succession of jobs carried him north to Arkansas and Missouri until he reached Chicago and its South Side black belt in 1940. Seven years later he joined a new type of migration, from Chicago to a small rural Michigan community where colored people had bought land and taken over the township offices, as the white population retreated before their advance. It was here, in Calvin Township, Cass County, that I met Suggs in 1952. He died three years later,

The Negro

a day laborer with a dozen young children, after deeply tasting life as a prison guard, semipro baseball player, minstrel show performer, soldier, short-order cook, valet and handyman, railroad brakeman, ditch-digger, foundry worker, and sometimes just a "spo'ting man." Unquenchable, infectious, optimistic, uninhibited, Suggs bubbled over with high spirits, particularly when some small audience appreciated his humor, but he excelled too in dark and occult matters.

Suggs symbolizes the unity beneath the seeming diversity of Negro folk expression. His life and lore were all of one piece, the saga of the southern-born migrant Negro of modern times. Facile in so many different traditional forms, he himself made little distinction among them, and what is true for Suggs appears true in general. Observers have commented on the extreme fluidity of Negro songs, which seem more like impromptu recombinations of well-known snatches and sentiments than fixed and crystallized texts. The same comment can also be applied to tales, now that the full repertoire is coming to light. Incidents and traits are continually shuffled and shuttled between Old Marster and the Rabbit and Colored Man and the preacher. But the larger forms too—dance, song, tale, sermon, belief, folk history—continually merge with each other.

A consideration of one form of Negro folk utterance soon leads into another. Discussing the "Negro Folk Rhymes" he had gathered together, Talley described the musical measures (¾ or ⁴⁄₄) into which they fitted, the feet-tapping dances that counted out the rhymes, the fiddle and banjo tunes to which they were often sung, the folk instruments that furnished accompaniment, the children's ring games they flavored, the Brer Rabbit stories in whose plots they played key parts, the wise sayings to which they were often compressed, the evening sings at which they were introduced by song leaders to start off the group. The rhymes themselves vary from small animal and bird fables like "Possum Up the Gum Tree," to ballad-like pieces of vivid drama, and even to ordinary vendors' cries chanted with infectious rhythm:

> Here's yō cōl' ice lemonade,
> It's made in de shade,
> It's stirred wid a spade.
> Come buy my cōl' ice lemonade.
> It's made in de shade
> An' sōl' in de sun.
> Ef you hain't got no money,
> You cain't git none.
> One glass fer a nickel,
> An' two fer a dime,
> Ef you hain't got de chink,
> You cain't git mine.
> Come right dis way,
> Fer it shō' will pay
> To git candy fer de ladies
> An' cakes fer de babies.

The distinction between the religious and social songs of the Negro is by no means as hard and fast as the classifiers would make out. Even in their *Slave Songs* of 1867 the editors noted how the same song might shift from a spiritual to a military march. The church service and the dance party present points of analogy; both are complexes in which various elements of Negro vocal music, bodily movements, and rhythmic narrative all blend. In the one case, the combination is wrought through the cry of the folk spiritual, the shouts and contortions of the happy, the parables of the preacher; in the other, it is achieved through the taps of the dancers,

The Negro

the balladry and lyrics of the songs, the tunes of fiddle and banjo, the shouted encouragement of the bystanders. New Orleans jazz bands were inspired by Negro revivalist church music, and now instrumental music re-enters Negro churches. The ring shout amounts to a secularized church dance. Stanzas from spirituals sprout onto animal jingles, church songs do duty as work songs, shouts and patting songs enliven the church atmosphere. The ready transition from heavenly to earth-bound sentiments is seen in the innumerable rollicking verses signed with the chorus, "When the Good Lord Sets You Free," examples of which we have given from Suggs. James Weldon Johnson sees a common "swing" rhythm in spirituals and secular folksongs, with the bodily movements in the first instance centering on swaying head and torso, and in the second on patting hands and feet.

Rhymes are sung, intoned, hummed, and recited and run the gamut from story to song. Occasionally I have heard colored people without a voice for singing recite a song in rhythmic prose; John Blackamore did this with the ballad of the bad man "Stagalee," and Mary Richardson lightly hummed the popular nursery song "The Frog Went A-Courting." The same text can appear in alternate forms. Blackamore related the saga of Brother Bill, the rampaging Negro cowboy, as a "toastie" (the rhymed recitation, often scatological, so popular at Negro parties); but Suggs told it to me as a tall tale. One form indeed, the cante-fable, unites the prose tale with little interspersed rhymes and chants which are sung or intoned by the narrators. When the rabbit in the hollow log converses with the waiting fox, or taunts the short-legged hedgehog, or cries out mournfully after the farmer has tied him to a limb, the storyteller breaks into a whiney chant. Some of the most delectable Negro stories hinge on cries of animals and fowls rendered with expert mimicry as human words. Thus in one favorite tale the rooster crows

Is the preacher g-o-o-o-ne?

in a high-pitched quavering wail straight out of the barnyard.

Conversely, the Negro singer interrupts his song to discourse on its theme. Lead Belly does this with his "Talking Blues," and also in his own rendition of the Child ballad known as "The Hangman's Tree" (No. 95), which he calls "De Gallis Pole." Suggs presents the fight between the grizzly bear and the preacher moaning, "Oh Lord, if you don't help me, at least don't help this grizzly bear," in a song that trails into prose.

The chant or cry that often flavors a Negro tale also enjoys an independent life. Sometimes wordless, sometimes joined to brief texts, the cry is lyric folk music, capable of musical scoring, and expressing intense emotions of grief, joy, despair. During and since slavery times the cry has been heard with astonishment by the white man, who gave it such names as "cornfield holler," "nigger squall," "piney-woods whoop," "roustabout drunk-yell," and "loud mouthing." Willis Laurence James, listing these epithets in his clever article on the Negro folk cry, speaks of the southern Negro's urge to chant his words when hawking wares in the street, dropping the leadline in the Mississippi, preaching a fiery sermon, giving out square dance calls, umpiring a baseball game. Where the white officer barked commands to his soldiers, the Negro noncom sang them out. Spirituals, work songs, blues, jazz, all build upon the lyric cry. When Cab Calloway formulated his

'Hi-dee hi-dee ho," he was simply molding a cry to the rhythms of his band.

In the folk sermon, chanted with accelerating fervor by the Negro preacher, folklorists now recognize a traditional if fluid form. The rhythmic phrasing and biblical metaphors of the preacher, punctuated by the antiphonal responses of the congregation, mount into a giant swelling cry of exultation and ecstasy. Folktales reflect the folk sermons, and when American Negroes tell the preacher jests popular in Europe since the Middle Ages, they insert the chanting of the preacher and shrieking of the sinners from their own cultural experience.

Set phrases move casually from one Negro folk form to another. A parody on "Reign, Master Jesus, Reign!" (in Talley's *Negro Folk Rhymes*) concludes with the field hand praying for rain; Old Marster overhears him.

> "Oh rain! Oh rain! Oh rain, 'good' Mosser!
> Dat good rain gives mō' rest."
> "What d'you say? You Nigger, dar!"
> "Wet ground grows grass best."

This incident turns up separately as a trickster tale in the Old Marster cycle.

Tales can expand popular sayings, and wise saws can summarize tales. "Eating further up the hog" is now an expression in general usage, but a Negro protest tale employs the phrase literally. A hired hand, whose boss feeds him only leftovers from the hog's carcass, finally quits the job, buys a piece of land, and does well enough to purchase some swine of his own. Meeting his old boss one day he says he is eating further up the hog now, dining on spare ribs, backbone, pork chops, middling. Similarly, the saying "Well, 'Ole Man Know-All' is Dead," alludes to a rhyme about an omniscient prattler who knew too much for his own good and drowned fording a creek instead of crossing on the bridge.

Fictional tales, true experiences, and popular beliefs continually cross into each other's territory. The belief in the spirit or the hoodoo leads into a true story of black magic or spirit visitation; and the supernatural folktale may be told as a real occurrence. Mary Richardson, who grew up in northern Mississippi and later migrated to Chicago and Michigan, related the international tale of the witch-cat for fact. A servant cuts off the paw of a mischievous cat, which turns to a woman's hand with a gold ring on one finger; subsequently the mistress of the house takes to bed, until she is found with one hand severed. Mary declared this happened in North Carolina in the Bissitt house where her grandmother worked as a house slave. Spook stories of haunted houses are told both as awesome spectral visions of the night and as hilarious jocular fictions. The colored raconteur blurs the twice-told tale and the personal experience, which contain similar elements of horror, supernaturalism, and humor.

So the forms and ingredients of Negro folklore coalesce and mingle. From European, African, and American folk materials, and from the vicissitudes of his own life under slavery and quasi-freedom, the southern Negro has developed a rich complex of unified folklore whose parts intertwine in a many-veined, dazzling filigree.

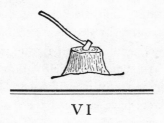

VI

A Gallery of Folk Heroes

Early in the nineteenth century and continuing into the twentieth, heroes began to rise from the varied folkstuffs accumulating on the American continent. Native humor, regional types, frontier life and lawlessness, the emerging Negro, and the mass media have shaped these heroes, who are particularly subject to the opposing pulls of American folk and mass culture.

When a close-knit group of people spins tales and ballads about a character celebrated in their locality or occupation, a true hero of the folk comes into existence. Such a one is Barney Beal of Beals Island. If the hero's fame spreads into subliterary channels, like county histories or chapbooks or dime novels, which enlarge the circle of his admirers through printed means but on levels close to folk groups and influential on local tradition, we may call him a legendary hero. The pre-Civil War Davy Crockett fits this description. When feature writers and resort promoters and movie producers flourish the name and invent the deeds of the hero in order to attract public interest, their creation becomes a mass-culture hero. Of this model, Paul Bunyan is the archetype. Because Americans today, in the glory of their national maturity, yearn for swashbuckling and sentimental heroes whom they may cherish, the hucksters have supplied their wants. If one Paul Bunyan book succeeds, a dozen more spring up to share the market. The student of folklore wishes to ascertain the extent of folk tradition in these highly publicized heroes. Each case needs to be analyzed separately, to unscramble its mixture of oral, legendary, and popular elements.

American field collectors have found surprisingly little trace of heroes in oral tradition. Vaunted pioneers like Daniel Boone and Kit Carson live in books, not in tales, whereas oral anecdotes about local characters ridicule and spoof rather than exalt their figures. One type of local celebrity, the strong man renowned for feats of lifting, fighting, and hunting, does thrive orally in numerous communities, but in the form of isolated incidents rather than connected sagas. Stories of big eaters also verge on the fabulous, without ever producing a full-fledged carnivorous hero. Sometimes a spinner of tall tales adopts an autobiographical approach and casts himself in the role of conquering hero, and to the extent that listeners repeat his wonders, he makes himself into a folk hero. In the case of Davy Crockett, the he-man, the regional eccentric, and the Münchausen figure all merged to create a genuine frontier folk and legendary hero. Then national publicity transformed him into a mass hero. Therein lies the difference between Crockett and Paul Bunyan, whom advertisers and journalists developed from a mere trickle of oral tradition into a household name. There never was a Paul Bunyan, as there was a David Crockett, but the origin of the hero does not affect the genuineness of his folk quality. He may be historical or fictional. But to qualify as a true champion of the folk he *must* be the subject of their tales.

Several common elements link the various types of American folk and mass heroes, whether comic demigods, Münchausens, Robin Hood outlaws, or noble toilers. All exalt physical virtues, and perform or boast about prodigious feats of strength, endurance, violence, and daring. Even Johnny Appleseed vanquishes the dangers of the wilderness through sheer stamina and pluck. As the critic Leo Gurko has pointed out, the popular hero on every level of American life glorifies brawn and muscle in contrast to mind and intellect: Clark Gable in the movies, Babe Ruth and Jack Dempsey in sports, Ernest Hemingway and his he-men in highbrow literature, Tarzan of the Apes in lowbrow literature, Paul Bunyan and his ilk in folklore, Superman in the comic books. America's idols all rise from the ranks of the common man and exhibit the traits and manners of unwashed democracy, spitting, bragging, brawling, talking slangily, ridiculing the dandy, and naïvely trumpeting their own merits. "Be sure you're right, then go ahead," said Davy Crockett. "There's no mistake in Sam Patch," announced Sam Patch. All the heroes display humor, even the deadly intense outlaws, who joked in the midst of mortal danger. Coarse jests clung to Johnny Appleseed and John Henry before the sentimentalists refined them away, and we still sing the libelous version of the ballad of "Casey Jones."

American "folk heroes," then, partake of many elements, ranging from local tradition to high-pressure publicity. In most cases they fail to qualify as genuine products of oral lore, a matter that may pain the folklorist, but which will intrigue observers of American civilization. We will here look at the general configurations of the hero types, and consider more closely one hero in each mold.

NINETEENTH-CENTURY RINGTAILED ROARERS

Before the Civil War four shaggy heroes shaped by the newly risen native humor soared into prominence. Two came from the western frontier, and two from eastern cities, but all swaggered and crowed in the same vainglorious fashion, and each deified the common man. Davy Crockett was a Tennessee bear-hunter, Mike Fink a Mississippi keelboatman, Sam Patch a Rhode Island cotton-spinner, and Mose the Bowery "b'hoy" a New York City fireman. We know them chiefly from antiquarian sources that testify to the hold they once exerted on the popular imagination. Their feats and escapades appeared on the humbler levels of print, in almanacs and jest books and newspapers, or in the rudest of one-act farces performed for Bowery loafers and gawking countrymen. The Americans who relished their antic adventures knew nothing of the unborn science of folklore. Educated in classical mythology, they rarely attempted highflown comparisons for their half-horse, half-alligator originals. The journalist Joseph Field did liken Fink to Jason questing for the Golden Fleece, or to a Scandinavian river-god, but the elegant demigods of antiquity bore little relation to these homebred gamecocks. Based on actual personalities, the legendary figures perfectly caught the spirit of the times. In the decades after the War of 1812 we think of a strident young nationalism, of a surging westward push, of the emergence of the common man. Crockett and

A Gallery of Folk Heroes

Fink, Patch and Mose shocked the genteel sensibilities of eastern aristocracy with their ruffian antics and rowdy Jacksonian fervor. They were bullies and brawlers and inane daredevils who could shoot farther, jump higher, dive deeper, and come out drier than any man this side of Roaring River.

Davy Crockett.—Curiously the boom that first catapulted Davy Crockett to national fame in the 1830's repeated itself in 1955. The Tennessee bear-hunter originally captured national attention through a cascade of manufactured publicity. From the stimulus provided by the television and cinema films of Walt Disney, Crockett again became known to millions of Americans. A juvenile audience relishes the motheaten conception of the frontier hero who fights Indians, kills b'ar, and dies gloriously. But that image of Davy bears only a small and skimpy resemblance to his fabulous nineteenth-century portrait.

The process of legend-building began with the election of the backwoodsman to Congress in 1827. Already in the 1820's journalists and travelers had noticed a new kind of American, an "original" cradled and nurtured in the trans-Appalachian clearings, half a horse and half an alligator, with an added touch of snapping turtle. Now this b'ar-hunter had marched head on into the nation's capital as duly elected representative of the people. The press found delicious copy in reporting his alleged quips and gaucheries. When Crockett broke with Andrew Jackson, his fellow westerner, for opposing the Bank of the United States, the Whig party eagerly embraced this potential vote-getter from the newly enfranchised West. Publicists went to work to exalt further the salty personality of their recruit, whose backwoods wisdom was turned towards praise of Whig policies and abuse of the Democrats. This ferment culminated in popular books that crystallized further the image of Crockett.

The *Sketches and Eccentricities of Colonel David Crockett of West Tennessee* (1833) brought together in patchwork fashion ephemeral anecdotes that had circulated in the papers and by word of mouth. Various strains of native humor issue from the intrepid hunter. He periodically recites Dutch dialect stories, then in vogue. He speaks in the frontier vernacular, and cites as "one of our backwoods sayings" the proverb "Lay low and keep dark, stranger, and *prehaps* you'll see some fun." In the White House, he astonishes the President's son with accounts of backwoods amusements, and tells of a female frolic on the cleared ground, where the women jig with such enthusiasm that the following morning Davy raked up handfuls of toe nails. The sinister figure of the Yankee clock-peddler emerges in a baleful light, performing his tricks and knavery, and Davy makes no bones that "the backwoodsmen, even the half-horse, half-alligator breed, when boasting of their exploits, always add, 'I can stand anything but a clock peddler.'" Throughout the book Davy crows and brags in the western tradition. He boasts how his powerful grin could bring a coon down from a tree, although on one occasion he mistook a knothole for a coon's eye and grinned all the bark off. A rumor spread that the President had authorized Davy to wring the tail off a comet.

Presumably to counteract the misrepresentations of the anonymous author in the *Sketches,* Crockett next year took up pen himself to set the record straight in an *Autobiography.* Thomas Chilton, Congressman from Kentucky, collaborated with him on this new work, which contributed further to the burgeoning legend and would eventually win a permanent place in American literature. A connected narrative and a taut style replace the loose and scrappy composition of the *Sketches*, although some of the same expressions and anecdotes remain. Davy continues to brag western fashion and to despise skinflint Yankees. What especially gives sauce and tang to the *Autobiography* is a wealth of homespun proverbial expression. Crockett customarily speaks and thinks in vivid metaphor: as dry as a powder horn; as cool as Presbyterian charity; as thick as Kentuck land titles; as sharp as a steel trap, and as bright as a pewter button; as little use as pumping for thunder in dry weather. To make his point he invokes old saws and adages: salting the cow to catch the calf; a fool for luck, and a poor man for children; a new country where every skin hangs by its own tail; a short horse is soon curried. He indulges in far-fetched hyperbole: "we would give him a little of the hurricane tipp'd with thunder"; "lean, lank, labbersided pups, that are so poor they have to prop up again a post-and-rail fence, 'fore they can raise a bark"; "a chap just about as rough hewn as if he had been cut out of a gum log with a broad-ax"; "had brass enough in his face to make a wash kettle." Davy's sayings express the personality coming to focus in the two books, a self-reared woodsman, courageous physically and morally, "determined to stand up to my lick-log, salt or no salt."

While the contents of the *Autobiography* are devoted mainly to bear hunts and politicking in the backwoods, a sequel, *Col. Crockett's Exploits and Adventures in Texas* (1836), carries Davy onto the plains. The later narrative, fabricated by Richard Penn Smith, graphically describes prairie scenes and the angular characters Crockett met on his way to join the Texan army. In a postscript an "eyewitness" relates Davy's murder at the hands of Santa Anna's Mexicans. This spectacular death salvaged the reputation of the Tennessee congressman, who had failed of re-election in 1834. Now his heroism at the Alamo won the heart of the nation.

One more step determined the apotheosis of Crockett. As newspaper stories had grown into books, so now the books spread into comic almanacs. Already in 1835 a slender, closely printed almanac had issued from Nashville, titled *Davy Crockett's Almanack, of Wild Sports of the West, and Life in the Backwoods,* adorned with fearsome woodcuts. This first almanac drew largely from the *Autobiography* for its material, and announced that Crockett would write additional scenes and episodes for each annual issue. The preface to the 1837 almanac explains that the Colonel had prepared copy for several future issues before his death, and so the series continued with the additional momentum gained from his stand at the Alamo. From 1837 on the "heirs of Col. Crockett" instead of "the author" appear on the title pages as the publishers. These Nashville imprints lasted through 1841, when the firm of Turner and Fisher distributed a rival Crockett almanac in New York, Philadelphia, and Boston. This firm, and others, kept publishing Crockett almanacs until 1856, when the annual series abruptly terminated. The tales and woodcuts developed the legendary implications of the figure outlined in the *Sketches* and the *Autobiography* and transformed Crockett into a swashbuckling demigod of American hue but with international counterparts.

In the almanacs the heroic and the comic aspects of Davy are sharply drawn. The tales concentrated on his prowess as a hunter and fighter, his hostility to Yankees and sharpers, his salty and extravagant speech. Eventually the characterization reached the point of caricature; the language dissolves into absurd misspellings, the adventures move to faroff lands and fantastic climaxes. Sometimes the narratives treat Crockett in the third person, as in the *Sketches,* and sometimes they are told in the first person, as in the *Autobiography,* while on occasion they describe backwoods zoölogy and customs and never mention Crockett. By 1856, when the slavery controversy smothered the frivolities of Yankee and frontier humor, the almanacs had elaborated an intricate and many-sided legend.

This union of the western hero with the subliterary almanac proved a brilliant success. Through much of the colonial period the almanac had performed yeoman service for American farmers. The "packhorse" of early American letters Moses Coit Tyler had called it, for the humble almanac entered homes that owned no book but the Bible. Farmers scanned closely the weather prophecies and zodiacal signs and planting hints for the coming year, and in between they lingered over verses, epigrams, facetiae, and fables. Almanac publishers like Nathaniel Ames and Robert B. Thomas expanded these departments, until the almanac blossomed into a vigorous specimen of agricultural literature. Benjamin Franklin appreciated its possibilities for disseminating homespun wit and wisdom, and by the early decades of the nineteenth century the almanac had come to function as jestbook and chapbook. "Colonel Crockett" and his "heirs" adapted an instrument particularly congenial to the American people for their special purpose of enlarging the fame of a homespun hero.

The new tide of native American humor, fed by Yankee springs and western tributaries, flowed naturally into such cheap printing outlets. Newspapers, periodicals, jokebooks, and paperbacks carried the yarns popular in campfire and country-store circles, and followed oral rather than literary conventions. Accordingly the Crockett almanacs dispensed with any connected narrative and treated their hero episodically, in single actions and escapades, as though these were separate yarns. They ignored and scorned literary refinements, as did Davy himself. On the level of print, the almanac writers—whoever they were—stayed close to popular sources and annexed a good many floating tales and motifs from oral tradition.

For all their disjointed and uneven quality, the almanacs display consistent themes and attitudes. The Crockett they create speaks with the brash and strident voice of Jacksonian America. Davy represents frontier crudity, violence, anti-intellectualism, chauvinism, and racism. He butchers the varmints of the forest, sneers at book learning and educated Easterners, despises niggers, Injuns, and Mexicans, and arrogantly trumpets the supremacy of Uncle Sam in foreign lands. Confronted by the Emperor of Haiti, whose black subjects were all abjectly kneeling, Davy announced, "I am Col. Davy Crockett, one of the sovereign people of Uncle Sam, that never kneels to any individual this side of sunshine." Then when the Emperor ordered his field hands against the stranger, he demolished the whole army with two sun-dried sugarcanes. In the name of freedom and patriotism, Davy rants and kills. Those characteristics which Frederick Jackson Turner associated with frontier society emerge in garish colors in the almanacs; Crockett is self-reliant and individualistic, scornful of cultural institutions, intensely confident and braggart, and a thorough nationalist.

A Gallery of Folk Heroes

While exemplifying American traits, the Crockett legends at the same time fall within universal patterns of the heroic epic. All folk epics spring from the fluid state of society which Hector and Nora Chadwick call the Heroic Age. Peoples of the Heroic Age live restlessly, ready to migrate, to raid the cattle of a neighboring community, to wage battle. Always some outstanding champion rockets to legendary fame; to him alone are attributed the marvelous feats attached to lesser heroes, and in the course of centuries the bards and tale-tellers weave a mighty saga about the conqueror. Eventually a chronicler or poet sets down the cycle in writing, adds continuity and polish, and bequeaths to the world an *Iliad*, an *Odyssey*, a *Beowulf*, a *Mahabharata*. Sometimes the legends fail to reach epic perfection and remain in arrested literary forms, like the scattered ballads of Serbian Marko Kralyevic, the sagas of Icelandic Grettir the Strong and the Celtic Cu Chulainn, or the romances of the German Siegfried and the Arabian Antar.

All these heroes exhibit strikingly similar developments. They grow from a basis of fact but assume extraordinary proportions. Each begins his career with precocious deeds of strength and in manhood slays dreaded warriors and monsters in gruesome single combats described with bloody detail. Before engaging in combat, they recite an awesome list of their feats and talents. As befits their age, the heroes hunt, drink, play at rough sports, and make love with enormous gusto. Especially are they proud of possessing the fleetest steed, the surest weapon, and the trustiest dog in the land, all of whom bear pet names and share in the hero's adventures. At some point the invincible champion wanders off to remote and exotic countries, to engage in new exploits and best more adversaries. The day comes when the hero, for he is mortal, must die, and since no single man or beast can kill him, he succumbs to over-whelming odds, or treachery, or witchcraft, sometimes in combination. Achilles and Siegfried, Beowulf and Cu Chulainn, Grettir and Marko, all follow this pattern.

And so does Davy Crockett. The frontier that bred him belongs to the Heroic Age of American culture, when migratory men lived dangerously on the border strip between wilderness and civilization. Warfare with Indians and the hunting of wild game kept frontiersmen on their mettle. In his *Autobiography* Davy tells of planting and tending his corn, but chiefly he wanders from his home base, to fight against the Creeks with Jackson, to pursue bear, or to explore new land. Already in his lifetime the Colonel had acquired legendary renown, not only for the prowess of an Achilles but for the cunning of a Ulysses. (Lacking funds, he bought drinks for his constituents with the same coonskin given anew to the unsuspecting Yankee grog-seller. When his bullet flew clear of the shooting board and could not be found, he inserted another into the center hole of the target while pretending to probe for his dead shot.) After Crockett's death, the juicy yarns circulating throughout the southwestern frontier clustered more thickly than ever about his name, the best known in the region, and legend soon engulfed fact.

In the United States, by contrast with other civilizations, printing existed concurrently with the Heroic Age, and frontier whoppers found their way into print in a few years instead of after many centuries. Still, the almanac tales rest upon a firm oral base, and tall stories about Davy are even today told in the Ozarks. Some of the almanac narratives clearly reproduce wandering folktales.

Whatever the mixture of traditional and invented elements in

A Gallery of Folk Heroes

the legendary life of Crockett, its outline reads like a true folk epic. Infant Davy was rocked by water power in a twelve-foot cradle made from the shell of a six-hundred-pound snapping turtle, varnished with rattlesnake oil, and covered with wildcat skins. He was weaned on whiskey and bear's meat. At six he began to hunt varmints from the back of his dog Butcher. In full manhood he hunts and fights in riproarious fashion and boasts prodigiously. "In one word I'm a screamer," he bragged, "and have got the roughest rocking horse, the prettiest sister, the surest rifle and the ugliest dog in the district. I'm a leetle the savagest crittur you ever did see. For bitters I can suck away at a noggin of aquafortis, sweetened with brimstone, stirred with a lightning rod, and skimmed with a hurricane. I can walk like an ox, run like a fox, swim like an eel, yell like an Indian, fight like a devil, spout like an earthquake, make love like a mad bull, and swallow a nigger whole without choking if you butter his head and pin his ears back." Like other vainglorious epic heroes, Davy cherished his rifle Killdevil, his knife Big Butcher, the longest in all Kentucky, and his faithful dog Teazer, who could throw a buffalo, and who drowned in the Mississippi when Davy sent him under and forgot to order him up again. In his conquests, Davy ventures ever farther afield and leaves the backwoods to wrestle anacondas in Brazil and outdive pearl-divers in Japan.

In his amours Davy tracked the doughty dames of the backwoods as relentlessly as he trailed any b'ar or pant'er. His sweethearts included Lottie Richers, the Flower of Gum Swamp, who chased a crocodile until his hide came off, and wore a necklace of human eyes she had pulled out, and Sal Fungus, who could sink a steamboat, blow out the moonlight, tar and feather a Missouri Puke, and ride a painter bareback.

211

American Folklore

The girl Davy wed, Sally Ann Thunder Ann Whirlwind Crockett, once battered the redoubtable riverboatman Mike Fink so unmercifully that he swore he had been chawed up by an alligator. When Davy tried bundling with one of these backwoods belles, he found her under-petticoat was made of briar bushes woven together and concluded that he might just as well embrace a hedgehog.

In the course of the legends, Davy assumes godlike command over the elements and the natural universe. He rides up Niagara Falls on the back of an alligator, slides down Mont Blanc ahead of an avalanche sled-fashion on a Rocky Mountain Indian, escapes from a tornado by mounting a streak of lightning, and drinks dry the Gulf of Mexico. In his most glorious feat, Davy saves mankind when the earth had frozen fast in its axis. He climbed up the peak of Daybreak Hill, squeezed bear's oil on the axis, and returned with a piece of sunrise in his pocket.

A pantheon of lesser demigods gathers about Crockett and joins his escapades. Ben Harding met the Colonel when both were floating down the Mississippi, and they immediately became as fast friends as a tame hawk and a blind rooster. Although himself a member of Congress from Kentucky and an alligator crossed with snapping turtle, Ben followed the sea and felt uneasy in the woods. As Davy said, "My cousin and crony Ben Harding was very savagerous at climbing a ship's mast, and treeing a squall; he could catch a whale by the throat, and squeeze or flog several casks of oil out of him, if not more. But when it came to walking up the tall masts of the backwoods, he was like a sucking colt in a cow stable, turning every way but the right way." On the Big Muddy, however, Davy and Ben felt equally at home. When a western steamer refused them passage because Crockett wanted to bring his pet bear Death Hug aboard, they fashioned their own craft out of a hollow gum tree, and put Death Hug at the stern to steer with his tail and hold up the American flag, while Ben and Davy paddled past the aristocratic steamer in sassy triumph. Mike Fink, king of the Mississippi keelboatmen and a legendary figure in his own right, saunters through several almanacs, and gave Davy his only defeat in a shooting match. Mike shot half the comb out of his wife's hair and asked Davy to finish the job. "No, no, Mike," he protested, "Davy Crockett's hand would be sure to shake if his iron was pointed within a hundred miles of a shemale, and I give up beat."

History had provided a thoroughly appropriate death for the frontier hero, surrounded by a savage horde in a mission fort but dauntless and defiant to the last. The almanac account adds some embroidery. While the Colonel draws a lead on one Mexican and stabs another, a rascal runs his bayonet through Crockett's back, "for the cretur would as soon have faced a hundred live mammoths as to have faced Crockett at any time. Down fell the Colonel like a lion struck by thunder and lightning." A dirge mourns the passing of the celebrated warrior. "Thar's a great rejoicing among the bears of Kaintuck, and the alligators of the Mississippi rolls up their shining ribs to the sun, and has grown so fat and lazy that they will hardly move out of the way for a steamboat. The rattlesnakes come up out of their holes and frolic within ten foot of the clearings, and the foxes go to sleep in the goose-pens. It is because the rifle of Crockett is silent forever, and the print of his moccasins is found no more in our woods."

The legends of Davy Crockett correspond in detail after detail to the great folk epics from Europe and Asia. If they seem crude and clownish by comparison, it must be remembered that all popular epics begin in humble and comic form. Frequently a wild poetic imagery, reminiscent of the *Kalevala* in its rich natural metaphor, illuminates the almanac tales. Had some artist, steeped in the traditions and talk of the nineteenth-century frontier, combed away the dross in the cycle, and strung together exploits in some semblance of harmony, the epic implicit in the Crockett legends might have flowered. In their present form they still remain a powerful revelation of the American genius.

TWENTIETH-CENTURY COMIC DEMIGODS

A whole new pantheon of humorous heroes made their debut before the American public in the present century. At their head strode Paul Bunyan, a giant lumberjack accompanied by a mammoth blue ox, and in his wake marched a host of imitators, colossi all: Pecos Bill, the supercowboy of the Southwest, riding a mountain lion with barbed wire reins; Old Stormalong, king of Yankee sailors, steering a vast ship whose masts were hinged to let the moon pass by; Joe Magarac, an iron puddler, squirting molten steel through his fingers to form rails; Febold Feboldson, titan of the Nebraska wheat farmers, tying tornadoes into knots as they swept across the plains. In some respects these oversized demigods resembled the Salt River roarers, for they too exuded might and bestrode the elements. But these surface similarities conceal major differences in folk process. Paul Bunyan and his fellows rest on little or no oral tradition and on no historical prototypes. The spirit of gargantuan whimsy oozing through the contemporary heroes reflects no actual mood of lumberjacks, cowboys, or steelworkers but only the childlike fancies of money-writers. Indeed the chief folklore connected with them lies in the mistaken idea that they are folk heroes—an idea widely held by schoolteachers, librarians, and the public and assiduously fostered by writers and promoters. The names and antics of these occupational giants have now elbowed aside the Greek and Roman gods and myths who once dominated the minds of American children.

A little research however has shown that these heroes originate in the brains of journalists and authors. Annie Christmas, supposedly a legendary whore of New Orleans, evolved from the artful pen of Lyle Saxon, the Louisiana local color writer, in a sardonic moment of tomfoolery. Joe Magarac, widely touted as an industrial folk hero of Hungarian steelworkers, hatched in the fancy of Owen Francis, who named his hero with the Slavic word for "jackass" and launched him in *Scribner's* magazine. Pecos Bill came to light in the *Century* magazine, contrived by Edward O'Reilly, pretty much from whole cloth. A lawyer named Paul Beath conjured up Febold Feboldson, juvenile writer Margaret Montague invented a West Virginia Bunyan called Tony Beaver, and Jeremiah Digges even devised a sea-going cowboy, Bowleg Bill, who straddled giant tunas. The nation demanded demigods, to reflect its massive triumphs in subduing the continent and conquering its foes, and professional writers furnished them ready made.

Paul Bunyan first appeared in a full-length book in 1924, and set the archetype for the twentieth-century folk hero, a good-natured giant breathing 100 per cent Americanism and playfully tampering with man and nature. Bunyan books promptly multiplied, and so did a host of imitation heroes. By 1930 Frank

Shay could exhibit a whole gallery of comic demigods in *Here's Audacity!*, and similar volumes soon followed. Children's authors fastened on this new vein, and one after another issued book after book on the same shopworn heroes, devoid of any field sources and derivative from previous writings. Management smiled on these super-productive, contented work giants; the Red River Lumber Company adopted Paul Bunyan as its advertising symbol, and the United States Steel Corporation sponsored Joe Magarac cartoons. Aware now of "folklore," the American public appreciated this new-found heritage of native, all-conquering demigods who coyly reflected American power, efficiency, and indestructibility.

The manufacture of a twentieth-century folk hero can best be seen in the success story of Paul Bunyan.

Paul Bunyan.—A slender trickle of oral tradition can be detected beneath the torrent of printed matter about Paul Bunyan. Old Paul first entered print in a feature article written by James McGillivray for the Detroit *News-Tribune* of July 24, 1910, titled "The Round River Drive." McGillivray came from Oscoda in northeastern Michigan and had logged in white pine lumber camps around the state. He was working as a night reporter when at three o'clock one morning his editor, Malcolm Bingay, later a well-known columnist for the Detroit *Free Press*, suggested that his news-hungry staff try writing features for the Sunday magazine section. Thereupon McGillivray set down a series of casual yarns about Paul Bunyan and his camp. Later in life he recalled how he first heard these stories.

My first knowledge of such a lumbercamp character now known as Paul Bunyan came to me when I was scaling logs at the logging camp of Rory Frazer, twenty-two miles east of Grayling on the north branch of the Au Sable river. I was then thirteen years of age, but big, like an adult man. . . . The men had a lounging shanty by themselves, removed from Rory's domicile, and hardly an evening went by that some lumberjack did not bring out some new angle on the prowess of a mythical 'Paul Bunyan.' I had never heard the name before, despite the fact that I lived in the renowned lumber-mill area of Oscoda-Au Sable, twin towns that led the world in saw-mill production back in the eighties.

One piece of corroborative evidence from 1910 affords another glimpse into the early oral tradition. A diary kept by a young schoolteacher, Edward O. Tabor, who spent a summer working as a lumberjack at Palmer Junction, Oregon, records some wonderful fragments about Paul and his blue ox. Otherwise only a handful of field-collected tales exist, nearly all of a relatively late date, and therefore open to suspicion of literary contamination, since the Paul Bunyan legend entered so many channels of print.

In 1914 a small thirty-page booklet of postcard size, *Introducing Mr. Paul Bunyan of Westwood Cal.*, reached the desks of lumber dealers and sawmill operators. A former lumberjack from northern Minnesota, W. B. Laughead, who had become an advertising executive for the Red River Lumber Company in Minneapolis (later of Westwood, California), prepared the pamphlet and interspersed little Bunyan anecdotes and cartoons among the eulogies of his company's product. Laughead probably saw a versified rendition of McGillivray's "The Round River Drive," that appeared in *The American Lumberman* for April 25 of that year. A second booklet followed in 1916, but the third issue in 1922, larger and handsomer, with a colored cover and the title *The Marvelous Exploits of Paul Bunyan*, put Paul on the map. Instead of circularizing only his customers, Laughead now offered the brochure freely to the public and disposed of a printing of ten thousand copies so quickly that he had to order five thousand more. The company issued ten subsequent editions at intervals of two or three years, and shortly before its dissolution brought out a thirtieth-anniversary edition in 1944, *Paul Bunyan and His Big Blue Ox*. Laughead's drawing of Paul Bunyan, as a moon-faced axman with a stovepipe cap and flaring whiskers, became the trade-mark of the company, and Laughead found himself in later years the target of eager inquiries from folklore researchers. When I visited him in California in 1939, he disclaimed much knowledge about Paul Bunyan or folklore, but did say he had invented the name of "Babe" for the blue ox and had thought up minor characters, such as Johnny Inkslinger, the camp secretary, and loggers Shot Gunderson and Chris Crosshaul.

Following the success of Laughead's brochures, Paul Bunyan tales mushroomed rapidly in the nation's press. West coast newspapers ran Paul Bunyan columns, to which readers con-tributed; interpretive articles appeared in magazines like the *New Republic* (1920), and the *Century* (1923), country weeklies carried boiler plate stories (prepared by news agencies for sale to small newspapers) about the giant woodsman, and soon came two full-length books in 1924 and 1925, both titled *Paul Bunyan*, and both written by Seattle authors, Esther Shephard and James Stevens. These established the appeal of the lumbering deity in the bookstores, and scarcely a publishing season passed that did not add a new title to the Bunyan bibliography. By 1947 this literature had grown to such proportions that a dreary anthology of *Legends of Paul Bunyan* offered extracts from dozens of writers who had exploited Old Paul. None of the Bunyan books listed inform-ants or furnished details of field collecting, and their contents

A Gallery of Folk Heroes

obviously veered far from the rough talk of woodsmen. Actually most books containing Paul Bunyan stories are written for children.

Unexpectedly I gained a first-hand insight into one of these books. During a field trip to Upper Michigan in 1946, I met Stan Newton of Sault Ste Marie, who had just completed *Paul Bunyan of the Great Lakes*. Since I had interviewed scores of old lumberjacks in that area, and secured a negligible handful of Paul Bunyan tales, I asked him wonderingly where he had obtained his material. Mr. Newton readily acknowledged it all came from a Paul Bunyan column he had conducted in a promotional magazine, *The Upper Peninsula Development Bureau News,* to which contributors sent in any tale they cared to hitch onto Bunyan. Mr. Newton had included the Russian people in his dedication and arbitrarily assigned the origin of Old Paul to a medieval Russian dragon-slayer, Ilya Murometz, thus hoping to tap the Russian market.

Paul Bunyan books are patched together in just this kind of casual fashion. They range in format from a colored booklet with cartoon drawings distributed through the dime stores, to a privately printed quarto volume in slip cover from the Derrydale Press. Most volumes repeat or elaborate on certain stock themes: the size of Paul's camp and its accouterments; the eating and hauling feats of Babe the blue ox; talents and troubles of the camp crew; ways in which Paul created American geography, by dragging his peavy (the lumberjacks' spiked pole) behind him to form the Grand Canyon, or logging off North Dakota, or inadvertently starting the Mississippi River from a leak in Babe's water tank. What kernels of oral folklore, if any, can be picked out from this amorphous literature? Since newspaper and advertising men first captured

American Folklore

Bunyan tales, the folklorist today must separate the wheat of tradition from the chaff of journalism.

The Detroit newspaper article and the Oregon diary of 1910 provide our earliest and surest evidence of oral lumberjack tales. Both mention specific informants. Tabor remembers a longbow artist named Duffy who could "give the story the proper flavor," and McGillivray did name some jacks who told Bunyan tales in Michigan in 1886.

Historically the Michigan tales put in print by McGillivray must precede those found in Oregon. His ten loosely joined anecdotes contain some well-known tall tales, like the stretching buckskin harness that contracts in the sun and draws its load into camp, and the giant tree around which two teams of axmen chop for four days without meeting each other. Technical descriptions of lumbering operations appear.

Bunyan sent me out cruisin' one day, and if I hadn't had snowshoes I wouldn't be here to tell you. Comin' back, I hit the log road, though I wouldn't knowed it was there but for the swath line through the tree-tops. I saw a whiplash cracker lyin' there on the snow. "Hello!" says I, "someone's lost their whiplash"; and I see it was Tom Hurley's by the braid of it. I hadn't any more'n picked it up, 'fore it was jerked out of my hand, and Tom yells up, "Leave that whip of mine alone, d——n ye! I've got a five hundred log peaker on the forty-foot bunks and eight horses down here, and I need the lash to get her to the landin'."

The lay reader gags at terms such as cruising, swath line, whiplash, log peaker, but the story simply says a teamster was hauling a big load of logs toward the river landing underneath a snowdrift. This is an old whopper in American folklore. We have met the tale of the mired traveler, whose hat alone shows above the ooze, in Paulding's play *The Lion of the West*, on the lips of Nimrod Wildfire. The folktale floated into the lumber camps and was recast into lumberjack idiom.

A Gallery of Folk Heroes

Besides already traditional tales, McGillivray set down some novel incidents destined for many literary repetitions. The account of the giant hotcake stove greased by Negro cookees with hams strapped to their feet has notably prospered, and Laughead illustrated the windy in his initial booklet of 1914. McGillivray's title story of "The Round River Drive," describing Paul's spring drive the winter of the black snow along a circular river with no outlet, has also entered the Bunyan canon.

The Oregon diary designates Paul Bunyan as "the first logger in the West." His blue ox ate carloads of potato peels and bales of hay, was currycombed with a garden rake, and made footprints large enough to drown men who fell into them. The big camp appears, with waiters on roller skates and windmills that pumped water for the crew three hours before breakfast. An unusual entry mentions Paul's son and his forty-eight-inch threshing machine in Dakota; he used eighty-five three-horse teams to carry away the grain. Paul logged off and farmed the Dakotas, and then dug out Puget Sound with the blue ox's help, in order to float the big logs. Clearly the Oregon lumberjacks coming to the Pacific Northwest from the Great Lakes states brought with them some Paul Bunyan motifs which they adapted to the new country.

A few rare flashes of oral vitality show Paul as an ingenious Yankee. In 1916 a professor of literature, Homer Watt, obtained a lumberjack tale with the authentic ring. To break a great jam in the Wisconsin River, Paul stationed the ox in front of the pile, and peppered him with rifleshot; the ox switched his tail furiously, to fend off the flies, drove the stream backwards, and dispersed the jam. Then Paul took the ox out of the stream and the logs resumed their normal flow. As Daniel G. Hoffman has pointed out, this tale displays

Yankee shrewdness rather than sheer brawn; in Paul's usual conception he would simply tear the jam apart barehanded. Another oral anecdote reported by Watt tells how Bunyan cheated his men out of their spring pay. He rushed into camp shouting that the law was about to arrest them for cutting on government pine. Each man seized what camp property he could carry and they made off in different directions. Thirty years later I heard a close variant in French-Canadian dialect pinned onto a wily lumbercamp boss in Escanaba, Joe LeMay. This incident obviously has survived in lumberwoods lore, but no Paul Bunyan books depict their hero in this knavish light.

In the books the brief oral anecdotes are lengthened into chapter-long episodes. Paul moves from a shadowy background position into front center. The technical language of white pine logging vanishes, to be replaced by the arch vocabulary of children's picture books. A host of secondary characters and beasts takes up the slack. The resulting fare is uniformly banal and tedious.

Oral tales about Bunyan can still be heard. Off-color stories, none of which reach print, can alone be trusted as genuinely oral. A veteran woodsman, Archie Garvin, gave me this bit of Bunyan lore in Menominee, Michigan, in 1946.

The Blue Ox used to look fancy when he went out with nine bales of hay stacked on one horn and seven bags of feed on the other. Every time he'd crap it'd take the crew three days to swamp around the pile. During the Winter of the Blue Snow, one of Paul's men climbed a tree and couldn't get down. It was so cold that Paul told him to pass water. He did, it froze, and the jack slid down on the icicle.

Other Paul Bunyan tales that circulate in the northwoods seem suspiciously close to print. Charlie Goodman, living in the lonely Lake Superior ghost port of Grand Marais after eighty-one years spent in the woods, told me several stories that McGillivray first set down. He knew about the giant griddle.

Paul Bunyan had a big camp when he lumbered down in lower Michigan. He had a table nine hundred feet long, and the waiters would grease the pancake griddle by skating around it with a ham on each foot. Then they'd skate down the table with the chuck, but even then sometimes it was cold before they got to the end of the table. They'd hold a washtub in each hand weighing a hundred and fifty to two hundred pounds, full of potatoes and meat, and skate right down the table, one behind the other, and distribute the chuck.

A new touch flavors this description, in the washtubs carried by the waiters. Another one Charlie tells seems a local variation upon the Round River drive. "They claim that Paul Bunyan had an underground current from Lake Superior to Big Spring. He had a drive on the J——[comic obscene] River; that's where the wild geese flies backwards to keep the sand out of their eyes—there's four miles of desert sand there. He drove the wrong man's logs and had to drive 'em back. They called it Paul Bunyan's Tagolder Drive; Tagolder is the commonest brush there is in swampy ground. That's why that current is flowing uphill." Perhaps the texts of McGillivray in 1910 and Charlie Goodman in 1946 reflect an oral woods tradition in northern Michigan, but the all-pervasive influence of mass publication and tourist promotion have hopelessly muddied the lore.

Not only men of the woods, but men of the cities narrate Paul Bunyan tales of a sort. These stories consistently deal with Paul's creation of local topographical features. Certain persons whose work involves public relations, or who have written about Paul Bunyan, make a practice of narrating Bunyan tales to clubs and organizations, and acquire some local celebrity as Bunyan storytellers. Such after-dinner speakers, catering to urban audiences of businessmen and housewives seeking light social entertainment, are far removed from the folk raconteur of the lumberwoods.

If Paul Bunyan possesses only a slight and insubstantial basis in folk tradition, he has achieved a considerable impact on American thought. In its later phase the legend bursts from print into a variety of art forms and pageants: sculpture, ballet, musical suite, lyric opera, folk drama, radio play, oil painting, lithography, wood carving, and even a glass mosaic mural celebrate the giant lumberjack and his blue ox. A practice of holding a "Paul Bunyan's Day," a gala community festival or carnival in honor of the timber god, originated in Brainerd and Bemidji, Minnesota, but spread east to Concord, New Hampshire, and west to Tacoma, Washington. At these ceremonies the carved dummy of a majestic Paul presides over an active scene of logging contests and woodsmen sports, such as birling, canoe-tilting, log-bucking, log-rolling, and log-chopping, or winter pastimes of skiing, bobsledding, and ice skating. Sometimes images of Paul are fashioned from snow or metal, or men of heroic proportions play Bunyan for a day. So fast and far had the "myth" spiralled upward into the popular imagination that figures of Old Paul adorned both the New York and the California World's Fairs of 1939.

Actually the nation's newspapers, rather than the lumberjacks of the northwoods, have nourished Old Paul in the hearts of his countrymen. Columns of Paul Bunyan stories ran in Washington and Oregon newspapers in the early 1920's and helped spread the fame of the colossus. By 1939, when I began subscribing to a news clipping bureau that snipped all references to Bunyan, his name had clearly become a journalistic commonplace, useful in feature stories, promotional material, and news items and pictures of all kinds. The clippings revealed the widespread invocation of Paul's name, the display of his image, and the public recital of his tales in many avenues of American life. Resort areas relied heavily on magical association with Paul, and Minnesota, Wisconsin, Michigan, California, and Washington all bid lustily for the giant's playground, "Paul Bunyan's land." Each new volume of Bunyan tales brought in its wake a stream of reviews eulogizing the patriotic deed of publication. Newspaper stories on the lumber industry and lumberjacks invariably cited Old Paul, as a symbol for all logging operations or for the individual woodsman. All sorts of fabulous personalities breaking into the news, from foreign folk heroes to American eccentrics, must needs be introduced as a rival to Bunyan. Paul does duty too as a colorful tag to describe a mammoth undertaking, an enormous object, or a powerful exaggeration. Headlines, leadoff sentences, and picture captions invoked "Shades of Paul Bunyan" to indicate the immensity of the world's largest cheese, cigar, or strawberry sundae or to introduce some prankish stunt, like a photograph of a tobacco-chewing fish. Occasionally the name of Paul is used with an adverse connotation, to lampoon a blowhard or braggart.

This bulky file of news clippings shows Bunyan in a new light and reveals his real role in American civilization. He is the pseudo folk hero of twentieth-century mass culture, a conveniently vague symbol pressed into service by writers, journalists, and promoters to exemplify "the American spirit." He means different things to different vested interests: the soul of the workingman to the *Daily Worker;* the efficiency of American capitalism to the lumber companies; a gargantuan comic dummy baiting tourists for resort owners; the invincible brute strength of America to some artists; a loudmouth, a fantasy, a Hercules, a woods deity, to other Americans. But no one knows very much about the legends of Paul and Babe. Americans as a people share no oral body of narratives about Paul, in the way that Indian tribes know trickster tales, and southern Negroes talk about Old Marster and John.

Twentieth-century America, ripe and self-confident after defeating the Kaiser and saving the world for democracy, thirsted for a New World Thor, or Hercules, or Gargantua to symbolize her might. And so Paul Bunyan, bursting into public view in the 1920's, filled the psychic need. Journalism and advertising spread his name across the land, with a few associated clichés about his uniqueness in American mythology. The hullabaloo penetrated all corners of American society and even impressed the lumberjacks. Professors and critics and composers swallowed the myth as eagerly as the man in the street. Artists yearning for indigenous materials strove earnestly to wrest some meaning from the legend to transmute into drama and opera, painting and sculpture, poem and dance. They could not realize that Paul Bunyan represented only the most obvious facts of American life—the worship of bigness and power, and the ballyhoo of salesmanship and promotion.

MÜNCHAUSENS

Some local yarn-spinners adept at autobiographical sagas initiate their own legends. Primarily storytellers, rather than participants in exciting events, they embroider ordinary incidents of their travels and occupations. "Oregon" Smith expatiated on the marvels of the Oregon country, Jim Bridger, the Rocky Mountain guide, enlarged the natural wonders of Colorado, Gib Morgan elaborated on techniques of oil drilling, John Darling embellished his farming and hunting exploits in the Catskills. Mostly, however, the exaggerators depend upon stock fictions current throughout the country, which they adopt as authentic personal experiences. This after all is the manner of that most redoubtable truth-twister, Baron Münchausen (Rudolph Eric Raspe, 1720–1797), whose solemn-faced *Narratives of His Marvelous Travels and Campaigns* in Russia made his name a synonym for gorgeous fabrications.

The storytelling heroes are remembered in their neighborhoods after their deaths for the wondrous tales they spun about themselves. A younger generation of local folk retell prize narratives, giving due credit to the master. "Gib used to like to tell this one." Obscure and humbly born, the Münchausens never attract public notice, but occasionally they drift into the net of folklore collectors. Folklorists, not writers or promoters, have placed them on record. Mody C. Boatright followed the spoor of Gib Morgan from the Pennsylvania to the Oklahoma oilfields; William H. Jansen gained a doctor's degree by pursuing the tales of "Oregon" Smith in Indiana and Illinois; Herbert Halpert bagged John Darling stories from old woodcutters and raftsmen in the western Catskills of New York.

Gib Morgan.—Although he has made no impact on the general public, Gib Morgan stands as the only tall-tale hero of occupational lore with satisfactory folk credentials. The field and library work of Mody Boatright, the Texas folklorist, has uncovered a wide spate of whoppers told by Gib in which he portrays his adventures as a cable driller in the oil industry. Morgan's own life paralleled the rise and phenomenal growth of oil drilling as big business, and he turned his storytelling talents into the technical aspects of labor in the oil fields. Old-time drillers and tool dressers and producers remember and retell his yarns. They do not narrate floating stories that gravitate to Gib, but recall fanciful exploits Gib wove about himself.

Gilbert Morgan was born in Callensburg in western Pennsylvania in 1842 and six years later moved with his family to nearby Emlenton, which he called home throughout his life. In this scraggly country of miserable farmers and bark peelers Gib grew up to young manhood. He left to fight in the Civil War and on his return found western Pennsylvania in the throes of an oil boom. Thenceforth the oil fields claimed his energies. He married, but the early death of his wife left him rootless and he became a boomer, an oil gypsy, who followed the new strikes in Ohio and West Virginia and Pennsylvania. Apparently he never went to Texas. He retired in 1892, and spent his last years in old soldiers' homes, dying in one in 1909.

A trimly built man of average height, dark complexion, alert grey eyes, and a heavy mustache, Gib is remembered first and last as an inveterate raconteur. He began yarning to buoy up his comrades in the Tenth Pennsylvania Reserve Infantry, and he ended his days surrounded by laughing veterans; in the oil fields he continually entertained his fellow workers with extravagant tales. Friends urged he write them down, but the few he did publish in a booklet called *Useful Information for Oil Men* (1898), while they suggest Gib's imaginative powers, chiefly demonstrate the ineffectiveness of the oral artist who turns author. A widely traveled little anecdote that always

A Gallery of Folk Heroes

fastens onto champion American liars pays tribute to Gib's storytelling fame. "Gib, tell us a lie," some buddies asked him in Macksburg, Ohio. Soberly Gib replied, "I can't tell you a lie now. I've just got word that the cable clamps have slipped and killed my brother at the well." Later the chastened loafers learn that Gib had indeed told them their lie.

The tall tales Gib Morgan left in oral tradition follow two main patterns. One group he picked up from already existing tradition, and these include familiar hunting and fishing windies and fool yarns he heard in western Pennsylvania or on his travels. Among the classic American fictions, Morgan retells whoppers of the split dog, who ran into a sapling splinter, and was patched together by Gib with two legs up and two legs down, so that thereafter he outran any rabbit in the Allegheny valley by turning cartwheels (see "The Diverting Club" in chapter ii, and the New Mexican tale in chapter iii); the speedy greyhound tied to the train Gib was riding on, who trotted alongside on three legs to cool off a hot box on a car wheel; the giant catfish Gib landed with a spool of drilling cable for a line, a steamboat anchor for a hook, and a young steer for bait, whose removal from the river caused the water level to drop two feet; his shot with a twenty-four-barrel fowling piece that buried him in pigeons seventy-two feet deep and knocked him through the top soil and three feet into the hardpan, the first time he emptied the barrels. Such time-honored lies Gib managed to invest with a freshness of detail and extravaganza.

The bulk of Morgan's recorded tales concern his experiences in drilling for oil wells. These windies apparently grew from the fertile brain of their narrator, who inflated the sensational incidents of the oil industry to the point of fantasy. True wonders did occur, and the New York *Herald* soberly reported an oil gusher striking corn whiskey, when the rig inadvertently drilled into a moonshiner's cave. Hoaxes flourished in the oil fields, and burlesque prospectuses announced companies that would drill entirely through the earth to China, and that owned wells producing cooking butter, cod liver oil, and the milk of human kindness. Gib developed stories not out of whole cloth, but from materials and circumstances at hand, and used them to top blowhards. When city men boasted about their fine horses or splendid hotels, Gib countered with tales about his favorite horse Torpedo, twenty-two yards long, whom he threw in reverse instead of turning around, or his forty-story hotel mounted on a turntable to give every guest a room with southern or eastern exposure. When a tough foreman bragged that he had killed a man, Gib described the fight he had had with a Negro at the bottom of the Ohio River for two weeks, while the spectators along the banks cheered as pieces of white and black flesh alternately rose to the top.

In many tales Gib performs miraculous feats of drilling. When a geologist mistakenly located a well on tope of Pike's Peak, Morgan managed nevertheless to sink a well from the mountaintop. He strikes buttermilk champagne, and horse urine in the Fiji Islands, and rubber in South America. In Big Toolie he located a giant tool dresser who could grease the crown pulleys of the derrick from the ground. Gib lost Big Toolie when he shipped him back to America under the ocean, in a pipeline which forked at St. Louis; Toolie's left leg started for New York and his right for Chicago, and he was not subsequently seen in one piece. In Strickie, Gib found a monstrous boa constrictor he could use in place of the regular steel cable and with his help brought in a beautiful well. Most of Gib's fictions involve a close knowledge of drilling operations, and therefore ring true; only a skilled oilman could sufficiently understand the terms and the situations to relish their humor. The fifty-odd yarns credited to Gib Morgan definitely belong to an occupational folk cycle, for, excepting a few standard tales and motifs, they reflect the technology of a specialized craft.

NOBLE TOILERS

Three dissimilar figures of the nineteenth century, a western tree-planter, a Negro laborer, and a railroad engineer, symbolize the glories of dedicated toil. In 1873 John Henry died with his hammer in his hand, his heart bursting as he outsmote the white man's steam drill. In 1900 Casey Jones, a daredevil who raced his engine against the clock to keep ever on schedule, saw a caboose loom ahead in the darkness, and stayed in his cab long enough to pull the airbrake and save his passengers. They found Casey with an iron bar through his neck, one hand on the bell cord, the other on the throttle. Johnny Appleseed met his Maker peacefully in 1845 on the Indiana frontier, after a lifetime tramping through the Ohio Valley wilderness planting apple orchards for his fellow man. The three toilers were actual persons who first gained folk fame from their physical powers, and then in the present century were sentimentalized into noble mass heroes. Single ballads catapulted John Henry and Casey Jones into legend after their sacrificial deaths, while the romancers and poets fastened onto Appleseed.

The later sentiment has obscured the earlier lustiness. Violent jests and bawdy ballads burgeoned in the Big Bend Tunnel in West Virginia, where John Henry pounded rock among a thousand half-naked laborers newly freed from slavery. An undercover song about Casey Jones, to which his widow objected, pays tribute to the engineer's prowess as lover. And Johnny Appleseed was truly earthy before the popular culture transformed him into a saccharine saint of the orchards.

Johnny Appleseed.—By a process similar to the journalistic and artistic development of Paul Bunyan, the itinerant sower of apple seedlings, John Chapman, has soared into the public fancy. Where Bunyan represents destructive power, Johnny Appleseed connotes sweet fertility. Barefoot he wanders through the frontier forests of Ohio and Indiana, looking for likely places to plant his nurseries, clad in a mushpot hat and a coffeesack garment. He carries Swedenborgian tracts, which he expounds to pioneer families as he lies on the plank floor of their cabins. Indians and wild beasts harm him not, and he in turn injures none of God's creatures. When accidentally the heel of his scythe kills a snake, he weeps. Once a pompous evangelist berated his frontier audience for their vanity, asking "Where now is there a man who, like the primitive Christians, is traveling to heaven barefooted and clad in coarse raiment?" Johnny stepped forward and said, "Here's your primitive Christian." During the War of 1812 he traversed the Ohio frontier, warning isolated families of danger from England's Indian allies. Johnny never married, because his youthful love went west and died before he found her. He himself dies reading the Bible while apple blossoms swirl to the ground outside his door. A modern Saint Francis of Assisi, Johnny lived to befriend humanity and replenish the earth. The Midwest owes her lush orchards to Johnny, and more than one starving pioneer blessed him on finding apple trees in the wilderness.

So runs the modern version that constantly reappears in mass and local media. This syrupy image varies considerably from the known facts. John Chapman was born in Leominster, Massachusetts, of Yankee stock, in 1774. His father, made out to be a Revolutionary hero, actually was released from service because of mismanagement of military stores. The son's history is a blank from his birth till 1797, when he appears in northwestern Pennsylvania, perhaps attracted by new land openings. Records and reminiscences fill in his career from then on, as he wandered and paddled through central and northwestern Ohio, and in his last years in Indiana, where he died near Fort Wayne in 1845. He did present a queer appearance, and travel in solitary fashion along the frontier leasing land and planting nurseries, and the sobriquet John—later Johnny—Appleseed was bestowed upon him by pioneer folk. On the other hand, he was no self-made pauper who gave away apple trees and seeds and shoes to the needy, but a fairly successful businessman who accumulated twenty-two properties of nearly twelve hundred acres. He did not originate the planting of apple orchards in the West, but followed methods well established for two generations. His one contribution lay in moving his nurseries west to keep abreast of the receding frontier. Nor was Johnny a hermit, but a sociable fellow who spent a good deal of time with his half-sister and her family in Perrysville and Mansfield, Ohio. He did give a false alarm of Indian danger in 1811, and a real one in 1812, traveling from Mansfield to Mount Vernon on the Ohio border to rouse the community; but in the retellings, separate incidents and alarms have been condensed into one grand race of warning, with echoes of

Paul Revere. The idyllic death of Johnny is pure improvisation.

This sentimentalizing of the apple-sower resulted from literary not folk causes. Robert Price, the most careful biographer of Chapman, has demonstrated that oral tales about Johnny did at one time circulate among Ohio pioneer families, and that these tales bear little relation to the later saccharine accounts. Early traditions "suggest hearty and brawny tales," according to Price, and center on Chapman's stamina in the face of hardship and privation. They tell that he drank and hint at a libidinous interest in women. One oral account collected in the Ozarks in 1931 by Vance Randolph, from a hillman who had heard it forty years before, preserves this coarser vein. The Ozarker debunks a newspaper story about Johnny wearing a tin pan on his head and a gunnysack round his middle and walking barefoot from Pennsylvania through the woods. Johnny dressed like anybody else and wore Choctaw moccasins. His wife was a full-blooded Choctaw, and when she and her baby died, Johnny went balmy. He had returned east to obtain dogfennel or "feverweed," which he claimed would make a tea to cure his wife's malaria. Finding her dead on his return, he went around the country planting this weed. Instead of Johnny Appleseed he should be called Johnny Feverweed. The queer fellow called rattlesnakes his brothers and said he hoped to marry three angels in heaven.

In this oral narrative Johnny appears as a harmless and useless eccentric, with normal physical appetites and crazy notions. Hundreds of local character anecdotes throughout the country poke fun at similar figures. But literary romancers went to work on Johnny, and submerged the folk tradition under a blanket of sentiment. As early as 1817 legends about the sower of apple seeds, who "actually thawed the ice with his bare feet," found their way into the report of a Swedenborgian society in Manchester, England. In America, Johnny Appleseed seems not to have stimulated the almanac and newspaper humorists who developed Davy Crockett and Sam Patch. Instead, an antiquarian volume of 1847, a preacher's novel of 1858, and the reminiscences of a frequent contributor to mid-century ladies' annuals, Rosella Rice, shaped his posthumous portrait in Ohio. Then in 1871 an article in *Harper's New Monthly Magazine* by W. D. Haley, "Johnny Appleseed, a Pioneer Hero," gathered together these threads into a narrative of universal appeal, drenched in bathos. The tin-pot hat, bare feet, religious tracts and apple seeds promptly became permanent literary fixtures. Another minister, Newell Dwight Hillis, introduced his novel of 1904, *The Quest of John Chapman*, with a glowing tribute to "the Patron Saint of the American Orchards—a man altogether unique, picturesque, pathetic, and broken-hearted. Save Colonel Clark, he is the most striking man of all the generation that crossed the Alleghanies." Hillis then constructed a tale of tragic love to explain John Chapman's life of abnegation.

Poets and horticulturists especially have wept over the nurseryman, who becomes a fertility symbol for all America. Some thirty poets have eulogized Johnny, particularly the modern troubadour, Vachel Lindsay, who saw a kindred spirit in the itinerant orchardist. Almost any journalistic story involving apples, or orchards, or trees, or planting and sowing, invokes the name of Johnny Appleseed. As one playwright pointed out, in a play contrasting Old Paul and Johnny, Bunyan destroyed but Appleseed planted trees. Kate Smith's radio show and Walt Disney's movie *Melody Time* have successfully squeezed further teardrops from the Appleseed story. An advertisement in the *Saturday Evening Post* for November 12,

1949, by the John Hancock Mutual Life Insurance Company showed a bareheaded, barefooted Johnny swinging joyously between rows of fruit trees, above the caption, "He planted seeds for us to reap." Ohio has declared a "Johnny Appleseed Day" on the anniversary of his birth, and Indiana dedicated a two-hundred-and-fifty-acre park to his memory.

OUTLAWS

The legendary group most firmly anchored in history are the border outlaws who spread terror throughout Missouri, Texas, and New Mexico in the decades after the Civil War. They speedily passed from local to national celebrity, and dime novels, movies, and other mass media transformed them into American Robin Hoods. While a tremendous promotion through the printed word and the movie screen has familiarized the public with the names of Jesse James, Billy the Kid, and Sam Bass, in their home territories people talked about them with the authentic accents of folk narrative. Tense moments in the lives and especially the deaths of the three outlaws powerfully affected the folk mind.

This memorable trio of bandits followed parallel paths to legendary fame. Historically they enacted their brief lives in similar environments: the blood-soaked farmlands of western Missouri where feuds of the fratricidal war kept smoldering; the thinly settled territory of New Mexico, rent by a shooting war between rival merchant-gangsters; and the plains of northern Texas, overrun with cattle rustlers and horse thieves. On these lawless frontiers the Wild West of the movies actually existed. Accounts of the bad men read like Icelandic sagas, compelling and hypnotic in their stark annals of shootings, holdups, skirmishes with enraged posses, massing of punitive forces, and finally the betrayals of the heroes. No subtleties of character emerge in these sagas, only a succession of bare names and violent scenes, with the figure of the outlaw-hero growing in intensity through the narrative, while lesser members of the gangs run off or get killed or go straight or turn coat. A great suspense gathers, for we know the hero must forfeit his life in its youthful vigor and prime; but who can outdraw or outwit the master bandit?

In the answer to this question lies the chief explanation for the ascent of the three desperadoes from murky history to glowing legend. Like the champions of all the great folk epics, they died by foul means. As Siegfried was daggered in the back by his best friend, and Achilles was pierced by the arrow of skulking Paris, so Jesse was shot from behind by a comrade under his own roof, and Sam Bass was lured into ambush by a confederate whose life he had spared. Pat Garrett, while wearing the badge of the law, shot William ("the Kid") Bonney from the cover of darkness as he stepped into the room of a friend. The Judas character of the informer enters conspicuously into the legends, and his ignoble end properly fits his cowardly deed. Robert Ford never realized the glory and cash he expected to reap as the killer of Jesse James. He drifted from traveling stage shows to gambling halls and saloons, and got himself shot in a dive. Jim Murphy received his pardon for robberies committed while a member of Sam Bass's gang, but his old cronies and the Texas Rangers alike scorned him, and he perished miserably a year after betraying Sam, from poison he apparently drank deliberately. Posterity remembers Bob Ford and Jim Murphy only as cowardly skunks in the ballads about Jesse and Sam. Pat Garrett enjoyed celebrity for a number of years, and Teddy Roosevelt called on him personally and awarded him a postmastership. In the course of time Pat's fame waned while the Kid's grew, and Pat turned sour. He made the mistake of badgering a young tenant farmer of his, who retorted sharply; stung beyond control, Pat drew, but the younger man drew faster, shot Pat dead, and was acquitted in court on the plea of self-defense.

Legend looked kindly on their premature deaths and softened the histories of the three, badmen. *They* never betrayed a friend. They loved their mothers and wives and sweethearts; they were polite to women and kindly to cripples; they had a sense of humor. A Missouri farmer musing about the James Boys told Homer Croy: "They didn't ever cause farmers any trouble. Mostly they robbed banks and railroads and express companies that had plenty of money." The defender of Jesse points out that he never stole cattle or wantonly murdered like the despicable Kid. The apologist for Bonney declares the Kid never robbed innocent people like Jesse, but merely helped himself to cattle that freely roamed the range. History can justly regard Jesse, Sam, and the Kid as pariahs and sadists, but legend sees a spirited youth laughing as he gallops from a red-faced posse of respectable citizens toward the inevitable doom ahead.

Jesse James.—Many facts are now known about the career of Jesse Woodson James. He was born in Clay County, Missouri, in 1847, and northwestern Missouri remained his home territory until his death. His father, who died in Jesse's childhood, was a Baptist preacher, and his mother was raised in a Catholic convent. The border warfare in Kansas and Missouri between Confederate raiders and Union troops blooded young

A Gallery of Folk Heroes

Jesse, who saw his foster father hung up till nearly dead and his mother and sister jailed, while Yankees bayoneted the boy for fun, in their search for Confederate sympathizers. At fifteen he joined the noted guerrilla leader Quantrill, with whom he rode and fought and killed along the farm lanes and timbered country of mid-Missouri and learned the tactics that served him in his later years. This was a war of ambush and the sudden strike and the rapid melting away into the darkness, and the slaughter of defenseless prisoners. Twice Jesse suffered grievous wounds through the lung, once when carrying a flag of truce. He emerged from the strife a killer, with personal rather than sectional hatreds, that continued unabated after the Confederate surrender. The State of Missouri refused to grant full amnesty to Confederate soldiers and guerrillas, barred them from professional careers, and threw them in jail on flimsy pretexts. In a sense Jesse continued to fight the war, relying on old guerrilla friends and supporters to protect his flanks and furnish him intelligence.

Banks, an impersonal and unloved target, and bankers, a species of Yankee reptile who strangled the impoverished farmers, now became the enemy. Bandits screamed the rebel yell at the novel American bank robbery, in Liberty, Missouri, early in 1866. Frank James, who took part, showed kid brother Jesse his share of the spoils. Before the year was over Jesse, at nineteen, participated in his first armed robbery. The James's farm possessed fine riding horses, and the open country, largely free from fences, permitted horsemen to scatter in all directions. Jesse James had found his profession.

His bank-robbing technique followed a successful master-plan. A group of five or six well-mounted strangers rode into a town in Missouri or Kentucky or Arkansas, wearing the

linen dusters of traveling cattle-buyers. The ample folds of
these dusters concealed six-shooters and pistols. One man saun-
tered into the bank to the cashier's window and asked to have
a hundred-dollar bill changed. Two stood at the door to keep
out intruders, and two or three stayed on their mounts in the
street to watch for trouble. Jesse usually held up the cashier,
the most ticklish part of the job. When he opened the safe to
get change, Jesse pulled his gun, and demanded the full contents. At Gallatin, Missouri, in 1869, he deliberately shot an
unresisting cashier, apparently mistaking him for an old enemy. In time he added trains and stagecoaches to his prey, holding out a grain sack invitingly for the passengers' "contributions." In these holdups Jesse and his boys shot whoever
resisted.

One tragic episode helped to smother the resentment rising
against the James Boys, and keep them in the role of the per-
secuted. On a night in January, 1875, a band of Pinkerton
detectives stole up to the house near Kearney where Frank
and Jesse lived with their mother, stepfather, and young half-
brother, and hurled a bomb through the window. (The Pinkerton Agency claims it was an illumination device.) When
Jesse's mother pushed it into the fireplace, the bomb exploded,
tearing off her arm and fatally piercing the boy. Frank and
Jesse had ridden away shortly before. In the letters he wrote
to newspapers, establishing his alibis on the occasion of bank
robberies, Jesse mentioned this outrage with righteous fury
and accused his hunters of being the lawbreakers. The manner
of Jesse's death crystallized this idea.

The turning point in his successful and arrogant career came
when Jesse ventured into the untried territory of Minnesota.
His famous raid on Northfield in 1876 ended in disaster for

the band, when alert citizens fired back at the robbers and trailed the three Younger brothers to a slough, where they killed one and captured the others. Jesse, who had wantonly murdered the cashier, made his getaway with Frank. For several years the brothers lay low and attempted to farm in Tennessee. Finally Jesse rented a house on a hill in St. Joseph, Missouri, grew a beard, took the name of Howard, and attempted to rebuild his gang. A former associate, Charles Ford, brought his nineteen-year-old brother Bob to meet Jesse and join his outfit. Jesse invited the two brothers to live with him until plans had matured for the next holdup, little suspecting that Bob Ford had discussed the shooting of the outlaw with Governor T. T. Crittenden of Missouri, who promised him immunity and gave him a detective's badge. The cleancut, boyish youth found his opportunity the morning of April 3, 1882, when Jesse laid aside the holster he always wore, to mount a chair and dust a picture. Bob Ford walked behind him and shot his host in the back of the head with a pistol given him by Jesse. The governor promptly pardoned Ford, who then toured the country re-enacting the murder.

Four hundred and fifty dime novels and half a dozen Hollywood movies celebrated the fictional feats of Jesse, but the folklorist notes the ballads and legends that kept Jesse's fame alive in oral tradition. Countless tales reshaped Jesse into a romantic outlaw. In his valuable book *Jesse James Was My Neighbor* (1949), Homer Croy sets down dozens of such stories and identifies the speakers. Yet he declares, "I am not putting in this book any legends or folk tales," failing to recognize that these word-of-mouth narratives bear the unmistakable imprint of folklore. They invariably portray Jesse as kind and generous, intrepid and uncanny, and they contain most improbable incidents. In his role as humanitarian, Jesse saves a Negro boy from a mob, releases a captured Union soldier who had come home to see his mother, refuses to rob a preacher, and gives a poor widow eight hundred dollars to pay off a skinflint mortgage-holder, whom Jesse promptly robs as soon as the widow pays him. Raconteurs also tell how Jesse threw trailing posses off his scent by shoeing his horse backward, and sprinkling the blood of a wild hog along a false turn. The mysterious stranger who stares down Omaha Charlie, the poolroom bully, or moodily leaves the town of Cumberland Furnace when he learns the safe is empty, must indeed have been the renowned outlaw. Ubiquitous Jesse sits next to Billy the Kid at Sunday dinner in a New Mexico hotel.

In certain legends Jesse displays a wry humor. He informed a Pinkerton detective he met in a bar that he was agent for a tombstone company; the detective said that he hoped to meet Jesse James before he died, and Jesse later wrote him that he had, and could now die comfortably. Another time Jesse walked home with a scared poolplayer to protect him from robbers. One widely known folktale entered the Jesse James tradition. An old maid sits in a railroad car being held up by the James Boys, even though a panicky fellow passenger says Jesse will rape her and that she must flee. "Jesse James is the one who's running things here," she sternly informs the meddler.

A new Jesse James tale unexpectedly came my way from the prolific Negro storyteller, J. D. Suggs, who had lived some years in Missouri. There he had heard of a secret tunnel by which Jesse made his escape after a holdup.

A Gallery of Folk Heroes

Jesse James had his home twenty miles down from Cairo on the Missouri side of the Mississippi River, about five miles south of Wyatt. The Cotton Belt railroad runs through there, and then you leave it and go down the river. Jesse'd rob the Illinois Central and row himself across the river to the willows, and he'd disappear. He had a tunnel there going underground to the well in his house. Or if they'd surround the house he'd go into the cistern, and swing off before he'd get to the water and crawl into the tunnel. Wasn't no levee on the Mississippi then.

Reason I know is that in '47 I was at Wyatt cooking for Morowe Levee Company, and the house burned down. And when they 'xamined it they could see the tunnel in the cistern. You could still go about a hundred yards in it each way.

Besides the oral legends, three other folklore developments have sprouted from Jesse's grave. The treasure that he buried in numerous caches continues to lure diggers, especially in the Ozark hills. In the tradition of the Returning Hero, who reappears after his alleged death to defend his people in time of crisis, ancient warriors have announced that Jesse James lives on in their emaciated frames. The last claimant, one year past the century mark, interviewed reporters while breakfasting off whiskey and doughnuts, but proved ill acquainted with his own past. Finally, two forms of the ballad of Jesse James have pushed firmly into folk tradition. They portray Jesse as a noble-hearted friend of the poor, and glorify the Mr. Howard who was shot by a dirty little coward.

VII

Modern Folklore

For two and a half centuries the American people were predominantly agricultural and rural, a nation of husbandmen. The city served as a marketplace for the countryside. Northerners and southerners alike tilled the soil. The outdoor occupations of lumbering, mining, cattle-raising, sailing before the mast, loomed large in the economy. All these conditions appeared propitious for folklore, whose students regarded the hinterland as its proper habitat. Then in the decades following the Civil War, the center of gravity rapidly shifted from country to city, from farm to factory, from old-fashioned ways to new-fangled inventions. A society of hustle and bustle took over the stage; the organization man succeeded the frontier individualist; the tradition-directed pockets of American life dwindled before the onward march of the other-directed generation. How in the face of mobility, technology, mass media and mass conformity could folk traditions breathe and survive? And could one speak of "modern" folklore when by definition folklore must have demonstrated its ability to live among human beings for a considerable time?

Folklorists have not attempted to answer these questions, tacitly assuming that the mass culture of contemporary America is traditionless. Yet, paradoxically, vast bodies of folklore have coagulated in the midst of urban industrial America, and intimately touch the lives of city dwellers, college youths, and service men and women.

FOLKTALES AND LEGENDS OF THE BIG CITY

Because the wonder tale and the animal fable have so preoccupied the scholars, no one has pointed out that the twentieth-century American is a tremendous storyteller and story-listener. He specializes in jokes, snappy and drawn-out, lily white and darkly off-color. They cover the major themes of modern life—religion, politics, business, as well as sex—and they are told incessantly, in private parties and at public gatherings. All age groups and both sexes relish jokes. At social get-togethers, old friends loyally tell each other the latest good one, and new acquaintances break the ice with a gag. One funny story automatically evokes another, and the swap session is under way: in the office, the car pool, the Pullman smoker, the convention hotel, at the cocktail party, the lodge luncheon, the church supper. In the Madison Avenue culture of the soft sell, with its premium on being-one-of-the-boysmanship, every personage deals in public relations, and every public speaker must relax his audience with laugh-provoking jests. The college professor, putting on a show for his tuition-paying clients, sandwiches in dabs of learning between tasty anecdotes. The insurance salesman softens his client with a belly laugh. Politicians, ministers, bankers, executives, and fund-raisers, all must turn storyteller and pray for a laugh. "That reminds me of a little story," begins the after-dinner speaker, and the audience, glutted with creamed chicken and peas, sink back torpidly waiting the signal to participate with forced guffaws in the rigid ritual of American banquetry. A rabbi, an educator, and a sales promotion manager of my acquaintance maintain elaborate files of comic anecdotes to insert in speeches.

President Conant of Harvard, whose address to his first graduating class, among whom I was numbered, left some doubt as to his staying power, had turned into a poised and fluent platform humorist when I heard him again fifteen years later. Among the string of stories and anecdotes he unreeled to a summer school convocation was included the witticism, apropos of the revolutionary decision permitting Radcliffe girls to attend classes with Harvard students, that not Harvard but Radcliffe was coeducational. Later I read the same story in *Newsweek* attributed to President Pusey, who may have inherited his predecessor's story files along with his august position.

The objection will certainly be made that contemporary American jokelore owes much to the mass media of radio, television, and journalism, and cannot properly be called an oral folk tradition. This objection will not stand up before closer inspection. Much jokelore—like folklore in general—is obscene, and so is barred from the mass media. Vaudeville and literary styles often impose special requirements on their material that differ from the needs of oral folk style. A joke has to be tailored to Jack Benny's personality, by his highly paid gag-writers. On the other hand, radio comedians like Bob Burns and Sam Levenson have indeed dipped into their own personal knowledge of folk humor in the Ozarks hills and on New York's Jewish Lower East Side. The folk can on occasion feed the mass media, and equally the media can feed back into oral lore, but a selective process is at work on both sides; folk and mass culture coexist peaceably and on friendly terms. The joke one tells at a party is much more frequently a good one the teller has heard than one he has read; he remembers the gestures, intonation, delivery of the previous raconteur along with the punch line, but all these personal touches are lacking in print, invisible on radio, and contrived on television. Finally we can document the unsuspected antiquity of a good many current jokes. The *Reader's Digest* and the jokebooks pick up old chestnuts *after* they have aged and actually furnish proof of their oral fame. Nor do good stories cease to be told in their original circles once they have lodged in print. Jokebooks are tiresome to read, but fresh, live, crackling jokes are endless fun to hear.

One example must here suffice. A story of great popularity in our present society revolves around a boastful man who claims he knows all the important people worth knowing. This boaster goes by different names; one is Harry Garrett. A skeptical friend challenges Harry to make good his contention. Harry calls on Roosevelt in Washington and Churchill in London, who slap him cordially on the back. Finally he flies to Rome to see the Pope and appears on the balcony with him overlooking St. Peter's Square, where His Holiness is about to bless a vast assembled multitude. Harry's friend, swallowed up in the crowd below, peers up at the two remote, dim figures

American Folklore

and then asks an Italian beside him who they are. "I don't know who the fellow with the beret is," the Italian replies, "but the one alongside him is Harry Garrett."

This story is told with innumerable variations. Sometimes it is given in Jewish dialect, and The Man-Who-Knows-Everybody is a Jewish merchant. The names of the prominent personalities change—Eisenhower has begun to replace Roosevelt —save for the Pope, around whom the climax and the punch line center. A history professor who first related the yarn to me included Mussolini with the Pope in the final scene, thus dating his version twenty years back to his college days in Brooklyn. My sales promotion friend from General Motors used his rendition on his auto dealers, to underscore the techniques of salesmanship through contacts. The story has traveled. In the Philippines it is attached to the scapegrace culture hero Juan Pusan; I heard it given at a party in Tokyo by an American serviceman; it is known in Great Britain with reverse English. A humble Irishman receives invitations to visit the priest of his parish, the bishop of his diocese, and finally the Pope at the Vatican, with the customary denouement. But instead of proclaiming his self-importance, he reiterates his unworthiness.

This is a modern American folktale. Its appeal lies in a comic exaggeration of American business values: getting ahead by knowing the right people, by having "contacts" in high places. Where in the British version the hero is a shrinking violet, in the American examples he is a loud and self-confident blowhard. Harry Garrett is indeed America's supersalesman, the Yankee peddler updated and slickened with twentieth-century know-how.

Modern Folklore

If jokelore has won a stable twentieth-century audience, pushing to the side its rival story forms from earlier eras, jokes themselves flutter in the breezes of fashion. In the last thirty years we have seen the mysterious emergence and recession of several joke cycles: the idiocies of little Audrey and the little moron; the long-drawn-out pointlessness and unbearable pun-lines of the shaggy dog story; the grisly humor of little Willie verses and "sick" jokes ("Otherwise how did you enjoy the play, Mrs. Lincoln?"). The fads come and go, but the relish for the pithy comic story remains an essential element of modern living.

City folk all know about jokes, even if they have not considered them as folktales, but they are unaware of another kind of traditional narrative which crosses their tongues. The legend —the story which never happened told for true—has anchored itself in the metropolis in urban guises. Certain stories will traverse the country, acquiring local details in each new city, and circulating among sophisticated city-dwellers as an extraordinary event, whose accuracy no one doubts. Such legends fasten particularly onto the automobile, chief symbol of modern America. In the tale of The Ghostly Hitchhiker, a fair young maiden signals for a lift from two youths returning home from a dance. They let her into the back seat and drive to the address she requests. On arriving, they discover the back seat is empty. In perplexity the lads knock on the door of the girl's supposed home, and explain to the gray-haired lady who answers what has happened. She beckons them to follow her into the living room and points to a framed picture of a young girl, whom they immediately recognize as their hitchhiker. "This is my daughter," announces the old lady

American Folklore

gravely. "She died in an accident on the corner where you met her, six years ago. Others have had the same experience as you."

Sometimes one of the youths lends the shivering girl a coat, which she takes with her into her house. He calls back the next day to retrieve his coat, and finds it wrapped around the tombstone of the long-dead girl.

The "Ghostly Hitchhiker" has been reported over one hundred times, and has been analyzed into four distinct subtypes. It is found as far as Hawaii, where a rickshaw supplants the auto, and is traced back to the nineteenth century, in America, Italy, Ireland, Turkey, and China, with a horse and wagon picking up the benighted traveler.

Another automobile legend, "The Death Car," first came to my attention in 1944, through the casual reference of a colleague in Lansing, Michigan. He said the Buick dealer downtown had been receiving numerous telephone calls about a second-hand car in which a man had died, and which was supposedly available for fifty dollars, because the death smell could not be removed. This was in wartime, when the automobile factories had gone into tank production, and no new cars were being made. Nonplussed at the phone calls, the dealer could only deny knowing anything about such a car.

Subsequently I learned that the same rumor had spread through many other cities, chiefly in Michigan. In every instance the person who related the story believed a Death Car had been offered for sale cheaply, and sometimes had even attempted to locate and purchase it, but never had anyone actually seen and smelled the automobile. Some students were highly indignant when I pointed out their accredited report as an example of a modern legend in our own midst. Meanwhile the variants accumulated in my archive, referring to different cities, different makes of car (though Buick predominated), different sales prices, and different causes of death. The driver had been shot at the wheel by a dude hunter in northern Michigan during the deer-hunting season; he had locked himself in his garage and inhaled carbon monoxide from the car engine; he had perished from thirst crossing the California desert when his car ran out of gas. Always some time elapsed before the automobile and the corpse were found, hence the pervasive stench of death.

In 1953 I was collecting Negro folklore in the tiny community of Mecosta in central Michigan, where a colony of colored people had settled on the sand barrens shortly after the Civil War. Called on to speak on folklore before the crowd that gathered on Old Settlers Day, I related the case of the depreciated Buick, as an instance of contemporary folklore. That evening some of the young fellows pulled me aside and politely explained that the incident had occurred in their town. A white man named Demings, who owned a 1929 Model-A Ford, committed suicide in it in 1938, after his girl, Nellie Boyers, had a spat with him on a date. He chinked up all the cracks under the seat and on the floorboards with concrete, and then sniffed a hose he had connected to his tailpipe, while the motor ran. This was in August, and the car and the body were not found until hunting season in October. A guide kept returning to the spot where Demings had pulled the car off the road into the brush, and seeing the car would say,. "That fellow's always hunting when I am." Finally he investigated.

This Model-A was painted all over with birds and fish, and was quite an eye-catcher. A used-car dealer in Remus sold the car to Clifford Cross, who tried every expedient to eradicate the smell. He reupholstered and fumigated the interior, in vain, and finally had to drive around in midwinter with the windows wide open. At length he turned the car in for junk.

I talked with Clifford Cross and his friends who had ridden in the Ford. Here was the first verified case of the Death Car. Did this modern big-city legend originate with an actual incident in a hamlet of two hundred people in a rural Negro community and by the devious ways of folklore spread to Michigan's metropolises, and then to other states? Unlikely as it seems, the evidence from many variants, compared through the historical-geographical method of tracing folktales, calls for an affirmative answer.

In recent years a street in Detroit has gained the reputation of being haunted. Different streets in several sections of the city are named and the details vary, but all accounts agree that a little girl was struck and killed by a hit-and-run driver, and that ever since cars driving over that street hear bumps from the child's body dragging behind the fender. Some say that one of her arms was cut off and that the arm is thumping against the doors of passing cars. Others ascribe the bumping noise to a curse placed on the road by the mother (or the father). In several versions the girl was riding a bicycle when the speeder ran her down, and she knocked vainly on his door to attract his attention, before losing her balance and falling under the wheels of the car. So many drivers heard the knocks that complaints reached the Detroit Department of Roads, who tore up and repaved the street, but the knocks continued. The legend reached the Detroit papers, and curious drivers thronged the street, causing so much traffic that a policeman had to be stationed there. A number of my students drove down the street in question, and all without exception reported the thumps. Some suggested natural explanations, such as air pockets in the cement or cracks in the pavement. The legend has traveled to nearby Ann Arbor, Michigan, and Toledo, Ohio.

Rumors spread about remarkable inventions which would improve automobiles, A carburetor that will give fifty miles to the gallon is being kept off the market by the big oil companies. But an experimental model inadvertently slips into a customer's hands, who informs his dealer with astonished delight about the fine mileage he has been getting. Hastily the dealer offers another car in exchange, saying this model was not intended for sale. Similar stories deal with the tire that will never wear out, and the razor blade that will last forever. These reports are thoroughly credited and told with circumstantial detail.

Department stores as well as automobiles attract modern legends. Certain famous stores, like the lavish Nieman-Marcus in Dallas, grow into public institutions as well as merchandise marts and acquire a legendary aura. Tales circulate of the princely shopper who purchased three vicuña coats at one time, and of the oilman who ordered an electric comforter for his pet lion. Other stories go the rounds from Macy's in New York to Hudson's in Detroit to Marshall Field's in Chicago. A well-dressed dowager pays for a small purchase with a hundred-dollar bill. The clerk takes it to the cashier to be checked, and the dowager screams her indignation. The bill is good, and milady stalks off in a huff. Next day she returns to the same counter, presents another hundred-dollar bill for a trinket, and this time is promptly given her change by the abashed clerk. But this bill is counterfeit.

A ubiquitous department store legend concerns the Dead Cat in the Package. Intending to dispose of her deceased pet, an elderly spinster wraps Tabby up in brown paper and goes downtown. She tries to leave the package in a street car, but another passenger returns it to her. She is about to throw it in a garbage can when she sees a policeman eying her suspiciously. Finally she enters a department store, and while making a purchase, has her parcel stolen by a shoplifter. The store detective, noticing the theft, immediately instigates a search. At length the shoplifter is discovered in the ladies' room, in a hysterical condition, with the dead cat on her lap. In some versions, the old lady returns home without having been able to dispose of the package, opens it for one last look at pussy, and finds a leg of mutton.

The recurrent motif of the hair-turned-white enters another macabre legend. In J. L. Hudson's Department Store in Detroit, a woman entered an elevator car before it had completely stopped, and was caught with her body hanging inside the shaft and only her head visible to the passengers inside. The body fell down the shaft twelve floors, while the head was decapitated and rolled into the car. The hair had turned completely white from the shock, and all the women in the car fainted. Another account places the blame on a careless operator, who closed the doors too soon. A third party states, "This really happened in Flint, in the building where my father worked. And it wasn't due to a careless operator. The cable broke and that is why the car fell."

THE FOLKLORE OF COLLEGE STUDENTS

When she comes tripping by, stone lions will bark. A Revolutionary War cannon will fire out. Two facing statues will solemnly dismount from their pedestals, walk to the center of the courtyard, and clasp hands in congratulation. A series of boulders, delicately balanced atop each other by nature's art, will suddenly collapse. When she gazes their way, the Flattop Mountains will turn purple with rage.

On college campuses throughout the country these various signs will greet her achievement. For she will be the first virgin to graduate from the university. One report states that the teetering rocks on the University of Alabama campus did once topple to the earth, when an undefiled soul passed by. It belonged to a young man.

Every college and university in the land possesses some odd faculty member whose behavior makes legends. At Exeter I remember hearing tales about an extremely cross-eyed Latin master, whom we called "Squint" among ourselves. Enraged in class one time, Squint glared at a squirming student and roared, "Look out, I've got my eye on you!" "Which eye?" the student asked innocently. In another irate mood Squint commanded, "You in the back row stand up," transfixing a malefactor with his wrathful gaze. Thereupon six students stood up. I always accepted these stories as gospel until recently, when I began to see the ways of college folklore.

At Harvard a number of anecdotes cluster around the historian Albert Bushnell Hart, who kept pottering about the library after his retirement. Folklore says that from force of habit he took careful notes on all the books he handled each afternoon and then tore all the notes up before going home. A curious librarian noticed him browsing in the fine arts section for several days and examined the books Hart had been using. Around every nude figure he found a penciled circle—proof of Hart's ever-youthful outlook. Resurrected to present a paper at the installation of a high school principal, Hart dutifully read the speech his secretary had typed for him, including the two carbon copies she had forgot to remove.

The classic absent-minded professor story concerns the pundit who drove his car to a destination, took a train back, and bawled out his wife for not meeting him at the station with the auto. A variation on this theme recently appeared in the *Harvard Alumni Bulletin,* which reported that Professor William J. Cunningham, holder of the chair in transportation at the business school, had dropped his wife at a mailbox and then continued on his journey. Some time later he noticed her absence and informed the police. But I have heard the same story told on a mathematics professor of the University of Michigan, whose wife went to the restroom when he stopped for gas and came out to find him gone. Worse yet, she had newly arrived in this country and could speak no English.

Professors are important, campus-wise, chiefly because they give grades. How they arrive at their decisions, folklore alone knows. The old story of course is that the prof throws the bluebooks down the stairs, and gives *A*'s to those which land at the foot, *F*'s to those at the head. Or he throws them at the ceiling, and whichever stick receive an *A*. A Harvard tale has chemistry professor J. P. Cooke distributing his papers to his family; he gave the *E*'s himself, his son-in-law the *D*'s, and so on up to the baby, who being the slowest marked the *A*'s. From way back I recall the tale of the professor who customarily placed his papers in two heaps, representing the good and the bad students. When he came across an error by a good student he disregarded it, saying "He knows better than that." When he saw a correct answer by a poor student he marked it wrong, saying "He couldn't have meant that."

Examinations, the source of grades, provide folktales. Around

Modern Folklore

Harvard they still talk about Robert Benchley's feat in handling a question in American diplomatic history on rights to the Newfoundland fisheries. Benchley knew nothing about the matter, so he wrote, "This question has long been discussed from the American and British points of view, but has anyone ever considered the viewpoint of the fish?" He proceeded to give it, and was awarded, appropriately enough, a *C*.

There is a sheaf of stories about the dumb star-athlete. His coach instructs him to sit next to the class grind for the crucial exam. Forty-nine questions the two answer identically. On the fiftieth the brilliant student writes, "I don't know the answer to this," so the athlete puts down, "I don't know the answer either." Then they tell of the football star who received such encomiums in the press that the dean asked the coach, "Won't all this praise go to his head?" "No," said the coach, "he can't read."

As the prof is lowly and comical, so the coach is lofty and admired. Which college president was it whose salary was raised to make it equal that of the football coach? Anyway tales constantly spring up of coaches' magic. For instance, Adolph Rupp, the wizard basketball coach at the University of Kentucky, lays his luck to the fact that the door to his office is exactly six feet high. If an ambitious freshman enters without stooping, Rupp doesn't even bother to stand up and shake his hand. Bennie Bierman of the University of Minnesota used a similar technique in culling football talent. On a scouting trip he drove through a farm area until he came to a young fellow plowing. He asked him, "Where is the university?" and if the young man pointed the direction with his hand, Bierman drove on. If however, he lifted his plow to show the direction, Bierman stopped to explain how attractive his attendance at the university could be. This plow-lifting stunt is told on several European folk heroes.

Deans too grow into legends, and the dean of women leads all the rest. Her advice to new coeds echoes across the country. Never wear patent leather shoes on a date; they reflect. Never wear a red dress; it inflames. Don't eat olives; they're passion pills. Always carry along a telephone book (or a newspaper, or a copy of the *Saturday Evening Post*) in case your date asks you to sit on his lap. A coed must turn the picture of her boy friend to the wall before undressing at night.

In spite of these warnings, coeds do manage to have some fun. Just becoming a coed involves certain traditional procedures that the lady dean would be horrified to learn. A mild one is that at Michigan State University, where a girl becomes a coed when kissed in the shadow of Beaumont Tower at the stroke of midnight. At Purdue the requirements are more demanding. Girl kisses boy under the arch of the clock tower at Havoline Hall, on the first stroke of the chimes at midnight. Then both race across campus to John Purdue's grave and commence more serious business before the last chimes strike.

A grisly legend that turns up in various forms is known as the Fatal Fraternity Initiation. The pledge is tied to a chair, blindfolded, and told that his arm is to be cut open. The back of the blade is pressed against his skin, while a wet towel is hung over a chair and drips into a bucket, to simulate bleeding. The actives tell the pledge they will return later. When they come back in a couple of hours, the boy is dead. Sometimes the pledge is led blindfolded to the edge of a supposed cliff, and drops two feet to die of shock. Or he is to be singed with a hot poker, which is pressed against raw meat at the same time that a piece of ice is held on the pledge's skin. He smells the burning meat, thinks it is his own flesh, and crumples up dead. In a sorority initiation the pledge was blindfolded and told to shake the hand of a dead man. The actives thrust a pickled hand they had swiped from the laboratory into her hand, then ran out of the room and locked the door. In the morning they found their sister with snow-white hair, nibbling on the pickled hand. A Harvard man varied this stunt by gluing a coin to a pickled hand and breezily extending it to a toll-gate keeper from his car window. Coin and hand came away in the keeper's grasp, and he dropped dead from shock.

On various campuses a pledge is enticed to see the widow, or the farmer's daughter, or the trucker's wife. She is lonely and friendly, soft and cuddly. Eagerly the pledge accompanies his pals to her abode on the edge of town. But alas, the father, or husband, returns unexpectedly, cursing and shooting, and young Lochinvar takes off into the night with buckshot dancing around his heels, and no inkling that it is all a put-up job. This haze at least does not end fatally, save for the freshman's hopes.

Campus cries form still another aspect of collegiate tradition. At Harvard "Rinehart" rallies the mob for action and thus memorializes a lonesome alumnus. Poor Rinehart, lacking friends, would go beneath his window and call out his own name, to make the neighbors think him popular. Some say that he actually was popular. At the University of California the cry is "Pedro," and the explanations myriad. Pedro is the ghost of a student who dropped dead from the shock of getting all A's and now assists cramming undergrads when they call him in their distress. Or he is the ghost of an Indian whose tepee was razed to build the library, and who still hangs angrily about. Or again he is the date of a girl who found herself locked out of the dorm and called after him in despair. Anyway "Pedro" voices the soul yearnings of Berkeley bookworms on soft spring nights.

Anyone who would penetrate the mind of American collegians must know their songs. The undergraduate inherits a spirited grab-bag of folksongs from upperclassmen and sings them lustily at dorm bull sessions, beer busts, fraternity and sorority parties, and most any convivial occasion. The tunes are standard Tin Pan Alley stuff latched on to parodies and originals. The texts rise up spontaneously and spread mysteriously. Some classics seem to be familiar to college students everywhere; one fall coming back from Europe on a ship carrying fourteen hundred assorted students, I saw casual groups form on deck and join into lyric after lyric without benefit of songbooks or prompters. Most of the songs wouldn't look well in print anyway.

The *leitmotif* in college balladry is love, but not Tin Pan Alley or Hollywood brands of love. Dimpled, cherubic coeds sing the praises of an earthy, physical passion, of an insatiable sex mania. One group of their songs twines around wicked women and their lures: Flamin' Mamie, "a love scorcher and a human torture"; Mimi the College Widow, who taught the boys anatomy; Gumdrop Sal, the friendly Eskimo Queen, whose husband stayed out all night, in a land where the nights are six months long. But the chief beguiler, head and fins above the rest, is "Minnie the Mermaid."

> Many's the night I spent with Minnie the mermaid,
> Down at the bottom of the sea.
> She forgot her morals, down among the corals,
> Gee but she was good to me.

Modern Folklore

Many's the night when the pale moon was shining,
Down on her bungalow.
Ashes to ashes, dust to dust,
Two twin beds and only one of them mussed.

Oh it's easy to see she's not my mother,
'Cause my mother's forty-nine.
And it's easy to see she's not my sister,
'Cause I'd never give my sister such a helluva good time.

And it's easy to see she's not my sweetie,
'Cause my sweetie's too refined.
She's just a cute little kid who never knew what she did,
She's just a personal friend of mine.

In reverse plot stands the well-known fate of "The Lady in Red," reduced to begging a night's shelter under the bar. The moral to overambitious coeds: beware the ways of college men, "and how they come—and go."

There are various apostrophes to beer, gin, rum, and whiskey and an epic ballad about an Irish wake.

The night that Paddy Murphy died
I never shall forget,
The whole damn town got stinkin' drunk,
And some ain't sober yet.
The only thing they did that night
That filled my heart with fear,
They took the ice right off the corpse
And put it in the beer.

CHORUS:

That's how they showed their respect for Paddy Murphy,
That's how they showed their honor and their pride,
Ho-ho-ho, that's how they showed their respect for Paddy Murphy,
On the night that Paddy died.

When they finished with the beer they started on the corpse.
They took him from his coffin and put him on the porch,

And then they went next door and stole a neighbor's pig
And brought it back to Paddy's house and tied it on his leg.

A college story about Paddy Murphy says that he came to the States from County Cork, spent his life cheating on and beating up his wife, and died of acute alcoholism. His relatives assembled for a handsome wake. They duly passed the body and kissed the forehead, when cousin Maureen felt a movement and screamed to Mrs. Murphy, "He's hot, he's hot!" "Hot or cold, he goes out in the morning," said the grieving widow.

At Northwestern University the alcoholic exploits of Paddy Murphy receive each fall appropriate funeral rites, sponsored by the local Sigma Alpha Epsilon chapter. A procession three blocks long files from the chapter house to the outskirts of Evanston, the marchers festooned in green and tearfully draining beer bottles as they follow the corpse, itself composed of dead beer bottles, with a red lamp bulb for a nose. Upon reaching the grave, which has been dug by pledges, the mourners light candles and break into the Paddy Murphy song. An active attired in priestly robes renders the service, paying tribute to Paddy's inspiring and heroic drunks. En route to the grave the Sigma Chi's attempt to purloin the corpse, and so seriously do the ΣΑΕ's defend their honor that in 1945 one circled the procession in a plane to warn his fellow actives of the enemy's approach.

The group loyalties of college folk find expression in odes of sentiment and corny humor to fraternities and sororities and to the alma mater. Serious songs of love and devotion are used to serenade the newly pinned coed or to entertain a visiting sorority. They crawl with romantic clichés. But the undergrad has no scruples about parodying himself and will compose such a slurring "Ode to a Sigma Chi" as this:

Modern Folklore

The girl of my dreams has bobbed her hair
And dyed it a fiery red,
She drinks, she smokes, and she tells dirty jokes,
She hasn't a brain in her head.
The girl of my dreams is a cigarette fiend,
She drinks more booze than I.
But the girl of my dreams is not what she seems,
She's the sweetheart of six other guys.

College students possess a lively and varied miscellany of games. The folklorist, himself bound by tradition, has concentrated on children's games, which have now acquired the respectability of lavish comparative annotation, but the traditional pastimes of undergraduates have gone unheeded. In other-directed university life, where students prepare for the years ahead with extensive extracurricular socializing, games play a vital role. They introduce the sexes, drain off the energies of high-voltage adolescents, and supply the gaiety necessary to sustain the American ethos of happiness and good times. The games begin in grade school and high school, and broaden out in the enforced congeniality of sorority, fraternity, and dormitory mixers and house-party galas. Kissing games like "Spin the Bottle" and "Wink-um" commence in the early teens, and speed up into raucous beer-bust entertainments in the college years. Some common mental games like "Guggenheim," "Ghosts," and "Geography" are found in the college repertoire, but for the most part new and energetic creations regale the crowd. There are practical jokes, burlesque skits, dialogues, stunts, divinations, dance routines, mystery and logic puzzles, and hearty drinking games. Physical action, through mimicking, gesticulating, and athletic drinking, sparks the hilarity.

The date, the crush, the steady, and the future mate dominate the thoughts of undergraduates, who borrow from age-old divination rituals to ascertain their future paths of love. Indeed with the increasing precocity of American youth, these games of prophecy take on urgency among high school teen-agers, and even grade-schoolers. "Some children base their friendship towards the opposite sex upon the answers to this game," writes a college student, describing an ingenious "Method for Telling Whether or Not Your Loved One Loves You," through manipulation of the letters in lovers' names.

From the many hours whiled away on coke dates, a modern form of "He loves me, he loves me not" has developed, with drinking straws replacing flower petals. Upon finishing her drink, the coed twists the straw around each of her fingers in turn, while repeating:

> He loves me, he don't,
> He'll marry me, he won't,
> He would if he could, he could if he would,
> But he won't.

The line she utters as she reaches the end of the straw gives the prophecy. But there is more to come. A girl friend names the ends of the straw for two boy friends. Betty Coed presses her two index fingers on the middle of the straw and flattens it out toward the ends. The prophecy applies to the boy named for the end of the straw she flattens first. Now she tears the straw in two and forms a cross. She folds the ends over and over, taking a new end each time, until the four last tag ends remain. Then, wishbone fashion, she pulls one of these ends while her friend pulls another, making her wish. If both girls have hold of the same piece, the wish is doomed. If however lover girl pulls a free piece, her wish will come true, provided she places it in her shoe and keeps it there until fulfillment. Many a girl has worn out her piece walking on it in her shoe.

Modern Folklore

Another modernized love forecast replaces horses with automobiles. To discover the man you will marry, count one hundred red convertibles, look for a redhaired woman wearing a purple dress and a man with a green tie, and then wait for a boy to speak to you. The first one who does will become your husband. This divination is allied to the popular kissing game of "Padiddle," which permits the boy friend to kiss his date after spotting a one-eyed convertible and crying "Padiddle."

Drinking games mark off the men from the boys and the coeds from the bobby-soxers. The basic formula upon which the game patterns are built is simply chug-a-lug, which can serve as a game in itself. Each drinker in the group must down his glass, or bottle, in one fell gulp. Should he set his glass down with any beer remaining, he must pay for the next round. To chug-a-lug has thus become a verb of considerable collegiate import, and serves as the penalty for more ritualized drinking ceremonies, like "Cardinal Puff," the beer-bust classic. Seeking to become a cardinal, the candidate, seated among his peers in a jolly tavern, orders a round of beers, and solemnly intones, "Here's to Cardinal Puff for the first time this evening."

> Then he drinks *one* sip of the beer.
> He taps the table *once* with his glass.
> He hits the table *once* with one finger of his right hand.
> He hits the table *once* with one finger of his left hand.
> He taps the floor *once* with his right foot.
> He taps the floor *once* with his left foot.
> He rises up in his seat and sits down *once*.

Then he repeats the procedure, doubling and tripling the actions. Upon any mistake, he must chug-a-lug his glass and begin afresh with a new stein. If he completes his part successfully, he is a Cardinal Puff, and the play passes to the person on the left. When whiskey is consumed instead of beer, the player becomes a bishop. There are of course variations in the rites of tapping, rising, and holding the glass. In the version known as "Colonel Powwow," all present imitate the actions of the Colonel. If anyone laughs he must chug-a-lug. In "Cardinal Poof" the group in unison exclaim "Here's to Cardinal Poof," and take five successive drinks, upon which everyone turns his glass upside down on the table; if a rim is left, the procedure must be repeated, until the rimless drinker qualifies as a Cardinal Poof.

Adept at converting innocent lore to the services of demon beer, the tavern crowd has seized on a tantalizing tongue-twister for another excuse to chug-a-lug. The leader utters the first line of the teaser, each participant repeats it, the leader then gives the second line, and so until the tenth and last line, with the usual penalties for miscues. Here is one version of the twister:

A big fat hen.
A couple of ducks.
Three brown bears.
Four furious fire fighters.
Five fat females feeling fine.
Six simple simons sitting on a stump.
Seven sexy Siamese sailors sailing the seven seas.
Eight elongated elephants elevated on an elevator.
Nine nymphonious nude nymphs nibbling on the nemises of nothing.
Ten twin turtles tootling "Twilight Time" on twenty twinkling trumpets.

The verses change madly. Other last lines are:

Ten tiny Turks tripping through the trees.
Ten titanic taliputs tooting into Tucson on Tuesday at ten a.m.
Ten Turkish tankers transporting tanks to Tunis at ten on Tuesday.

Modern Folklore

College students have their serious moments. The proof can be seen in a recent game fad to sweep the campuses, requiring serious intellectual concentration. Known as parlor mysteries, logic games, or thought puzzles, they are calculated to sharpen the ratiocinative powers of the students, who must deduce a logical conclusion from illogical facts. Logic games are a modernized riddle with a shaggy-dog twist. Example: A lawyer and a doctor were having lunch together, when the doctor suddenly looked up and exclaimed, "My God, there's my wife!" The lawyer pulled out a gun and shot the doctor. Why? Answer: The lawyer was a woman in love with the doctor and didn't know he was married. Or this one: A man living in an apartment building on the tenth floor took the elevator down every morning, but on returning in the evening he rode up only to the fifth floor, and walked the rest of the way. Why? Answer: The man was a midget, the elevator was self-operated, and he could only reach to the fifth button. Of the fifty odd logic puzzles, the murder of the one-armed man is as far-fetched as any. Why did four sailors kill and chew off the arm of a man found dead in the streets of London? Answer: They had been shipwrecked on an island and forced to eat one of their own arms to survive when a passing ship ignored their distress signal. Upon finally being rescued, they swore to chew off the right arm of any sailor they met from the vessel that had left them stranded.

The enterprising folklorist need not journey into the back hills to scoop up tradition. He can set up his recording machine in the smokeshop or the union grill.

American Folklore

With the radical if reluctant change initiated in 1939 from demilitarization to peacetime drafts and a large standing army, a standing body of folklore also took its station on the American scene. Vast numbers of men now regularly serve in the Army, Navy, Marines, and Air Force, and uniformed women make up the WAC's, WAVE's, and WAF's. The Second World War, the Korean conflict, and the Cold War have maintained wartime tension for two decades. A military tradition has indeed come to roost in the peace-loving Republic. The armed services constitute an occupational in-group, comparable in folklore terms to cowboys, lumberjacks, and sailors, and even more to college students, since a fairly rapid change in personnel takes place, although the framework of the tradition remains constant. The undergraduates and draftees stay in harness long enough to inherit the existing lore and pass it on to their successors.

Volumes of floating lore swirl through the armed services. American soldiers, sailors, and airmen turn to humorous expression as relief from boredom, irritation, and tension. The experiences of war spew up countless exploits and escapes enshrined in legend. Rumors and hoaxes travel furiously in the atmosphere of global propagandistic warfare. The imminent presence of death brings to the fore age-old beliefs in talismans and amulets, signs and omens, jinxes and jonahs. Men living in barracks or in combat units form natural human channels for the transmission of oral lore. They swap ribald jokes and sensational incidents, play rough tricks on recruits, and sing lustily on the march. The presence of women in the armed

Modern Folklore

forces adds new material to time-honored themes of barracks yarns. Specialized groups of technicians and fighting men develop traditions of their own: paratroopers, Seabees, submarine crews. Certain colorful and salty personalities grow toward folk-hero status. An occupational folk speech takes form in the vocabularies of servicemen.

Out of this vast welter of jokes, gags, gripes, rumors, customs, and song parodies, the folklorist finds many items that clearly qualify as oral, traditional, and widely traveled. They have risen from incarnations in earlier wars, or are found in variant forms among all the services, or penetrate to the civilian population. The influence of print needs to be considered, with war humor gaining currency in four hundred service newspapers and magazines, the mass media of civilian life, and such widely read collections as Bennett Cerf's *The Pocket Book of War Humor*. On the other hand, from its licentious nature much service humor can never see print. An intermediary form between the spoken and the printed tale is the polysyllabic burlesque of military orders and regulations and the sophisticated verse satire of top brass, which are surreptitiously copied and circulated in typescript form.

The examples of service folklore that follow were collected by me personally or come from unpublished variants in the Indiana University Folklore Archives.

Because of the close connections between military and civilian lives in the United States, where the soldier is a uniformed youth rather than a professional warrior, certain army folktales pass muster among the people at large. We think of the Kilroy gags, or witticisms about the Pentagon, or cracks concerning second lieutenants and ensigns. One story of Pentagon snafu I heard as a civilian on three different occasions, always told as actuality:

There were some funny classification mixups during the war. A math professor by the name of W. E. Smith was commissioned at Fort Schuyler and then sent to Washington to get his orders. He expected to teach math in one of the naval programs, as there was then a serious shortage of instructors. However, his orders instructed him to proceed to Boston and board a destroyer, where he would find further orders. This considerably surprised him, but his friends insisted that Washington knew what it was doing and that the matter would duly be explained. He went to Boston, boarded the destroyer, and opened his second orders, which read that he was to command the ship in convoy duty to England. Smith called the junior officers together, explained to them his situation, and told them to tell him what to do. He stayed in his cabin all the trip to England. On subsequent trips he learned his way around, took actual command, and shot down several subs.

Some time later Smith received another call to Washington. As he was waiting outside the designated office, he saw another lieutenant pacing up and down and muttering angrily to himself: "How can they do that to me, me a graduate of Annapolis and they send me to teach mathematics at college. And I haven't had any math since my freshman year!" Smith, interested on hearing this, asked the man his name, and learned that it too was W. E. Smith.

This legend embodies the general American distrust of bureaucracy and military brass, symbolized by the hapless Pentagon. An unverified rumor alleged that a messenger boy entered the Pentagon one day and came out two weeks later, bearded, the message undelivered, and he promoted to lieutenant colonel.

The origin of GI itself is credited to the First World War. Instead of originating in the last conflict as a shortening of "Government Issue," one tradition assigns the initials to "Galvanized Iron." In the training camps of the 1917 war, soldiers sat on galvanized iron pails in lieu of proper latrines, and there shot the bull, hence the term GI.

One of the most popular folktales of the last war dealt with the "Kush-Maker." A draftee in the Navy states his occupation as a "kush-maker"—or kletch, splooch, kaplush, gleek, kaswish, kloosch, squish; the designation varies in every telling. Not wishing to show ignorance, the CO assigned the man to duties in the hold, where he remained until the admiral came to inspect the ship. Running down the ship's roster, he spied the kush-maker, and demanded an explanation. The kush-maker is summoned forth, and makes elaborate preparations for the display of his special skill; in the end a complicated steel sphere is hoisted over the ship's side, or even lowered from an airplane, into the water below, making the sound of "kush," or its equivalent. Curiously, a comparable tale, attached to a blacksmith, is credited both to Davy Crockett and Abraham Lincoln.

In occupational folklore, the greenhorn becomes the butt of many errands for plausible sounding but nonexistent tools, like a left-handed monkey wrench. Rookies and raw recruits in the services fall heir to this traditional role. They are sent for a shore line, a bunk-stretcher, buckets of propwash, a skyhook, ceiling jacks to raise the ceiling in poor flying weather, striped paint, a gun to shoot the sun. The classification officer informs the hillbilly trainee that openings in aerial submarines are filled, but that he might qualify for underwater aircraft. A smart aleck at the classification center is offered a position as "Tester of Rejected Parachutes," with this inducement: "You know, nylon is scarce, and we want to be sure that we're not throwing away good chutes. The plane lets you go from ten thousand feet, so there's plenty of time for them to open.

American Folklore

Of course when you land you have to fill out sixteen different forms giving all the details of the jump. However, if the chute doesn't open you don't have to fill out the forms." This hoaxing recalls the oft-told tale of the raw paratrooper whose regular and emergency chutes both fail to open on his first jump. Much disgusted, he mutters on his way down, "And I'll bet that truck they promised would pick me up when I landed won't be there either."

What may have originated as a scare story told a trainee grew into a legend associated with nearly every training camp in the United States. It was told me for true in 1943 by a student in my Army Specialized Training Program (ASTP) class. Trainees taking basic infantry training were required to crawl through an infiltration course covered with barbed wire entanglements and land mines, while machine guns fired live ammunition thirty-six inches above their heads. One rookie had penetrated the barbed wire and crawled to within fifteen feet of the end of the course, when he found himself facing a rattlesnake. Panic-stricken he stood up, and the machine guns cut him in two. The rattlesnake at Fort Riley, Kansas, changes to a cottonmouth moccasin in Georgia, a side-winder at Fort Sill, Oklahoma, an armadillo at Fort Hood, and a gila monster at Camp Carson, Colorado. As told in the Marine Corps, a marine marching in column up a steep incline suddenly faced a ten-foot rattlesnake, coiled to strike. He chose to leap several hundred feet over the cliff, rather than suffer the rattlesnake's bite. Still another variant has the trainee taking part in night maneuvers in Arizona, under the false impression that live ammunition was being fired. As the soldier moved cautiously toward an enemy machine gun nest, a shell burst close by him, illuminating the area. He glimpsed a foxhole nearby, and dove for the bottom. The foxhole was actually a rattlesnake nest, and he was instantly bitten to death. In a combat version, the accidental death is reversed into a miraculous escape. A young private was lying in a foxhole in New Guinea under heavy fire from the Japanese, when he beheld a deadly coral snake inches away. In terror he jumped to his feet and ran to another foxhole, while machine gun bullets shot him three times through the legs. The doctors said later that he could not possibly have run upon his shattered limbs.

Goldbricking furnished a favorite theme for stories of the enlisted man, and contributed choice folktales about medical discharges. One elaborate stratagem has the goldbricker ride an imaginary motorcycle all over camp, in close order drill, on long hikes, in the mess hall. He mounts it, gives a kick or two, and starts off, holding the handlebars and put-putting with his mouth. Called in by the CO, he rides into his office, screeches to a halt, jumps off, and salutes smartly. The CO puts him in the hospital for observation, and the soldier rides happily up and down the corridors, leaving the cycle at the foot of the bed. Once he bumped into a nurse and muttered something about "These damn women drivers." On another occasion he screamed that someone had stolen his machine and searched everywhere before he finally found it under the bed. At length the hospital psychiatrists decided he must be loony and granted his discharge on a section eight (insanity). He mounted his motorcycle, rode to the hospital entrance, parked it by the gate, and walked off. "Hey, don't you want your motorcycle," the orderly yelled after him. "No thanks, I don't need it any more," answered our hero.

The serviceman has his deeply serious side, and duly honors the ways of propitiating fate. Soldiers in the European

Theater turned their rings and identification disks toward home. As the war neared its close, a few foolhardy GI's turned their rings and tags toward Berlin. Many soldiers were killed in the last days of the war.

Navy men on shore leave abhor whistling, if there is a ring around the moon or when an outfit is being shipped out. Someone whistled the day an outfit sailed for the Pacific zone, and that outfit was lost at sea. Aboard ship no one ever whistles.

Flyers on completing their flying time always give a gift, of clothes or trinkets, to pilots still on missions, to pass on their good luck. During their missions they wore the same suit of underwear, to preserve their luck. The candy bar they received before taking off they never saved to eat on the homeward leg; this was tempting fate.

On hospital grounds, animals were harbingers of death. A cat came into the ward of a veterans' hospital in the Bronx in the summer of 1948 and stopped at the bed of Private Lonze Warner, wounded by shrapnel. Four days later Warner died.

A vast miscellany of songs floats up from the barracks and quarters of servicemen. They include popular hits, old standbys, parodies, originals, bawdy ballads, college songs. Some of these pieces qualify as folksongs, and the most representative folksong is known by its chorus, "Gee mom, I want to go home." Adopted by the Army, Navy, and Marines, this lugubrious plaint echoes such favorite ballads of the cowboys as "The Old Chisholm Trail" and of the lumberjacks as "The Shantyman's Life," which recite in doleful stanzas the hardships of a particular calling.

Modern Folklore

"I Don't Like Navy Life"

They say that in the Navy
The biscuits are so fine
But one dropped off the table
And killed a pal of mine.

CHORUS:

I don't like Navy life.
Gee Mom, I want to go
Right back to Quantico,
Gee Mom, I want to go home.

They say that in the Navy
The pay is very fine.
They give you fifty dollars
And take back forty-nine.

They say that in the Navy
The coffee is so fine.
It's good for cuts and bruises
And tastes like iodine.

They say that in the Navy
The chicken is so fine.
A leg dropped off the table
And started marking time.

. . . . .

They say that in the Navy
The clothes are mighty fine,
But I need Lana Turner
To fill out part of mine.

. . . . .

Lethal missiles and engines of death have rendered war more
terrifying than ever, but a softer element has entered too, with

the induction of women into the services. The following lament reflects the change in atmosphere.

> There's lipstick on the drinking fount,
> There's talcum on the bench,
> There's cold cream on the service plate,
> Hand lotion on the wrench,
> And Evening In Paris scents the air
> That once held the lube oil's smell,
> I just picked up a bobby pin.
> Believe me! War is hell!!

The present chapter has merely sampled the folklore of modern life. Large areas of contemporary American civilization are surely rich in traditions which yet remain to be collected. We can think of labor unions, white-collar occupations, the sports and entertainment world, as such areas. We know little about the folklore that feeds popular prejudices. If mobility has tended to diminish the sense of traditional roots, it has created another kind of lore, the hokum and blarney delighting the tourist. The wonders of the New World that seventeenth-century travelers reported to astonished Europeans live on still in the twentieth-century America of production miracles, success stories, fabulous fortunes, and Hollywood heroes.

A Last Word on Folklore

What are the future prospects for America's multihued and variegated folk traditions? Beyond question the forces of technology are stirring up the quiet, long-standing pools of regional culture where folklore breeds so abundantly. Even in my own collecting span I have seen giant bridges tie down to earth three lonely paradises: the Upper Peninsula of Michigan, Dauphin Island off the Alabama Gulf shore, and Beals Island high on the Maine coast. Increasingly have I contended with the din of radio and the mesmerism of television when informants were at home, and fretted when they were out, because the automobile has given wings to the old tale-tellers and ballad-singers, who refuse to sit peacefully in wait for the collector.

Yet the collector too benefits from technology. He now goes into the field highly mechanized and ready to cope with his fugitive sources. Equipped with a battery of tape recorders, from a tiny Wollensak to a majestic Ampex, plus a still camera, and on special occasions a motion picture rig, he can snare his informant in a trice, capture his voice and image on tape and film, and return home to process his loot at leisure in the archives.

In spite of the accelerated pace of modern living, which seems to strike at our roots and very identity, the folklorist marvels at the tenacity of tradition. Veer off the main highway for a little distance, and the civilization of rocket ships and automation suddenly melts away. All this time the legend of Barney Beal has flourished in coastal Maine, coincident with the manufactured hullabaloo about Paul Bunyan. The back-country speech of Lincoln echoed through the White House in the plain accents of Harry Truman, whose folk appeal was much misunderstood by the columnists and businessmen. Read reporter John Hersey's account of one day he spent with President Truman, and you can see in the Missouri President's peppery idioms and barnyard metaphors the Lincolnesque folk flavor. In the anonymous submerged mass of our population, the old folklore continues still with undiminished vitality. Only yesterday, as I write this, a woman downtown related a macabre legend of five babes drowned by their unwed mother in a rain barrel and hidden in the stairwell woodbox of a Kentucky log cabin, where their wailings chilled the inmates until the bones were discovered and buried. "That wasn't superstition, that really happened." The idea that folklore is dying out is itself a kind of folklore.

Important Dates

1647 Spectral ship sighted over New Haven harbor

1675 Prodigies herald King Philip's War and Bacon's Rebellion
John Josselyn, *An Account of Two Voyages to New England* (traveler's tales of New World wonders)

1684 Increase Mather, *An Essay for the Recording of Illustrious Providences* (supernatural legends)

1692 Trial of Susanna Martin for witchcraft in Salem, Massachusetts

1709 John Lawson, *Lawson's History of North Carolina* (marvelous accounts of natural history)

1754 Windham Frog Fright (enduring legend of how the inhabitants of Windham, Connecticut, mistook thirsty frogs for Indians)

1765 John Bartram, "Remarkable and Authentic Instances of the Fascinating Power of the Rattle-Snake over Men and Other Animals," *Gentleman's Magazine*

1781 Samuel Peters, *General History of Connecticut* (fabulous legends, such as the Windham Frog Fright)
The Blue Hen's Chickens from Delaware utter frontier boasts after winning the battle of King's Mountain

1787 Royal Tyler's *The Contrast* presents the first stage Yankee

1808 "The Diverting Club" (early tall tales published in the *American Magazine of Wit*)

American Folklore

1817　James K. Paulding, *Letters from the South* (contains early tall tale humor)

1821　Alphonso Wetmore's *The Pedlar* produced in St. Louis (a whole gallery of native folk types)

1828　Mike Fink legends first written down, in Morgan Neville, "The Last of the Boatmen," *Western Souvenir*

1829　Sam Patch jumps to his death over the Genesee Falls in Rochester

1831　*The Lion of the West* by James K. Paulding brings Nimrod Wildfire (modeled on Davy Crockett) to the stage

　　　The New York *Spirit of the Times* founded by William T. Porter

1832　Jim Crow dance step introduced by Daddy Rice as blackface entertainment

1835　First Crockett almanac published in Nashville, Tennessee

1843　*Yankee Blade* starts publication in Waterville, Maine, edited by William Mathews

1846　"Folk-Lore" coined in England by William J. Thoms

1848　*A Glance at New York in 1848* by B. A. Baker brings Mose the Bowery "b'hoy" to the New York stage

1859　Harden E. Taliaferro, *Fisher's River (North Carolina) Scenes and Characters* (sketches of Southern humor drawing from oral folklore)

1867　William F. Allen, Charles P. Ware, and Lucy M. Garrison, *Slave Songs of the United States* (first collection of Negro folksongs)

1871　"Johnny Appleseed—A Pioneer Hero," first popular presentation of the orchard planter (died 1845), by W. D. Haley, in *Harper's New Monthly Magazine*

1873　John Henry defeats the steam drill in the Big Bend Tunnel, West Virginia

1878　English Folk-Lore Society founded in London

1880　Joel Chandler Harris publishes *Uncle Remus, His Songs and His Sayings*

1882　Francis James Child begins publication of *The English and Scottish Popular Ballads*

　　　Jesse James shot in the back by Robert Ford in St. Joseph, Missouri

Important Dates

1888   American Folklore Society founded and *Journal of American Folklore* begun

1893   International Folk-Lore Congress held at Chicago under the auspices of the Chicago Folk-Lore Society

      Los Pastores (*The Shepherds' Play*) first reported in the United States by John G. Bourke, *Journal of American Folklore*

1900   Casey Jones dies at the throttle in the cab of his railroad engine in a collision in Vaughan, Mississippi

1908   First collection of cowboy songs, by N. Howard Thorp, *Songs of the Cowboys*

1909   Texas Folklore Society organized

1910   Paul Bunyan breaks into print, in the *Detroit News-Tribune*, July 24, "The Round River Drive," by James McGillivray

1914   *Introducing Mr. Paul Bunyan of Westwood, Cal.*, first of the Red River Lumber Company advertising booklets by W. B. Laughead

1916   Cecil Sharp begins collecting of English ballads in the Southern Appalachians

1928   Archive of Folk Song established in the Music Division of the Library of Congress

1934   John A. and Alan Lomax begin collecting songs in Southern Negro prisons

1936   The *Motif-Index of Folk-Literature* completed by Stith Thompson

1937   *Southern Folklore Quarterly* begun

1942   First Folklore Institute of America held at Indiana University

      California Folklore Quarterly begun (altered to *Western Folklore*, 1947)

1945   *New York Folklore Quarterly* begun

1949   Doctoral program in folklore established at Indiana University, first in the United States

1951   *Midwest Folklore* begun (expanded from *Hoosier Folklore Bulletin*, 1942)

1958   *Northeast Folklore* begun

1960   Doctoral program in folklore established at University of Pennsylvania

American Folklore

1966 First American Folklife Festival sponsored by the Smithsonian Institution, Washington, D.C.

1968 Urban Folklore Conference at Wayne State University

1969 Conference on American Folk Legend at University of California at Los Angeles

1970 Doctoral program in folklore established at University of
Texas

1973 Conference on Folklore in the Modern World at Indiana
University

1975 Team project to collect urban and industrial folklore in the
Calumet region of northwest Indiana funded by the National Endowment for the Humanities

1976 American Folklife Center established in Library of Congress

Bibliographical Notes

For the reader who wishes to pursue the study of folklore in general terms the following titles are suggested. *Folklore and Folklife, An Introduction*, edited by Richard M. Dorson (Chicago, 1972), presents an overview of the subject written by professional folklorists. Individual chapters deal with the genres of folklore and techniques of studying them, and contain annotated bibliographical references for further reading. Chapters are grouped under the headings Oral Folklore, Social Folk Custom, Folk Arts, Material Culture, and The Methods of Folklife Study. Alan Dundes's selection of published articles and essays, *The Study of Folklore* (Englewood Cliffs, N.J., 1965), offers a high level of theoretical discussion with useful prefatory notes. In *The Study of American Folklore* (New York, 1968), Jan Brunvand explains the general categories of folklore and illustrates them with American examples. An older book in an older tradition, A. H. Krappe's *The Science of Folklore* (New York, 1930), omits American material but does offer an introduction to the comparative study of oral folklore based on European scholarship.

The bible of the folklorist is Stith Thompson's six volume *Motif-Index of Folk Literature* (Bloomington, Ind., and Copenhagen, Denmark, 1955–58)—a dictionary, an encyclopedia, and a vast bibliography of folklore themes all in one. It serves as companion to *The Types of the Folktale* (Helsinki, 1961), an index of European tale-types which Thompson revised from the original 1910 catalogue of the Finnish folklorist Antti Aarne. Of special pertinence for the student of American folklore is Ernest W. Baughman's *Type and Motif-Index of the Folktales of England and North America* (The Hague, 1966). These indexes represent the most ingenious tools developed by folklore scholarship to identify narrative traditions and study them comparatively. An index for legends prepared by Reidar Christiansen, *The Migratory Legends* (Helsinki, 1958) is based primarily on Norwegian examples.

Folklorists have devoted much attention to particular genres of oral tradition, especially the tale and the ballad. In *Folktales and Society* (Bloomington, Ind., 1969) Linda Dégh has written an exemplary account of storytellers and their audiences in a Hungarian Szekler community. The older work of Stith Thompson, *The Folktale* (New York, 1946), discusses the forms of oral narrative and the historical-geographical method of tracing their origin and diffusion. The Folktales of the World series, under the general editorship of Richard M. Dorson (Chicago, 1963 to date), presents traditional narratives collected in a given country with comparative notes to the tales; twelve volumes have been published to date, for Chile, China, England, France, Germany, Greece, Hungary, Ireland, Israel, Japan, Mexico, and Norway. A comprehensive collection edited by Dorson, *Folktales Told around the World* (Chicago, 1975), reprints one or two tales from each of the series volumes but in the main offers previously unpublished oral narratives in the same format.

For ballads the classic collection was made by Francis J. Child, *The English and Scottish Popular Ballads* (10 parts, 1882–98). The set has been reprinted by photo-offset in three volumes by The Folklore Press and Pageant Book Company (New York, 1956). A convenient one-volume selection was made by Helen Child Sargent and George L. Kittredge (Boston and New York, 1904). Anthologies which enlarge the Child canon are MacEdward Leach, *The Ballad Book* (New York, 1955), and Albert B. Friedman, *The Viking Book of Folk Ballads of the English-Speaking World* (New York, 1956), both with useful introductions. Important indexes for identifying ballads have been prepared by Tristram P. Coffin, *The British Traditional Ballad in North America* (1950; rev. 1963), and G. Malcolm Laws, *Native American Balladry* (1950; rev. 1964) and *American Balladry from British Broadsides* (1957). All these are publications in the Bibliographical and Special Series of the

Bibliographical Notes

American Folklore Society. A general account of balladry and ballad collectors in England and the United States is Evelyn K. Wells, *The Ballad Tree* (New York, 1950), and a detailed critical history is Donald K. Wilgus, *Anglo-American Folksong Scholarship Since 1898* (New Brunswick, N. J., 1959).

Other important studies are Albert B. Friedman, *The Ballad Revival* (Chicago, 1961); Claude M. Simpson, *The British Broadside Ballad and Its Music* (New Brunswick, N. J., 1966); David C. Fowler, *A Literary History of the Popular Ballad* (Durham, N. C., 1968); and David Buchan, *The Ballad and the Folk* (London, 1972). Scholars now recognize the indivisibility of song text and tune, and Bertrand Bronson has achieved a fitting complement to Child in his *The Traditional Tunes of the Child Ballads*, 4 vols. (Princeton, 1959–72). A survey of texts and tunes in terms of their aesthetics is provided by Roger D. Abrahams and George Foss in *Anglo-American Folksong Style* (Englewood Cliffs, N. J., 1968).

Proverb and riddle studies have been the special subject of Archer Taylor, a master folklorist of the past generation. *The Proverb* (Cambridge, Mass., 1931) is a meaty series of essays (the most useful edition is *The Proverb and Index to "The Proverb"*, [Hatboro, Pa., 1962]). *A Dictionary of American Proverbs and Proverbial Phrases, 1820–1880* (Cambridge, Mass., 1958), which Taylor coauthored with Bartlett J. Whiting, lists proverbial expressions from many literary sources. Taylor's *English Riddles from Oral Tradition* (Berkeley and Los Angeles, 1951) is a monumental work of classification.

For the reader interested in myth and mythology, terms that the folklorist uses cautiously, a few titles may be suggested that reveal the diversity of viewpoints and approaches. Two symposia are *Myth: A Symposium*, edited by Thomas A. Sebeok (Bloomington, Ind., 1958), and *Myth and Mythmaking*, edited by Henry A. Murray (New York, 1960). Geoffrey S. Kirk, a classicist conversant with folklore and anthropology, explores *Myth, Its Meaning and Functions in Ancient and Other Cultures* (Berkeley, 1971). The once dominant place of mythology in academic and philosophical thought and in literary expression is demonstrated in *The Rise of Modern Mythology, 1680–1860* (Bloomington, Ind., 1972), a volume of selections edited and with excellent introductions by Burton Feldman and Robert D. Richardson.

American Folklore

Some of the best writing on folklore was done by English folklorists in the nineteenth century. They are discussed in my *The British Folklorists: A History* and their works are sampled in my two-volume edition of *Peasant Customs and Savage Myths* (both Chicago, 1969). The folklore theories of the "Great Team" of Victorian folklorists—Andrew Lang, George Laurence Gomme, Edwin Sidney Hartland, Edward Clodd, and Alfred Nutt—are well worth reading today.

A few reference works on American folklore not mentioned in the chapter notes may be cited here. The giant *Bibliography of North American Folklore and Folk Song* by Charles Haywood (New York, 1951; new ed., 1961) is marred by misprints and loose definition of folklore and is now dated. Some useful bibliographic aids are Tristram P. Coffin, *An Analytical Index to the Journal of American Folklore*, 70 vols. (Philadelphia, 1958); James T. Bratcher, *Analytical Index to Publications of the Texas Folklore Society* (Dallas, 1973); Robert Wildhaber, "A Bibliographic Introduction to American Folklife," *New York Folklore Quarterly* 21 (1965): 259–320. An annual classified and annotated bibliography of North and South American folklore appeared in the *Southern Folklore Quarterly* from its inception in 1937 until 1972; however, the latest bibliographer, Merle E. Simmons, published *Folklore Bibliography for 1973* as a separate volume (Bloomington, Ind., 1975). Covering a single region, an extensive inventory with lively notes is Vance Randolph's *Ozark Folklore: A Bibliography* (Bloomington, Ind., 1972). A handy general reference tool in essay form has been prepared by Jan H. Brunvand, *Folklore: A Study and Research Guide* (New York, 1976). A surprising number of *Folklore Theses and Dissertations in the United States* (Austin, Tex, and London, 1976) are uncovered by Alan Dundes.

Unfortunately many readers have been misled by titles of books purporting to offer accurate materials of American folklore. The series of treasuries compiled by Benjamin A. Botkin, beginning with his *A Treasury of American Folklore* in 1944, is intended for entertainment, and only a fraction of its contents qualifies as folklore. Juvenile "folklore" books have no validity. Just as the historian demands documentary evidence and the anthropologist requires controlling data, so the folklorist must supply credentials for his materials. These consist of authentic field texts obtained

through dictation or tape recording, adequate comparative annotation, and references to the authoritative indexes now available.
Texts secured from early printed sources can be properly documented through such tools as Thompson's *Motif-Index*.

Besides knowing how to use the tools, the folklorist in America
needs to determine the theoretical basis for his research. If he collects merely for the sake of collecting, he remains a hobbyist. In
"A Theory for American Folklore," in *Journal of American Folklore*, vol. 72 (July 1959), I considered existing schools of folklore
in the United States and proposed a new synthesis. The future
American folklorist should be trained both in comparative folklore and in American history in order to relate the special problems of folklore in the United States to the special conditions of
American civilization.

The "Theory" article, with other writings elaborating on its
premises, is reprinted in my *American Folklore and the Historian*
(Chicago, 1971). Further thoughts of mine on American and international folklore are collected in *Folklore: Selected Essays* (Bloomington, Ind., 1972) and *Folklore and Fakelore: Essays toward a
Discipline of Folk Studies* (Cambridge, Mass., 1976). A subsequent
hypothesis building on the "Theory" article divides American history into four chronological periods, each having a lifestyle and
folklore which reflect its dominant character; this thesis provides
the frame for my *America in Legend* (New York, 1973). A rich
and rewarding exploration of the legend concept as it applies to
the United States is available in *American Folk Legend: A Symposium*, ed. Wayland Hand (Berkeley and Los Angeles, 1971). The
contributors deal with broadly theoretical and specifically regional
legend themes, but all agree that, for the United States at any rate,
these themes transcend narrow categories. One absorbing psycho-
cultural study of a pervasive belief which germinates legends is
Water Witching U.S.A., by Evon Z. Vogt and Ray Hyman (Chicago, 1959). The interweaving of folk beliefs, personal experiences,
and local legends about the dead is skilfully presented by Lynwood
Montell in *Ghosts along the Cumberland: Deathlore in the Kentucky Foothills* (Knoxville, 1975). Folklorists in the United States
have not by and large related their theory-building to American
folklore, a point evident in the thoughtful overview "American
Folklore and American Studies," by Richard Bauman and Roger

American Folklore

D. Abrahams with Susan Kalcik, in *American Quarterly* 28 (1976): 360–77. Articles and essays of two regional folklore interpreters are reprinted in Louise Pound, *Nebraska Folklore* (Lincoln, Nebr., 1959), especially commendable for its studies of white origins of Indian pseudolegends; and in *Mody Boatright, Folklorist*, ed. Wilson M. Hudson (Austin, Tex., 1973), which reflects Boatright's Texan and southwestern interest in frontier humor and oilfield lore. Miscellaneous articles are brought together in two volumes titled *American Folklife*, ed. Don Yoder (Austin, Tex., 1976), and *American Folk Medicine: A Symposium*, ed. Wayland D. Hand (Berkeley and Los Angeles, 1976). The directions in which theoretically-minded American folklorists, who subscribe to what I have called the contextualist school, are moving can be seen in such volumes as *New Perspectives in Folklore*, ed. Américo Paredes and Richard Bauman (Austin, Tex., 1972); *Folklore, Performance, and Communication*, ed. Dan Ben-Amos and Kenneth S. Goldstein (The Hague and Paris, 1975); and *Folklore Genres*, ed. Dan Ben-Amos (Austin, Tex., 1976).

Festschrifts for American folklorists contain writings of value on American materials. See *Folklore in Action: Essays for Discussion in Honor of MacEdward Leach* (Philadelphia, 1962); *Folklore & Society: Essays in Honor of Benj. A. Botkin*, ed. Bruce Jackson (Hatboro, Pa., 1966); *Folklore International: Essays in Traditional Literature, Belief, and Custom in Honor of Wayland Debs Hand* (Hatboro, Pa., 1967); and *Folklore Today: A Festschrift for Richard M. Dorson*, ed. L. Dégh, H. Glassie, and F. J. Oinas (Bloomington, Ind., 1976).

Turning from theory to collections, we find some volumes organized according to state, although the folklore of one state is to a large extent interchangeable with that of another. Noteworthy is *The Frank C. Brown Collection of North Carolina Folklore*, 7 vols. (Durham, N.C., 1952–64), edited by a group of eminent folklorists. See also Fred W. Allsopp, *Folklore of Romantic Arkansas*, 2 vols. (New York, 1931); *Texas Folk and Folklore*, ed. Mody Boatright et al. (Dallas, 1954); *Kansas Folklore*, ed. S. J. Sackett and W. E. Koch (Lincoln, Nebr., 1961); *A Treasury of Nebraska Pioneer Folklore*, comp. Roger L. Welsch (Lincoln, Nebr., 1966); George G. Carey, *Maryland Folklore and Folklife* (Cambridge, Md., 1970). The most successful collections follow subregional contours, e.g.

Bibliographical Notes

Emelyn E. Gardner's *Folklore from the Schoharie Hills, New York* (Ann Arbor, Mich., 1937).

In the past three decades the rapid acceleration of interest in American folklore on all levels has produced a number of centers for the study, collection, and publication of folklore materials. Indiana University was the first institution in the United States to offer master's and doctor's degrees in folklore, and at this writing (May 1977) enrolls annually over 150 graduate students seeking higher degrees and some 3000 students in all courses. On that campus are edited the *Journal of the Folklore Institute* by Richard M. Dorson, *Indiana Folklore* by Linda Dégh, and *Folklore Forum* and *Folklore Preprint Series* by folklore graduate students. Also on campus are located the Folklore Archives for manuscripts and the Archives of Traditional Music for tapes. The University of Pennsylvania and the University of Texas now also offer doctor's degrees in folklore, and the master's in folklore is offered at the University of California at Los Angeles, the University of California at Berkeley, the University of North Carolina, and Western Kentucky State University. Over two hundred American colleges and universities currently schedule courses in folklore.

Folklorists not only hold faculty positions but are beginning to find openings for their skills in the federal and state governments. An Act of Congress of January 1976 established an American Folklife Center in the Library of Congress to preserve and disseminate folklore and folklife materials. State folklorists have received positions in Maryland, Tennessee, and Minnesota. The Smithsonian Institution in Washington, D.C., has full-time and part-time folklore collectors on its staff. Some pioneer and folklife museums, such as Conner Prairie Settlement in Noblesville, Indiana; the Ozark Folk Center in Mountain View, Arkansas; and the Farmer's Museum in Cooperstown, New York, have recruited professional folklorists.

The following notes cite works from which I have chiefly drawn for the individual chapters. Information added is bracketed following the original notes.

CHAPTER I

The seventeenth-century writings upon which this chapter is largely based may be consulted in my anthology, *American Begins*

(New York, 1950), where the sources are fully cited. The pertinent chapters are "Natural Wonders," "Remarkable Providences," "Indian Conceits and Antics," and "Witchcrafts" (chaps. 2, 3, 5, and 7). A valuable assembling of early zoölogical marvels to which I am indebted is by James R. Masterson, "Travelers' Tales of Colonial Natural History," *Journal of American Folklore* 59 (1946): 51–67, 174–88. George Lyman Kittredge has provided an encyclopedia of folklore motifs in *Witchcraft in Old and New England* (Cambridge, Mass., 1929) and an entertaining miscellany of folk notions current in eighteenth-century New England in *The Old Farmer and His Almanack* (Cambridge, Mass., 1904). This last work refers to the corpse gushing blood at the murderer's touch, in the chapter "Murder Will Out" (pp. 71–77). My other examples come from *Sir Walter Scott's Minstrelsy of the Scottish Border*, edited by T. F. Henderson, III (Edinburgh, London, and New York, 1902), pp. 241–45, in the "Notes on Earl Richard"; and *The Frank C. Brown Collection of North Carolina Folklore*, vol. 1 (Durham, N.C., 1952), pp. 639–40, "Murderer Betrayed by Victim's Blood." My *Jonathan Draws the Long Bow* (Cambridge, Mass., 1946) presents witch, devil, and specter legends of colonial New England in chap. 2, "Supernatural Stories," pp. 25–68. In "Comic Indian Anecdotes," *Southern Folklore Quarterly* 10 (1946): 113–28, I have followed the tradition of Indian dolt and knave from colonial to modern times. [This essay is reprinted in my *Folklore and Fakelore* (Cambridge, Mass., 1976), pp. 269–82.]

CHAPTER II

A seminal work in considering the humor of the folk Yankee and the western roarer is Constance Rourke, *American Humor* (New York, 1931). In his lengthy critical introduction and source selections, in *Native American Humor* (*1800–1900*) (New York, 1937), Walter Blair gives heed to oral folk humor. Franklin J. Meine offered a rich selection from the "Spirit of the Times" in his *Tall Tales of the Southwest* (New York, 1930), choosing literary rather than folkloristic narratives. Arthur Palmer Hudson concentrated on Alabama, Mississippi, and Louisiana for *Humor of the Old Deep South* (New York, 1936), and Thomas D. Clark emphasized the social history of the Old Southwest as revealed in humorous tales

Bibliographical Notes

and anecdotes, in *The Rampaging Frontier* (Indianapolis and New York, 1939). Although restricted to the printed humor of one state, James R. Masterson's *Tall Tales of Arkansaw* (Boston, 1943), provides a generous and well-documented inventory of popular and folk humor. In *Folk Laughter on the American Frontier* (New York, 1949), a thoughtful group of essays with a Texas accent, Mody C. Boatright moved closer than these previous anthologies to the track of oral tradition. An important study on *William T. Porter and the "Spirit of the Times,"* by Norris W. Yates (Baton Rouge, 1957), looks closely at the editor, his correspondents, and their techniques in developing the "Big Bear" school of American humor.

A number of journal articles have probed early newspaper files for folk and subliterary humor. In an all-too-rare kind of study, "Specimens of the Folktales from Some Antebellum Newspapers of Louisiana," *Louisiana Historical Quarterly* 32 (1949): 723–58, Arthur K. Moore identified folktale types in humorous and serious newspaper narratives. George Kummer excavated comic tales from early Ohio newspapers and travelers' writngs in "Specimens of Ante-Bellum Buckeye Humor," *Ohio Historical Quarterly* 64 (1955): 424–37, and Philip D. Jordan culled from Ohio and Indiana newspapers in "Humor of the Backwoods, 1820–1840," *Mississippi Valley Historical Review* 25 (1938): 25–38. Georgia received attention from Eugene Current-Garcia in "Newspaper Humor in the Old South, 1835–1855," *Alabama Review* 2 (1949): 102–21, and a single North Carolina newspaper yielded rich gleanings to Eston E. Ericson, in "Folklore and Folkway in the Tarboro (N.C.) *Free Press* (1824–1850)," *Southern Folklore Quarterly* 5 (1941): 107–25. That folk humor could be found also in the newspapers of the Far West and the East was shown by Randall V. Mills in "Frontier Humor in Oregon and its Characteristics," *Oregon Historical Quarterly* 43 (1942): 339–56, and R. M. Dorson in "Yorker Yarns of Yore," *New York Folklore Quarterly* 3 (1947): 5–27.

Other articles have considered folk elements in the writings of individual southern humorists. Harden E. Taliaferro, although omitted from Meine's *Tall Tales of the Southwest,* caught the attention of Ralph S. Boggs, in "North Carolina Folktales Current in the 1820's," *Journal of American Folklore* 47 (1934): 269–88; B. J. Whiting in "Proverbial Sayings from Fisher's River, North Carolina," *Southern Folklore Quarterly* 11 (1947): 173–85; and James H. Penrod, "Harden Taliaferro, Folk Humorist of North Carolina," *Midwest Folklore* 6 (1956): 147–53. Henry Clay Lewis, who wrote under the pseudonym of "Madison Tensas," was discussed by John Q. Anderson, in "Folklore in the Writings of the 'Louisiana Swamp Doctor,' " *Southern Folklore Quarterly* (1955): 243–51. Anderson also studied the *Yazoo Sketches* of little-known William C. Hall for an intriguing report on "Mike Hooter—the Making of a Myth," *Southern Folklore Quarterly* 19 (1955): 90–100. James H. Penrod isolated "Folk Humor in *Sut Lovingood's Yarns*," in the *Tennessee Folklore Society Bulletin* 16 (1950): 76–84. Among a number of related articles by Penrod, "Folk Motifs in Old Southwestern Humor," *Southern Folklore Quarterly* 19 (1955): 117–24, may be cited. Walter Blair analyzed T. B. Thorpe's classic sketch in "The Technique of 'The Big Bear of Arkansas,' " *Southwest Review* 28 (1943): 426–35. As I indicated in the text, this group of studies is not uniformly successful.

The flood of studies and anthologies dealing with southwestern humor has completely overshadowed the ante-bellum folk humor of New England. I tried to redress the balance in *Jonathan Draws the Long Bow* (Cambridge, Mass., 1946), which reprinted Yankee yarns and tall tales from the *Yankee Blade* and other down-East publications. The *Yankee Blade* and its versatile editor, William Mathews, have not attracted further scholarly interest.

For early traces of native folk humor, Blair's chapter on "Beginnings (1775–1830)" in *Native American Humor*, pp. 17–37, is suggestive and amply documented. My quotations on "the blue hen's chickens" are taken from the *Narrative of the Battle of Cowan's Ford, February 1st, 1781, by Robert Henry, and Narrative of the Battle of Kings Mountain, by Captain David Vance*, published by D. Schenck, Sr., Greensboro, N.C., March 28, 1891, pp. 28, 37, 38. Herbert Halpert has written on "The Blue Hen's Chickens" in *American Speech* 26 (1951): 196–98, as a still current phrase. The full text of "The Diverting Club" is printed in R. M. Dorson, "Two City Yarnfests," *California Folklore Quarterly* 5 (1946): 72–82. Floyd C. Watkins called attention to "James Kirke Paulding's Early Ring-Tailed Roarer," in *Southern Folklore Quarterly* 15 (1951): 183–87.

Few studies have dealt with folk humor in the American drama.

Bibliographical Notes

See R. M. Dorson, "The Yankee on the Stage," *New England Quarterly* 13 (1940): 467–93; "Mose the Far-Famed and World-Renowned," *American Literature* 15 (1943): 288–300; "Sam Patch, Jumping Hero," *New York Folklore Quarterly* 1 (1945): 133–51. [The material from these articles, with illustrations from contemporary sources, appears in my *America in Legend* (New York, 1973), pp. 92–121.] The unpublished dissertation by Merl William Tillson, *The Frontiersman in American Drama* (University of Denver, 1951), contains useful material on "the Yankee gone West" as portrayed on the stage. Tales, dialogues, and play scenes associated with Yankee Hill and Dan Marble are reprinted in *Life and Recollections of Yankee Hill; together with Anecdotes and Incidents of His Travels,* edited by W. K. Northall (New York, 1850); and Jonathan F. Kelley, *Dan Marble: A Biographical Sketch* (New York, 1851). The text of Alphonso Wetmore's *The Pedlar: A Farce in Three Acts,* published by John A. Paxton (St. Louis, 1821), is available on microprint in "Three Centuries of American Drama," edited by Henry W. Wells (New York: Readex Microprint, 1954). James N. Tidwell has discovered and printed a manuscript of James Kirke Paulding's *The Lion of the West* (Stanford, Calif., 1954). Brief remarks on "The Ring-Tailed Roarer in American Drama," by Stuart W. Hyde, appear in the *Southern Folklore Quarterly* 19 (1955): 171–78.

A comprehensive treatment of a neglected field is William Murrell, *A History of American Graphic Humor,* 2 vols. (New York, 1933–38). Vol. 1 concerns the period 1747–1865.

[The scholarship on humor of the Old Southwest has reached the point where not only the humor itself but also critical interpretations of it can be anthologized, and this is what Thomas Inge has done in *The Frontier Humorists: Critical Views* (Hamden, Conn., 1975). The book contains essays appraising southwestern humor in general, individual humorists, and the continuities of that humor in post-bellum fiction, plus a comprehensive bibliography by Charles E. Davis and Martha B. Hudson, "Humor of the Old Southwest: A Checklist of Criticism." The anthologizing of southwestern humor has continued in such selections as Hennig Cohen and William B. Dillingham, eds., *Humor of the Old Southwest* (Boston, 1964), and John Q. Anderson, ed., *Frontier Texas 1830–1860* (Dallas, 1966) and *With the Bark On* (Nashville, 1967).]

American Folklore

A meaty introduction to the history, theology, and folk culture of German Pennsylvania is Fredric Klees, *The Pennsylvania Dutch* (New York, 1951). The annual publications of the Pennsylvania German Folklore Society, issued since 1936, and the Pennsylvania German Society, initiated in 1890, are storehouses of information on all aspects of traditional culture of their people. Excellent collections of various forms of folklore are available. For folk narrative there is Thomas R. Brendle and William S. Troxell, *Pennsylvania German Folk Tales, Legends, Once-upon-a-Time Stories, Maxims and Sayings* (Norristown, Pa., 1944). For folk beliefs there are Edwin M. Fogel, *Beliefs and Superstitions of the Pennsylvania Germans* (Philadelphia, 1915); Thomas R. Brendle and Claude W. Unger, *Folk Medicine of the Pennsylvania Germans: The Non-Occult Cures* (Norristown, Pa., 1935); D. E. Lick and Thomas R. Brendle, "Plant Names and Plant Lore among the Pennsylvania-Germans," in vol. 33 of the Pennsylvania German Society Publications (Reading, Pa., 1923). Proverbial lore is fully treated by Edwin M. Vogel in *Proverbs of the Pennsylvania Germans* (Pennsylvania German Society, 1929). Folk art is lavishly presented in Frances Lichten, *Folk Art of Rural Pennsylvania* (New York and London, 1946) and *Folk Art Motifs of Pennsylvania* (New York, 1954), and Henry Kauffman, *Pennsylvania Dutch: American Folk Art* (New York and London, 1946). These can be supplemented with a number of individual monographs, e.g., Preston and Eleanor Barba, "Lewis Miller, Pennsylvania German Folk Artist," in vol. 4 of the "Pennsylvania German Folklore Society Publications" (Allentown, Pa., 1939), and vol. 18, Preston A. Barba, *Pennsylvania German Tombstones: A Study in Folk Art* (Allentown, Pa., 1953). For folksong, two authoritative chapters in *Pennsylvania Songs and Legends*, edited by George Korson (Philadelphia, 1949), are "Pennsylvania German Songs," by Thomas R. Brendle and William S. Troxell, and "Amish Hymns as Folk Music," by J. William Frey (pp. 62–128, 129–62). The biographical story of a Catholic orphan brought up in an Amish household, as told by Joseph W. Yoder in *Rosanna of the Amish* (Huntingdon, Pa., 1941), is rich in Amish folk custom. A general sampler is provided in John

Bibliographical Notes

Baer Stroudt, *The Folk-Lore of the Pennsylvania-German* (Lancaster, Pa., 1915).

Single-handedly, Vance Randolph has collected all kinds of Ozark folklore. A vast miscellany of traditional songs is presented in his *Ozark Folksongs,* 4 vols. (Columbia, Mo., 1946–50). Localized folktales, about a hundred in each swatch, appear in *Who Blowed Up the Church House?, The Devil's Pretty Daughter, The Talking Turtle,* and *Sticks in the Knapsack* (New York, 1952, 1955, 1957, and 1958); the first three are annotated by Herbert Halpert, and the fourth by Ernest W. Baughman. *We Always Lie to Strangers* (New York, 1951), synopsizes and discusses Ozark tall tales. *Ozark Superstitions* (New York, 1947) is an abundant and well-organized harvest. In *Down in the Holler: A Gallery of Ozark Folk Speech* (Norman, Okla., 1953), Randolph enlisted George P. Wilson as collaborator. I have also consulted the six volumes of *Unprintable Ozark Folklore* which Mr. Randolph deposited in the library of the Sex Research Institute of Indiana University in 1954. The close associate of Mr. Randolph, Otto Ernest Rayburn, has published *Ozark Country* in the American Folkways Series (New York, 1941), emphasizing the role of tradition and custom in daily life. Printed sources are culled in Fred W. Allsopp, *Folklore of Romantic Arkansas,* 2 vols. (New York, 1931), and James R. Masterson, *Tall Tales of Arkansaw* (Boston, 1943).

Splendid resources are available for the Spanish-Mexican folklore of the Southwest. *An Annotated Bibliography of Spanish Folklore in New Mexico and Southern Colorado,* prepared by Marjorie F. Tully and Juan B. Rael (Albuquerque, 1950), is a useful and indeed unique regional folklore bibliography. A sampling of the traditions, partially translated, is provided by Aurora Lucero-White Lea in *Literary Folklore of the Hispanic Southwest* (San Antonio, 1953). Juan B. Rael offers a giant haul of folktales in *Cuentos españoles de Colorado y de Nuevo Méjico,* 2 vols. (Stanford, 1957), with English summaries. Arthur L. Campa has critically discussed and illustrated *Spanish Folk-Poetry in New Mexico* (Albuquerque, 1946), and Juan B. Rael has singled out one poetic form in *The New Mexican Alabado* (Stanford, 1951). For the folk drama, a convenient starting point is the *"Los Pastores" Number: Folk Plays of Hispanic America,* in *Western Folklore* 16 (October 1957). The important study there by John E. Englekirk, "The Source and Dat-

American Folklore

ing of New Mexican Spanish Folk Plays" (pp. 232–55) supplements his earlier essay, "Notes on the Repertoire of the New Mexican Spanish Folktheater," *Southern Folklore Quarterly* 4 (1940): 227–37. A useful composite synopsis of known texts and performances is given by Thomas M. Pearce in "The New Mexican 'Shepherd' Play," *Western Folklore* 15 (1956): 77–88. The first modern American recording of the drama, by Captain John G. Bourke, was translated and published by M. R. Cole as memoir 9 of the American Folklore Society, *Los Pastores* (Boston and New York, 1907). Some excellent articles on various aspects of southwestern Spanish lore appear in the *New Mexico Folklore Record* (1946–56). In vol. 2 (1947–48), pp. 58–65, T. M. Pearce gives a New Mexican text of "Los Moros y los Cristianos: Early American Play." John D. Robb in his intriguing article "The Sources of a New Mexico Folksong," vol. 5 (1950–51), pp. 9–16, traces the history of the "Corrido de la Muerte de Antonio Mestas," and furnishes an English translation in his *Hispanic Folk Songs of New Mexico* (Albuquerque, 1954), pp. 52–57. Holy folk festivals of the Mexican population in San Antonio, Texas, are described, too preciously, by Julia Nott Waugh in *The Silver Cradle* (Austin, 1955). The folk psychology of the Border Mexican toward the Anglo-Texan is revealed in the admirable study by Américo Paredes, *"With His Pistol in His Hand": A Border Ballad and Its Hero* (Austin, 1958). The old troubadour of New Mexican territorial days, Charles F. Lummis, is really the first folklorist of New Mexico, and I have quoted from his chapter, "New Mexican Folk-Songs," in *The Land of Poco Tiempo* (New York, 1893), pp. 215–50. Helen Zunser's superb folklore vignette, "A New Mexican Village," appeared in the *Journal of American Folklore* 48 (1935) 125–78.

All students of America folklore appreciate the splendid treatment of Mormon folk traditions by Austin E. and Alta S. Fife in *Saints of Sage and Saddle* (Bloomington, Ind., 1956). The authors thoroughly demonstrate the interaction of American history and Mormon folklore. Important individual articles by Austin Fife are "The Legend of the Three Nephites among the Mormons," *Journal of American Folklore* 53 (1940): 1–49; "Popular Legends of the Mormons," *California Folklore Quarterly* 1 (1942): 105–25; "Folk Songs of Mormon Inspiration," *Western Folklore* 6 (1947): 42–52 (with Alta S. Fife); "Folk Belief and Mormon Cultural Auton-

Bibliographical Notes

omy," *Journal of American Folklore* 61 (1948): 19–30; "A Ballad of the Mountain Meadows Massacre," *Western Folklore* 12 (1953): 229–41. A fascinating study is Hector Lee, *The Three Nephites: The Substance and Significance of the Legend in Folklore* (Albuquerque, 1949). Levette J. Davidson published "Mormon Songs" in the *Journal of American Folklore* 58 (1945): 273–300.

A sampling of the tales, beliefs, and songs I collected in Jonesport, Washington County, Maine, in July 1956, is published in the *Proceedings of the American Philosophical Society* 101 (1957): 270–89. Six additional texts of Curt Morse are printed in my "Mishaps of a Maine Lobsterman," *Northeast Folklore* 1 (1958): 1–7. This field trip was made possible by a grant from the American Philosophical Society. The history and cultural setting of the Maine coast area are described by Horace Beck in *The Folklore of Maine* (Philadelphia and New York, 1957), a semipopular treatment.

[Field-collected texts for the regions discussed in chap. III, save for the Ozarks, are set down in my *Buying the Wind: Regional Folklore in the United States* (Chicago, 1964). Additional resources given for the five regions considered in chap. III follow.

GERMAN PENNSYLVANIA: John A. Burrison, "Pennsylvania German Folktales: An Annotated Bibliography," *Pennsylvania Folklife* 15, no. 1 (Autumn 1965): 30–38, contains 55 entries from general sources and 284 entries from the files of *The Pennsylvania Dutchman* for 1949 to 1956 and for *Pennsylvania Folklife* for 1957 to 1964. A folklife history of the Pennsylvania Dutch people with copious illustrations has been written in personal terms by John J. Stoudt in *Sunbonnets and Shoofly Pies* (Cranbury, N.J., 1973).

THE OZARKS: Vance Randolph continues to add to his output. *Hot Springs and Hell, and Other Folk Jests and Anecdotes from the Ozarks* bolsters the jokelore, with comparative notes (Hatboro, Pa., 1965). *Ozark Folklore: A Bibliography* (Bloomington, Ind., 1972), the well organized results of an exhaustive sleuthing through all manner of publications, demonstrates Randolph's facility with printed as well as oral sources. And his typescripts of Unprintable Ozark Folklore are finally becoming printable, with *Pissing in the Snow and Other Ozark Folktales* being published by University of Illinois Press (Urbana, 1976).

SPANISH NEW MEXICO: Stanley L. Robe has compiled a valuable *Index of Mexican Folktales, Including Narrative Texts from Mex-*

American Folklore

ico, Central America, and the Hispanic United States (Berkeley, 1973). An urban collection of Spanish texts with English summaries is Elaine K. Miller, *Mexican Folk Narrative from the Los Angeles Area* (Austin, Tex., 1973). Américo Paredes has assembled 66 songs of the Lower Rio Grande Border recorded between 1750 and 1960 in *A Texas-Mexican Cancionero: Folksongs of the Lower Border* (Urbana, Ill., 1976).

José E. Espinosa has described and reproduced paintings and statues of New Mexican folk artists in *Saints in the Valleys: Christian Sacred Images in the History, Life, and Folk Art of Spanish New Mexico* (Albuquerque, 1960, 1967). A comprehensive, detailed account of *Popular Arts of Spanish New Mexico*, covering work in wood, mud, textiles, hides, paper, and straw, with many illustrations, has been written by Elizabeth Boyd (Sante Fe, 1974).

UTAH MORMONS: *Lore of Faith and Folly*, ed. Thomas E. Cheney (Salt Lake City, 1971) is an uneven collection of articles produced by members of the Folklore Society of Utah, touching on Mormon pioneer, local family, and folk history. Cheney has also published *Mormon Songs from the Rocky Mountains* (Austin, Tex., 1968), and *The Golden Legend* (Santa Barbara and Salt Lake City, 1974), the latter a choice collection of anecdotes, unfortunately lacking field data and comparative annotation, about the indecorous elder of the Mormon Church, J. Golden Kimball. Showing the ubiquity of Three Nephite stories, William Wilson recorded a sheaf of them in Bloomington, Indiana, in "Mormon Legends of the Three Nephites Collected at Indiana University," *Indiana Folklore* 2–3 (1969–70): 3–35. Wilson has also written "The Paradox of Mormon Folklore," in *Essays on the American West*, ed. T. G. Alexander (Provo, Utah, 1976), pp. 127–47; the article illustrates how devout believers transmit folklore both supportive and seemingly subversive of Mormondom. Wilson introduced a special Mormon folklore issue of *Utah Historical Quarterly* (vol. 44 [Fall 1976]) with his article "The Study of Mormon Folklore," and also contributed "A Bibliography of Studies in Mormon Folklore" to the same issue (pp. 389–94). Jan Brunvand has provided *A Guide for Collectors of Folklore in Utah* (Salt Lake City, 1971), which necessarily stresses Mormon matters, and he has donated a reassuring essay, "Modern Legends of Mormondom, or Supernaturalism is Alive and Well in Salt Lake City," to *American Folk Legend: A*

Symposium, ed. W. D. Hand (Berkeley and Los Angeles, 1971), pp. 185–202. That Mormon supernatural belief is alive elsewhere is evident in the article of Roger M. Thompson, "The Decline of Cedar Key: Mormon Lore in North Florida and Its Social Function," *Southern Folklore Quarterly* 39 (1975): 39–62, which discusses legends explaining the decline of Cedar Key as a consequence of its residents rejecting Mormon missionaries.

MAINE COAST YANKEES: Genealogical facts about Barney Beal's family tree are gathered by Velten Peabody in *Tall Barney's People: A Genealogy* (Williamsville, N.Y., 1974). The same author gives details of Barney's life and tales of his exploits based on nine interviews with descendants of Barney, and adds valuable photographs and sketches, in *Tall Barney* (Williamsville, New York, 1975). I present more of my Jonesport field materials in *Buying the Wind* (Chicago, 1964), chap. 1, "Main Down-Easters," pp. 21–105.]

CHAPTER IV

The regional-immigrant traditions of Michigan's Upper Peninsula form the subject of my *Bloodstoppers and Bearwalkers* (Cambridge, Mass., 1952), but most of the dialect humor was published separately in "Dialect Stories of the Upper Peninsula," *Journal of American Folklore* 61 (1948): 113–50. Unique is Phyllis H. Williams, *South Italian Folkways in Europe and America* (New Haven, 1938), undertaken as a study in applied folklore. The fine early article by Henry R. Lang on "The Portuguese Element in New England" appeared in the *Journal of American Folklore* 5 (1892): 9–18, and the Portuguese-American tale collection of Elsie Clews Parsons was published as memoir 15 of the American Folklore Society, *Folk-Lore from the Cape Verde Islands* (Cambridge, Mass., and New York, 1923). Part 1 contains English translations. The ballad of Oleana is presented in Theodore C. Blegen and Martin B. Ruud, *Norwegian Emigrant Songs and Ballads* (Minneapolis, 1936), a collection of popular rather than folk poetry. Scandinavian-American folklore has received some modest attention. For the Norwegian tradition see Ella V. Rølvaag, "Norwegian Folk Narrative in America," *Norwegian-American Studies and Records* 12 (Northfield, Minn., 1941): 33–59, and Jan Brunvand, "Norwegian-American Folklore in the Indiana University Archives," *Midwest*

American Folklore

Folklore 7 (1957): 221–28. For some Swedish and Danish material, see Albin Widen, "Scandinavian Folklore and Immigrant Ballads," *Bulletin of the American Institute of Swedish Arts, Literature and Science* (Minneapolis), n.s. 2, no. 1 (January–March 1947): 1–44. For the Finnish tradition, Aili K. Johnson has written three superior studies, "Finnish Labor Songs from Northern Michigan," *Michigan History* 31 (1947): 331–43; "Lore of the Finnish-American Sauna," *Midwest Folklore* 1 (1951): 33–39; and "The Eyeturner," ibid., 5 (1955): 5–10 (Finnish trickster tales from Upper Michigan about Konsti Koponen). Polish-American tales collected by R. M. Dorson from a Polish storyteller living in Michigan are printed in "Polish Wonder Tales of Joe Woods," and "Polish Tales from Joe Woods," *Western Folklore* 8 (1949): 25–52, 131–45. The Irish story of "Seán Palmer's Voyage with the Fairies" appears on pages 36–42 of R. M. Dorson, "Collecting in County Kerry," *Journal of American Folklore* 66 (1953). The provocative article by Marvin K. Opler on "Japaneses Folk Beliefs and Practices, Tule Lake, California," is in the *Journal of American Folklore* 63 (1950): 385–97.

Dorothy Demetracopoulou Lee has written a series of articles on the acculturation of Greek-American lore in the Boston area: "Folklore of the Greeks in America," *Folk-Lore* 47 (1936): 294–310; "Greek Personal Anecdotes of the Supernatural," *Journal of American Folklore* 44 (1951): 307–12; "Greek Tales of Priest and Priestwife," ibid., 60 (1947): 163–67. My field texts recorded from the Corombos family in Iron Mountain, Michigan, are published in *Fabula* 1 (Berlin, 1957): 114–43.

A comparative study by Svatava Pirkova-Jakobson, "Harvest Festivals among Czechs and Slovaks in America" (*Journal of American Folklore* 59 [1956]: 266–80) takes its ethnographic data from communities in Chicago, New York City, Heightstown in New Jersey, and Detroit. Mrs. Jakobson concludes that in these transplanted festivals "gradual change can be observed from ritual to drama." In the same number appears "Some Czech-American Forms of Divination and Supplication," by Lawrence F. Ryan (pp. 281–85), describing practices in Iowa and Minnesota connected chiefly with Christmas and Easter.

[Book-length interpretive collections by professional folklorists of immigrant-ethnic folk materials have now begun to appear. A model for its kind is Carla Bianco's *The Two Rosetos* (Blooming-

Bibliographical Notes

ton, Ind., 1974), a study of Italian folk culture as transferred from the peasant village of Roseto, Italy, to its offshoot colony in the town of Roseto, Pennsylvania. Bianco skilfully synthesizes field data, ethnographic background, and analytic commentary on the lifestyle of the Americanized Rosetans, who continue Old World folk-religious festivals and beliefs, such as the veneration of saints and madonnas, while accepting New World values of hustle, bustle, and good fortune. Concentrating on one traditional institution among southern Italian village immigrants in Philadelphia, Elizabeth Mathias reveals that they borrow not the peasants' but the landowners' (*signorini*) funeral model and maintain it through the third generation ("The Italian-American Funeral: Persistence Through Change," *Western Folklore* 33 [1974]: 35–50). Unlike these Italians, the Hasidim of Brooklyn strove mightily to retain their orthodox form of Judaism as practised in eastern Europe, and insulated themselves from their neighbors, even from non-Hasidic Jews, as Jerome Mintz shows in *Legends of the Hasidim* (Chicago, 1968). In spite of their success in preserving their institutions of the miracle-working rebs and their courts, some American elements have crept into their folkways. A briefer account of a different but comparable orthodox people isolated inside a metropolis is Willard B. Moore, *Molokan Oral Tradition: Legends and Memorates of an Ethnic Sect* (Berkeley and Los Angeles, 1973). The Molokans emigrated to Los Angeles from Russia in the early 1900s as a tightly knit Spiritual Christian community. Unlike these ethnographic reports of societies in transition, the collections from Detroit made by Susie Hoogasian-Villa, *100 Armenian Tales and Their Folkloristic Relevance* (Detroit, 1966) and Harriet Pawlowska, *Merrily We Sing! 105 Polish Folksongs* (Detroit, 1961), present merely texts of "memory culture" from Old World folk-knowledge having relatively little vitality in the United States.

References follow to a few articles with suggestive theoretical implications. In "Immigrant Folklore: Survival or Living Tradition," *Midwest Folklore* 10 (1960): 117–23, Elli Kaija Köngäs Maranda relates an unexpected encounter with an isolated Finnish woman in Vermont who narrated a number of Enemy Cycle and treasure tales which she had not told for over forty years. Maranda conjectured that functionless tradition does survive without use in isolation, at least in its original tongue. A new perspective on immigrant-ethnic folk studies advocates attention to new forms as well as to retentions and survivals of old forms; see Linda Dégh, "Approaches to Folklore Research among Immigrant Groups," *Journal of American Folklore* 79 (1966): 551–56, based on field-work among Hungarians in the Calumet region of northwest Indiana, and Robert B. Klymasz, "From Immigrant to Ethnic Folklore: A Canadian View of Process and Transition," *Journal of the Folklore Institute* 10 (1973): 131–39, which generalizes about traditional, transitional, and innovational layers of folk materials, using a study of Ukrainians in western Canada.]

CHAPTER V

The bibliography of Negro folklore is extremely rich. A number of important studies and collections are mentioned in the text and need not be repeated here. Constance Rourke has a suggestive chapter, "That Long-Tail'd Blue," in her *American Humor* (New York, 1931), pp. 77–104, but overpresses the debt of blackface minstrelsy to plantation Negro folklore. *Tambo and Bones* by Carl Wittke (Durham, N.C., 1930), pithily traces the history of American stage minstrelsy. An informative article by Hans Nathan discusses "The First Negro Minstrel Band and Its Origins," *Southern Folklore Quarterly* 16 (1952): 132–44. A convenient reprinting of *Slave Songs of the United States*, by William Francis Allen, Charles Pickard Ware, and Lucy McKim Garrison, has been issued by Peter Smith (New York, 1951). Relevant biographical and literary facts are assembled by Stella B. Brookes in *Joel Chandler Harris— Folklorist* (Athens, Ga., 1950). The life history of Huddie Ledbetter is given in John A. and Alan Lomax, *Negro Folk Songs as Sung by Lead Belly* (New York, 1936). Some useful information on the origin of the blues appears in the sketchily written *Father of the Blues*, by W. C. Handy (New York, 1944). The periodical literature on Negro folklore contains much excitement, but suffice it here to acknowledge my debt to Willis L. James, "The Romance of the Negro Folk Cry in America," *Phylon* 16 (1955): 15–30.

A bibliography of Negro folktale collections is given in my *Negro Folktales in Michigan* (Cambridge, Mass., 1956). For historical, textual, and bibliographical reference, Newman I. White's *American Negro Folk-Song* (Cambridge, Mass., 1928), remains, in spite of its age and its bias, the most useful song collection. Chap. 1, "The Negro Song in General" (pp. 3–30), is a meaty historical survey.

[The resources for the study of black folklore have been enriched by Bruce Jackson's anthology of material from early publications, *The Negro and His Folklore in Nineteenth Century Periodicals* (Austin, 1967), and by Alan Dundes's anthology of twentieth-century writings, *Mother Wit from the Laughing Barrel: Readings for the Interpretation of Afro-American Folklore* (Englewood Cliffs, N. J., 1973). A magnificent collection of raw primary data for Negro folk belief has been accumulated by an Episcopalian clergyman, Harry M. Hyatt, in his four volumes of transcribed tape-recorded interviews titled *Hoodoo-Rootwork-Witchcraft-Conjuration* (Hannibal and St. Louis, Mo., 1970–74). In *Blacking Up* (New York, 1974) Robert Toll has examined closely the evolution of blackface minstrelsy techniques. Folktales I collected in Arkansas and Mississippi are added to my Michigan findings in my *American Negro Folktales* (Greenwich, Conn., 1967). A pioneer work on urban black tales and toasts by Roger Abrahams is *Deep Down in the Jungle: Negro Narrative Folklore from the Streets of Philadelphia* (Hatboro, Pa., 1964; rev. ed., Chicago, 1970). Collections of toasts from black prison inmates appear under the titles *"Get Your Ass in the Water and Swim Like Me"* (Cambridge, Mass., 1974), by Bruce Jackson, and *The Life, the Lore, and Folk Poetry of the Black Hustler* (Philadelphia, 1976), by D. Wepman, R. B. Newman, and M. B. Binderman. The dispersion of United States Negro spirituals around the world has been documented by John Lovell, Jr., in *Black Song: The Forge and the Flame* (New York, 1972). Analyses of the Old Marster and John cycle have been made by Harry Oster in "Negro Humor: John and Old Marster," *Journal of the Folklore Institute* 5 (1968): 42–57, which contains texts spoken or sung with guitar accompaniment, and by Bruce D. Dickson, Jr., in "The 'John and Old Master' Stories and the World of Slavery: A Study in Folktales and History," *Phylon* 35 (1974): 418–29.

An impressive examination, *Black Thought and Black Consciousness: Patterns of Afro-American Folk Thought*, by Lawrence Levine (Oxford, 1977), represents a pioneering use of the full corpus of black folklore by an American historian.]

American Folklore

NINETEENTH-CENTURY RINGTAILED ROARERS: Reprintings from the Crockett almanacs are available in R. M. Dorson, ed., *Davy Crockett, American Comic Legend* (New York, 1939), and Franklin J. Meine, ed., *The Crockett Almanacks, Nashville Series, 1835–1838* (Chicago, 1955). My views on "Davy Crockett and the Heroic Age" originally appeared in the *Southern Folklore Quarterly* 6 (1942): 95–102; and I gave the almanac sources of my edition in "The Sources of *Davy Crockett, American Comic Legend*," *Midwest Folklore* 8 (1958): 143–49. Walter Blair and Franklin J. Meine first wrote up the Mike Fink legends in narrative form in *Mike Fink, King of Mississippi Keelboatmen* (New York, 1933), with a valuable bibliography, and have recently published the sources, in *Half Horse Half Alligator: The Growth of the Mike Fink Legend* (Chicago, 1956). My articles on Sam Patch and Mose the Bowery "b'hoy" are listed in the notes to chap. II, above.

TWENTIETH-CENTURY DEMIGODS: The one scholarly study is by Daniel G. Hoffman, *Paul Bunyan, Last of the Frontier Demigods* (Philadelphia, 1952), which provides a well-classified bibliography. The earliest unvarnished account of Bunyan tales, from the diary of an Oregon lumberjack, is in Edward O. Tabor and Stith Thompson, "Paul Bunyan in 1910," *Journal of American Folklore* 59 (1946): 134–35. Interesting for the history of the promotion of the legend is Max Gartenberg, "W. B. Laughead's Great Advertisement," *Journal of American Folklore* 63 (1950): 444–49. The journalistic inflation of the hero is documented in R. M. Dorson, "Paul Bunyan in the News, 1939–1941," *Western Folklore* 15 (1956): 26–39, 179–93, 247–61 (reprinted in Dorson, *Folklore and Fakelore* [Cambridge, Mass., 1976], pp. 291–336).

MÜNCHAUSENS: Mody C. Boatright has furnished biographical facts and oral texts in *Gib Morgan, Ministrel of the Oil Fields* (Texas Folk-Lore Society Publication 20, 1945). I recorded some Gib Morgan tales in Michigan from the Texas-born wife of one of my students. On the basis of eighty-two oral texts, William H. Jansen wrote a doctoral dissertation, "Abraham 'Oregon' Smith: Pioneer, Folk Hero, and Tale-Teller" (Indiana University, Bloomington, 1949), and published an article, "Lying Abe: A Tale-Teller and His Reputation," in *Hoosier Folklore* 7 (1948): 107–24. Other

Bibliographical Notes

tales are printed in Herbert Halpert and Emma Robinson, "Oregon Smith, an Indiana Folk Hero," *Southern Folklore Quarterly* 6 (1942): 163–68. A fine collection of oral tales is rendered by Herbert Halpert in "John Darling, a New York Münchausen," *Journal of American Folklore* 57 (1944): 97–107, and other tales and facts about Darling are in Harold W. Thompson, *Body, Boots and Britches* (Philadelphia, 1940), pp. 131–36.

NOBLE TOILERS: Robert Price has written a biography of *Johnny Appleseed, Man and Myth* (Bloomington, Ind., 1954), that does not fully explore the folklore aspects. He has accumulated a useful list of the miscellaneous printed references to the saintly hero in *John Chapman: A Bibliography of "Johnny Appleseed" in American History, Literature and Folklore* (Paterson, N.J., 1944). Two scholarly investigations are *John Henry, Tracking Down a Negro Legend*, by Guy B. Johnson (Chapel Hill, 1929), and *John Henry: A Folk-Lore Study*, by Louis W. Chappell (Jena, Germany, 1933). There is no proper folklore study of Casey Jones, but useful facts are gathered in Fred J. Lee, *Casey Jones: Epic of the American Railroad* (Kingsport, Tenn., 1939).

OUTLAWS: Folklorists have paid little heed to the bad men, possibly suspecting that they are dime-novel rather than folk heroes. A beginning is made by George D. Hendricks in *The Bad Man of the West* (San Antonio, 1941). A good many oral legends are cited by Homer Croy in *Jesse James Was My Neighbor* (New York, 1949), although the author explicitly denies any folklore impurities in his book. In 1956 I recorded two Jesse James legends from eighty-one-year-old Frank Sherman, who claimed to be related to Jesse, in Rhode Island. A distinct service has been performed by J. C. Dykes in his *Billy the Kid: The Bibliography of a Legend* (Norman, Okla., 1952), by bringing together the many fugitive and disparate items that surround the subliterary bad man.

GENERAL: The role of the hero-making process in American civilization is treated in rich detail, and with implications for the folklorist, by Dixon Wecter in *The Hero in America* (New York, 1941), and Leo Gurko in *Heroes, Highbrows and the Popular Mind* (Indianapolis and New York, 1953).

[Folklorists employing proper field methods are bringing to light local folk heroes unknown to the national public. A Maine lumberjack who died in 1892 when only thirty but who inspired legendary tales of his extraordinary and even diabolical powers has been placed on record by Roger E. Mitchell in a monographic field study, *George Knox: From Man to Legend* (Orono, Maine, 1970), published by the Northeast Folklore Society. A comparable field report, this time of a Münchausen figure who died in 1939 at eighty-three, also published by the Northeast Folklore Society, is C. Richard K. Lunt, *Jones Tracy: Tall-Tale Hero from Mount Desert Island* (Orono, Maine, 1968). On the opposite coast, in a mountainous area of southwest Oregon, a contract mail carrier named Hathaway Jones (1870–1937) spun windies about his adventures, which have been salvaged, mostly in journalistic elaborations, by Stephen Dow Beckham in *Tall Tales from Rogue River: The Yarns of Hathaway Jones* (Bloomington, Ind., 1974).

On the interpretive side, Roger D. Abrahams has considered the roles of American folk heroes in several thoughtful essays: "The Changing Concept of the Negro Hero," *Tennessee Folklore Society Publications* 31 (1962): 119–34; "Some Varieties of Heroes in America," *Journal of the Folklore Institute* 3 (1966): 341–62; and "Trickster, the Outrageous Hero," in *Our Living Traditions,* ed. T. P. Coffin (New York, 1968), pp. 170–78. Abrahams sees American folk heroes as being permanently rebellious. Other analytical essays are by Robert Byington, "The Frontier Hero: Refinement and Definition," *Singers and Storytellers,* Texas Folklore Society Publications vol. 30 (Dallas, 1961), pp. 140–55; and William M. Clements, "Savage, Pastoral, Civilized: An Ecology Typology of American Frontier Heroes," *Journal of Popular Culture* 8 (1974): 254–66. The conclusion of Kent L. Steckmesser in "Joaquin Murieta and Billy the Kid," *Western Folklore* 21 (1962): 77–82, is that newspapermen developed the legend cycles of the two outlaws. Unfortunately in his own book, *The Western Hero in History and Legend* (Norman, Okla., 1965), he construes legend in the journalistic and literary sense and never touches folk sources.]

CHAPTER VII

Some of the material in this chapter is drawn from my articles, "The Folklore of Colleges," *American Mercury* 68 (1949): 671–77, and "Folklore at a Milwaukee Wedding," *Hoosier Folklore* 6 (1947): 1–13. The Indiana University Folklore Archives is rich

Bibliographical Notes

in college and GI traditions turned in to me by over a thousand students enrolled in my folklore classes at Michigan State University; for a description of the contents, see R. M. Dorson, "The Michigan State University Folklore Archives," *Midwest Folklore* 5 (1955): 51–59.

City lore is beginning to receive some attention. The now classic legend of "The Vanishing Hitchhiker" was first presented by Richard K. Beardsley and Rosalie Hankey in the *California Folklore Quarterly* 1 (1942): 303–35. These authors added "A History of the Vanishing Hitchhiker," in ibid 2 (1943): 13–26, and Louis C. Jones entered revisions with "Hitchhiking Ghosts in New York," ibid 3 (1944): 284–92. Jones has a chapter on "The Ghostly Hitchhiker" in his book of New York ghost tales, *Things That Go Bump in the Night* (New York, 1959), pp. 161–84. James Howard gathered "Tales of Neiman-Marcus" in *Folk Travelers* (Texas Folklore Society Publication 25 [Austin and Dallas, 1953]), pp. 160–70. Albert H. Carter has set down "Some Folk Tales of the Big City" in *Arkansas Folklore* 4 (15 August 1953) 4–6. Alexander Woollcott included five irrepressible city legends in *While Rome Burns* (New York, 1934), pp. 75–99.

One text of the pickled-hand legend, from thirteen Indiana variants in his possession, was printed by Ernest W. Baughman in "The Cadaver Arm," *Hoosier Folklore Bulletin* 4 (1945): 30–32. This believed prank is popular around medical school and hospitals as well as on campuses. Half a dozen versions of "Going To See the Widow" have been published since 1951. The most recent example, under that title in *Western Folklore* 17 (1958): 275–76, refers back to earlier texts in *Western Folklore* and the *Journal of American Folklore*. There is an unpublished text in the Indiana University Folklore Archieves. Sixteen variants of the fatal fraternity initiation form the basis of the article by Ernest W. Baughman, "The Fatal Initiation," *Hoosier Folklore Bulletin* 4 (1945): 49–55. Archer Taylor considered the University of California cry of "Pedro, Pedro!" in *Western Folklore* 6 (1947): 228–31.

Service folktales crop up in Bennett Cerf's *The Pocket Book of War Humor* (New York, 1942). William H. Jansen pointed out the parallel between the GI "klesh-maker" story and David Crockett's blacksmith "skow-maker" story, in "The Klesh-Maker," *Hoosier Folklore* 7 (1948): 47–50. From his personal collection,

American Folklore

William Wallrich published 168 parodies and other service songs, in *Air Force Airs: Songs and Ballads of the United States Air Force, World War One through Korea* (New York, 1957). Texts of "The Coffee that They Serve You" and "Murgatroyd the Kluge Maker" appear in Agnes N. Underwood, "Folklore from G. I. Joe," *New York Folklore Quarterly* 3 (1947): 285–97.

[Modern and urban folklore have come into their own since the first edition of *American Folklore*. Papers from the Conference on Folklore in the Modern World held at Indiana University in Bloomington in 1973 are published in *Folklore in the Modern World*, ed. Richard M. Dorson (The Hague and Chicago, 1978); the papers deal with the city, industrialism, mass media, and nationalism. In *Urban Folklore from the Paperwork Empire* (Austin, Tex., 1976), Alan Dundes and Carl Pagter demonstrate that in city life today a great deal of nonoral folklore (comic letters, gags, cartoons, squibs, lampoons, and comparable matter) circulates through typewriter, ditto-machine, Xerox, and other forms of mechanical reproduction. Contributors to *The Urban Experience and Folk Tradition*, ed. Américo Paredes and Ellen Stekert (Austin, Tex., 1971), covered such topics as southern Appalachian folk medical practices, ethnic mixing, black ghetto riots viewed as performances, and hillbilly music, all occurring within city limits, but this symposium must be regarded as a preliminary effort. In *Urban Blues* (Chicago, 1966), Charles Keil has skilfully traced the remolding of southern folk blues performers into popular recording artists in Chicago studios. The journal *Indiana Folklore*, founded and edited by Linda Dégh in 1968, contains excellent texts and annotations of modern urban legends.

For further examples of college folklore see Richard M. Dorson, "Folklore of the Youth Culture," in *America in Legend* (New York, 1973), pp. 257–309; J. Barre Toelken, "The Folklore of Academe," in J. H. Brunvand, *The Study of American Folklore* (New York, 1968), pp. 317–37; Lydia Fish, "The Old Wife in the Dormitory: Sexual Folklore and Magical Practices from State University College," *New York Folklore Quarterly* 28 (1972): 30–36; Bruce Jackson, "The Greatest Mathematician in the World: Norbert Wiener Stories," *Western Folklore* 31 (1972): 1–22; D. K. Wilgus, "More Norbert Wiener Stories," ibid., pp. 23–25; Joyce Glavan, "Sorority Tradition and Song," *Journal of the Ohio Folk-*

lore Society 3 (1968): 192–98; James T. Bratcher, "The Professor Who Didn't Get His Grades In: A Travelling Anecdote," in *Diamond Bessie and the Shepherds*, ed. Wilson M. Hudson, Publications of the Texas Folklore Society, vol. 36 (Austin, Texas, 1972), pp. 121–23.

Samples of automobile legends and lore can be found in B. A. Botkin, "Automobile Humor: From the Horseless Carriage to the Compact Car," *Journal of Popular Culture* (1968): 395–402, and Stewart Sanderson, "Folklore of the Motor-Car," *Folklore* 80 (1969): 241–52. For war folklore see Sandi Morgen, "Antiwar Protest Songs: Folklore in a Modern Age," *Folklore Annual*, 2 (1970), pp. 73–80; Henry E. Anderson, "The Folklore of Draft Resistance," *New York Folklore Quarterly* 28 (1972): 135–50; and Catherine H. Ainsworth, "American Folktales from the Recent Wars," ibid. 29 (1973): 38–49.

Jokes are winning serious attention from folklorists, notably in the two gargantuan, erudite, and inimitable treatises of Gershon Legman, *Rationale of the Dirty Joke* (New York, 1968) and *Rationale of the Dirty Joke, Second Series* (New York, 1975); through a Freudian lens Legman sees the modern American dirty joke as a projection of homoerotic impulses. Theoretical articles examining jokelore in cultural and functional terms are Francis Lee Utley and Dudley Flamm, "The Urban and the Rural Jest," *Journal of Popular Culture* 2 (1969): 563–77; Jan H. Brunvand, "The Study of Contemporary Folklore: Jokes," *Fabula* 13 (1972): 1–19; Elliott Oring, "Everything Is a Shade of Elephant: An Alternative to a Psychoanalysis of Humor," *New York Folklore* 31 (1975): 149–59. Useful classifications are Jan H. Brunvand, "Classification for Shaggy Dog Stories," *Journal of American Folklore* 76 (1963): 42–68; and William M. Clements, *The Types of the Polack Joke*, Folklore Forum Bibliographical and Special Series, vol. 3 (November 1969).]

Table of Motifs and Tale Types

This table lists motifs and tale types in the order of their mention in the text. References are to Stith Thompson, *Motif-Index of Folk-Literature* (6 vols.; Bloomington, Ind., 1955–58), and Antti Aarne and Stith Thompson, *The Types of the Folk-Tale* (Helsinki, 1928).

CHAPTER I

Table of Motifs and Tale Types

Table of Motifs and Tale Types

313

Table of Motifs and Tale Types

Table of Motifs and Tale Types

Table of Motifs and Tale Types

Acknowledgments

In a coffee-shop in Tokyo, an excellent vantage point from which to consider American civilization, Dan Boorstin and I talked about this book. His ideas were enormously helpful.

Indiana University has generously provided me with all necessary research facilities, including graduate students in folklore to read my manuscript with gimlet eyes—Jerome Mintz, Jan Brunvand, and Joseph Hickerson—and a tireless secretary, Laura Jane Houser.

The folklore fraternity are all my benefactors, through their writings, papers, and discussions ranging from formal symposiums to late evening shoptalks.

Index

Index

Anne Arundel County, Maryland, 53

Annie Christmas, manufactured folk heroine, 215

Antar, Arabian folk hero, 209, 210

Apparitions, 19, 33–34

Appleseed, Johnny; *see* Johnny Appleseed

Arabia, 66

Arabian Nights, 189

Arizona, 272

Arkansas, 60, 75, 90–100, 192, 239

"Arkansaw Traveler, The," 91

Ashe County, North Carolina, 32

Ashe, Thomas, traveler, 42–43

Astronomical Diary and Almanac, 60

Athens, 159, 160

Athletes, folklore of college, 257–58

Atkinson, Sarah, colonist, 38

Atlanta Constitution, 174

Atlantic Monthly, 173

Au Sable River, 217

Augusta, Maine, 56

Austin, Mary, 107

Autobiography, of David Crockett, 204–5, 206, 207

Azores, 145

Babcock, Maud May, and the legend of the Three Nephites, 117

Babe the Blue Ox, 217, 218, 219, 221, 222

Bacon's Rebellion, 11, 33

Bahl, Joseph, 90

Baker, Benamin A., playwright, 64

Baker, Jim, character in folktale, 62

Ballads: hero, of John Henry, Casey Jones, Jesse James, 201, 231, 243; among the Mormons, 119–20; Negro, 196; in the Ozarks, 93; among the Pennsylvania Germans, 86–87; Scandinavian immigrant, about America, 150–52; in the Spanish Southwest, 110–11

Ballanta, N. G. J., folksong collector, 177

Bambakou, Greece, legends of, 156–62

Bangor, Maine, 125, 131

Bar Harbor, Maine, 122

Bardis, Jim, 158

Barnett, Morris, playwright, 66

Bartram, John, colonial author, 12

Bass, Sam; *see* Sam Bass

Bath, Maine, 162

Beacon, Joseph, colonist, 33–34

Beal, Ami B., informant, 129

Beal, Barney, folk hero, 134, 199, 278; discussed, 124–28

Beal, George, character in Maine legend, 129

Beal, Manwaring, 125

Beal, Napoleon, informant, 125, 126

Beal, Riley, informant, 125–26, 127–28

Beale Street, Memphis, 191

Beals Island, Maine, 122–29, 278

Bear, in folktales, 11–12, 62, 71

Beath, Paul, 214

Beaufort, Port Royal Island, South Carolina, 176

Beaver, Tony; *see* Tony Beaver

Belmore, Captain, character in Maine legend, 129

Bemidji, Minnesota, 224

Benchley, Robert, 257

Benny, Jack, 246

"Ben's First Visit to the Theatre," 66

Beowulf, 60, 210

Beowulf, 209

Berks County, Pennsylvania, 76

Berkshire Hills, 58

Berlin, 274

Bermuda Islands, 30

Bethlehem, Pennsylvania, 77

Beverley, Robert, colonial author, 11, 14, 17, 19

Bickford, Thomas, colonist, 21

320

Index

Index

Index

and the Davy Crockett legend, 206–8, 211–13; as a vehicle of folk humor, 60–63

Crockett, Davy; see Davy Crockett

Cross, Clifford, informant, 251

Crosshaul, Chris; see Chris Crosshaul

Crowley, Cam, character in Maine legend, 129

Croy, Homer, and the Jesse James legend, 238, 241

Crystal Falls, Michigan, 152

Csanok, Poland, 153

Cu Chulainn, Celtic folk hero, 209, 210

Cuentos españoles de Colorado y de Nuevo Mejico, 107

Cunningham, William J., character in folktale, 256

Cures, 17–18, 85

Daboll, Nathan, almanac publisher, 45

Daily Worker, 226

Dallas, 183, 253

Danckaerts, Jasper, colonial author, 19, 29, 36

Darley, Felix O. C., illustrator, 67

Darling, John, storyteller, 227

Darwin, Erasmus, 1

Dauphin Island, Alabama, 277

Davenport, John, 34

Davy Crockett, 47, 50, 61–63, 64, 199, 200, 201, 202, 235, 270; *Autobiography*, 204–5, 206, 207; discussed, 203–14; Heroic Age patterns of, 209–14; historical career, 203–6; literary and legendary development, 204–14

Davy Crockett's Almanack, of Wild Sports in the West, and Life in the Backwoods, 206

"Dead Cat in the Package, The," 253–54

"Death Car" legend, 250–52

Delaware, 15, 41

Delaware Indians, 15

Delaware River, 76

Dempsey, Jack, 201

Department stores, legends of, 253–54

Derby, Connecticut, 40

Detroit, 220, 252, 253, 254

Detroit *Free Press*, 216

Detroit *News-Tribune*, 216

Davis, Jefferson, 72

Devil, the, 8, 18, 23–24, 27, 35, 36, 37, 82, 83, 84, 100, 102, 104, 106, 119, 169

"Di Matztown Cornet Band," 87

Dialect and Folk-Lore of Northamptonshire, The, 1

Dialect, Pennsylvania Dutch, 78, 81

Dialect stories: Dutch, 46; French-Canadian, 139–40, 222; Indian, 21–23; Jewish, 141; Mexican, 107–8; Upper Peninsula, 137–41; Yankee, 66

Digges, Jeremiah, 215

Disney, Walt, 203, 235

Dissinger, Moses, preacher-hero in folktales, 83–84, 98

"Diverting Club, The," 44, 81, 229

Divination: among college students, 264–65; among Greek immigrants, 163

"Dixie Land," 87

Dodge, Hiram, Yankee character, 66

Dog: in proverbs, 78–79; in tall tales, 44, 81, 93, 108, 229

Dog Ghosts and Other Texas Negro Folk Tales, 180

Doggett, Jim, storyteller, 60

"Donderback's Machine," 98–99

Douglas, Stephen A., 71

Douglass, Frederick, 170

Downer, Robert, colonist, 38

Dreams, 22, 27, 45

"Drei Wochen vor Ochsdren," 86

Drinking games, 265–66

"D'r zwitzerich Danzer," 87

Duke University, 178

Dutchman, as comic type, 46

323

Index

Dutiful, Deuteronomy, Yankee character, 66

Dwight's Journal of Music, 173

Egypt, 161

"Egypt," in southern Illinois, 75

Eilischpijjel, trickster-hero, 80–81, 82

Eisenhower, Dwight D., 248

Eliot, Abigail, colonist, 29–30

Eliot, John, 27

Emmett, Dan, minstrel, 172

England, 2, 10, 23, 28, 65, 90, 97, 168, 185, 235, 270

Englekirk, John, folklorist, 104

Escanaba, Michigan, 222

Essay for the Recording of Illustrious Providences, An, 25

Eulenspiegel, Tyl; *see* Tyl Eulenspiegel

Euphemisms, 95

European folktales: in ante-bellum humor, 59, 62; among immigrants, 147, 152–53, 164–65; among Negroes, 189; among Pennsylvania Germans, 80, 82–83

Evanston, Illinois, 262

Evil eye, 156, 162–63

Examinations, in college folklore, 256–57

Exeter; *see* Phillips Exeter Academy

Fairies (Irish folk belief), 152

"Fakelore," 4, 214–16

Farmer's Almanack; see Old Farmer's Almanac

"Fatal Fraternity Initiation, The," 258–59

Fayetteville, Arkansas, 99

Feast of the Madonna del Carmine, 144

Feast of San Gandolfo, 144

Febold Feboldson, manufactured folk hero, 214

Ferguson, Major Patrick, 42

Festivals: among Italian-Americans, 144; of Paul Bunyan, 224

Field, Joseph, southern humorist, 202

Fiji Islands, 230

Fink, Mike; *see* Mike Fink

Finland, 3, 149, 150

Finnish-American folklore, 139, 149–50

Fisher, Miles Mark, folklorist, 179

Fisher's River (North Carolina) Scenes and Characters, 59

Fisk University, 175, 178, 179

Flattop Mountains, 255

Flint, Michigan, 254

Florida, 180

Fogel, Edwin M., folklorist, 78

Fogo Island (Cape Verde Islands), 146, 147

Folk arts, of Pennsylvania Germans, 87–90

Folk beliefs: among Greek-Americans, 160–64; among Italian-Americans, 142–44; among Japanese-Americans, 149; among the Pennsylvania Dutch, 84–85; among servicemen, 273–74

Folk Beliefs of the Southern Negro, 177

Folk Culture on St. Helena Island, South Carolina, 177

Folk cures, for convulsions, 85

Folk drama, 103–7

Folk epics: compared with Crockett almanac tales, 209–14; compared with outlaw legends, 237

Folk foods, 144

Folk heroes, 124–28, 199–243

Folk history, of a Greek-American family, 157–62

Folk-music instruments, 111–12

Folk rhymes, Negro, 193–95

Folk sayings, Negro, 197–98

Folk speech: in the Blue Hills, 59–60; used by Lincoln, 71–72; among Portuguese-Americans, 146

Folklore; *see* Anecdotes; Ballads; Festivals; Folk arts; Folk beliefs; Folk drama; Folk heroes; Folksongs; Folktales; Legends

Folk-Lore (journal), 1

Index

Index

Index

Index

Jansen, William H., folklorist, 227

Japan, 65, 148

Japanese-American folklore, 148–49

Jazz, 182

Jefferson, Thomas, 14–15

Jesse James, outlaw hero, 236; discussed, 238–42: folklore elements, in humor, legend, ballad, 242–43; life and death, 238–41

Jesse James Was My Neighbor, 241

Jewish dialect stories, 141, 248

Jim Crow, minstrel dance, 172

Jingles: Negro, 182; in the Ozarks, 98; in the Upper Peninsula, 139

J. L. Hudson's Department Store, Detroit, 253, 254

Joe Magarac, manufactured folk hero, 214, 215, 216

John Hancock Mutual Life Insurance Company, 236

John Henry, folk hero, 182, 231, 232

"John Henry" (ballad), 182, 201

John Henry: Tracking Down a Negro Legend, 177

Johnny Appleseed (John Chapman), folk hero, 201, 231; discussed, 232–36

"Johnny Appleseed, a Pioneer Hero," 235

"Johnny Berbeck" (or "Johnny Verbeck"), 99

Johnny Inkslinger, and Paul Bunyan, 218

Johnson, Guy B., folklorist, 177, 179

Johnson, James Weldon, folksong collector, 178, 195

Johnson, Norman, informant, 137

Johnson, William, 22

Joke cycles, fads in, 249

Jokes, and mass media, 246–67

Jonathan Draws the Long Bow, 125

Jonathan Ploughboy, Yankee character, 49, 65

Jones, Casey; *see* Casey Jones

Jones, Charles C., folklorist, 176

Jonesport, Maine, 122–29

Jonny-Cake Papers, The, 132

Joplin, Missouri, 98

Josselyn, John, colonial author, 8, 10, 11, 13, 18, 35

Journal of American Folklore, 176

Journal of a Residence on a Georgian Plantation in 1838–1839, 170

Judas character in outlaw legends: Robert Ford, 237; Pat Garrett, 237–38; Jim Murphy, 237

Jung, Carl Gustav, 5

Kaler, Paris, character in Maine legend, 129–30

Kalevala, 214

Kalm, Peter, colonial author, 12

Kansas, 71, 83, 238, 272

Kearney, Missouri, 240

Kelley, Warren, of Head Harbor, Maine, 128–29

Kemble, Fanny, as commentator on Negro folklore, 170

Kennebec, Maine, 126, 127, 132

Kenny, James, colonial author, 13

Kentucky, 14, 42, 43, 62, 64, 70, 71, 72, 74, 90, 130, 168, 204, 239, 278

Kentucky, University of, 257

Kerr, Orpheus C., 69

Kidd, Captain, 65

Kilroy, 269

Kilton, Charles, informant, 126

Kimball, J. Golden, character in Mormon folktales, 120–21

King Philip, Indian chief, 22, 31

King Philip's War, 22, 24, 31, 33

King's Mountain, South Carolina, 42

Kinney, Aaron, storyteller, 53

Kipling, Rudyard, 167

Kitsune-tsuki (Japanese folk belief), 148

Kittery, Maine, 121

Klees, Fredric, 78

Knott, Father Edward, 30

328

Index

Index

Lumberjack folklore, 220–23
Lummis, Charles F., as commentator on New Mexican folk music, 111

Mabinogion, 189
McGillivray, James, and the Paul Bunyan legend, 216, 217, 220
Machias, Maine, 122, 129
Macksburg, Ohio, 229
Macy's Department Store, New York, 253
Märchen, 152; *see also* European folktales
Maga (Italian folk belief), 143–44
Magarac, Joe; *see* Joe Magarac
Magisses (Greek folk belief), 155
Magnalia Christi Americana, 26, 34
Mahabharata, 209
Maine, 9, 19, 20, 28, 53, 55, 56, 121–34, 162, 277, 278
Maine coast folklore: anecdotes of local characters, 131–33; coastal legends, 124–33; folk belief in calling the spirits, 128–29; strongman legends of Barney Beal, 124–28
Maki, Herman, informant, 150
Malden, Massachusetts, 33
"Man Who Knows Everybody, The," 247–48
Manabozho, Ojibwa Indian trickster hero, 168
Manchester, England, 235
Mansfield, Ohio, 233
Marble, Dan, Yankee actor, 65–67
Marquette County, Michigan, 149
Mark Twain; *see* Clemens, Samuel L.
Marko Kralyevic, Serbian hero, 209
Marshall Field and Company Department Store, Chicago, 253
Martin, Mary, colonist, 31
Martin, Susanna, witch, 37–38
Martha's Vineyard, Massachusetts, 57

Marvelous Exploits of Paul Bunyan, The, 217
Maryland, 17, 29, 30, 37, 53
Massachusetts, 25, 26, 29, 58, 121, 135, 145, 146, 172, 233
Massachusetts Bay, 8, 10, 24, 37, 121
"Master Thief, The," 189
Mather, Cotton, 13, 16, 20, 25, 27, 31, 33, 34, 36, 37
Mather, Increase, 25, 26, 28, 36
Mathews, William, newspaper editor, 55, 69
Mati (Greek folk belief), 163
Mecosta, Michigan, 251
Melody Time, 235
Memphis, Tennessee, 181, 191
"Memphis Blues," 191
Mennonites, 77
Menominee, Michigan, 222
Merman, 9
Merztown, Pennsylvania, 87
Mestas, Antonio, subject of *corrido*, 110
"Method for Telling Whether or Not Your Loved One Loves You," 264
Mexico, 101, 102, 103, 105; Gulf of, 130, 212
Michigan, 22, 53, 71, 75, 99, 136, 149, 152, 156, 159, 192, 198, 216, 219, 220, 222, 223, 250, 251, 252, 253, 277
Michigan, University of, 256
Michigan State University, 156, 258
Mike Fink, folk hero, 48, 62, 98, 202, 203, 212, 213
Milwaukee, 153
Miller, Lewis, folk artist, 89
Minneapolis, 217, 225
Minnesota, 224, 225, 240
Minnesota, University of, 257
"Minnie the Mermaid," 260–61
Minstrel humor, 171–72
Miracles: of epidemics halted, 160–61; of fog concealing a besieged city, 160; of the gulls and crickets, 113; of an Indian cured, 30

Index

Mississippi, 13, 14, 16, 43, 57, 96, 99, 177, 183, 190, 192, 196, 198, 202, 212, 213

Mississippi River, 42, 60, 62, 219, 243

Missouri, 51, 90, 98, 113, 181, 190, 192, 211, 236, 238–42, 278

Moby Dick, 60

Modern folklore: of the big city, 245–54; of college students, 254–67; of servicemen, 268–76

Modern Language Association, 183

Mohawk Indians, 18, 22

Mohawk River, 22

"Mojo, The," 189

Monongahela River, 42

Mont Blanc, 212

Montague, Margaret, 215

Montanus, Arnoldus, colonial author, 13

Montgomery County, Pennsylvania, 76, 81

Moors and Christians, 105–6

Moravians, 77–78

Morgan, Gilbert; *see* Gib Morgan

Morganfield, Kentucky, 132

Mormon folklore: historical ballad, 119; legends of the Nephites, 115–18; songs about Brigham Young, 120; yarns of J. Golden Kimball, 120–21

Morse, Curt, storyteller, 126, 130–33

Mose the Bowery "b'hoy," folk hero, 63, 68–69, 202, 203

Mose among the Britishers, 69

Moseley, Captain, colonist, 21

Mount Teddon, 19–20

Mount Vernon, Ohio, 233

Mountain Meadows, Utah, 119

"Mountain Meadows Massacre," 119–20

Münchausen, Baron, 14, 44, 57, 200–201, 227

Mules and Men, 180

Murometz, Ilya; *see* Ilya Murometz

Murphy, Jim, and the Sam Bass legend, 237

Murphy, Paddy; *see* Paddy Murphy

Mussolini, Benito, 248

My Bondage and My Freedom, 170

Nantucket, 146

Narragansett, Rhode Island, 26

Narratives of His Marvelous Travels and Campaigns in Russia, 227

Nasby, Petroleum V., 69

Nashville, 61, 68, 206

Nasser, Gamal Abdel, 3

Native American Humor (1800–1900), quoted, 43

Nauvoo, Illinois, 113

Navaho Indians, 166

Nazareth, Pennsylvania, 77

Nebraska, 214

"Necessities of Life, The," 95

Negaunee, Michigan, 139

Negro chant or cry, 196–97

Negro Folk Rhymes, 178

Negro folklore: blues, 181–82, 191; cante-fables, 195–96; folk music, 173–74, 193–95; folk rhymes, 193–95; folk sermons, 52, 197; folksongs, 169–71, 172–73, 183–84, 190–91; folktales, 175–76, 180–81, 186–91, 198; spirituals, 178–80; sources of, 168–71, 186; "toasties," 195

Negro Folktales in Michigan, 180

Negro and His Songs, The, 177

Negro Myths from the Georgia Coast, 176

Negro Slave Songs in the United States, 179

Negro Tales from Pine Bluff, Arkansas, and Calvin, Michigan, 180

Negro Workaday Songs, 177

Nephites, in Mormon legend, 115–18

Neraidos (Greek folk belief), 155, 162, 163

New Bedford, Massachusetts, 145, 146, 147

Index

New England, 8, 10, 11, 15, 16, 21, 24, 25, 26, 28, 31, 34, 35, 37, 38, 40, 48, 55, 65, 91, 95, 173, 185
New-England Almanac, 45
"New-England's Crisis," 22
New Guinea, 273
New Hampshire, 36, 58, 121, 224
New Hampshire Neighbors, 58, 158
New Haven, 27, 34, 48, 144
New Jersey, 12, 75
New Mexico, 101–12, 113, 236, 242
New Netherlands, 13, 29, 45, 76
New Orleans, 182, 183, 191, 215
New Orleans *Picayune*, 51
New Orleans *Sunday Delta*, 53
New Orleans *Weekly Delta*, 67
New Republic, 218
New York, 37, 44, 54, 55, 58, 66, 113, 114, 206, 224, 227, 230
New York *Atlas*, 58
New York City, 61, 63, 64, 144, 152, 156, 158, 171, 172, 202, 247, 253
New York *Herald*, 230
Newfoundland, 8
Newport, 146, 147
Newspapers, as sources for folklore, 50–58, 224–26
Newsweek, 246
Newton, Stan, and the Paul Bunyan legend, 219
Niagara Falls, 15, 65, 212
Niebelungenlied, 32
Nieman-Marcus Department Store, Dallas, 253
"Night That Paddy Murphy Died, The," 261–62
Nights with Uncle Remus, 176
Nikanape, Illinois Indian chief, 16
Niles, Abbe, 178
Nimrod Wildfire, stage hero, 49, 63, 64, 68, 220
Ninjitsu (Japanese folk belief), 148
Noita (Finnish folk belief), 137
North Carolina, 14, 17, 32, 40, 51, 59, 74, 90, 97, 198
North Carolina, University of, 177
North Dakota, 219, 221

Northampton (Massachusetts) *Hampshire Gazette*, 45
Northfield, Minnesota, 240
Northwestern University, 179
Norwalk (Ohio) *Experiment*, 52
Norwalk (Ohio) *Observer*, 51
Norway, 150
Norwegian-American folksong, 150–51
Numskull tales, 80–81, 82–83

"Ode to a Sigma Chi," 263
Odum, Howard W., folklorist, 177, 192
Odyssey, 124, 209
Off-color folklore, 94, 100, 222
Ohio, 51, 54, 113, 228, 229, 231, 232, 233, 234, 236, 253
Ohio River, 42, 62, 181
Ohio Valley, 231
Oil drillers' folktales, 229–31
Ojibwa Indians, 22, 136, 166, 167, 168
Oklahoma, 90, 167, 227, 272
"Old Chisholm Trail, The," 274
Old Farmer's Almanac, 44, 60
Old Marster and John, Negro story cycle, 186–90
Old Stormalong, manufactured folk hero, 214
Old Southwest, humor of, 58–63
"Oleana," 50, 151
Olmsted, Frederick Law, traveler, 168–69
Omaha Charlie, and the Jesse James legend, 242
On the Trail of Negro Folk-Songs, 178
Oñate, Don Juan de, 101, 106
"Onct I Had a Sweetheart," 191
Opler, Marvin K., folklorist, 148, 149
Ordimalas, Pedro de, trickster hero, 107
Oregon, 217, 220, 221, 224
"Oregon" Smith; *see* Smith, Abraham
O'Reilly, Edward, 215

332

Index

Index

334

Index

Robinson, Rowland, 58
Rochester, New York, 65
Rockland, Maine, 126, 127
Rome, 247
Roosevelt, Franklin D., 247
Roosevelt, Theodore, 238
Rosanna of the Amish, 85
Roughead, Robin, correspondent, 57
"Round River Drive, The," 217, 221
Rupp, Adolph, in college folklore, 257
Russia, 3
Russell, William Howard, newspaper correspondent, 69
Ruth, George Herman ("Babe"), 201

Sagola, Michigan, 153
St. Helena, South Carolina, 172
Saint Helena Island Spirituals, 177
St. Joseph, Missouri, 241
St. Louis, 47, 230
St. Louis *Pennant*, 54
St. Louis *Reveille*, 51, 58
Saints' legends: about Johnny Appleseed, 232; about St. Haralampos, 160–61
Salem, Massachusetts, 37, 185
Salisbury, Massachusetts, 37
Salminen, Emmanuel, seer, 149–50
Salt Lake City, 119
Sam Bass, 236, 237, 238
Sam Patch, folk hero, 65, 201, 202, 203, 235
Sam Patch in France, 65
Sam Patch, or the Daring Yankee, 65
San Francisco, 144, 147
San Juan, New Mexico, 101
San Nicolao (Cape Verde Islands), 146
San Rafael, New Mexico, 104, 106
Sandusky, Ohio, 52
Sandwich, New Hampshire, 58
Santa Anna, General, 206

Santa Cruz, New Mexico, 110
Santa Fe, 101, 104
Sault Ste Marie, Michigan, 219
Sausaman, John, 31–32, 33
Satan; *see* Devil
Saturday Evening Post, 235, 258
Saxon, Lyle, 215
Saxon, Missouri, 190
Scarborough, Dorothy, folklorist, 178
Schlauraffenland, 150; *see also* Cockaigne
Schoolcraft, Henry Rowe, 136
"Schpinn, Schpinn," 86
Scottish examples of the bleeding corpse, 32
Schulz, Christian, traveler, 43
Schuylkill River, 82
Scribner's, 215
Sea serpent, 8
Seattle, 218
Second Book of Negro Spirituals, The, 178
Second Shepherd's Play, 189
Seer, 149–50
Selemna, Greece, 155
Selzer, Christian, folk artist, 89
Severn River, 53
Sgraffito, 89
Shaggy-dog stories, 71, 249
Shakespeare, William, 32
"Shantyman's Life, The," 274
Sharp, Cecil, folklorist, 2
Shattuck, Lige, trickster, 57
Shay, Frank, folklorist, 216
Shephard, Esther, 218
Shot Gunderson, and Paul Bunyan, 218
Shreveport, Louisiana, 183
"Sick" jokes, 249
Siegfried, Teutonic folk hero, 209, 210, 237
Silver Lake, Utah, 117
"Simon Slow's Visit to Boston," 66
"Sir Hugh and the Jew's Daughter," 100
"Sister Nance and the Ager," 54

335

Index

336

Index

67; of Paul Bunyan, 219–23; rich soil, 52, 64; the "shakes," 53–54; speed, 71

Talley, Thomas W., folklorist, 178, 193, 197

Tarboro (North Carolina) *Free Press,* 51–52

Tarzan of the Apes, 201

Taylor, Archer, folklorist, 97

Tennessee, 54, 61, 62, 90, 98, 181, 202, 203, 241

Texas, 104, 106, 168, 180, 183, 227, 228, 236

Texas Rangers, 237

Theater, in relation to folklore, 63, 67

Thomas, Robert B., almanac publisher, 44, 207

Thompson, Harold W., folklorist, 58

Thoms, William John, folklorist, 1

Thor, 226

Thorpe, Thomas Bangs, southern humorist, 60

Three Years in Arkansas, 92

Time, 184

Times (London), 69

"Titanic, The," 182

"Toastie," form of Negro folklore, 195

Tobacco, in colonial reports, 10–11

Tokyo, 248

Toledo, Ohio, 253

Tompson, Benjamin, 22

Tomteguber (Swedish folk belief), 137

Tongue-twisters, 266

Tony Beaver, manufactured folk hero, 215

"Tough Stories, or, Some Reminiscences of 'Uncle Charles,'" 56

Transformation, in folktales and ballads, 189

Travelers' tales, 9–16, 42–43, 54

Trickster tales: of Davy Crockett, 61, 210; of goldbrickers, 132, 273; "How Big Lige Got the Liquor," 57; of Old Marster and John,

186–90; of Paul Bunyan, 221–22; of Yankees, 45–46, 48

Truman, Harry S., 278

Tule Lake, California, 148, 149

Turner, Frederick Jackson, 208

Turner, Nat, 180

Tuskegee Institute, 175

"Twa Magicians, The," 189

"Two White Springs, The," 96

Tyl Eulenspiegel, 80; see also Eilischpijjel

Tyler, Moses Coit, 207

Tyler, Royall, playwright, 47

Ulysses, 209, 210

"Uncle Frost Snow," 59

Uncle Lisha's Shop, 58

Uncle Remus: His Songs and His Sayings, 174

United States Steel Corporation, 216

Upper Peninsula of Michigan, 75, 99, 136–41, 149, 152, 219, 277

Upper Peninsula Development Bureau News, 219

Useful Information for Oil Men, 228

Utah, 112–21

Utah, University of, 117

Vanderbilt University, 179

Vasa, Gustav, Swedish folk hero, 137

Vergennes, Vermont, 58

Vermont, 44, 51, 58, 71, 158

Vermont Wool Dealer, 66

Virgin coed, legend of, 254–55

Virginia, 11, 12, 15, 19, 20, 29, 30, 33, 37, 40, 42, 44, 74, 168

Virginia Minstrels, 172

Volkskunde, 2

Voris, Jim, 163–64

Vrykólakas (Greek folk belief), 155, 162–63

Wallaschek, Richard, musicologist, 179

Walton, George, colonist, 36

337

Index